It Happened One Semester

What Reviewers Say About Aurora Rey's Work

Sweat Equity

"Rey (*Roux for Two*) stresses the importance of building something to last in this torrid home renovation romance. Rey makes the chemistry between Maddie and Sy obvious and immediate, leading naturally to plenty of creative and exciting sex scenes, but tempers the hot-and-heavy goings-on with emotional intelligence that makes the relationship feel as sturdy as a load-bearing wall. Readers will never doubt that a happy ending is on its way, but they'll love watching it come together."—*Publishers Weekly*

Greener Pastures

"I was hooked on this from the very first moment and enjoyed it so much I couldn't put it down. It had everything I want from a romance and everything I have come to know and love in Aurora Rey stories. Definitely recommend this amazing story and for romance readers, it's another must read!"—*LESBIreviewed*

You Again

"*You Again* is a wonderful, feel good, low angst read with beautiful and intelligent characters that will melt your heart, and an enchanting second-chance love story."—*Rainbow Reflections*

Twice Shy

"[A] tender, foodie romance about a pair of middle aged lesbians who find partners in each other and rediscover themselves along the way. …Rey's cute, occasionally steamy, romance reminds readers of the giddy intensity falling in love brings at any age, even as the characters negotiate the particular complexities of dating in midlife—meeting the children, dealing with exes, and revealing emotional scars. This queer love story is as sweet and light as one of Bake My Day's famous cream puffs."—*Publishers Weekly*

"This book is all the reasons why I love Aurora Rey's writing. It's delicious with a good helping of sexy. It was a nice change to read a book where the women were not in their late 20s–30s…" —*Les Rêveur*

The Last Place You Look

"The romance is satisfying and full-bodied, with each character learning how to achieve her own goals and still be part of a couple. A heartwarming story of two lovers learning to move past their fears and commit to a shared future."—*Kirkus Reviews*

"[A] sex-positive, body-positive love story. With its warm atmosphere and sweet characters, *The Last Place You Look* is a fluffy LGBTQ+ romance about finding a second chance at love where you least expect it."—*Foreword Reviews*

Ice on Wheels—*Novella in* Hot Ice

"I liked how Brooke was so attracted to Riley despite the massive grudge she had. No matter how nice or charming Riley was, Brooke was dead set on hating her. A cute enemies to lovers story."—*Bookvark*

The Inn at Netherfield Green

"I really enjoyed this book but that's not surprising because it came from the pen of Aurora Rey. This is the kind of book you read while sitting by a warm fire with a Rosemary Gin and snuggly blanket." —*Les Rêveur*

"[Aurora Rey] constantly delivers a well-written romance that has just the right blend of humour, engaging characters, chemistry and romance."—*C-Spot Reviews*

Lead Counsel—*Novella in* The Boss of Her

"*Lead Counsel* by Aurora Rey is a short and sweet second chance romance. Not only was this story paced well and a delight to sink into, but there's A++ good swearing in it and has lines like this that made me all swoony because of how beautifully they're crafted." —*Lesbian Review*

Recipe for Love

"*Recipe for Love* by Aurora Rey is a gorgeous romance that's sure to delight any of the foodies out there. Be sure to keep snacks on hand when you're reading it, though, because this book will make you want to nibble on something!"—*Lesbian Review*

"So here's a few things that always get me excited when Aurora Rey publishes a new book. …Firstly, I am guaranteed a hot butch with a sensitive side, this alone is a massive tick. Secondly, I am guaranteed to throw any diet out the window because the books always have the most delectable descriptions of food that I immediately go on the hunt for—this time it was a BLT with a difference. And lastly, hot sex scenes that personally have added to my fantasy list throughout the years! This book did not disappoint in any of those areas." —*Les Rêveur*

Autumn's Light—*Lambda Literary Award Finalist*

"[*Autumn's Light*] was another fun addition to a great series." —Danielle Kimerer, Librarian (Nevins Memorial Library, Massachusetts)

"Aurora Rey has shown a mastery of evoking setting and this is especially evident in her Cape End romances set in Provincetown. I have loved this entire series…"—*Kitty Kat's Book Review Blog*

Spring's Wake

"[A] feel-good romance that would make a perfect beach read. The Provincetown B&B setting is richly painted, feeling both indulgent and cozy."—*RT Book Reviews*

"*Spring's Wake* has shot to number one in my age-gap romance favorites shelf."—*Les Rêveur*

Summer's Cove

"As expected in a small-town romance, *Summer's Cove* evokes a sunny, light-hearted atmosphere that matches its beach setting. …Emerson's shy pursuit of Darcy is sure to endear readers to her, though some may be put off during the moments Darcy winds tightly to the point of rigidity. Darcy desires romance yet is unwilling to disrupt her son's life to have it, and you feel for Emerson when she endeavors to show how there's room in her heart for a family." —*RT Book Reviews*

"From the moment the characters met I was gripped and couldn't wait for the moment that it all made sense to them both and they would finally go for it. Once again, Aurora Rey writes some of the steamiest sex scenes I have read whilst being able to keep the romance going. I really think this could be one of my favorite series and can't wait to see what comes next. Keep 'em coming, Aurora."—*Les Rêveur*

Crescent City Confidential—*Lambda Literary Award Finalist*

"This book blew my socks off. …[*Crescent City Confidential*] ticks all the boxes I've started to expect from Aurora Rey. It is written very well and the characters are extremely well developed; I felt like I was getting to know new friends and my excitement grew with every finished chapter."—*Les Rêveur*

"This book will make you want to visit New Orleans if you have never been. I enjoy descriptive writing and Rey does a really wonderful job of creating the setting. You actually feel like you know the place."—*Amanda's Reviews*

Built to Last

"Rey's frothy contemporary romance brings two women together to restore an ancient farmhouse in Ithaca, N.Y. …[T]he women totally click in bed, as well as when they're poring over paint chips, and readers will enjoy finding out whether love conquers all." —*Publishers Weekly*

"I adored every minute of this story and it left me feeling all warm and fuzzy, even when the drama hit because these characters gave me so much hope for happiness. A great read, very enjoyable, and highly recommended."—*LESBIreviewed*

Winter's Harbor

"This is the story of Lia and Alex and the beautifully romantic and sexy tale of a winter in Provincetown, a seaside holiday haven. A collection of interesting characters, well-fleshed out, as well as a gorgeous setting make for a great read."—*Inked Rainbow Reads*

By the Author

Cape End Romances:

Winter's Harbor

Summer's Cove

Spring's Wake

Autumn's Light

Built to Last

Crescent City Confidential

Lead Counsel (Novella in The Boss of Her collection)

Recipe for Love: A Farm-to-Table Romance

The Inn at Netherfield Green

Ice on Wheels (Novella in Hot Ice collection)

The Last Place You Look

Twice Shy

You Again

Follow Her Lead (Novella in Opposites Attract collection)

Greener Pastures

Hard Pressed

Roux for Two

Her Brother's Girlfriend (Novella in All for Her collection)

Renovation Romances:

Sweat Equity

Good Bones

Fixed Up

It Happened One Semester

Written with Jaime Clevenger

A New Leash on Love

Frosted by the Girl Next Door

A Convenient Arrangement

Love, Accidentally

It Happened One Semester

by

Aurora Rey

2025

IT HAPPENED ONE SEMESTER

ISBN 13: 978-1-63679-814-1

This Trade Paperback Original Is Published By
Bold Strokes Books, Inc.
P.O. Box 249
Valley Falls, NY 12185

First Edition: October 2025

Credits
Editors: Ashley Tillman and Cindy Cresap
Production Design: Susan Ramundo
Cover Design By Inkspiral Design

Acknowledgments

I had some trepidation about writing a book set on a college campus. So much good material, so much potential for using said material to bite me in the ass. I think I managed to channel the essence without getting myself into trouble. Higher ed is a truly great place to work. And like so many jobs, utterly absurd at the same time. I'm grateful for the students and colleagues I've had through the years, even the ones worthy of Shit Professors/Students/Administrators Say.

Thanks as always to Ash, Cindy, and the folks at Bold Strokes Books who create the books and get them out into the world. I am so grateful for the passion and energy that goes into getting so many important stories published. Thanks especially to Ash for taking such delight in making me feel old.

And to you, dear readers. A million thank yous are not enough. None of this would matter without you.

Dedication

For all the staff who keep the trains running

Chapter One

@shitprofessorssay: Summer is for research. And by research, I mean day drinking.

Hudson buttoned her shirt all the way up before frowning in the mirror and undoing the top one. She smiled and buttoned it again. Then frowned and unbuttoned it a second time.

It was fine. She would be fine. It was Pride, not an inquisition. A Pride she'd never been to before, but really, what better way to get to know the town she now called home? She'd enjoy the parade, chat up a few people at the various booths, and get to know the queer scene. It was the sort of thing she'd encourage a shy baby queer in one of her classes to do. And if an awkward eighteen-year-old could handle it—and she believed deeply they could—so could a newly minted tenure-track assistant professor. Even if she had to do it alone.

It was the alone part that gave her pause. Between her undergrad years at Cornell and doing her PhD at UC Berkeley, she'd never been without a bevy of fellow queers for any and all social functions. In fact, she'd had to go out of her way to get any alone time that didn't entail holing up to write papers or work on her dissertation. Even her stint as a post-doc at UC Santa Barbara had come with a community of fellow academics—queer and otherwise—all hustling their way onto the job market.

Not the case anymore. She had a place of her own finally, but she'd lived in Ryekill all of two weeks. Other than members of the search committee that hired her and her dad's friend who would now be one of her colleagues, she didn't know a soul.

"But that's why you're going to Pride. To be with your people. And maybe make a friend," she said.

Hudson fastened and unfastened the top button of her shirt once more, then briefly entertained leaving the top two open, before ultimately deciding to leave the single top one undone. A non-statement, or at least as much of a non-statement as a short-sleeve button-down covered with tiny rainbow flags could be.

She checked her hair one last time, glad the one barber shop she'd found in town turned out to be queer-friendly. Something about a fresh haircut made her feel confident, and she could use all the help she could get. Too bad new social settings couldn't be as easy as giving a paper at a conference.

After a parting promise to Gertrude that she wouldn't be bringing any women home, Hudson topped off the cat's kibble bowl, grabbed her keys, and let herself out the back door. The drive to the park at the edge of town took all of five minutes, but she added an additional one or two to take the winding road along the edge of campus.

Coteau College was exactly what you'd expect an elite liberal arts college nestled in the Hudson Valley of New York to be. Most of the campus consisted of old brick buildings with ivy creeping up their walls. The rest were quaint but thoroughly remodeled residence halls, a state-of-the-art science building, and a brand-new fitness center. It had a robust endowment and a commitment to excellence in both teaching and research. In other words, the stuff academic dreams were made of.

At the park, Hudson secured a spot in the makeshift grass lot—between an ancient Subaru and a gorgeous Land Rover that probably cost more than her annual salary. She did a final check of her hair in the rearview mirror and gave herself a nod of reassurance. It was Pride. How hard could it be?

Since the festival schedule kicked off with the parade, she strolled over to the four-block strip of Cedar Street that made up the route. The local chapter of SAGE marched first—two dozen or so seniors wearing matching T-shirts and rainbow feather boas. Hudson cheered, grateful so many more of this generation of elders were around to share their wisdom but also simply around.

A gaggle of drag queens came next in a homemade float, blasting "We Are Family" from a pair of speakers mounted on the back of the pickup hauling them. Musicians, dancers, and community groups filed past, carrying balloons and waving rainbow flags. It was a far cry from New York City Pride, or the Prides she'd gone to in California. But it was exuberant and, in a way, much more her speed.

When the last makeshift float passed, the crowd dispersed. Hudson wandered, a little sad to be solo but enjoying the sense of community all the same. She talked up folks at a few of the booths, taking cards from the people and businesses that would become part of her life in Ryekill.

A banner bearing the Coteau College emblem caught her eye. A pair of what she assumed to be students and three adults chatted with themselves and any passersby who paused in front of their table. Hudson made her way over, excited but nervous. Silly really, since these were her people. And yet not silly, since she felt the weight of making a good first impression.

One of the students caught her eye first and flashed a thousand-watt smile. "Happy Pride," they said.

"Happy Pride." Hudson stepped the rest of the way up to the booth. "Are you a student at Coteau?"

"Sophomore biology major." They puffed out their chest ever so slightly, making Hudson smile. "Premed."

"Nice." She hooked her thumb at her chest. "New professor. English."

"Oh, nice. My man Dwayne is an English major. He's around here somewhere." They made a show of looking around. "I'm Asher. They/them."

"Hudson. Greene. She/her."

"Bet." Asher bopped their head. "Are you looking to connect to the community?"

"I am. Tell me everything."

They chatted for longer than Hudson would have expected, and Asher introduced her to Davina, an anthropology professor, and Eric, who worked in res life. She got info on the LGBT resource center, the faculty/staff affinity group, and the welcome social that would happen the first week of classes. She'd just started to walk away when Asher caught her attention.

"I need a humanities elective in the fall. I'm not loving the philosophy class I got into. Maybe I'll switch into one of yours."

Hudson got a little swell of excitement anytime she had the chance to hook a non-major. "I'd love that. No hard sell, but my survey of American lit will only have women and queer writers as required reading."

"No shit. I mean, no way."

It was her turn to do the head bop. "It'll be a lot of fun, and I think at least half the kids in it will be non-majors."

"I'm totally switching. I'm going to tell Dwayne he should take it, too."

"The more the merrier. Especially when it comes to family." Hudson leaned in like they were trading secrets. "Y'all don't say that anymore, do you?"

Asher gave a sheepish shrug. "I know what it means though."

"I'll make you a deal. I'll introduce you to some cool queer books and you can hook me up on Gen Z slang." She tried, but it changed so damn often.

"Facts."

That one, at least, she knew. "I'll see you in August, then."

Hudson continued her meander, a swell of optimism about starting her career at Coteau making her buoyant. During her job search, she'd been focused on the reputation of the department—well-resourced and with a solid reputation for quality publications and high-profile conference proceedings. Neither were givens at small liberal arts colleges.

There was also the fact that Lawrence Michaelson, a family friend since before she was born, had been a fixture of the Coteau College English Department for close to four decades. It was like starting at a new school and already having a buddy. A buddy old enough to be her father, but still. She considered him a mentor as much as an honorary uncle.

And now she'd gotten a taste of how welcoming and robust the queer community on campus was. She hadn't expected unwelcoming. In fact, she'd ruled out both conservative institutions and conservative parts of the country when starting her job search. It was a risk, but she'd had the luxury of living her whole life in blue states and had no desire to do otherwise. And she'd made enough of a name for herself that she'd been recruited pretty heavily by Coteau and a couple of other institutions.

Coteau, an hour north of the City and two from her parents' place on Long Island, was shaping up to hit all her wickets and then some. It was so satisfying to have chosen well, and to be back on the East Coast.

Rather than heading home, Hudson wandered over to the row of food trucks assembled on the far side of the festival. Definitely more fun than her fridge of salad makings and leftovers. And maybe—just maybe—she'd stick around long enough to check out the dance party slated to start at sundown.

❖

Callie stepped back from the Planned Parenthood booth and scanned the crowd. It was a good turnout this year, likely fueled by the absolutely glorious weather. Winters might be brutal, but the northeast sure knew how to do summer. She didn't get it off like students and faculty did, but she made the most of every moment she had.

She'd already run into a handful of students—a few who stuck around to take a summer course or two and a few who preferred lingering on campus to whatever awaited them at home. It made her sad that so many of the latter seemed to be the queer kids, but she was glad Coteau kept its doors open and made a year-round safe space for those who needed it.

"Dean Shaw!"

Whatever Callie's feelings about academic rank and title might be, it still gave her a surge of pleasure to hear her own. Some faculty might not consider the dean of advising a real dean, but since she technically outranked them in the college org chart, that was their problem and not hers. Besides, it was students' opinion and respect she most valued. She turned in the direction of the voice and found herself face-to-face with the co-presidents of the Rainbow Alliance. She wasn't sure which of them had called to her, but it didn't really matter. "Hey, Dwayne. Hey, Asher."

"Your dress is amazing." Asher flicked a finger up and down to indicate Callie's outfit. "We think you should wear it one of the days of orientation."

She glanced down. The rainbow fabric had been stitched on the bias, creating a bold chevron pattern. "A bit loud for work, I'm afraid. Aesthetically, I mean. Not politically."

Both Dwayne and Asher laughed. "Bet," Asher said.

Dwayne nodded. "Bet."

Callie smiled at both the slang and the echoed sentiment. "Are you having a good Pride?"

They nodded. Asher tipped their chin. "Are you going to the dance?"

The dance served as the finale of the day and consisted of a DJ and several disco balls under a huge tent set up at the center of the park. Since she'd essentially given up late nights at the club, it was one of the few times a year she got to dance in that bass-fueled bump and grind that reminded her of her own days as a college student, reveling in exuberant queerness until the wee hours. "I wouldn't miss it."

They squealed their delight and promised to see her there, even if it required waving at her from the underage side. Callie promised to keep an eye out for them, then headed over to the Coteau booth for the closing volunteer shift. It wouldn't be dark for hours yet, but the sun had shifted behind the towering oaks and maples that edged the park, and the festival started to wind down. She helped pack up and carted a couple of the boxes to her car.

Satisfied she'd done her gay civic duty, she texted Sasha, Coteau's registrar and her best friend, who'd left briefly to take her nephew to baseball practice. They met up at one of the makeshift bars flanking the over-twenty-one section of the party. "Drink?" Sasha asked.

"Drink," Callie said.

Since their choices consisted of cans of beer or hard seltzer, she went with a seltzer. "God, this is terrible," Sasha said after a single sip.

"Did you expect otherwise?"

Sasha sucked her teeth. "Fair."

They hovered for the first twenty minutes or so, letting the crowd warm up and the sun go down. Callie didn't need alcohol to dull her inhibitions, but since she'd gone to the trouble of buying it, she figured she might as well drink it.

She and Sasha hadn't gone to school together, but they'd graduated the same year, and when a song from their college days came on, a single knowing look had them joining the fray. Callie thrust out her arms and sang along. She jutted her hips this way and that, letting the joy of the music pulse through her. They danced to that song and the next three, until sweat trickled down her spine and she felt lithe and free.

Sasha insisted on another drink, even if it was terrible, and they resumed their spot on the periphery, soaking up the joy of the night.

Sasha cleared her throat, punctuating it with an unsubtle flick of her finger in the direction of the bar.

"What?" Callie asked.

"Hottie at three o'clock, totally checking you out."

"Seriously?" Callie snickered. "Just because most of the people here are half our age doesn't mean we need to talk like we are."

"Speak for yourself. I'm all about pretending I'm twenty-two and looking to get laid." Pretending being the operative word. Sasha had gone through a nasty divorce in the spring and remained squarely in the stubbornly celibate phase.

"Hey, I never said I was against getting laid. I'm just happy to do it as my thirty-six-year-old self." If anything, she'd become more sexually adventurous since landing in her thirties. And she wasn't ashamed to say so.

"Well, I think you might have some willing company."

Callie turned in time to see an adorable butch giving her an appreciative stare. But instead of coming over, they shifted their attention to the beer in their hand. "A little skittish, no?"

Sasha quirked a brow. "We can't all be as brazen as you."

Callie's eye roll said all she had to say about that.

"Go on. Take pity." Sasha gave her a none too subtle elbow to the ribs. "Talk to them."

She would have even without the encouragement. Because as much as she loved a butch with swagger, she wasn't about to turn her nose up at one who invited her to make the first move. Especially one with a preppy aesthetic and a sexy ass fringe. She took a sip of the seltzer that, in fact, tasted nothing like a mojito and slowly crossed the dance floor to where they stood. "Hi."

They glanced down again, but only for a second. When they looked up, they gave Callie one of those smiles that might be shy or simply made to look that way. Either way, Callie ate it right up. "Hi," they said.

"I'm Callie." She extended a hand.

"Hudson."

Hudson's grip was firm but not aggressive, leaving Callie even more intrigued than she'd been with the smile. "Cute." And so gay.

"Family name," Hudson said with a what-can-I-say half shrug.

"She/her." She hooked a thumb at herself.

"Same."

"I don't think I've seen you in Ryekill before." Not that she knew every queer in town, but she certainly knew more than she didn't. "Visiting?"

"Just moved here," Hudson said.

"Ah. Welcome to town, then. And happy Pride."

"Thanks." Hudson's head tipped slightly. "Are you the official welcome wagon?"

Callie smirked. "I can be. Would you like to dance?"

Another tilt of the head. "Yes, I would."

This Hudson was shaping up to be the most adorable creature she'd bumped into in ages. Callie set her drink on the closest high-top table, happy for an excuse to abandon it. Hudson did the same with her beer and gestured for Callie to lead the way.

They started the way casual acquaintances might, smiling and moving in and out of each other's personal space. When the song ended, Callie looked to where she'd left Sasha, only to find her chatting with a trans guy from the admissions office.

"Can I get you another drink?" Hudson asked.

She didn't love her choices at the abbreviated bar, but that was no reason to say no. "You most certainly can."

It was hard to have much of a conversation with the music, but they chatted about the magic of queer spaces and how encouraging it was to see so many young people embracing their identities. They danced again. Closer this time, shifting with and eventually against one another. She made space for Hudson's thigh between her own, let her breasts brush ever so slightly against Hudson's chest.

As one song melded into another, Callie wondered whether Hudson would make a move. When the next one ended in a slightly more pronounced way, she took a tiny step back, thinking she'd suggest a break if nothing else.

"Do you maybe want to get out of here?" Hudson lifted a shoulder, like she might be referring to taking a stroll or hitting a diner instead of the more obvious insinuation. But the intensity in her hazel eyes told a different story.

Callie debated her options and decided against being coy. "My house is only a couple of blocks from here."

Surprise registered first, there was no mistaking it. And in the blink of an eye, Callie would swear she watched a whole internal debate play across Hudson's features. But instead of backing off or backing down, she gave Callie another of those killer smiles. And there was nothing shy about it. "I'd love that."

Chapter Two

@shitprofessorssay: Let me assure you, I am the leading expert in this field.

The walk to Callie's didn't take long, but it took them down one of the residential streets Hudson had yet to see. The houses—an eclectic mix of craftsman, Victorian, and bungalow styles—sat close together but were impeccably maintained. The night air cooled her skin even as the heat they'd generated on the dance floor held low in her belly.

Callie's auburn hair glowed in the moonlight, and Hudson imagined the soft waves sliding through her fingers. The vibrant colors of Callie's dress might seem muted now, but the fabric clung to her curves just as suggestively as when Callie moved against her while dancing. The faint scent of jasmine wafted between them, but Hudson couldn't tell if it came from a vine they'd passed or Callie herself.

Callie pointed Hudson up one of the front walks. After unlocking the door, Callie turned. "You're okay with dogs, right? Lucy is ten and super chill."

"Totally." Hudson nodded more eagerly than was perhaps necessary.

Callie flipped on a light and tossed her keys into a small basket on the console table. A beagle-something-mix appeared at their feet. "Hi, sweet girl. This is Hudson. Be nice."

Lucy was all wags and sniffs, and the second Hudson bent down to say hello, Lucy flopped onto her side and flashed her belly. "Hi, Lucy. It's so nice to meet you."

"Would you like something to drink?" Callie asked.

Hudson straightened and swallowed, throat suddenly dry. More alcohol was the last thing she needed, but having something to do with her hands appealed. Would it be weird to ask for water? "Sure."

"I've got wine and a reasonably stocked liquor cabinet. I've also got regular seltzer if you're more interested in hydrating at this point." Callie smiled, all easy confidence. "That's what I'll be having."

"Seltzer would be great. Thank you." She nodded, again with more enthusiasm than the situation warranted.

"Make yourself comfortable." Callie gestured to the sofa then disappeared through the cased opening that led to the kitchen.

Hudson considered her options and settled on the end of the sofa closest to the door. It also happened to be the end closest to the stairs. Lucy settled in her bed, not bothering to keep her eye on things. "You've got a great place," she said.

"Thanks." Callie returned with a pair of cans. "Pomegranate or pink grapefruit?"

"Either."

Callie handed her the pomegranate and opened the pink grapefruit. "Cheers."

They clinked cans and Callie settled on the sofa right next to her. Hudson took a long swig of seltzer, suddenly parched. The carbonation burned her throat even as the liquid soothed. Callie drank from her own can, then set it on the coffee table. She shifted ever so slightly closer, her thigh brushing Hudson's.

Even as Hudson's pulse ticked up a couple of notches, she couldn't help but admire Callie's skill. In feeling things out, in opening the door of possibility. Hudson wasn't without moves, but she did better after all the would-they, wouldn't-they was squared away. She set her drink next to Callie's and mirrored the move, adding a torso twist so she faced Callie more than the table or the fireplace on the opposite wall.

Callie responded in kind, turning her body and locking eyes with Hudson. She flicked her gaze to Hudson's mouth. Licked her lips.

Hudson moved an inch closer. "Yes?"

Callie merely nodded.

For all the moments of self-consciousness—today, in general—this didn't phase her. A beautiful woman, enthusiastic consent. She knew what to do with this.

The distance between them was barely a breath now. She closed it and covered Callie's mouth with her own. Callie's lips parted, invited her in.

Hudson would be hard-pressed to put her finger on exactly what the underlying notes were, but Callie tasted like summer, carefree and warm. She angled her head to take the kiss deeper, slid her fingers into Callie's hair. Callie sighed like she'd been waiting all night for that kiss.

When Callie's hand fisted in her shirt, Hudson moved closer. But instead of pressing in, Callie leaned back, pulling Hudson with her. Hudson took the hint, coming onto one knee and bracing herself over Callie's now supine body.

Callie moaned her approval. She released her grip on the fabric and slipped both hands under Hudson's shirt, running her fingers up Hudson's sides and over her back. Hudson let out a moan of her own.

With her left hand holding her up, Hudson had only the right to work with. But she wasted no time sliding it up Callie's thigh. Callie hooked her ankle over Hudson's ass, inviting her higher. Hudson accepted, running her fingers along the lacy edges of Callie's underwear.

Callie's hips arched and, even through her panties, the heat radiating from Callie's core stoked Hudson's arousal. Like blowing on embers to make a roaring fire. She caressed Callie from behind, keeping her fingers on top of the fabric. It was already soaked, and all Hudson could think about was plunging inside until Callie came undone.

"We should take this to my bed," Callie said, her voice already a little ragged.

Hudson pried herself away, knowing the payoff of more space and fewer articles of clothing would be worth it. "Yep."

She extricated herself from the sofa and held out a hand to help Callie. Callie held on, dragging her up the stairs without a second of hesitation. "Lights?" she asked after pulling Hudson through the door.

"Whatever." Enough spilled in from the hall that she could see what she needed to.

Instead of reaching for the switch, Callie started pulling at Hudson's clothes. She managed to rid Hudson of her shirt and sports bra before Hudson had a chance to even figure out how Callie's dress worked. Callie took a step back and pulled it over her head in one fluid motion. The move itself was sexy, but the sight of Callie in a plunging floral print bra and patching hip-hugger panties was enough to take her breath away.

Callie smiled like she knew exactly what Hudson was thinking and resumed dispensing with Hudson's clothes. After toeing off her shoes, Hudson stepped out of her shorts and boxers, kicking them to the side. As much as she enjoyed Callie's lingerie, the need to touch and taste won out. She brought her fingers to the little gold clasp that sat perfectly nestled between Callie's breasts, lifting her gaze to meet Callie's.

No words were exchanged, but there was no mistaking Hudson's request for permission or Callie's granting of it. Hudson flipped open the clasp, and Callie's breasts spilled out, luxurious and full. Callie slid the bra down her arms and tossed it aside, leaving Hudson free to cup one in each hand.

She dipped her head to take one taut nipple in her mouth and rolled the other between her finger and thumb. Callie let out a moan that went right to Hudson's clit, and Hudson was more than a little tempted to toss her on the bed and do something about it. Not exactly a good first date move, though, so she held off.

When she released Callie's nipple long enough to go in for another kiss, Callie saved her the trouble, guiding them both to the bed and pulling Hudson down on top of her. What had been sexy on the sofa was next-level erotic now. Skin on skin and the heat of their bodies and the scent of arousal starting to permeate the air.

Hudson resumed her worship of Callie's nipples, sucking and biting each in turn. She used her free hand to explore the swell of Callie's hip, her ass. Callie dropped her knee to the side, giving Hudson access to her center. Hudson took advantage, teasing the small patch of hair and caressing the impossibly soft skin on either side of Callie's pussy.

"Would you just fuck me already?" Callie said with a slightly frustrated laugh.

The final piece of the consent puzzle clicked into place and, with it, Hudson's confidence. "Oh, is that what you were after?"

Callie's eyes flickered open and her gaze locked on Hudson's. "Yes. Yes, it is."

Hudson ceased her lazy caresses and slipped a finger into Callie's wetness. Her clit was impossibly hard and the rest of her impossibly soft. Callie let out a low moan, and Hudson bit back one of her own. It would be so easy to lose herself in the feel of Callie under her hand.

But instead of getting lost, Hudson tuned in. To the tempo of Callie's body moving against her, to the fact that Callie made little sounds of pleasure on the downward strokes. With each clue, a micro adjustment, like tuning a priceless violin.

"More," Callie said, voice breathy but demanding.

Nothing micro about that. Hudson slid a second finger into Callie, reveling in the way Callie clamped around her.

"More," Callie said again.

Hudson obliged, adding a third. Callie rocked against her for a minute, then repeated her command. Again, Hudson obliged, getting onto her knees to give herself the leverage she needed. The change in angle also gave her the freedom to stroke Callie's clit with her thumb. Callie rose to meet each thrust with the sort of glorious abandon that fueled Hudson's desire even as it fed her.

Callie arched and held on a long, low moan. Watching and hearing and feeling Callie come was its own version of getting off. Hudson soaked it in and rode the wave of release with her.

When Callie's limbs went limp, Hudson settled next to her—revved up but also satisfied. They stayed like that for a moment, and she basked in Callie's aftershocks and the way her breathing slowly returned to normal. Callie rolled to face her, running her hand down Hudson's side and over her ass. Hudson let out a hum of pleasure.

"I'm so glad you made eyes at me across the dance floor," Callie said.

Hudson chuckled. "I'm so glad you noticed."

"Technically, my friend noticed. But I'll take credit for doing something about it."

Since first moves weren't her forte, that counted as a big perk in her book. "I'm so glad you did."

"I'd like to do something about this." Callie flicked a finger, indicating Hudson's body.

"Oh, yeah?" Making Callie come might be its own satisfaction, but she wasn't going to turn down reciprocation. "What did you have in mind?"

Callie dipped her head to suck one of Hudson's nipples. She paused, pulling back enough to make eye contact. "I was thinking of doing to you exactly what you did to me."

Hudson's pussy clenched, and her clit throbbed.

"With your preferred level of penetration, of course. I know what I like is a little, shall we say, extra for some."

It was a fair point, and one that turned Hudson on rather than leaving her self-conscious. "I'll stick with the clit and one finger, maybe two, if it's all the same to you."

"Oh, it's all good with me." Callie's hand left Hudson's ass and nudged her onto her back. She wasted no time, sliding her fingers over Hudson's sex and into her wetness.

"Good." Hudson let out a groan. "Very, very good."

❖

Hudson was true to her word, taking as good as she gave. She also used Callie's kneeling position to slip a hand between Callie's thighs and fuck her again, mirroring perfectly the rhythm and pace. Rather than distracting Hudson, it seemed to amplify her pleasure.

Hudson orgasmed with a force that had Callie quivering and coming all over again. She collapsed from her kneeling position onto her back, flopping one arm above her head. *Fuck, that was good.* Hudson might not win any prizes for making the first move, but she sure as hell knew what to do with the subsequent ones.

Hudson waited a beat, then propped on one elbow and regarded her with a satisfied smile. "Is that your way of tapping out?"

It wouldn't take more than about two minutes to let the sex high soften into the sated sleep that came with a couple of really good orgasms. But it had been ages since she'd invited a virtual stranger back to her house for a hookup, and it seemed like a shame to waste it. "Just catching my breath." She lifted a finger. "Unless you're done, of course. I'm perfectly content if that's the case."

"Not." Hudson pressed a kiss to Callie's shoulder. "The." She got to her knees and kissed between Callie's breasts. "Case." Straddled Callie's hips. "At." Pulled one of Callie's nipples into her mouth. "All."

"In that case." Callie thrust her pelvis against Hudson's before pulling her down for a kiss. She gently scratched along the back of Hudson's neck and buried her fingers in Hudson's hair.

Hudson lingered over the kiss for a moment, but then she started a slow descent down Callie's body. Her neck, her breasts. Her ribs, her belly. Callie spread her legs and Hudson settled between them. "Is this okay?"

Callie nodded, wanting to say something clever but not having enough blood flow to her brain to come up with anything.

Hudson didn't rush. She trailed a line of kisses from the swell of Callie's hip to the top of her thigh. Callie let her head fall back to the pillow and closed her eyes. Much like the first brush of Hudson's fingers over her, or the first thrust into her, the press of Hudson's tongue to her clit sent a jolt of electricity through her. But instead of the almost frantic rush to release, this felt like a languid and luxurious ride—sensuous and beckoning her to soak up every detail.

She undulated slowly, letting Hudson set the intensity and pace. She moaned. She sighed. She fell utterly under Hudson's spell.

Time spun out, and her surroundings blurred. All that remained was the sensation of Hudson's mouth on her. The sort of pleasure that had her drifting blissfully along and yet hyper aware. The sort of pleasure that made her understand why addicts chased the next fix.

When Hudson slid one and then a second finger into her, timing perfectly curved strokes with the lap of her tongue, Callie was done. She came in a rush, but rather than all at once, the orgasm rolled through her. It vibrated from her center in waves and made her feel like she was basking on a shallow beach as the tide swept over her in perfect rhythm.

The ripples finally subsided enough for Callie to get her bearings, and she let out a shaky sigh. She squeezed her thighs just tightly enough to signal Hudson. The second Hudson pulled away, Callie's whole body seemed to melt, limbs limp and torso heavy. "Fuck," she said in a low whisper, more for her own benefit than Hudson's.

"Yeah?" Hudson had moved up to lie alongside her.

Callie chuckled feebly. "It's cute that you ask as though you don't already know."

"I try to take nothing for granted." Hudson ran a finger along her collarbone. "Especially when it comes to sex."

She summoned the energy to open her eyes and turn her head. Hudson's words might have been humble, but her expression was anything but. Not many people could pull off smug without looking like a jerk, but Hudson could. If Callie had the strength to move, she'd be tempted to do something about it. "Yeah, but you know how to get a woman off. And you know sated when you see it."

"I like to think of it as a matter of attentiveness over skill, but thank you." Hudson smirked. "And you're welcome."

"Attentiveness is a skill," she said to be contrary.

"I'll give you that. You, however, are very easy to pay attention to."

Who'd have guessed the preppy and slightly shy hottie checking her out from across the dance floor would turn out to be one of the best fucks she'd had in recent memory? Or that she'd have so much fun in the process? "I hope you're going to let me return that favor."

"You don't have to." Hudson waited a beat, seeming to search Callie's face for something. "But I'm definitely not going to turn you down."

"Oh, good." Callie rolled to her side. "I hate being turned down."

Hudson chuckled. "Something gives me the feeling it doesn't happen very often."

"You'd be surprised." Not that she had a plethora of crash-and-burns. More that she probably put herself out there more than most, so the law of averages upped her tally on both sides.

"You give me some names and numbers. I'll be happy to call them up and tell them what a colossal mistake they made."

Callie laughed. "I can think of a few better uses for our time."

She slinked down Hudson's body. Hudson shifted up a bit, giving Callie enough room to settle comfortably between Hudson's thighs. The paleness of Hudson's skin was set off by the patch of dark hair and a stark contrast to the tan of her arms. Callie filed away the details, loving the way women's bodies could be so different and yet also the same.

She slipped her arms under Hudson's thighs, curling them up and around so she could have a nice hold. Hudson wiggled a bit, as though testing Callie's grip. She gave Hudson a gentle squeeze. "Is this okay?"

"Oh, yeah."

Callie smiled at Hudson's tone as much as her words. Mostly invitation, but there was the tiniest bit of challenge there, too. She could work with that. More, she liked it. "Preferences? Prohibitions?"

Hudson shook her head. "I'm pretty sure I want whatever you're offering."

Armed with that information, and with her desire to prove Hudson wasn't the only one who could be attentive, she pressed her tongue into Hudson's folds. Slow strokes, languid circles, a gentle suck. She tried them all, homing in on what made Hudson clench, what made her moan.

It didn't take long to find a rhythm. Hudson moved with her hypnotically, breaths shallow and punctuated with sounds of pleasure. Despite her best intention to keep her focus strictly on Hudson's reactions, she fell into a bit of a trance. Hudson's subtle musk, her salty sweet taste. Maybe not quite as good as being on the receiving end, but pretty damn close.

"Fuck. That's it. Yes."

Callie didn't even try to suppress a smile. But then she doubled down, matching the frenetic thrust of Hudson's hips and not worrying too much about getting enough oxygen. It didn't take long for Hudson's entire body to tense. She grasped at Callie's hair and growled, and Callie had the closest thing to an orgasm she'd ever experienced without direct stimulation.

Hudson went lax. Callie dropped her head onto Hudson's thigh and sucked in as much air as her lungs could process. *Damn.*

"Holy crap," Hudson said.

Callie laughed. "Yeah."

"I think I had an out-of-body experience."

"Really?" Callie crawled up the bed to lie next to Hudson. "Were you watching us from the corner like a voyeur?"

Hudson grabbed a lock of Callie's hair and gave it a gentle tug. "It's not nice to tease someone too sex-dazed to fight back."

Callie propped her head on her hand. "You started it."

"I was merely trying to give you a compliment."

"Oh, well, in that case, you can keep it simple and call me a goddess."

"Goddess, huh?" Hudson lifted her head long enough to press a soft kiss to Callie's lips. "All right. You are a goddess."

She pretended to be shy about it. "Aw, thanks."

"Seriously, though." Hudson shook her head. "Amazing."

Hudson let out what sounded like a happy sigh, but then frowned. Callie knew that look. "Can I get you a glass of water?"

"That would be great," Hudson said.

Callie climbed from bed. She started for the door but paused halfway there and turned. "And no pressure, but I'd love you to stay the night."

Hudson's features relaxed, and Callie congratulated herself on reading the situation correctly. "That would be great, too."

CHAPTER THREE

@shitprofessorssay: If I wanted to work in the summer, I'd have gotten a real job.

Callie woke to the sound of Hudson snoring beside her. She smiled, oddly charmed. It wouldn't be charming if she had to sleep next to it every day, obviously, but that was something she gladly didn't have to worry about.

She slipped out of bed, pulled on her robe, and headed to the kitchen, stopping in the bathroom to pee and brush her teeth. Some things were even more pressing than coffee. She let Lucy out, ground beans and put on a full pot, figuring she could use the leftovers for iced coffee if Hudson didn't want any.

It was too bad she hadn't been to the store. Offering overnight guests breakfast was a point of pride. She could always rustle up eggs. Or French toast. Or a bagel from the freezer. Pedestrian but passable.

"Good morning."

Callie turned to find Hudson fully dressed and sporting some genuinely epic bed head. "Good morning."

Hudson ran her fingers through her disheveled hair. The dark waves remained untamed. "I, uh, hope you haven't been up long."

"Not long at all." She gestured to the coffee pot and bowl of dog food on the counter. "Starting the morning putters."

"Oh." Hudson started. "I can get out of your hair."

Callie waved a hand. "I just got the coffee on. Would you like a cup?"

Hudson's gaze darted to the pot that had started to gurgle and send out its alluring aroma. She looked back at Callie, eager but wary. "If you're sure it wouldn't be too much trouble."

"I'm sure. I'd never send someone off after spending the night without at least that much."

Hudson's features softened. "That would be great."

"How do you like it?" Callie went for a smirk, believing it was never too early in the day for a little double entendre.

"Oh. Um. Black is fine."

Quips about the austerity of that preference flitted through her mind, but she held them in check. Was Hudson having regrets about last night? Perhaps the veil of shy and awkward returned in the light of day, or perhaps Hudson simply wasn't a morning person. Hopefully one of the latter. Even if they never crossed paths again, she didn't like to be something someone regretted. Though, honestly, in a town the size of Ryekill, chances were high they would. In fact, it was entirely possible—likely?—Hudson had moved to town because she'd been hired at the college.

Callie poured two cups of coffee, adding her favorite oat milk and brown sugar creamer to her own, and set all those thoughts aside. "Here you go."

Hudson had the grace to take it in both hands and offer a genuine smile. "Thanks."

"Feel free to sit." She gestured to the thrift shop table she'd refurbed the summer she bought the house. "There are also some chairs out on the back deck."

"This is great. Thank you."

Since the chairs outside would be all dewy, she didn't argue. Even though coffee outside was one of her favorite summer weekend luxuries. "I've just got to let Lucy in."

Hudson took a seat, and Callie would swear it was more to be out of the way than anything else. Funny how a person could take command in bed with such ease and be borderline meek after the fact. Of course, if she could only pick one, she'd take commanding and confident in bed any day of the week.

She opened the back door, and Lucy trotted in like she owned the place. Which she sort of did. Callie set down her breakfast, then joined Hudson at the table. They sat silently for a moment and Callie wondered once again if it was a morning thing or an uncomfortable thing that had Hudson so quiet. "It's going to be a gorgeous Sunday, I think," she said with all the cheerful banality she'd bring to a faculty/staff social.

"Is it? Oh, that's nice. I'll have to take my laptop outside."

Curiosity swirled, but Callie held it in check. Hudson had seemed reticent to talk much about herself the night before, and she doubted that would change now. "I do my best to leave mine at the office, but I'll definitely be outside. My conundrum will be whether to lounge in the hammock or yank out some of the weeds that seem much more eager to grow than my flowers."

Hudson chuckled. "Weeds are like that."

Since she didn't volunteer anything else, or ask any questions, Callie let it go. But before the lack of conversation could get weird, Hudson tipped back the contents of her mug and set it on the table. "Thank you for the coffee. It was exceptional."

"My pleasure. Can I—"

"I'll let you get on with your day." Hudson stood.

"Yeah. Sure." She certainly wasn't about to beg Hudson to stick around.

Hudson didn't take her time heading to the front door. She slid into her shoes and all but yanked it open. Callie hovered a couple of feet behind her. But just when she thought Hudson might bolt without so much as a backward glance, Hudson turned. She gave Callie a slow, appreciative once-over, and her eyes had all the confidence of the night before. Callie became acutely aware that the satin robe barely skimmed the tops of her thighs. "Thank you again for last night. I had a really great time."

"Thank you back, because the feeling is entirely mutual." Which it was, even if things had gone a little weird this morning.

Hudson seemed to realize she was staring and gave a brisk nod. "Enjoy the good weather."

"You, too." Callie offered a wave and resisted saying something about seeing each other around.

❖

Hudson retraced her steps from the night before. A cleanup crew was already at work in the park, breaking down the main tent and hauling away bags of trash and recyclables. Hers wasn't the only car abandoned in the lot, making her smile. She hoped their owners had spent their nights as pleasurably as she had.

She debated going home to change but decided she still enjoyed enough anonymity to buy groceries in the same clothes as the day before without anyone taking notice. She had a crap ton of work to do, and it would be silly to waste twenty minutes to avoid feeling self-conscious at the store.

Despite her commitment to efficiency, she wandered the aisles, tossing way more than she needed for the week into her cart. She'd yet to fully stock her new kitchen, after all, and the sauces and spices and staples she relied on wouldn't simply appear. And while the local market was a far cry from the sprawling Whole Foods she frequented in California, it boasted a nice balance—fresh produce, all the essentials, and more than a few things she'd missed or forgotten about during her time on the West Coast.

She got so caught up in the selection of mustards, she almost forgot where she was.

"You look like a local already." Henry Hazelton, chair of the Coteau College English Department—not to mention the person who'd hired her—offered a jovial smile.

Hudson started, almost dropping the jar of hot 'n' spicy she'd been studying. "Henry. Hi. Yes. Gotta get the fridge up to snuff."

"A woman after my own heart." He pointed to one with a bright red label. "If you want a local delicacy, try Noltz's. It'll clear out your sinuses and leave you wanting more."

She'd have taken the suggestion to be polite, but it sounded right up her alley. "Sold."

Henry gave a nod. "You won't be disappointed. You're all set with your office, right? You don't need to move in until August, but I imagine you might want to get settled in sooner than that."

Was it weird to admit she planned to be doing a lot of work there, too, even over the summer? "I am. I might be further along unpacking there than my house."

"Spoken like a true professor. I confess Storey is rather a ghost town in the summer, but Betty will be there. She's got an abbreviated schedule for June and July, but she's in more days than not."

Hudson was pretty sure she and Betty had been the only people to set foot in the building shared by the English, Philosophy, and Comparative Religions Departments in the last two weeks. "We've bonded over the belief that no classes or administrative tasks should happen before ten."

Henry laughed. "Remind me not to give you any eight a.m. classes next semester."

"I would absolutely teach at whatever time you assign." Hudson lifted both hands, afraid Henry might have taken the comment seriously and, by extension, think she was the sort of self-entitled new professor who presumed to make such demands.

Henry reached across his cart to clap a hand on her shoulder. "Relax. My goal is to protect my junior faculty, not torture them."

He had an earnestness about him that Hudson appreciated. It balanced out his middle-aged white-dude-ness. In addition to all the other reasons she'd chosen Coteau from the three offers she'd received, she really liked the vibe of the department. Reasonably diverse, not super competitive with one another, and with enough different research interests that she'd be one of only three faculty members with a focus on American literature. And as far as she could tell, her particular interest in queer and female writers was unique. What she might lose in esoteric banter she'd make up for in getting dibs on teaching in her preferred areas—at whatever time her chair deemed appropriate. "Well, this junior faculty member thanks you."

"Good, good. I'll let you get on with your shopping. I've got to get home myself before Isa thinks I'm stalling at the store to avoid mowing the lawn." He let out a self-deprecating chuckle. "You holler if you need anything. Otherwise, I'll see you in August."

She thought that might be a joke, too. The see you in August bit, not the comment about his chores or his wife's expectations. But when he didn't shoot her a wink or mime an elbow to her ribs, she realized he wasn't kidding. Full professor prerogative, apparently. Even if he was the chair of the department. Someday. "Hopefully I'll have my bookcases organized by then."

He did chuckle at that. "Nineteen years and mine are still a mess."

She liked that about him, too. Earnest, but a chaos Muppet deep down. "Oh, I was going to email you. Do you need to sign off on my syllabi before classes start?"

Henry's eyes narrowed, like the thought hadn't even occurred to him. "I suppose I should. Due diligence and all that. You send it to me when it's done, but I'm sure it'll be fine. You know where to find all the boilerplate mumbo jumbo, yes?"

Hudson wondered if the words "boilerplate" and "mumbo jumbo" had ever been used together. Then she wondered if she should mention that "mumbo jumbo" was one of those phrases not inherently racist but problematic enough to retire from daily use. She settled on neither—junior professor prerogative. "I do. Thanks."

"Excellent. Well, then. Enjoy the rest of your summer."

He continued down the aisle. Hudson did the same, making sure to turn her cart in the opposite direction. She finished her shopping, deciding to grab a rotisserie chicken on her way out to save her having to actually cook for the next few days.

She checked out and headed home, loving that the drive took all of ten minutes. She also loved taking her groceries in and putting them away exactly how she wanted. Sharing an apartment in Berkeley had been the financially responsible thing to do but also kind of a pain. Having her own space, even if it was a rental, was a delight.

Since it was, and she didn't need to negotiate her comings or goings or anything-in-betweens, she decided to take her comment to Callie to heart and take her lunch and her laptop outside. After a shower, though. A day of being outside followed by a night of sex and a morning in old clothes had left her feeling gnarly.

In the bathroom, she peeled off her clothes and turned on the taps. While waiting for the water to warm, she glanced in the mirror. And was promptly mortified by the reflection staring back. Her attempts to finger comb her hair had proven futile, or perhaps more accurately, temporary. Worse, the smudge of pink on her neck could be mistaken for nothing other than the lipstick it so obviously was.

Had Henry seen it? Had he taken one look at her and immediately known what she'd been up to the night before? Was he at home now, telling his wife about running into the new junior faculty member at the store after a night of debauchery? Was he judging her or, worse, laughing at her? Would he never take her seriously now?

"Whoa, there. Slow down, bud." Hudson spoke to herself the way she might try to calm a friend stuck in an anxiety spiral. It made her feel silly, but it worked.

It was fine. Everything was fine. She was a rising scholar, courted and hired for her impressive list of publications and her above average teaching evaluations. And she was an adult, free to do whatever she wanted in her free time. It wasn't like she was sauntering into Survey of American Lit looking freshly laid.

Hudson nodded to her reflection, soaked in the nod it gave her in return. Last night had been an aberration. A delightful aberration, but an aberration all the same. She had no plans to date or get involved with anyone, and least not during her first year on the tenure clock. And as gorgeous and deliciously distracting as her night with Callie had been, it wasn't who she was or what she was about. And it wasn't like she'd be seeing her again.

Chapter Four

@shitprofessorssay: I'll reply to your email on or about August 15, when I am contractually obligated to do so.

Callie shimmied her hips and trailed her hands up her torso before extending them overhead. A bead of sweat trickled down her spine and made her smile. She flicked her gaze to Iliana for the cue, then transitioned to a walking hip bump.

Right, left, right, left. Then the same move but in reverse. A four-point turn, followed by a spin. Chest circles, hip circles, and a series of rapid-fire Mayas. Iliana canted her head to the right, and the six women seamlessly slid in formation, ending with Callie in the lead position.

She led a series of moves, enjoying the freedom of taking the dance wherever her imagination suggested. Since she no longer had to watch for the cues, Callie studied her own form in the mirror. The front-tie top she wore accentuated her breasts and showed off her soft belly. The peasant skirt sat low on her hips. She'd come to love her curves, even if they only intimated an hourglass shape.

It had been quite a journey. She'd never suffered from the sort of crippling body image issues many women did. Her family was too loving for that sort of thing, not to mention too practical. Still, a couple of toxic relationships had done a number on her, and it took several years of therapy and self-exploration to come truly into her own. She now boasted the confidence that came from within rather than ticking boxes in the list of societal expectations. Most days, at least.

There was also the slightly perverse satisfaction of having a hobby that many of her stuffier, starchier faculty colleagues would find unseemly.

She finished her turn in the lead position and took her next spot in the formation. She danced the moves Sasha cued and allowed her mind to wander. As it had several times over the last few weeks, it led her right to thoughts of Hudson.

Well, thoughts might be an overstatement. Or perhaps an oversimplification. Because what she actually had were flashbacks, along with a few fantasies. Images, sensations—the sort that had her thighs clenching and wetness pooling between her legs. Honestly, there were worse ways to make it through a belly dance class. She liked leaning into the sensuality of it as much as the playfulness. And being turned on brought focus to each thrust and undulation of her body.

As it usually did, the hour flew by. When Iliana called it and cut the music, Callie grabbed her water bottle and chugged.

"Who wants to go out for drinks?" Iliana asked.

Callie raised her hand. "I do if drinks can also include falafel."

Iliana bumped her hip to Callie's. "I like the way you think."

Janina had to work at six the next morning and bowed out with a pout. Sara declined without explanation, but her eyes held mischief. She waited a beat, in true Sara fashion, then said, "I'm going to hang with a couple I met at Pride."

"Hang?" Sasha asked, never one to shy away from saying what everyone else was thinking.

Sara shrugged, all innocence. "I don't imagine I'll actually be hung, but I am hoping some rope is involved."

After a round of winks, nudges, and high fives, the group disbanded. Callie packed up her things and she, Sasha, and Iliana walked to Za'atar, the middle eastern restaurant a few blocks over. They got a table and ordered a bottle of wine and a bunch of dishes to share.

With the wine poured, Iliana raised her glass. "To boss babes and earth mothers and everything in between."

Callie clinked her glass to the others. That's why she loved this group of women—they were exactly that.

"So," Sasha said with a casualness Callie knew to be anything but. "Any developments on your Pride hookup?"

Iliana's gaze darted between them. "Hookup? I was not informed there was a hookup."

"That's because you were on vacation when I made the announcement." Callie winked. There'd obviously been no formal announcement, but she'd shared highlights at class the week after. And Iliana had been in Philly making nice with her in-laws.

"Unacceptable. I deserve a text or a recap at the very least," Iliana said.

The food arrived, and Callie made a show of studying the plate of baba ghanoush in front of her. She looked up to find Iliana staring at her with a mixture of impatience and expectation. "I had a hookup at Pride."

"And?" Iliana's impatience showed no signs of waning.

"And the sex was good enough that I'm still thinking about it."

"And?" Iliana asked.

Callie had no qualms playing coy, but she also didn't have a lot of additional details to share. "And that's it."

"Uh-uh. What's her name? Who is she? Where does she live? Where does she work? Will you see her again?" Iliana counted each question by ticking her fingers, then wiggled them. "Do you want to start with those, or should I continue?"

Callie grabbed a triangle of pita from the basket in the middle of the table and piled it with baba. She stuffed it into her mouth and made a show of chewing. Iliana mimicked the move, but in addition to the exaggerated chewing, she laced her fingers together and placed them on the table in front of her.

Callie took her time wiping her fingers on a napkin and taking another sip of wine. "Hudson and no, I didn't get her last name. As for the rest, no idea. She mentioned just moving here but didn't offer details, and I didn't ask."

Iliana shook her head. “Of course you didn’t.”

“I mean, chances are good she works at the college because half the people who live in Ryekill do. But she seemed skittish, so I didn’t go digging.”

“Skittish but good in bed?” Iliana looked dubious.

“That’s what I said.” Sasha lifted a hand to hide the fact that she was talking around a mouthful of stuffed grape leaf.

Callie shrugged. She’d been just as surprised. Pleasantly surprised, but surprised. “I don’t know what to tell you. It was like she was afraid to make the first move, or even the second. But once it was one hundred percent clear we were going to end up in bed together, she had the moves and the swagger to match.”

Iliana let out a wistful sigh. “That’s hot.”

“It was.” Callie reached for a falafel, breaking it in half to let some of the steam escape before taking a bite. She let out a moan of pleasure—part falafel delectation, part memory of her night with Hudson. “Why are these so good?”

“Because they’re fried with love,” Iliana said.

Since Iliana happened to be cousins with the owner of the restaurant, Callie accepted the assertion at face value. Though she could have argued it had more to do with the crap ton of garlic and fresh parsley. Either way, they hit the spot. She helped herself to another, making a mini sandwich with pita and tzatziki.

“Have you trolled the campus directory?” Iliana asked. “I can’t imagine there are too many Hudsons floating around.”

She wanted to say no, but the nonchalance would have been an act. “New faculty aren’t loaded until their contracts start.”

“Hmm. So, faculty not staff, you think?” Iliana lifted her chin at Sasha. “And when do contracts start?”

“My money is on faculty.” Sasha gave a knowing nod. “And the fifteenth.”

“That’s next week.”

Being thoroughly prepared didn’t seem to keep it from sneaking up on her. “Yes, and so is move-in, new student orientation, convocation, and the hundred or so other things that come with the start of the semester.”

"And new faculty orientation," Sasha said, as though that fact had only just occurred to her. "If she's new faculty, she'll be at that."

"Assuming she's a rule follower," Callie said, not acknowledging that both she and Sasha would be presenters at it.

Both Sasha and Iliana laughed. Sasha lifted her glass of wine at Callie. "Your favorite."

❖

The start of the semester remained a week away, but campus seemed to be coming alive, and Hudson was loving it. Most students hadn't moved in yet, but she'd seen several milling around the bookstore when she stopped by to check that what she'd ordered for her classes had come in. She crossed paths with close to a dozen people on her way across the quad, and nearly everyone returned her hello. Even Storey finally felt abuzz. Sure, it was the first department meeting of the new year, but still. She leaned into the vibe rather than the obligation that might be lurking behind it.

Hudson settled in and worked on her current paper, an exploration of Dorothy Allison's influence on queer literature in the twenty-first century. Even with having to pull herself out of the deep work groove, she got to the conference room early. Rather than take a seat, she hung around the refreshments to make small talk with Betty. One, because she'd spent more time with Betty over the summer than any of her faculty colleagues. Two, because department admins wielded more power than most people wanted to admit, and having an in with Betty counted almost as much as one with Henry. Three, sitting in someone's usual seat could make things weird. Faculty might be cutting edge scholars but most of them were also creatures of habit. The last thing Hudson wanted was to kick off the semester as the proverbial pea under some princess's pillow.

She'd hoped to bump into Lawrence, but he hadn't been in his office when she checked. He hadn't been in his office all summer from what she could tell. Not completely surprising, especially for a full professor likely beginning to entertain retirement, but disappointing. She'd known him her whole life, given that he and her father had been friends since college, and it gave her a thrill to think the honorary uncle she'd adored as a kid was now her colleague and, hopefully, mentor.

He'd yet to show up today, too, but other members of the department trickled in. She'd met most as part of her day-long campus interview in the spring. Henry, of course. Amber Jones, a stunning woman with waist-length braids who specialized in African American writers and Black feminist thought, came over to say hello and ask how she was settling in. She was joined by Esther Fielding, a Medievalist who managed to look the part in a flowing floral dress and a green velvet vest. Harrison Smith-White—complete with his trademark bowtie—gave her a friendly nod. And Layla Byrne, the creative writing professor with a specialization in speculative fiction who'd been on sabbatical, pulled her into a hug.

"Oh, damn." Layla released her and smacked a hand to her forehead. "I forgot I'm not supposed to do that without consent. Sorry."

"No apology needed." She appreciated the attempt at awareness, even if it landed a little late. "I would have consented."

Amber and Esther laughed. Esther said, "And that is Layla in a nutshell."

Hudson had done her homework. Layla had six novels under her belt and had written several episodes for the latest series in the *Star Trek* franchise. The fact that she was a bubbly eccentric inclined to give hugs was merely icing on the cake. "It's a pleasure to meet you."

Wesley Roberts and George Payne strode in next. Wesley gave her an eager smile. He was probably thrilled not to be the most junior member of the department anymore. George—or G.W., as his bio and the name plaque on his door referred to him—didn't even make eye contact. She'd have expected no less from the requisite douchey film studies bro.

Henry glanced at his watch as Lawrence joined, and Hudson couldn't help but notice the relieved expression on his face. Henry's, not Lawrence's. She couldn't make meaning from it, but she filed it away for future reference. In addition to being creatures of habit, faculty could be finicky. And departments were ecosystems where each element had to be kept in just the right balance. She intended to do her part to impress but also to play well with others.

"Shall we get started?" Henry moved to the head of the table and gestured for people to join him, which Betty took as her cue to hightail it out of there.

Lawrence caught her eye and winked, as though they were in on a joke together. She smiled, not quite sure what the joke was but thrilled to see him nonetheless. Everyone shuffled into the seats around the large table. Hudson hung back long enough to get a sense of things, then settled in an empty chair next to Lawrence.

"Well, look who's at the table," he said with a nudge of his elbow. "All grown up and ready to make her mark."

Hudson basked in the dad vibes even though she didn't want to lean on the personal connection, much less give the impression of doing so. "I'm going to do my best."

"Trust me, with these yahoos, it won't be hard."

He'd lowered his voice but not by much. Hudson stole a glance at Henry, who was looking their way with irritation. She cleared her throat and straightened her shoulders. Hopefully, Henry would take it as a sign of respect. And, hopefully, Lawrence wouldn't tease her after the fact for being a suck-up.

She opened the leather journal she used as her running list of things to note and do and picked up the hand-carved fountain pen her mom had given her for Christmas. But when she took a deep, ready-to-get-to-work breath, the exhale came out shaky.

In the flurry of greetings and getting her bearings, the weight of the moment only then hit her. She was sitting in her very first department meeting, a tenure-track assistant professor. The culmination of a decade of hard work and more than a few existential crises. The dream she'd nurtured since her very first lit class her freshman year at Cornell.

Holy crap.

Hudson sat a little taller in her chair and scribbled down everything Henry said. New system for scanning college ID for printer and copier jobs. Check. Process for requesting a TA. Check.

She actually knew most of it already, courtesy of her exhaustive study of the Coteau College website, the faculty handbook, and the hundred or so questions she'd asked Betty, but it never hurt to be thorough. She prided herself on being thorough, professionally and personally. Sexually.

Her mind had no rational reason to go there, but it did, flashing select moments of her night with Callie. Hudson hadn't seen her in the two months since, but it didn't stop Callie from invading her thoughts with inconvenient regularity. Eyes the color of polished mahogany, playful one minute and sultry the next. Those gloriously thick curls—just as rich but a few shades redder. The lithe movements of her body on the dance floor. In bed.

"There's not going to be a quiz." Lawrence leaned over to speak but didn't bother whispering.

After yanking her attention from the all too vivid images, Hudson offered him a half-smile, not wanting to be rude but refusing to get a reputation for being a cut-up at her very first department meeting.

"Good thing, or Professor Michaelson would have flunked out by now." Amber's deadpan delivery, paired with the look of utter disdain, would have sent Hudson slinking under the table had it been directed at her.

Lawrence merely looked bored. "I happen to have the answer key. Her name is Betty."

Hudson fought a cringe. The comment could pass for a compliment, at least to some. But it was rooted in the sort of arrogance that came with being someone like Lawrence. Someone comfortable with their privilege and status. It left a bad taste in her mouth even as she tried to set it aside.

"Betty is a rock star," Henry said, clearly trying to smooth things over.

"But not your personal assistant." Amber looked pointedly at Lawrence then, leaving Hudson to wonder if the antagonism preceded this meeting.

"Nah. That's what TAs are for." Lawrence chortled at his own joke.

Amber rolled her eyes. Several others sighed. Henry looked uncomfortable, then he cleared his throat. "Anyway, I think that about covers the housekeeping part of the agenda. What else?"

Esther raised her hand. "I thought we'd schedule the fall brown bags before the semester started and everyone's schedules got out of hand."

"Right, right." Henry smiled his affable smile, probably happy for the change of subject as much as the reminder.

"We have four first Thursdays. Any takers?"

Layla raised her hand, and Hudson did, too. She'd learned about the informal sharing of current research during her interview. Attending would be a great way to get to know her colleagues' interests, but presenting would hopefully solidify her status as a serious researcher while she ran the gauntlet that was journal submission.

"Excellent." Esther looked at the calendar in front of her. "Layla, I'll put you down for September since I'm sure you've got some juicy stuff to share. Hudson, are you okay with October?"

Hudson's brain had already started outlining her presentation. "Absolutely."

Harrison and Amber rounded out the schedule, and they moved on to committee assignments. Hudson tried to volunteer for Faculty Senate, mostly because it would look good on her CV. Henry steered her away, citing political landmines, and Esther promptly backed him up and said she'd do it. "We want you to get your feet wet before we throw you into the deep end."

In the end, she ended up on an ad hoc committee on advising. Not a huge commitment and mostly feel-good work around improving the student experience and bridging the gap between the faculty advisers students had in their majors and the centralized advising office. Definitely up her alley.

The meeting ended, and Hudson lingered, hoping to catch up with Lawrence. He clapped her on the shoulder and cited a one o'clock tee time. "We'll do lunch," he said, already halfway out the door.

She collected her things and tried not to be disappointed.

Amber caught her eye and pulled her aside. “I know you know him from some family connection or something, but I’d be careful about hitching your wagon to Lawrence.”

A knot formed in Hudson’s stomach. She had nothing but respect for Amber. On top of that, when a badass woman of color gave a word of warning about an old white guy, she was largely inclined to listen. How could she do that without throwing her father’s best friend under the bus?

“I know that puts you in a weird place, but he’s a dinosaur of the worst kind. You don’t want that rubbing off on you.”

Hudson wondered if Amber was referring to Lawrence’s behavior or his reputation. Not that it made much difference. “Thanks.”

Amber lifted a shoulder and flashed a wry smile. “Welcome to the department.”

Chapter Five

@shitprofessorssay: Faculty need other faculty members as friends. Who else are you going to go to the gym with in the middle of the day?

With the start of classes right around the corner, Storey began to feel like a hive of faculty activity. Hudson spent even more time in her office, working but also enjoying drop-ins from her colleagues. As much as she was looking forward to getting into the classroom, it was the sort of scholars-being-scholarly vibe that got her creative juices flowing and had her running ahead of schedule on the book chapter she had due in November.

She'd been invited to contribute to a collection of essays based on her dissertation—an exploration of subtle and not so subtle queer themes in the works of Edith Wharton. While she didn't plan to hang her whole career on exploring queer subtexts in classics of American literature, she wasn't about to pass up the chance to add a line to her CV with work she had, for the most part, already done.

Hudson hit command-S with a flourish. A satisfying gesture if technically unnecessary in the world of autosave. Intentional. Thorough. She liked being those things, even if she'd been called some less flattering synonyms a time or two.

When her phone flashed with a text notification, she happily scooped it up, prepared to brag about her progress to whoever had messaged her. Dad. Hudson smiled. If anyone could appreciate a little scholarly self-congratulation, it was him.

Lawrence says you're making a great first impression with the department.

Hudson frowned at the message, thoughts of her own exploits taking a back seat to the awkward interaction they'd had at the department meeting. It wasn't the observation that befuddled her so much as the context. Or perhaps lack thereof. Lawrence had treated the entire meeting as an inconvenience. He'd basically laughed at her for taking things seriously. She hadn't said as much to her parents, mostly because she still couldn't decide what to make of it. Part of her harbored hope it was an aberration, even if Amber's words of warning remained lodged firmly in her mind.

She cleared her throat and sat up straighter, like she'd been cold called on in class. *It was great to see him. Didn't get to catch up really but hoping to do lunch soon.*

Hudson hit send and slumped back in her chair. Then she laughed at herself for getting worked up. She might still want to impress them both, but it wasn't about that anymore. Of course, telling herself that didn't drive away the little voices in her mind—the ones that had been compelling her to overachieve for as long as she could remember and the ones telling her that praise and approval were better than any drug.

Deciding it might be a good time to call it a day, she closed her laptop and snagged her gym bag. Some good old-fashioned sweating would get her out of her head, and she'd been wanting to check out the campus fitness center. No time like the present.

Since she didn't know the locker room situation and would need to come back to her office anyway, she did a quick change in the corner, safely away from the frosted glass window of her office door. The trek across campus—complete with brilliant sunshine and a warm breeze—restored her good mood.

She walked into the fitness center and found it virtually empty. Two women on treadmills chatted with one another, and a guy with a ponytail rowed to nowhere with impressive gusto. No one else in sight. That wouldn't be the case once classes started, and she'd yet to decide whether working out with students crossed the line into weirdsville, but she'd cross that bridge when she got to it. For now, this was super convenient. Not to mention free.

Since the weather remained nice enough to enjoy cardio outdoors, she headed to the weight benches. She fished her earbuds from the pocket of her shorts, only to realize she'd neglected to charge them. Oh, well. She tucked them away and selected a pair of ten-pound dumbbells to start.

Hudson worked through sets of shoulder presses and flys, curls and rows. She'd been a bit lax over the summer and felt it. Her muscles burned and her breaths didn't seem to bring enough oxygen to the places she needed it. It was a good sort of pain, though. The kind that reminded her of what her body could do and why it was nice to have stamina. Things like hiking one of the High Peaks or swimming in open water. Like making love to a beautiful woman.

Hudson groaned at the thought. Other than her night with Callie, she hadn't had sex since moving to New York in June. Not that two months counted as a dry spell. Hell, she'd gone over a year a couple of times. No, the problem with the last two months was that being with Callie had been good. The kind of good that made it hard to think about anyone else and that made her solo endeavors feel woefully inadequate. And while she held firm her intentions of not getting involved with anyone for at least the next year, she'd experienced more than a few moments of regret they hadn't exchanged information or even broached the subject of getting together again.

To make matters worse, she was pretty sure that had been her doing. Callie hadn't expressed interest explicitly, but she'd offered breakfast. That had to count for something. But Hudson had been so flummoxed by the whole thing that she'd bolted like a bashful schoolgirl. Not her finest moment. And not one she could likely recover from should their paths ever cross again.

It was so uncouth.

Hudson groaned again, though it came out closer to a grunt as she strained through the last set of overhead presses.

"Easy there, cowboy."

Hudson started, and her gaze flicked in the direction of the voice. It belonged to a gloriously muscular woman with flame-red hair in a floral sports bra and matching pair of leggings. She'd taken up a spot on the next mat over, and Hudson hadn't even noticed. "Sorry. I, uh, was distracted."

"You'll distract yourself right into a rotator cuff tear if you're not careful." The woman smiled, and Hudson couldn't tell if it was a joke or genuine caution.

"That would be classic, wouldn't it? How did you hurt yourself? Well, I had these ten-pound weights."

The woman laughed. "You new on campus?"

"That obvious? Hudson Greene, English Department."

"Nice to meet you, Hudson Greene, English Department. Gwyn Bywood, Gender Studies."

Since they both held weights, they exchanged nods instead of a handshake. Hudson's gaze tracked to the pair in Gwyn's hands, and she realized they were twenty-fives. She looked more closely at Gwyn. Thick, taut muscles defined her arms and torso, and her quads stretched the fabric of her leggings. "You look like you know what you're doing," Hudson said.

"A decade of professional body building will do that to a girl."

"Wow." It proved oddly comforting to know she wasn't even in the same league.

Gwyn shrugged, but Hudson read it as playful more than dismissive. "Keeps things interesting. Academia can get a little dull, don't you think?"

She didn't think that at all. Of course, novelty might have something to do with it. "Ask me again in a decade."

Gwyn roared with laughter. "I thought you looked like fresh meat but figured it would be rude to say so."

Hudson laughed, too. She didn't mind being the butt of that sort of joke. Well, not if it was coming from a colleague like the one standing next to her. "I did a post-doc, but it's technically my first semester at my first real job."

"Aw. I remember those days."

Gwyn was definitely older than her, but not by that much. At least Hudson didn't think so. "Are you so very jaded now?"

"Depends on the day."

"Fair." Hudson racked her weights and began stretching. "So, do you come here when classes are in session?"

"I do." Gwyn's arms continued their fluid motions. "The convenience makes it worth the trouble of bumping into students."

"Yeah." She liked knowing at least one other faculty member felt that way, even if she'd yet to convince herself.

"Besides, it's fun to bench more than a bunch of twenty-year-old dudes."

"I suddenly have the urge to take up bodybuilding."

"Ha." Gwyn shifted her stance and switched to tricep curls. "If you want some pointers, let me know."

She couldn't tell whether Gwyn was serious, but the prospect of having a workout buddy appealed. "Do you take clients or are you taking pity on me?"

"Neither," Gwyn said with a knowing look. "I like your vibe."

Hudson's mind flashed to Pride, to referring to Asher and the folks at the Coteau booth as family. She had zero doubt that's what Gwyn meant now. "Well, then, I might take you up on that."

"We should grab coffee, too."

For a hot second, it seemed like Gwyn might be hitting on her. Which would be flattering if nothing else. But then Gwyn shot her a knowing look, one that said they'd be bros, despite Gwyn's more feminine presentation. That, she could do. And that, she realized with a smile, she'd like very much.

❖

Callie stepped back from the box of folders, neatly labeled with the names of the six hundred or so first-year students who'd be arriving on campus in a week's time. "Is it weird that we still hand out folders?" she asked.

Mari, the youngest member of the advising staff, shook their head. "I'm telling you. Kids like something concrete they can hold onto. It's a thing. I still have mine."

"You do not." Mari had graduated three years prior and gone off to grad school to get a master's in higher ed administration. They'd worked for Callie as a student, and Callie had jumped at the chance to bring them onto the professional staff in May.

"I do! I can bring it in and show you if you want." Mari lifted a hand. "I'm not saying that's normal. I'm peak nerd and don't pretend otherwise."

"Nerds forever." Callie lifted a hand, and Mari indulged her in a high five.

"Nerds forever," Mari echoed. "I'm serious, though. I think it's cool. Especially since it's full of both handouts and QR codes. You're speaking everyone's language."

Callie knew that wasn't true. Plenty of students would lose or toss theirs before classes even started. But for those who held onto them—those who used and connected with the resources they put together—it remained worth it. "We try."

"What else needs to be done?" Mari asked.

"I think we're ahead of schedule." They usually were, thanks to doing orientation programs enough years running to have a plan and timeline in place early. "Other than making labels for any last-minute deposits, we should be set."

"Cool, cool. I'm going to go work on my icebreaker for College 101."

"Sounds good. I'm going to work on my most definitely not an icebreaker for the new faculty orientation."

Mari snickered. "You mean you don't want to play identity bingo with a bunch of new professors?"

"Hmm. Let me think." She tapped the tip of her index finger to her chin. "I'll pass."

"I'm sure at least a few of them would be good sports about it."

Callie knew better than to get too snarky in front of her staff, especially about faculty. "You're right. Still, I'll throw my hat in with the students any day."

That got her a vigorous nod. "Totally."

Mari headed to their office and Callie to hers. She put the finishing touches on her PowerPoint for her segment of the new faculty orientation. As promised, not an ice breaker in sight. It was informative, though, and as interesting as a dozen slides about policies and procedures could be. Plus, she'd put a lot of effort into the advising as mentoring angle. That's really what she wanted the faculty to focus on anyway. As long as they weren't out there giving blatant misinformation about policies and procedures, she and her staff could handle the rest.

Speaking of faculty…

The fifteenth of August had come and gone, and Callie had resisted trolling for Hudson on the college website. But if there was a chance they'd cross paths the next day, she wanted to know it. She clicked over to the Coteau homepage and pulled up the directory. She chewed her lip for only a second before typing "Hudson" into the search box.

Hudson, Caleb – Junior, Mathematics

Hudson, Vivienne – Sophomore, Political Science

Greene, Hudson – Assistant Professor, Department of English

Bingo.

Callie sat back and mulled her discovery. Assistant professor of English. There were worse things. There were better things, of course, but that was hardly the point. The point was that she'd been right, and she would in fact see Hudson again. Because despite whatever offhanded comment she'd made about whether or not Hudson was a rule follower, she had no doubt that, on a campus the size of Coteau, they'd bump into each other eventually.

That said, she got big rule follower vibes from Hudson. Definitely not always the case with faculty—that's why she found them so frustrating at times. Not new faculty, though. They usually tried. They might be painfully naive in the process, but she could almost forgive them that. They spent years and years working on some research or other, then got teaching jobs, often without a lick of classroom experience. Or at least barely a lick.

It was like how people who were good at their jobs became managers with or without any ability to manage people. She'd made a point to not be that sort of manager, slowly building experience and taking whatever professional development opportunities came her way. She'd supervised students, then two entry level advisors as an assistant director. She might not have tenure, but she'd earned her Dean title fair and square. With it, the right to have zero patience with professors who couldn't be bothered. Or who thought having degrees and tenure earned them the right to look down on everyone else.

And why, exactly, was she going down this rabbit hole? No good reason. She knew herself and her worth, even with the weird class divide that seemed to exist between faculty and staff. And whether or not Hudson was cool about things or got all weird and distant, those things wouldn't change. In the meantime, she picked up her phone and dashed off a text to Sasha. *Hottie is a lit prof. Kill me now.*

That got her a string of laughing emojis and the expected questions. How did Callie feel about that? Was she going to reach out? Before or after new faculty orientation?

Callie considered her options. It felt a little stalker-ish to reach out to a one-night stand when they hadn't discussed getting together again. They hadn't exchanged last names, much less numbers.

I'm cool with seeing her again—sort of expected to. Will let it happen organically.

Sasha left her on read, which was fine. They were both supposed to be working. She turned her attention back to work, shifting to the resource guide her area and the Division of Student Affairs put together for faculty each year. Unlike the student version, she'd decided to keep the full hard copy intact. But she'd sprinkled in a few QR codes for good measure. Most new faculty were millennials, after all, if not Gen Z, and she didn't want to come across as a luddite.

I think you misspelled orgasmically.

One glance at the notification flashed on her phone and Callie let out a snort. She snatched it up and dashed off a *You think you're so clever.*

No delay in the reply this time. *I know I am.*

Unfortunately for you, I cannot be scandalized. Which might not be entirely true, but it would take a lot more than an implied Freudian slip.

It's hard not to take that as a challenge Sasha tossed back.

She'd walked right into that. Of course, Sasha would never do anything genuinely embarrassing, much less hurtful. It was nice to trust that even as they gave each other a hard time.

I can't wait to meet her. Sasha accompanied that with a wink and a declaration that the absence of a nudge emoji was an affront.

Callie conjured an image of Hudson. Well, a couple. The first was that shy look Hudson had shot her from across the dance floor. The second was the almost smug smile Hudson had after making Callie come. She sighed. *I hope she's cool.*

If not, I'm sure you can cull a few SPS posts from the wreckage.

Callie groaned. What had started out as a joke between a few of her higher ed friends—and an outlet for some of their frustrations with working in academia—had exploded into something much larger. Shit Professors Say had gained over a hundred thousand followers in its three years of existence. And while it collected quotes from institutions all over the world, its primary source of content and sole moderator was Callie herself. *That would be a very small consolation.*

What do you want, woman? Sabbatical?

Callie rolled her eyes. Sabbaticals were a common theme of SPS. Not that she had any issue with the practice itself. Hell, she'd gladly take one. The problem was the side effect. Namely, how far removed many academics were from the realities of how most people lived and worked. *Yes. Now go get your work done so we can go out for drinks later like the plebs we are.*

Plebs forever Sasha texted.

Callie smiled. *Plebs forever.*

Chapter Six

@shitprofessorssay: New faculty orientation is great. They tell you who to go to when you don't want to be bothered with administrivia.

Hudson arrived early, more out of habit than any real nerves. She'd done a version of faculty orientation during her time as a doctoral student, one of more than a hundred fresh-faced teaching assistants who'd be staffing a swath of the one-hundred-level courses offered to Berkeley undergrads. She'd been terrified then, but she'd come a long way.

Today was about learning the ropes of the Coteau systems, not about figuring out how to be a professor.

Since she was the only new hire in the English department, she scoped the other Precocious Pattys, trying to glean who might be in what discipline. She pegged the group of three women already chatting as social scientists and scolded herself for assuming the Asian guy with glasses was comp sci.

The tables were set up in a square with twenty or so seats arranged around the perimeter. A quarter of those had their backs to the teaching station, which she assumed would be in use, so she picked one along the far side. She offered nods of greeting when the women paused long enough to acknowledge her and settled in.

Others started to arrive, including someone from the provost's office who encouraged everyone to help themselves to the bagels and coffee in the back. Hudson didn't hesitate. She'd thrown a protein bar in her bag, but it had been a choice of convenience, not health consciousness.

The session started with a welcome from the provost herself, a vibrant Black woman who'd been promoted from the dean of faculty position when the prior provost resigned suddenly. Hudson was surprised she'd originally come from the Physics Department, mostly because she'd never met a physicist with such charisma. Though, to be fair, she'd only met a few physicists, so her sample size was decidedly small.

Human Resources came next, complete with a hard sell for the Employee Assistance Program. Hudson appreciated that, though she expected life on the tenure clock to be less stressful than on the job market, at least with the number of pubs she already had under her belt or pending. Student Affairs put in a plug for serving as faculty advisor to student orgs. Hudson made a note to check out what those clubs were, especially the ones geared to queer kids and outdoorsy things.

Last on the agenda before lunch was a joint presentation from the registrar and the dean of advising. Hudson wouldn't be assigned advisees in her first year, but it paid to know the systems and structures. She'd have to submit grades, obviously, but she'd learned students brought their questions to the faculty they felt safe with, regardless of who might have the official adviser title. Much like her relationship with Betty, it paid to have an in with the people in control of college administrivia.

Hudson sat a little straighter, prepared to pay extra attention and earn a few brownie points. But when the folks in charge of the session strolled in, it was all she could do not to fall out of her chair. Registrar Sasha Crane was the woman who'd caught Hudson staring across the dance floor and whispered it to her friend. And the Callie she'd hooked up with—and fantasized about ever since—was none other than Callie Shaw, Coteau College's dean of advising.

Even as echoes of *it couldn't possibly* flitted though her mind, the blare of *but of course it is* screeched to the forefront. Because

Ryekill was a small town, and Coteau was undoubtedly its largest employer. And because that's what she deserved for thinking she could have an anonymous hookup and leave it at that.

To make matters worse, Callie was even more gorgeous than Hudson remembered. No rainbow dress this time, but the black-and-white stripe echoed the style. And while the cut was less revealing, the overall look—professional without being severe—proved even more appealing. It took conscious effort to keep her mouth closed. Even then, she couldn't tear her eyes away. Which meant that when Callie's gaze landed on hers, she had no doubt she looked as gobsmacked as she felt.

Recognition flashed in Callie's eyes, but not surprise. Callie smiled, one of those knowing smiles that in any other circumstance would send Hudson's libido surging. Even in this painfully awkward circumstance, her mind flashed to Callie in bed, smiling up at her in playful challenge.

Was it possible to be completely aroused and utterly mortified at the same time? Apparently so.

Callie licked her lips and shifted her attention to the others in the room. She introduced herself and talked about her role and the advising center she oversaw. She handed things over to Sasha, and the two of them spent the next hour in easy, informative banter. Dates and deadlines, policies and procedures, tutoring and accessibility services.

Hudson would have been impressed regardless. Callie had poise but also finesse. She came across as an expert in her field without being stuffy or pedantic. Knowing this was the same woman who'd teased her, flirted with her, and given her a couple of her best orgasms in recent memory? It was almost enough to make her head explode.

It made paying attention more than a little difficult.

Hudson did her best, though. One, so she wouldn't embarrass herself any more than she already had. Two, because she needed to know the information being shared. She scribbled notes like her life depended on it, glad for the excuse to avoid eye contact as much as the record of what was said.

When Sasha and Callie wrapped their presentation, Hudson joined in the polite applause. The assistant from the provost's office stepped in to thank them and invite them to stay for lunch. Hudson's heart lodged in her throat, making her pulse thud in a way that surely must be visible to the naked eye.

Should she acknowledge knowing Callie or pretend they'd never met? What would Callie do? Was she half as floored as Hudson and simply better at hiding it?

Before she could sort out an answer to any of those questions, Callie and Sasha politely declined. They'd both volunteered to help with new student move-in, it seemed, and were due at one of the residence halls shortly. Relief and disappointment zipped through her in rapid succession.

Hudson settled on relief, if for no other reason than it was the sane choice. And she was nothing if not sane. Rational. Practical.

She had to remind herself of that fact throughout lunch and the remainder of the afternoon. It didn't help that she found herself at a table with a mediocre deli sandwich and four natural scientists. Or that the afternoon presentations included the faculty ombudsman talking about the grievance process and a well-meaning librarian whose doomsday presentation about AI made her want to poke her eyes out with a fork. Not that he didn't have some valid points, but damn.

Throughout it all, Callie remained front and center in her mind. Poised and professional Callie, playful and naked Callie. Callie in that flimsy excuse for a robe, making it almost painful for Hudson to leave the next morning. Callie who, if Hudson was being completely honest, had been front and center in her thoughts for far longer than the afternoon.

Not in some creepy obsessive way, obviously. More like she'd yet to make many friends so didn't have much else to think about when she wasn't thinking about work. Only those thoughts had been of the highly sexual and pleasantly distracting variety. Which was all well and good when Callie remained squarely in the category of virtual stranger.

Only Callie wasn't that now. Callie was a known quantity. Callie was…a colleague.

By the time Hudson got back to her office a little after three, she'd worked herself into a state. Enough of a state that she tried—and failed—to edit the same paragraph three times. She closed the document in disgust and stared at the photo from Redwood National Park she'd selected as her background image.

Should she let it lie? Maybe. Would she? As far as she was concerned, the unknown usually felt worse than something sucky but understood.

Hudson let out a grumbly sigh and clicked over to her email.

❖

Callie dropped into her desk chair with an exaggerated slouch. So much peopling.

It wasn't actually all that bad. The families moving in were great—excited and nervous and flabbergasted that someone with dean in their title was carrying their kids' laundry baskets and bed linens. And while she preferred working with students in general, the new faculty had better attention spans when it came to presentations. Or at least they were better at faking it. Good questions, genuine interest in student advising and support, and at least a dozen phones came out when she flashed the QR code to sign up for her fall advising intensive.

Oh, and Hudson.

Callie smiled at the memory. Genuine shock. She almost felt bad about it. But Hudson had been so damn cute, she hadn't been able to resist a sly smile. Which sent such a flush up Hudson's neck and across her cheeks it had Callie thinking about the last time she'd had Hudson's blood rushing all sorts of places.

Those memories left her squirming, but she couldn't even be mad about it. She'd take that flavor of karma any day.

But as much as she might like to spend the next however long in an NSFW daydream, she'd been away from her desk for hours and shuddered to think of the emails that had piled up in the interim.

So, she unlocked her computer like the responsible adult she was and skimmed the thirty-odd subject lines to begin triage.

She was the pinnacle of professional until Hudson's name caught her eye. Hudson's name and the subject line "Touching base." Curiosity took hold—along with an undoubtedly satisfied smirk—and she clicked on the message.

Hello Dean Shaw,

Thank you so much for your presentation at new faculty orientation. It was engaging and informative, and I so appreciate your commitment to student well-being and success. Obviously, I was surprised to see you again. I'm hoping we might connect and clear the air before the semester begins. Please let me know the best way to schedule a meeting. I look forward to that, and to working with you and your office.

Best,

Hudson Greene

Callie read the email a second time, guffawing at the same spot as the first time through. *Clear the air.* Then again at the sign-off. Not that she didn't bust out a *best* with the best of them. But with someone who'd fucked her halfway into the next week?

And what exactly did Hudson think was clouding said air? Embarrassment? Paranoia? Had she been carrying a flame around all summer and now wanted to act on it?

Callie drummed her fingers on the edge of her desk, debating how to reply. Well, probably best not to reply too quickly. She might get carried away and drop a warmest regards, and then where would they be?

Instead, she grabbed her phone and snapped a photo, which she promptly sent to Sasha with the caption *So this just happened.*

Sasha, being the most amazing friend she was, replied instantly. *Noooo.*

Callie laughed. *Oh, oh yes.*

You gonna...send her your scheduling link?

She laughed again, but this time it came out as a snort. *How do you make Outlook sound dirty?*

Sasha didn't miss a beat. *It's a gift.*

It had obviously been a joke, but the fact of the matter was that was the easiest way to schedule something. At least during business hours. And with someone she hadn't exchanged phone numbers with. Besides, Hudson had started it.

Callie dashed off a reply, mirroring Hudson's almost comical professionalism. And because she didn't feel the need to spend more time trying to set up a conversation than they'd spend actually having said conversation, she pointed out the link in her email signature that gave students and colleagues alike access to her calendar. She did, however, suggest they meet up at the café in the library instead of her office.

She took a photo of her reply before sending it to Hudson, then forwarded the image to Sasha. *Don't hate.*

I'm not hating, but I'm confused. Are you trying to be friendly or make sure you don't end up fucking on your desk?

Callie's jaw dropped, on principle more than being genuinely scandalized. *I would never.*

Never?

She chewed her lip and considered. *Fun fantasy but so impractical. Too many people on this campus with master keys.*

That got her a string of cry-laughing emojis and a *Truth.*

In the time it took them to have that exchange, a calendar invite popped to the top of her inbox. Callie clicked on it without bothering to set down her phone.

Hi Callie,

I have a feeling the first week of classes will be intense for both of us, so I snagged something for tomorrow. If that's not enough notice, please don't hesitate to decline and suggest an alternate. I'll be working on my syllabi but am completely flexible.

Hudson

For someone so reticent to make the first move, Hudson didn't waste time. At least she'd picked up the hint and reverted to first names. She might joke about it, but it actually did skeeve her out to have someone she'd slept with address her by her title. Callie accepted the invite with a "looking forward to it" and blocked the slots before and after as cushion to get across campus.

She texted an update to Sasha. Sasha laughed a bit more. They kvetched about how much work had to be done and agreed to do happy hour the next night to kvetch with wine and, since it promised to be interesting if nothing else, to process her coffee with Hudson.

With both sets of plans settled, Callie tuned her attention back to work. She had a training with her student peer advisers the next morning and then back-to-back sessions for new students on Friday. She could do both in her sleep, but she liked refreshing her slide decks and incorporating trendy references and memes. It gave her credibility—not as some old fart trying to be one of them, but to let them know she wasn't completely out of touch and had made an effort to relate.

That was how she approached all her work. Anything she could do to make herself and her office less austere and intimidating would increase the chances a nervous student would step through the door. And stepping through the door was the first step of connection, and connection was the number one indicator of student persistence. Her job didn't hang on retention numbers the way some of her colleagues' at other institutions did, but she cared what they were. Students—their struggles and their success—were the reason she came to work every day. In a world where many faculty looked at students as a necessary evil, or perhaps the cash cows that bankrolled their research agendas and summers off, that mattered. It was one of the few hills she'd die on, metaphorically at least.

Speaking of…

Callie picked up her phone and logged into the SPS account. A handful of notifications awaited her, including a couple of direct messages with particularly juicy quotes she'd add into the following week's schedule. Today, however, she had her own inspiration.

Not Hudson, though their exchange had been both the highlight and the pinnacle of absurdity in her day. No, that felt a hair too close to home. Instead, she typed out—verbatim—a request Sasha had gotten to ensure the enrollment of a course was held at twenty or filled to exactly twenty-four so group work could be assigned easily.

She scheduled the post to go live just after five and got back to her actual work, feeling good about her life and choices.

Chapter Seven

@shitprofessorssay: The only thing worse than dealing with students is dealing with other professors.

Hudson got to the Coteau Faculty Club a few minutes early, but she went ahead and swiped her ID at the cashier station set up at the door. Inside, she scanned for Lawrence. She didn't see him, but several of the tables were already occupied. Most people sat in pairs or groups, but a few were solo, reading or pecking away on their laptops.

The "Club" was little more than a private dining room adjacent to the main dining hall on campus. The offerings were identical, but faculty had their own salad bar and soup station, and they could order sandwiches or plates of whatever was being served on the buffet line that day. For a flat ten dollars, she could see why so many of her colleagues made it their regular lunch spot.

Classes hadn't started yet, but with orientation in full swing, the Club had resumed its regular hours. When Lawrence suggested it, Hudson hadn't hesitated. She snagged a table near the window and had no sooner pulled out a chair when Lawrence strolled in. He offered her a friendly wave and headed over.

"It's good to be back." Lawrence settled in the chair opposite Hudson like he was the guest of honor at a banquet, or perhaps presiding over something.

Hudson caught the eye of one of the servers scurrying around. Lawrence knew her by name. They ordered iced teas, and Lawrence went with the special of the day, roast chicken and mashed potatoes. Hudson opted for a turkey club, always happy to have a sandwich or a salad she didn't have to make.

When the server left, Hudson chuckled. "How often do you eat here?"

"Every day I'm on campus." He waggled his eyebrows. "And some days I'm not."

She couldn't imagine coming to the faculty dining room for lunch on a day she wasn't teaching or otherwise working, but it made sense for Lawrence. He and his wife had divorced back when Hudson was in high school. He'd never remarried, and something told her he wasn't especially skilled in the domestic sphere. "Is the food that good, or are you that much a creature of habit?"

"I reserve the right not to incriminate myself," Lawrence said with a self-deprecating shrug.

While they waited, several people came over to say hello. Mostly older faculty members, all male. Hudson told herself it was a coincidence and happily accepted the introductions. She didn't anticipate a lot of overlap with folks from other departments, at least in her first year, but it never hurt to know people. She'd wind up on committees with some of them, obviously, and a few would wind up on her tenure review when the time came.

"How are you settling in?" Lawrence asked.

"Good." Despite her disappointment in seeing neither hide nor hair of Lawrence along the way, Hudson didn't have to fake her enthusiasm. "I had my office all arranged by the start of July."

Lawrence shook his head. "I was talking about your house."

"Oh." She chuckled. "That was all arranged by August."

"Just make sure you don't spend more time in the former than the latter."

She had no intentions of becoming a workaholic, but it struck her as odd that he'd lead with that advice. She didn't fret being on the tenure clock, but that didn't mean it was easy. "I'll do my best."

"I'll let you in on a little secret." Lawrence leaned in like he meant it as more than a figure of speech.

Hudson played along, shifting her head close. "What's that?"

"Get yourself an eager TA. I pay mine twenty dollars an hour under the table when she maxes out on approved time, and she does everything." Lawrence leaned back and made a sweeping gesture with both hands. "Everything."

She nodded slowly, not sure what everything meant but pretty sure whatever it entailed broke any number of rules. Especially since TAs at a school like Coteau were simply junior and senior undergrads whose role was limited to things like tutoring and office help. They weren't allowed to do any real teaching or grading.

"I can see your wheels turning. Policy this and policy that." Lawrence pointed at her and made little circles with his finger. "I'm telling you, though. It's amazing. The girls especially."

Hudson's ick sensors flashed, and she didn't need a mirror to know her expression gave her away.

"Nothing untoward," he said quickly. "I'm not a lecher."

Relief washed through her, though a residue of disquiet remained. "Oh, I didn't think that." Or, at the very least, she was happy to be wrong.

"I mean things like grading. Maybe not upper-level stuff, but I haven't graded a one-hundred-level essay in a decade." Lawrence winked. "Or picked up my own dry cleaning."

The relief gave way to a slightly sick feeling. Sure, this was a whole lot better than sexual harassment or sleeping with students, but it was hugely inappropriate. Not to mention explicitly against policy. She tried for a casual chuckle. "I might be too much of a rule follower for that."

"If you want to get tenure, you're going to have to learn what to prioritize." He gave a dismissive shrug. "And what corners to cut."

She didn't believe that for a second, but she knew better than to objurgate a senior member of her department. Plus there was the matter of Lawrence being her dad's best friend. Still, she refused to go on record—even in the context of a private conversation—as agreeing with it. "I guess I'll just have to work extra hard."

Rather than taking offense, Lawrence laughed. "God, I miss that wide-eyed optimism."

Hudson went for a cringey smile, not sure whether he meant it as a compliment or insult. Did it matter? He was going to do things his way, and she was going to do things hers. And it wasn't like she was going to go tattling on him to HR or the chair or whoever one reported such things to. She was going to put her head down and mind her own business. Oh, and play the consummate colleague.

When they finished lunch, Hudson figured they'd walk over to Storey together, but Lawrence simply waved her off. "I gave Betty my syllabi to format and print. I'm heading to the golf course before I've got to work around the weather and my teaching schedule."

It wasn't like he didn't have a point. Fall would come blowing in before they knew it, and winter would be hot on its heels. If she had forty years of teaching experience under her belt, she might not feel the need for much prep either. Since she didn't even have one, they parted ways, and Hudson headed to her office solo.

She hadn't been lying when she told Lawrence she'd settled into it before her house. The old oak shelves were lined with books she'd been collecting since her undergraduate days, and the desk was home to a carefully curated collection of literary-themed tchotchkes, including the novelty bust of Virginia Woolf made of silicone whose mouth opened and closed from behind with a clothespin.

She had a couple of hours before she was scheduled to meet up with Callie and didn't plan to waste it. Her syllabi were done, but she wanted to add a few bells and whistles to her course sites. The time might be better spent writing, but she didn't entirely trust her capacity to concentrate.

Because Callie.

She was being ridiculous and knew it, but knowing and being able to stop herself weren't the same thing. Hopefully, getting together would be a reset. They could agree to be friendly, to keep things professional. Clear the air, she'd said, and she meant it. What other choice was there?

❖

Callie got to the library café a few minutes early, but Hudson was already there. Because of course she was. Clutching an iced coffee and looking like a student about to tell their parents they wanted to major in art instead of premed. She wore another of those short-sleeved button-downs, making Callie wonder if that was her unofficial uniform. This one had apples on it—very teacher's pet.

"I hope you haven't been waiting long," she said in lieu of a hello.

"Not at all." Hudson stood. "Can I get you something?"

Callie waved her off and got in line. She succumbed to the power of suggestion and got an iced coffee of her own, complete with caramel syrup and cream. Mostly because iced coffee deserved such things. And a little because she had no idea how this conversation was going to go. A little treat would ensure the time wasn't a complete waste no matter what unfolded. She snagged her drink from the end of the counter and returned to the table, wondering if Hudson would start the conversation or leave it to her.

After a pause that bordered on awkward, Hudson said, "So you work here."

"I do." Callie smiled. "Almost seven years now."

"Nice." Hudson nodded slowly and stared at her coffee.

"And, it turns out, you do, too."

Hudson's gaze shot up. "Yes. I do."

"A lot of people in Ryekill do, it seems," Callie said.

"Right." More nodding from Hudson.

"Such is the way of small college towns." Which maybe Hudson had never experienced before. Still, the queer world was its own version of that, wasn't it?

"For sure." Hudson blew out a breath. "I confess it didn't occur to me."

Callie tipped her head and almost felt bad about figuring it out and keeping it to herself. Almost. "Yeah."

Hudson looked up from her drink, hazel eyes intense. "Is that a problem?"

"Problem?" She resisted conjecture on the specifics of why Hudson so obviously thought it was.

"That we work together. After we, you know."

Callie laughed before she could help it. "The college would lose a lot of its faculty and staff if it was."

Hudson frowned.

"Sorry. I don't mean to be flip. You're obviously concerned." Which would be irritating if Hudson didn't look so damn adorable while doing it.

"I'm just…I'm new, obviously. I read the rules, and I understand there's no policy against it, but I don't know what the culture is. I don't want to put my foot in it before my first semester even starts."

Of course Hudson had read the rules. Even with how silly this whole thing felt, it was almost sweet. Hudson seemed as genuinely worried about Callie's reputation as her own. "I'd say dating within one's department or division can raise some eyebrows, but even that is quite common. Two chemistry professors got married last year."

Hudson's eyes widened, perhaps at the mention of marriage.

"Though more people date or hook up than walk down the aisle, obviously." She went for a playful wink. "As long as there's no drama or public shenanigans, it's fine. I promise."

"Shenanigans?" Hudson seemed less panicked but still a long way from relaxed.

"You know, like making out in the library café." She made a sweeping gesture to indicate their surroundings.

The panic returned to Hudson's features, as though Callie had suggested they do it right then and there.

"Which we're not doing, obviously." Callie lifted her hands in concession but couldn't resist a smirk. "We're just having coffee."

Hudson released a breath. "Right."

"Which is a bit out of character for me, but surely not enough to raise suspicion."

"Do you not get coffee?" Hudson frowned.

Callie tipped her head. "Not with faculty."

"Oh." Furrowed brows joined Hudson's frown.

"I don't get a lot of invitations." Callie shrugged, making sure to keep it playful. "From faculty at least."

"Do you think people will think us having coffee is strange?"

"Are you worried about what people might think?" Maybe an unfair question, but she reserved the right to be at least a little judgmental.

"I mean, some. It comes with the territory of being on the tenure track."

Callie resisted an eye roll. "Well, you have nothing to worry about. If anything, people will think you're an eager beaver."

Hudson cringed. "Gee. That's flattering."

"Would you rather they think we're fucking?" She shouldn't have said that, but Hudson walked right into it.

Hudson's eyes went huge. "No."

Callie laughed.

Hudson's frown returned, then she seemed to catch herself. "I definitely don't want people thinking that if I don't have the pleasure of doing it."

The brazenness of the comment caught Callie off guard, especially given the uptight vibes practically radiating off Hudson from the moment they sat down, but she recovered quickly. "That could be rectified, you know."

To her credit, Hudson didn't balk. "Is that a proposition?"

She hadn't gone from teaser to the one being teased, but it certainly felt like the tables had turned. Or perhaps they were simply coming onto equal footing. "Merely an observation."

"You don't think it's inappropriate?" Hudson's gaze remained intense, as though Callie might say more with her body language than her words.

"Last time I checked, you're not my student. Or my supervisor."

"True," Hudson said. "And vice versa."

"And vice versa." She didn't actually expect Hudson to go for it, but anything short of a full blown freakout felt like progress.

"Wait." Hudson's spine straightened, and it was peak adorable nerd. "Did you just ask me out?"

Callie wasn't one to play coy, but something about this situation—or maybe it was something about Hudson herself—made her want to be pursued. Wanted it to be all Hudson's idea. "I didn't."

"Oh."

"But I opened the door for you to." She canted her head. "If you're so inclined."

"I see."

"No pressure, though. I only want to make it clear I'm open to any of the possible permutations." More than open, if she was being honest. Hudson might be channeling anxious and uptight, but Callie knew what she could do when the lights went out and the clothes came off. Faculty or no.

Hudson leaned back, crossing her arms over her chest. "And what are those, exactly?"

It felt almost too easy to lay them out for Hudson to pick from. Of course, she hated when people insisted on making things difficult for no reason. "Well, we can pretend that night in June never happened and just be colleagues. We could be friends. Or friends with benefits." She shrugged. "Or we could date."

"You don't have a preference?"

She took a second to really consider the options, weigh the pros and cons. She'd practically made a side hustle out of poking fun at faculty, but most of them were decent. Not to mention the fact that they made up the majority of eligible queers who crossed her path. If she ruled them out, she'd find herself swimming in a very small pond. "I'm inclined to date. We had a good time, great chemistry."

"True." Hudson's smile made Callie think she was thinking about their chemistry, too.

She lifted a finger. "But I've worked in academia long enough to know there's a tendency for professors to take everything seriously. Themselves most of all. And I make a point of not doing that."

Hudson tipped her head. "Guilty as charged."

Callie couldn't help but be a little disappointed, but at least Hudson could admit it. "Which means I think the ball is in your court."

"I can work with that," Hudson said with a slow nod.

"Can you?" Only after she said it did Callie realize Hudson might construe the question as an insult. Or maybe a challenge.

Hudson lifted her chin ever so slightly. Definitely challenge. "I'd like to get to know you, spend time with you. Whatever ultimately unfolds."

Callie smiled. "And I can work with that."

"I'm sure the next week will be even busier for you than it will be for me. How about I text you when the dust settles?"

The mere fact that Hudson didn't center her own start of the semester put her leaps and bounds above some of the faculty Callie worked with. And that hot and cold thing Hudson had going—which should have annoyed the hell out of her—somehow worked. Maybe because both felt deeply authentic. Whatever it was, Callie couldn't seem to get enough. And now, it seemed, she didn't have to try. "I'll look forward to it."

Chapter Eight

@shitprofessorssay: I love the first day of classes. Everyone shows up, everyone has good intentions, and no one's grandma dies.

Hudson got to her classroom twenty minutes early, only to find another class still in progress. Even as she chuckled at her own tendency to over prepare, Callie's words echoed in her mind. Eager beaver.

Callie had been teasing her, but Hudson hadn't minded. She was an eager beaver. She wanted to make a good impression on her students and her colleagues. Because that's who she was as a person but also because, at a place like Coteau, things like teaching evaluations and amorphous measures of collegiality often made the difference between getting tenure and not. Even for people from high profile grad programs like Berkeley. Or maybe especially. Her advisor had warned her against being perceived as aloof and egotistical, expecting to rest on the laurels of her research.

The thing was, despite going to one of the top programs in the country, research took a back seat to teaching in her mind. It was interesting, sure, but it didn't change lives. Teaching did.

The door to the seminar room opened and students filed out. Hudson offered encouraging smiles, remembering how scary the first day of classes could be, and also knowing there was every chance she'd have one of those students in class herself, if not this semester, then another. That was the other draw of a liberal arts college. Smaller classes and the chance to get to know students over their four years.

Hudson strode in, hovering at a polite distance from the teaching podium. The professor there—an older Black woman she recognized from the faculty welcome mixer—collected her things. "Have a great class," the woman said in passing.

"You, too." Hudson cringed. "I mean, thank you. Hope you had a great class."

The woman smiled. "New faculty, right? I remember you being introduced at the party last Friday. But of course your name escapes me now."

Hudson nodded, happy the woman didn't simply roll her eyes and leave. She stuck out her hand. "Yes, Hudson Greene. English. It's a pleasure."

"Cassandra Njani. Psychology." Cassandra accepted the handshake. "First class?"

Hudson chuckled. "That obvious?"

Cassandra lifted her chin. "You got this."

"Thanks."

Cassandra left and Hudson blew out a breath. She did have this. This was her sweet spot. While it might be a new campus, she was more than accustomed to welcoming fresh faces and being the one to offer reassurance.

She shifted her focus to the circle of desks that took up the entire room. Most of them had filled. Asher, who she'd had to beg the registrar to let in, offered a grin and a wave. Hudson returned the greeting, glad they'd taken her up on adding the class.

She offered nods and smiles to the rest. Overall, they registered as less diverse than what she was used to, at least ethnically. And dressed for the taste of fall that upstate New York was known for, even in late August. But beyond that, familiar. Eager faces mixed with a few who looked like they'd just rolled out of bed. Brand new laptops and beat-up ones. Backpacks and messenger bags.

Hudson checked her watch and sat at the desk she'd claimed for herself at the front. "Good morning."

A halfhearted murmur of replies greeted her.

"I'm Dr. Hudson Greene. I'm an assistant professor in the Department of English and I use she/her pronouns. Welcome to Survey of American Literature. If that's not the class you're supposed to be in, now would be a good time to figure out where you should be instead."

One guy in sweatpants and a backward baseball cap yanked himself from the slouch he'd settled into. After a moment of frozen panic, he grabbed his bag and bolted from the room. Everyone else looked at one another, then her, then laughed.

"Jeez. You would have thought I said advanced astrophysics."

Another laugh.

"Okay, I'm going to assume the rest of you want to be here. Or at least mean to be. I know this fills the humanities slot for gen ed and some of you just want to get through. I don't expect you to fall in love with everything in the syllabus, but hopefully, by the time we're done, everyone will have read at least one thing they liked and one thing that made them think differently about the world. Deal?"

Students nodded their assent.

"Speaking of the syllabus, let's start with that." Hudson pulled out the stack of stapled papers. "I know it's old school, but I'm a millennial with a soft spot for analog, so humor me."

She passed them around, then walked through the reading list and the assignments for the course. "What you may or may not notice is that almost everyone we'll be reading is female. Those who aren't are queer. Many are people of color. That's intentional."

Most of her students flipped—or flipped back—to the list of texts. Several nodded, like the revelation came as a pleasant surprise. A few squirmed. She tried not to stereotype, but she could have picked out those that did before she'd opened her mouth.

"One of the things we'll tackle in class discussion is what it means to be part of the canon, who gets to decide, and why. That might make some of you uncomfortable. I hope you'll stick around anyway."

A guy in a Yankees jersey raised his hand, and Hudson braced herself before signaling him to speak. "Is there any poetry?"

She kept her amusement in check. She'd take that over worries about being too woke any day. "Only a couple of short ones when we cover the Harlem Renaissance."

He nodded slowly, seemingly satisfied with that.

"All the standard language about college policies and support resources is in the electronic version on our class site and linked with the QR code on the last page." She lifted a hand. "I said I was a millennial, not a boomer."

A few students snickered.

"Questions?"

No one raised their hand.

"I'm sure some will arise. That's what office hours and email are for. Please don't be afraid to use them. You can also use them to let me know if you're going to miss class or if you simply want to nerd out about books. I'm down for that. Now, let's get to know each other a bit since the goal for our class time is discussion more than lecture."

She kicked off introductions, sharing the requisite hometown, favorite book, and fun fact about herself. As the students took turns with their versions, including major if they had one, she scribbled copious notes. With only twenty-two enrolled in the class, she hoped to have names and faces down within the first week, and the personal details helped her more than any mnemonic she'd ever tried.

By the time they'd finished, only about twenty minutes of their fifty remained. She used it to set up the first reading, a pair of short stories by indigenous authors she'd selected as a foil to some of the more traditional Puritan fare. Knowing there was every chance a few kids would add—or drop—before they discussed it, she didn't go too deep into context, opting to end a few minutes early instead.

Most of her students hustled out, eager for a few minutes of sunshine or the opportunity to grab some caffeine before their next class. A couple lingered. The first wanted to set up a meeting to go over accommodations. Hudson pointed them to her scheduling link rather than office hours so they wouldn't be interrupted. The second, Ari, who'd used they/them pronouns, simply wanted to say hi and express excitement about the queer writers on the list.

"I was so expecting the same old cis white guys," Ari said with a shake of their head.

"I try." Hudson lifted a shoulder. "I don't know what class year you are, but I'm doing Queer Writers of the Twentieth Century, too. I'm pretty sure it's still open if you want something more focused."

"Oh, I'm in that, too." Ari shrugged. "An eager beaver, as my mom would say, when it comes to having queer profs."

Hudson laughed before she could stop herself.

Ari winced. "Is that weird?"

"Not at all. It's…that phrase keeps popping up this week." She pointed to herself. "Fellow eager beaver, apparently."

Ari's face relaxed into an easy smile. "Bet."

She loved a kid who could so readily flip between dated and current slang. "So, I'll catch you at two then, yes?"

"Yes, Professor, you will." Ari offered a wave and left.

Hudson collected her things and followed, opting to head back to her office for lunch and some final prep for her afternoon class. She passed Callie's building or, rather, the building that housed Callie's office and the rest of the advising center. She'd looked it up the day of faculty orientation, not to be creepy but so she could be better prepared for possible run-ins. And by better prepared, she meant less likely to make an idiot of herself.

No sign of Callie today, though. She was probably busy helping students finalize their class schedules and start the semester on the right foot. Still, Hudson couldn't help but glance at the tall windows surrounded with ivy and brick and wonder which one belonged to the woman who'd—how had she put it?—opened the door. To friendship, fucking, and possibly more. Hudson hadn't decided exactly where they'd land on that spectrum, but she looked forward to finding out.

❖

Callie handed the student across from her four late add forms. "If you get these signed by the faculty and back to me by Monday, and get your hold resolved by the end of next week, I'll approve them."

Tori nodded with a sniff. "I will. I promise. Thank you."

She held out the box of tissues, and Tori took one. Even when students got on her nerves with their immaturity or privilege, Callie's empathy remained dialed in. Becoming an adult was no joke. But for those juggling the stresses of college life with the added layer of family drama or financial challenges? Brutal. Still, she couldn't refrain from adding, "The legal people get very bent out of shape over this stuff, so the sooner the better."

Another nod. "I'm sorry."

"You don't need to apologize. I'm here to help. It's hard when the adults we count on drop the ball." Parental immaturity, on the other hand, got exactly zero understanding from her.

Tori blew out a breath. "Divorce is stupid."

Callie winced. She never pried about the underlying cause when students were blocked from registration due to financial holds, but many volunteered the details. "It is."

"My dad is such a dick." Tori shook her head. "Sorry. I shouldn't say that to you, but I can't help it."

"I'm not a counselor, but I'm happy to be a friendly ear."

Tori's expression grew serious. "Maybe I should talk to a counselor."

"Big fan." She hooked a thumb at herself. "While I was a student and as an adult. Navigating hard stuff is way easier with support."

"We went to family counseling before my dad left." Tori shuddered. "It sucked."

Callie offered a silent moment of gratitude her experiences with therapy had not been to hash through toxic family relationships. "Definitely don't let that dissuade you. One-on-one is all about you."

Tori rolled her eyes. "Yeah, that was not the case then."

"Do you want to book an intake appointment while you're here?"

"You can do that?" Tori seemed suspicious of the prospect.

She chuckled. "There's an online form. You can do it yourself, but it's sometimes easier to do it when it's already front of mind."

"Yeah. Okay."

Callie had Tori pull out her laptop and navigate to the page. While they were there, she pointed out some of the other wellness programming, including the stress management workshops.

"Thank you," Tori said when they'd finished. She tucked the blank forms and her computer back into her bag.

"It's what I'm here for. Literally." Callie offered a smile. "You can drop your forms at the desk, but make an appointment to come see me next week. I'd love to check in and make sure everything is squared away."

It was code for "make sure you're okay," but Tori seemed to warm to the idea. "I will."

"Good. Now go so you're not late to class."

Tori's smile was genuine, and she hurried out of Callie's office. Callie took a minute to enter notes, then went to the small reception area for the next student waiting for drop-in advising.

By the time five o'clock rolled around, Callie had met with twenty-two students—everything from last-minute schedule adjustments to existential crises about not wanting to be a teacher after all. She didn't love the pace or having to keep conversations to the issue at hand, but she did thrive on the problem solving. With the exception of one student who walked out in a huff after not getting an override into a closed class he wanted, everyone left her office in a better state of mind than when they'd arrived.

Callie made the rounds, catching everyone in the office before they headed out for the weekend. She nudged the few who seemed inclined to linger, reminding them everything would keep until Monday and that none of them were paid enough to answer work email on their phones. She might be, but it was one of her hard limits when it came to work/life balance. She wondered sometimes if people respected that or didn't actually notice.

She returned to her office and packed up her things. In addition to the prohibition on phone email, she usually made a point of not bringing her computer home over the weekend. But this time of year counted as one of her exceptions. There'd be at least a few students who would reach out in a panic about adding or dropping a class late, and she didn't mind doling out reassurances that she'd grant a grace day as long as the faculty signed off.

She strolled across campus, turning her face into the August sun as the clock tower chimed the quarter-hour. Dozens of students lounged on the grass of the quad, some studying and some only pretending to. One group tossed a Frisbee, and another kicked a Hacky Sack. It felt so timeless, and it made her heart happy, even if she was more than ready to unplug for a couple of days.

Sasha met her out front of the administration building—home to the registrar, the bursar, and financial aid—and they opted to walk to Ivy rather than attempt to find parking at the pub on the edge of campus. The happy hour crowd was respectable—mostly staff and faculty, but with a few students thrown in. The latter made her smile. They might be pregaming for frat parties that wouldn't start until later, but she liked to imagine most saw themselves as above all that, finally legal and grabbing a drink and early dinner before a poetry slam or movie at the arthouse cinema.

When Sasha elbowed her, Callie braced to see someone they mutually disliked. But instead of the loathsome chair of Faculty Senate or the condescending guy from Political Science, she spied Hudson. She wore a short-sleeved button-down—solid black this time—and looked like she'd just gotten a haircut. Callie knew what those close-cropped hairs at the base of her neck would feel like and the sound Hudson would make if she did, and her fingers itched to touch.

"Why are you groaning? I thought you'd be happy?" Sasha studied her, eyes narrowed.

"I'm not. Groaning, I mean. I'm fine."

"Ooh, are you having a worlds colliding moment? Is that the problem?"

As much as Callie was perfectly happy to hook up with—or even date—people who fell loosely into the category of colleague, she liked her boundaries firmly in place. Not a code of silence or anything, but not getting up close and personal at what amounted to the campus water cooler. "There's nothing to collide. We had coffee."

"Uh-huh. Coffee." Sasha laid the sarcasm on nice and thick.

"I just haven't decided whether she's going to be chill or not." In other words, Callie had yet to recover from the email after faculty orientation. Even if the coffee had gone better than expected.

"At least she's hanging out with cool people," Sasha said.

That part was true. The English Department was about fifty-fifty when it came to faculty Callie liked, and Hudson was currently sipping what looked like an old-fashioned with the good half. "And she's looking this way."

Looking and offering a casual nod of greeting that reminded Callie of the sexy and confident Hudson far more than the shy and awkward one. Callie returned the nod and figured that would be the end of it. Only it wasn't.

Hudson's gaze flicked to Sasha, and her eyes lit up like she'd spotted a long-lost friend. Hudson's eyes, not Sasha's, though one glance at Sasha said she was eating it up. Hudson said something to Amber and Layla, then headed their way.

"Incoming," Sasha said, as though Callie couldn't see it happening right in front of her.

When Hudson got there, her hello was warm and clearly directed at both of them. But her attention quickly settled, and it didn't settle on Callie. "I wanted to thank you again for your help with Asher last week. I met them this summer and all but insisted they take my class. It never occurred to me it would be full."

"Always happy to help, especially when you're willing to take everyone on the waitlist. You made five students very happy."

"The more, the merrier, I say." Hudson lifted a finger. "I might not feel that way when it comes time to grade papers, but that's a problem for later me."

Sasha laughed. Callie did, too, since it would be rude not to. Oh, and because it was funny. When did Hudson become funny? Funny in a ha-ha way, not an oh-dear way. And why hadn't Sasha mentioned this little exchange that had left Hudson feeling like they were BFFs?

"Don't let me keep you, I just wanted to say that in person," Hudson said.

"You can call either one of us anytime." Sasha wagged her thumb between herself and Callie.

"Oh, I most definitely will." Hudson looked at Callie then. She smiled, and Callie would swear there was the tiniest hint of promise in it that had nothing to do with Callie's role or her office.

"Good first week of classes, then?" Callie asked. The last thing she wanted to do was talk shop at five thirty on a Friday, but she wasn't sure what else to say.

"Fantastic," Hudson said without hesitation. "How about for you? Not too busy, I hope?"

The fact that she even asked earned her some points. Not that Callie was keeping score. "The usual. I think we put out all the fires."

"No small feat, I'm sure." Hudson lifted both hands. "Well, look, I don't want to keep you from your well-earned cocktails. You two enjoy your evening, and your weekend."

And with that, she was gone.

Sasha barely waited until Hudson was out of reasonable earshot to say, "Well, that was interesting."

Callie raised a brow. "It was basic colleagues-in-passing banter. There was literally nothing interesting about it."

"You said she was awkward." Sasha pointed—not subtly, by the way—in the direction Hudson had gone. "That was not awkward."

"I said she was awkward about the fact that she'd hooked up with a colleague without realizing it. She was borderline flirty by the end. She practically invited me out."

Sasha frowned. "It was more fun to think of her as a colt not quite sure how to use her legs."

"Maybe for you. I much prefer the version I'm likely to have sex with again." She motioned to a spot that opened at the bar. "Come on. Drinks are on me."

Chapter Nine

@shitprofessorssay: Please come to class prepared so I don't have to.

After her morning class, Hudson headed back to Storey for office hours. Just like the first week, no one came. Not even Asher or Dwayne—who'd added her upper-level queer lit seminar—stopped in to say hello. She resisted the inclination to be down about it. She'd yet to build the kind of rapport that would inspire students to drop in just to chat. And with the first paper deadline still three weeks away, not even the high achievers were in the weeds of working on it.

She used the time to prep for her afternoon class and eat an early lunch. Despite her initial inklings to frequent the Faculty Club often, most days it was easier to hole up in her office and work. Not that she was a monk about it. She had a massive casement window that offered a view onto the quad, framed with tendrils of ivy that played into every professor fantasy she'd ever had. And while it was ancient and more than a little stubborn about opening, she'd brought in some silicone spray and managed to crack it enough to let in the late summer breeze.

Hudson also used the time to send a couple of pseudo-flirty texts to Callie. She didn't always get instant replies, based on when Callie had meetings, but the back and forth throughout the day seemed to work for both of them and didn't invite the shenanigans that texting in the evening sometimes could.

The problem was, the more they texted, the more Hudson craved those shenanigans. Well, not those specifically. But shenanigans in general. Ideally, the kind that came with close proximity and little clothing. As much as she didn't want to be the one with hangups, a niggling voice remained in the back of her mind. It sounded a lot like a robot cautioning danger.

And yet Callie's words remained just as insistent. "I'd be inclined to date" paired with the simple but effective "the ball's in your court." Hudson had said she could work with that, but she'd proceeded to sit on her hands for the better part of two weeks. She'd let the niggling voice win even as Callie's playful smile and lush curves occupied nearly as many of her thoughts as work had.

The scales finally tipped.

Hudson followed up her pseudo-flirty text with a question about whether the semester had settled into its groove yet. And another about whether Callie might like to get together over the weekend. There. That was more like it. She'd just finished congratulating herself on being bold when a new message came through. It was from Gwyn, though, not Callie.

Don't be like this. LOL.

Hudson glanced at the screen shot that accompanied the text. It was clipped from a social media account, and the text of it read: *No class this week. I'll be in Barcelona for a conference. Yes, a conference. That's it.*

Hudson chuckled, then squinted at the slightly blurred account name. Shit Professors Say. Ha.

She replied with a laughing emoji and a *Clearly I'm going to the wrong conferences* before toggling over to the platform app and doing a search. Boom. The profile picture was from an early aughts movie featuring a gaggle of purportedly brilliant academics who couldn't find their way out of a paper bag. She shook her head, equal parts amusement and cringe.

A few minutes of scrolling had her both laughing out loud and legitimately cringing. Some of the quotes felt too absurd to be real but most landed with an almost painful accuracy. Whoever compiled these knew academia well.

Hudson's finger hesitated over the follow button. It felt like a betrayal almost, like succumbing to the antics of the class clown. But even if she didn't want to support anyone who genuinely denigrated her profession, she really really didn't want to become the kind of professor accounts like these mocked. Besides, Gwyn had sent it to her. Gwyn might have an irreverent streak, but she was respected—on campus as much as in her field.

Callie's face popped into her mind, the mischievous expression she'd sported when they'd met for coffee. She'd called Hudson an eager beaver, but she might as well have said Goody-Two-shoes. Hudson's earnestness and tendency to follow the rules had earned her the moniker more than once. But while she didn't mind being called earnest, she hated the idea of being a killjoy.

She followed, imagining it would make Callie proud. At the same moment, a reply from Callie flashed in her notifications. *What did you have in mind?*

Hudson contemplated what to suggest, from the most insipid—like another coffee date—to a euphemistic Netflix and chill. Since the phrase was likely as dated as it was dubious, she settled on a proposition somewhere in the middle. She leaned back in her chair and threaded her hands behind her head, pleased with herself on being both interesting and clever. And not obviously horny. She enjoyed the state for about three seconds before glancing at the clock on her desk and realizing she'd almost made herself late to her afternoon class.

Almost.

Fortunately, it was in Storey and only a flight of stairs away. She hustled down and still made it to the room just as the prior class filed out. A few of her fellow eager beavers hovered in the hall. She offered hellos and bland questions about their weekends, then gestured for them to lead the way in.

Once everyone was settled, she pulled out her copy of *The House of Mirth*, complete with several dozen Post-It flags color coded by the themes she wanted to highlight over the course of class discussion. "Okay, folks. How are we feeling about Lily Bart so far?"

❖

The second week of classes passed more quietly than the first. A few students scrambled to add and drop classes late, and a few power planners were already looking ahead. Callie loved helping them sort out the feasibility of double majors and semesters abroad, and she loved asking the kinds of questions that helped undecided students uncover academic and professional paths that spoke to them.

By Wednesday, things felt settled enough that, when Sasha invited her for lunch and offered to order in sushi, Callie didn't even hesitate to say yes. She walked into Sasha's office to find a platter of mixed rolls and a container of seaweed salad already arranged on the little conference table in the corner.

"Wow," Callie said. "You fancy."

Sasha grinned. "I can be."

Callie sat and helped herself to a spicy tuna. "Yum."

Sasha filled her plate. "I confess I have an ulterior motive."

Callie, who'd pinched a bit of wasabi and was smearing a bit over her next selection, paused. "Who fucked up and what do you need me to fix?"

Rather than the sheepish or exasperated look Callie expected—looks that usually went with sharing some mistake someone made that they had to make right—Sasha's expression held glee. "Not a thing."

"What is it then? Is something going on with you?" There'd been many angsty and emotional processing sessions leading up to and in the aftermath of Sasha's divorce, but it had been months since things had been so dire.

"God, no. I'd need a personal life for that to be the case."

Callie chuckled. "Okay, then. What is it?"

"Just a juicy little SPS nugget for you." Sasha's innocent delivery implied it was neither just nor little.

"Go on."

"A certain newly hired faculty member might have mentioned in passing that her dad's best friend happens to be a member of her new department." Sasha plucked a California roll with her chopsticks and popped it in her mouth.

Callie blinked a few times as Sasha's words percolated, along with her overt not naming any names. "Hudson?"

Sasha nodded. "She told me herself."

"She did?"

"Well, in a joking way. Like, she knew no favors had been called in and he hadn't even been on the search committee, but still."

She didn't doubt Hudson had been hired on her own merit, but it left Callie with her own sense of but still. "That's weird."

"Right? But great for a post." Callie mimed typing. "Yes, my dad's best friend was on my hiring committee. What does that have to do with my opposition to legacy admissions?"

Callie snickered. "Yeah. That's really good."

Sasha grinned. "You're welcome."

Callie picked up her phone and tapped her way to a blank SPS post. But with her thumbs hovered over the keyboard, ready to type, she hesitated. "I don't know. It feels weird."

Sasha narrowed her eyes. "Weird to have it posted or weird for you to do the posting?"

"The second." Because the sentiment was totally on brand for SPS.

"Gimme." Sasha held out her hand and made grabby motions.

Callie handed over her phone and Sasha typed. "Done." She handed the phone back. "And since you didn't post it, you're officially absolved."

Since technically every post on Shit Professors Say was anonymous and scrubbed of any truly personal detail, it didn't take much for her to accept Sasha's assertion and think nothing more about it. They finished lunch and parted ways with promises to see each other at dance later. Callie had no sooner made it back to her office when a text notification caught her eye.

"Speak of the devil," she murmured to her herself with a smile.

A few hours later, she arrived at the dance studio with some scoop of her own.

"Hiking?" Sasha's voice was as incredulous as the look on her face. Her tree pose wobbled slightly, but she held it.

Callie held her own tree pose. She didn't love the group yoga sessions as much as a carefree shimmy and shake, but she couldn't deny it was good for her flexibility. Not to mention her core. "Why do you sound so shocked? I hike."

"I'm not questioning your athleticism."

"I'm outdoorsy, too, you know. I grew up twenty miles from Mount Marcy. I've done five of the High Peaks." Not that she did a lot of that these days, but she didn't doubt she still could.

"I don't know what any of that means, but I'll take your word for it." Sasha hoisted herself from child's pose to downward dog.

Callie did the same, reminding herself to rotate her shoulders back and her hips open. "I like to hike."

Janina, who'd gotten her official yoga instructor certification over the summer and was leading the group, transitioned into a series of sun salutations. Sasha and Callie followed, and the conversation paused. Athleticism or no, sun salutations did not mess around.

Half an hour later, after several glorious minutes of corpse pose, Callie and Sasha strolled out of the small dance studio a few blocks from campus. "So, is it a date?" Sasha asked.

"Is what a date?" Callie asked back, knowing full well what Sasha was talking about.

"Hiking." Sasha shook her head. "It's so lesbian."

Callie pouted. "It is not."

"Isn't a date or isn't lesbian? I've got arguments prepared for both."

Callie stopped walking and snickered. The snicker turned into a full-on giggle, and she didn't try to stop it.

Sasha got a few steps ahead, then stopped and turned. "What?"

She pressed her lips together and schooled her features into something slightly more serious. "I love you."

"I know. I love you, too." Sasha canted her head. "Are you changing the subject?"

"No." She caught up to Sasha and they resumed walking. "I genuinely love you. And I genuinely love that you're prepared to fight me on both points. It's peak best-friend."

"Lesbian best friend," Sasha said.

"Obviously."

Sasha shrugged. "So, which isn't it?"

"Lesbian." Callie rolled her eyes on principle more than out of any real conviction.

"Of course it is." Sasha thrust out both arms, clearly willing to belabor the point. "There will be boots and probably flannel. You can talk about whose cargo shorts have more pockets and see who has the bigger carabiner."

She stopped walking again. Debates like these were one of their love languages, so she balled her fists and planted them on her hips rather than conceding. "That's so offensive. You know I don't own cargo shorts."

Sasha cackled. "And let me guess, it's not about the size of your carabiner but what you can do with it?"

Callie caught up to her and laughed because it was terrible but also hilarious. And, to a certain extent, true. Point definitely to Sasha.

They got to Sasha's car first and stopped once again. "So, it's not a date?" Sasha asked.

"I never said that. I simply took issue with you calling it a quintessentially lesbian date."

"So it is a date." Sasha leaned against her driver's side door, clearly more interested in their conversation than going anywhere.

"I don't know. And I don't know if Hudson does either." She shrugged, telling herself it was a matter of intrigue and not Hudson being wishy-washy. "But I'm open."

"Yeah you are." Sasha's inflection made even the banal confirmation seem sexual.

"She's really good in bed." No point pretending that wasn't her primary motivation.

"And you don't care that she's faculty?" Sasha asked.

She didn't dislike all faculty. Hell, she didn't dislike most. It was simply that they tended to be clueless about how most people lived and worked. And those who were obnoxious managed to be epically so. She stood by that, even if her prior attempts at dating them had all crashed and burned. “As long as she’s not trying to give me a lecture while she’s making me come.”

Sasha’s shoulders dropped. “I’m serious.”

“I am, too. Is she relationship material? I have no idea. If we spend enough time together for that to be on the table, I’ll decide. For now, I’ll take the fucking.”

“And the hiking?”

Callie’s own shoulders fell. Technically, that’s what was on the table—hiking. She’d gotten a little ahead of herself with thinking and talking about fucking. Though something told her it wouldn’t be too hard a sell. She squared her shoulders and smiled. “And the hiking.”

Chapter Ten

@shitprofessorssay: Oh, what are journal articles to rocks and mountains?

Hudson pulled into Callie's driveway and debated texting her or simply waiting. Callie saved her the trouble of deciding by coming right out. She turned and said something into the house before closing the door, and Hudson smiled. It was nice not to be the only one who said goodbye to their pet when leaving.

Callie strode to the passenger seat, and Hudson took the ten or so seconds to appreciate Callie's legs. The hiking boots and shorts left just enough to the imagination. And the ponytail she sported made Hudson's fingers itch to tug the hair tie free.

She cleared her throat, though it was for no one's benefit but her own. Hiking. She'd invited Callie to go hiking.

Even as she told herself that, she admitted it was a load of shit. Not the hiking part. She genuinely loved spending a few hours walking through the woods. It was the idea that she'd had no other motive. That was the bullshit part.

For the millionth or so time, Callie's words echoed in her mind. "Friends with benefits," she'd said. "Or we could date." Hudson hadn't known what to say at the time, but she'd yet to stop thinking about the possibilities. Along with Callie's assurances that they were colleagues in the loosest sense of the word.

She'd wanted to act on the possibilities Callie had so effortlessly laid out, but the prospect of a traditional date had felt off. Just as inviting Callie over—or inviting herself to Callie's—seemed presumptuous. So here she was, picking up Callie and not Gwyn or Layla or anyone else she'd befriended and could have asked to join her to wander amongst the trees. Picnic lunch and the hike itself the absolute last thing on her mind.

"Hi," Callie said brightly as she opened the door.

Hudson's adrenaline surged as Callie slid in. Just a hike. For now. "Hi."

"Interesting choice for a first date. Or is it a second?"

Damn, the woman did not waste time. Though, if she was being honest, it was refreshing that Callie didn't beat around the bush. Or at least it was now that she wasn't freaking out over the prospect of the bushes. "I thought we could do the get to know you part and see how it goes."

Callie quirked a brow. "So, you consider stamina on the trail more telling than what I might order at a restaurant?"

She'd certainly never say that, but it held a kernel of truth. "Clearly."

"I feel like I should confess I haven't done a ton of hiking around here," Callie said.

"I promise the spot I picked isn't too strenuous."

"Oh, I didn't mean that." Callie smirked. "Though, I'm not sad to be leisurely."

"What did you mean?" Hudson asked.

"I meant I grew up in the Adirondacks so most of my hiking has been there. I did my first High Peak when I was fifteen."

"Impressive." She'd been somewhat athletic as a kid, but the outdoorsy part had come later. "I promise this is not that."

"Like I said, not sad about being leisurely."

"Well, I packed a picnic, so I think leisurely is a pretty safe bet."

"Ooh, a picnic. Why didn't you lead with that?" Callie wiggled her butt back and forth, sort of a seated happy dance.

Hudson tried not to think about that wiggle in a different context. "If I'd known that was going to be your reaction, I might have."

She drove along with the help of GPS, turning from one state or county route onto another. It took less than an hour to arrive at the trailhead parking area. As promised in the various guides she'd researched, signs pointed to various loops, but there was no mention of Huckleberry Point. "It's about four and a half miles round trip for the one I picked, and the view at the top is supposed to be spectacular. But we can do one of the shorter trails if you'd prefer."

Callie grinned. "If I get a gorgeous view and a break for lunch, I'm totally game. I'll even help carry stuff."

Hudson worked her arms through the straps of the backpack and clipped the one across her chest. "I got it, but thanks."

They walked about ten steps before Callie stopped. "Not to be weird, but do you have TP in there?"

She puffed out her chest. "I do. And hand sanitizer and a poop shovel should the need arise."

Callie smacked her lips. "You know, the shovel itself might not be sexy, but hiking with someone so prepared is."

An eager beaver compliment if ever she heard one. "I'll take it."

They started the trail in earnest, side-by-side when the path was wide enough and Hudson in the lead otherwise since she'd researched what markers to follow. She checked in with Callie on the pace a couple of times, just to be sure. After the third, Callie planted her hands on her hips and gave her a dubious stare.

"Sorry," she said, even though Callie hadn't actually complained.

"I need you to trust me to communicate." Callie smirked. "Just like in bed."

Hudson choked, not because they'd struggled to communicate in bed but because they'd done so seamlessly once they'd gotten there. Well, that and the fact that Callie was mentioning being in bed so casually. "Right," she finally managed.

"Though I do appreciate your meticulousness."

She laughed at herself because it seemed like the most graceful response. "Thanks, I think."

Callie flicked her fingers to signal Hudson to resume walking, which Hudson did. "It's a compliment. Mostly."

They walked on, pausing here and there for Hudson to double check her notes or to strategize the best way to pick their way across a tiny stream without getting their feet wet. It truly was a lovely hike, even if she found herself wishing for a different sort of physical exertion. "So, when did you decide you wanted to be a dean of advising?" Hudson glanced over her shoulder with a smile.

"I didn't." Callie quirked a brow.

She stopped, making Callie all but run into her. "Wait. What?"

Callie, who'd recovered from the near collision quickly, folded her arms. "When did you decide you wanted to be an English professor?"

"Sixth grade."

Callie pressed her lips together, making Hudson wonder if it was to suppress a laugh. "Are we almost to the lunch spot? Because this sounds like a story, and I want to hear it."

Hudson shrugged. "It's not anything exciting, really. I already loved books. And my father is a professor. To my eleven-year-old brain, he got to study as a job, and I thought that was pretty much the coolest thing ever."

Callie's features softened. "That's cute."

She made a show of standing a little taller. "Thank you. Most people think it's nerdy."

"Oh, it's definitely that, too. They're not mutually exclusive, at least not in my book."

"That's a relief."

Callie quirked a brow. "I'd be in the wrong line of work if I felt otherwise."

Hudson nodded her agreement and started walking again. "If you didn't decide you wanted to be a dean of advising, how did you become one?"

"I definitely did not grow up in a family of professors." Callie chuckled, but it had a trace of an edge to it. Not defensive, but maybe dismissive. "But I liked being in college. Not just the being a student part. It felt like the time where you became who you were going to be, you know?"

She turned back to smile again. "I do."

"I decided to do a master's in higher ed administration. My first job happened to be in advising and it clicked."

"Huh."

"Does that surprise you or give you anxiety?"

Hudson chuckled at being so easily pegged. "I'm going to plead the Fifth."

"Perhaps that's wise," Callie said.

She didn't get the chance to form a comeback. Without fuss or fanfare, the trail opened to a clearing with a sweeping view of the Catskills and the Hudson River. "Wow."

"Wow indeed."

They stood like that for several minutes, drinking it in. Finally, Hudson suggested they eat and scoped a fallen log to sit on. She pulled the various baggies and containers from her pack—cheese and crackers, nuts and dried apricots, olives. "I have a thermos of wine if you're interested, but I understand if you'd rather stick to water."

"I think we deserve a little wine, don't you?"

Hudson popped open the collapsible tumblers she'd brought and poured them each a glass. They clinked cups and ate, talking about everything and nothing. Other than not knowing whether they were going to act on the attraction simmering between them, Hudson couldn't think of much that would have made the day better.

When they'd polished off most of the food, Callie kicked her feet out in front of her and turned her face to the sun. She took a deep breath, looking every part the contented cat, before returning her gaze to Hudson. "Thank you for lunch. Much snazzier than I was expecting."

"That's me. Snazzy."

"Should we start back?"

"Probably." Hudson waited a beat, then decided to take her chances. "I'd kind of like to kiss you, though."

"Would you, now?" Callie seemed surprised by the declaration but pleasantly so.

She nodded. "I'd like to do more than kiss you, actually, but I'm not much of an exhibitionist, and the ground is overrated."

Callie's pupils dilated slightly, and a flush bloomed at the base of her throat. "What are you proposing?"

"How about dinner, and maybe more, at my place?"

Callie looked her up and down, slow enough to send a flush creeping through Hudson as well. "I think you should probably kiss me now, though."

"Yeah?" Hudson asked.

"Just to make sure the chemistry is still there."

Hudson had zero doubts on that front, but she wasn't about to turn down an opportunity to get her mouth on Callie's. "So, for science?"

Callie stood. "For science."

Hudson got to her feet and closed the short distance between them. "I have to say, for someone who'd devoted her life to the humanities, I love science."

Callie's eyes sparkled with a mixture of amusement and arousal. The combo proved pretty damn intoxicating. "For someone who spent way too much time researching the least science-y option to fulfill her natural science requirement, same."

They stood mere inches apart now. Hudson would swear she could feel the warmth radiating from Callie's skin. She took her time, drinking in the anticipation in Callie's eyes. The desire.

Callie's lips parted slightly. Was she even aware of it? Or was she driving Hudson wild on purpose? When push came to shove, it hardly mattered. Because Callie was driving her wild, but she'd also given Hudson license to act on it.

Hudson leaned in, delighting in the way Callie's eyes fluttered closed. Not surrender, exactly. Acquiescence perhaps. Invitation.

She kissed Callie softly. It had been a couple of months, and she wanted to see if Callie's lips under hers felt as good as she remembered. Or, perhaps more accurately, as good as she'd fantasized about.

Somehow, it was better.

Callie's mouth yielded to hers, but only for a moment. Before Hudson could take the kiss deeper, Callie's tongue darted out to trace the edge of her lip. Assertive. Eager.

Hudson let out a groan and sucked Callie's bottom lip between hers. Callie leaned into her, pressing already hard nipples to Hudson's chest. Hudson slid her hands around Callie's waist, pulling the full length of their bodies together. Callie's tongue played along hers, teasing. Teasing and tempting Hudson to do a lot more than kiss. The trail wasn't all that public, right?

Realizing how close she was to tossing her rules about what constituted suitable behavior, Hudson broke the kiss. Callie regarded her with hungry eyes, her breaths coming shallow and fast. She left no doubt about what she might be willing to do in the middle of the woods.

"I think we should head back," Hudson said reluctantly.

Callie merely nodded.

"For what it's worth, I don't want to stop. But if we did that for much longer, I'm not sure I'd be able to."

The heat didn't fade from Callie's eyes, but a smile played at the corner of her mouth. "Sounds like we're on the same page."

❖

"No pets?" Callie asked, not surprised but a little disappointed by Hudson's seemingly empty house.

"A cat. She's shy around strangers, but you may see her before the evening is up." Hudson's affectionate smile said loads.

"What's her name?" Callie asked, mollified.

"Gertrude."

"Gertrude?" She tried and failed not to laugh.

Hudson cleared her throat. "After Gertrude Stein."

Of course.

"I considered naming her Edith, since Edith Wharton is my favorite writer, but that felt a little too obvious."

Callie did chuckle then. "And you'd never want to be obvious."

Hudson's eyes narrowed. "You're making fun of me, aren't you?"

"I would never." She cocked her head. "Except when you do the most professor thing ever and name your cat after a famous lesbian intellectual."

"To be fair, it's the most queer professor thing ever."

It was absurd but also kind of charming. "Touché."

Hudson gestured to the kitchen. "I'm going to pull the chicken out to take the chill off and chop vegetables for the couscous. Glass of wine?"

"Absolutely. Can I help?"

"I got it." Hudson poured them each a glass of chardonnay and gestured back to the living room. "Make yourself comfortable."

Callie accepted the glass. "Don't mind if I do."

Instead of settling on the sofa, Callie wandered, studying the contents of Hudson's bookcases with curiosity. Lots of books, which was to be expected. They weren't all classic literature or academic esoterica, though. Bird books and fishing books sat nestled next to cocktail guides and a couple of Brene Brown's latest works. There was a whole shelf of worn sci-fi paperbacks, too. "You can learn a lot about a person by looking at what they put on their shelves," she said after catching Hudson peeking at her through the cased opening.

"Agreed." Hudson returned her attention to the cutting board. "What are you learning about me?"

Scattered amongst the books were family photos. One of Hudson at what looked like her college graduation and another more recent one with her in doctoral robes. In both, she was flanked by parents beaming with pride. Interesting that she'd chosen to display milestones instead of something like a vacation. "You're a nerd, but I already knew that. Quite diverse in your interests, which is a pleasant surprise. And I'm guessing you're an only child whose parents put a lot of stock in accomplishments."

"Impressive." Hudson stepped out of the kitchen, platter of chicken in hand. "Why do you say only child?"

She pointed to one of the photos. "I see pictures of you with what I assume are your parents. So, either you don't have siblings, or you don't like them very much."

Hudson laughed. "Sound logic, though I have a brother. I'm not sure why I don't have any pictures of him up. What about the accomplishments part?"

"Well, of all the moments in your life to put on display, you picked graduations."

Hudson's eyes narrowed, and she frowned. "What do you have pictures of?"

"Family camping trips mostly. Oh, and my sister's kids."

"Well, sure. If my brother had kids, I'd definitely have pictures of them." Hudson continued to frown.

"Hey, I'm not knocking your pictures. Or what they symbolize. Graduations are a big deal." Though she hadn't even attended the commencement ceremony when she finished her master's degree.

"I guess they were. Like I said earlier, my dad is an economics professor."

"Right." She tried for an encouraging nod. "It totally makes sense that academic milestones are the ones that feel the most important."

"I honestly never really thought about it. I mean, we do family vacations and stuff. I guess I take more pictures of scenery than us."

"Nothing wrong with that. I have a camera roll full of sunsets over various lakes in the Adirondacks."

"See, now you're speaking my language." Hudson smiled, and it went all the way to her eyes.

"Look at that. We agree on something." It was a weird choice of phrase, given that they hadn't actually disagreed about anything.

If it landed that way for Hudson, she didn't acknowledge it. She angled her head toward the sliding glass door. "I'm going to go turn on the grill. I can't wait to see what else you glean from my shelves."

Callie continued her perusal, not just of the bookcases but the room as a whole. Hudson's style was classic and skewed slightly masculine. The couch looked deep and comfortable—and a hell of a lot more expensive than the IKEA model currently gracing her living room. A big leather ottoman stood in for a coffee table. A few of the accent pieces looked antique but lived in. It made her wonder if they'd come from family or if Hudson had sought them out and chosen them for herself.

She wandered into the adjacent dining area that connected the living room to the kitchen. The table there sat six and also looked antique. A series of black-and-white photos caught her eye. They depicted the same stretch of beach at different moments, the mixture of tumultuous and serene striking.

"Did you take these?" She pointed to them when Hudson came inside.

"I wish. A friend from high school is a professional photographer. That's Sunset Beach in Montauk."

Of course it was. "It's beautiful."

Hudson stepped into the kitchen and grabbed the plate of chicken. "Not as dramatic as what you see on the West Coast, but I'm partial to it."

Hudson went back out to the grill, and Callie studied them a bit more. She'd never been to Long Island, had never felt the need. When she had the desire—and means—to go to a real beach, Cape Cod was her shore of choice. Easier to get to, oddly, but also home to Provincetown. And if she had to choose between chichi beach town and gay beach town, she was going to pick gay every damn time. Even if it happened to be a little chichi, too.

It felt like only a matter of minutes before they sat at that lovely table. Callie expected the food to be serviceable, but it was delicious. The chicken had been both marinated and grilled to perfection, and the addition of fresh herbs and toasted pine nuts took the couscous to the next level. "You're quite the cook."

Hudson's smile was sly. "You sound surprised."

She clicked her tongue. "Not surprised that you can, just that you're so good at it."

Hudson gave a slight bow. "I'll try to take that as a compliment."

The teasing tone reminded Callie that, while her first impression may have been the opposite, Hudson had a confidence about most things that was, for lack of a better term, hot as fuck. "You definitely should."

"Anything else you want to compliment while you're at it?"

"Depends. How assertive are you going to be about taking me to bed when we're done with dinner?"

Hudson leaned forward, and her eyes darkened. "How assertive do you want me to be?"

Callie swallowed, her arousal going from a two to about a two thousand in an instant. "Take the level you think I want and double it." She cocked her head. "Maybe triple."

Hudson nodded slowly. "Noted."

She smiled, her libido revving as high as her imagination.

"Hey, Callie?"

Something about the way Hudson said her name sent a delicious shiver up her spine. "Yes?"

"Finish your dinner."

Chapter Eleven

@shitprofessorssay: The only thing more satisfying than a really good fuck is telling reviewer #2 to go fuck himself.

Despite her suggestion, and despite the roaring in her ears since Callie's comment about being assertive, Hudson didn't rush. She took Callie's hand and led her upstairs, much the same way as Callie had done with her that first night. The thrill of novelty might be gone, but the anticipation of knowing exactly what she would do to Callie—of what Callie would do to her—more than made up for it. She offered a prayer of thanks to the goddess that they'd kept the hike tame, and that the fatigue she felt was the sort to dissolve with the right enticement.

The sun had only begun to set, casting her bedroom in a warm glow. Hudson wasted no time going to the bed and yanking down the covers. She didn't release Callie's hand.

"Nice," Callie said.

"I'm not sure this counts as assertive. At least not yet." Though she had no shortage of ideas.

"I was talking about your sheets."

Hudson glanced down, forgetting which set of her admittedly out of control collection she'd picked out for the week. White with little green pine trees. She chuckled. Better than the sloths in pajamas she'd just taken off. "Thanks."

"But you do get points for not letting go." Callie gave her hand a squeeze.

"I'm going to, but only long enough to get you naked."

Callie released her grip on Hudson's hand. Hudson went right for Callie's shirt, tugging it over her head and tossing it onto the chair in the corner. Underneath, Callie wore a soft cotton bra in pale green. That went, too.

"Wait," Callie said.

Hudson paused, hands poised barely an inch above Callie's breasts. "Why do I feel like this is a test?"

Callie laughed and the subtle shift of her body pressed her nipples to Hudson's palms. Hudson bit back a groan. "No test, I promise."

"What, then?" She'd stopped second-guessing Callie's desire, so it had to be something else.

"Shower. I really want a shower."

"Seriously?"

"I got sweaty." Callie made a show of smelling her armpit. "And smelly."

Of the many ways she could play this, one quickly rose to the top. "Only if we get to shower together."

Callie's grin spread slowly, but it grew, lighting up her entire face. "What a fantastic idea."

She took Callie's hand again and all but dragged her to the bathroom, letting go to flick on the water and rid Callie of her remaining clothes. "Now me."

Callie smirked at the directive but wasted no time getting Hudson naked. Hudson pulled back the curtain and gestured for Callie to go first. Callie stepped in, dunked her head, and let out a groan of pleasure. Hudson quickly followed.

"If you're going to make that sound under some hot water, I'm going to have to up my game."

Callie gave Hudson a salacious onceover. "I'm pretty sure whatever we get up to after this will feel even better."

She slipped her arms around Callie's waist and pulled her close. "Who says we have to wait until after?"

From the look on Callie's face, she'd managed to surprise her. Hudson got a feeling that didn't happen very often. She took advantage, cupping the back of Callie's neck and pulling her in for a kiss. She slid her other hand down to Callie's ass.

"Mm-hmm."

Hudson felt Callie's hum of approval more than she heard it. As tempting as it was to drop to her knees and take what she wanted, she'd promised Callie an actual shower, and she intended to deliver. She broke the kiss and murmured in Callie's ear. "Turn around."

Callie smirked. "Kinky."

Hudson tried for a stern look. Callie giggled but did as she'd been instructed. Hudson squirted a blob of shampoo into her palm and worked it into Callie's hair. Callie moaned. "You're easy," Hudson said.

"Yep."

She massaged Callie's scalp, then had her turn to rinse. Suds sluiced down both their bodies, slicking their skin and filling the shower with the fragrance of rosemary and mint. She added conditioner next, then soaped Callie's body from head to toe, lingering longer than necessary on Callie's erect nipples. "Now me."

The command got her the same smirk as before, but once again, Callie did as she was told.

Once they were both clean and rinsed, Hudson pulled Callie close. She pressed her hand to the apex of Callie's thighs. "Would you like to get out now, or would you like me to fuck you in the shower?"

"Bed." Callie's voice was breathy. "Please."

Hudson's insides clenched. God. What was it about a woman saying please?

She turned off the water and pulled back the curtain, then handed Callie one of the towels she'd grabbed from the closet. "Would you like one for your hair?"

Callie, who'd been drying her face, lowered the towel in her hand. "How'd you know?"

"I've been with enough femmes to learn a thing or two."

Callie bent over long enough to twist the towel around her head, and then held out her hand. "Major brownie points."

Hudson handed her a second towel and went to work drying herself. "What are these points good for?"

"Depends. What do you want?"

She tipped her head back and forth. "If last time is anything to go on, I think we might already be on the same page."

Callie—looking equal parts adorable and sexy in her matching towel wrap and turban combo—gave her a long, slow once-over. "I'm all in on a repeat performance. With room for improvisation, of course."

"Of course." Hudson didn't bother with the robe she kept on the back of the door. "Shall we?"

Callie shed the towel on her head and did a quick finger comb of her hair. "I'm right behind you."

Back in her room, Hudson considered Callie's words from earlier—the part about a repeat performance but also the part about being assertive. *Take the level you think I want and double it.*

"Why do you look like you're plotting?" Callie, still wrapped in the other towel, regarded Hudson with amusement.

"Because I am." Hudson narrowed her eyes slightly. "How do you feel about toys?"

"In general, or do you have something particular in mind?"

She lifted a shoulder. "Depends on your answer."

Callie's eyes narrowed slightly. "I love to be on the receiving end of a strap, but mostly I want to get my mouth on you."

Damn. "Those things don't have to be mutually exclusive, do they?"

"They do not." Callie bit her lip. "Can I go down on you first? It's such a turn-on."

Hudson couldn't suppress a chuckle. "Of course."

"What? Why are you laughing?"

"I'm finding it hard to be assertive when you keep coming up with such good ideas."

"Oh." Callie frowned.

"I'm not complaining, mind you. Simply observing."

"Okay." Callie inhaled deeply, connected the middle finger and thumb of both her hands, and closed her eyes—a picture of meditative calm. "I'm ready."

"Ready?" Hudson asked.

"For you to boss me around."

She laughed again. "How do you manage to be funny and sexy at the same time?"

"It's a gift," Callie said without missing a beat.

They stood for a moment, silent. Not a test, exactly, but Hudson was curious. Callie opened her mouth but closed it again, like she sensed Hudson's thoughts. Hudson smiled. "How about you get naked for me?"

Callie arched her brow and proceeded to give Hudson a strip show. No small feat, given she was only wearing a towel. And again, sexy without being overly serious. So damn effective. Callie struck a pose. "Better?"

"Much. And since you're so good at it, I'll let you get rid of mine while you're at it."

Callie didn't waste time, but she worked in a flourish or two, flicking the towel from around Hudson's waist and strutting around like a show girl.

"Very nice. Now, would you like to lie on your stomach or your back?"

It was infinitely satisfying to watch Callie's face as she extrapolated meaning from the two options. "Back," she said with a sly smile.

"Why don't you get comfortable, then?"

Callie pulled the covers the rest of the way back and climbed in, situating herself a couple of feet down from the head of the bed. "How's this?"

"Perfect." As aroused as she was, Hudson didn't lose sight of it being their first time in this particular arrangement. "You'll tap on my thigh if you need space or air or anything else."

"I will." Callie tipped her head. "But I won't."

Hudson trusted Callie to know the difference. She joined Callie in bed and had no sooner positioned herself over Callie's face than

Callie's tongue found her. She braced one hand on her thigh and one on the headboard. "Fuck."

Callie hummed her pleasure but didn't let up. She licked and sucked like she'd spent years dedicated to the study of Hudson's body—how it worked and what it liked and what got her off. Hudson murmured encouragements disguised as demands, wanting to uphold her end of the bargain. But mostly she let Callie do what Callie wanted to do.

That included Callie wrapping her arms around Hudson's thighs and holding tight. It included Callie's tongue circling Hudson's clit and then plunging into her opening. It included the most erotic noises she'd ever heard from someone on the giving end of things. And it included Hudson trying and failing spectacularly to hold her orgasm at bay.

She couldn't bring herself to be sad. Coming hard and fast meant she recovered quickly, and in a matter of minutes, she had Callie bent over the bed, legs spread in delicious invitation. Yeah, definitely not sad.

"I'm too sensitive to use the vibrator I keep in my harness. I'm going to use it on you unless you tell me not to."

"Depends. What will you do if I beg you to let up?"

She stroked the cock standing erect between her thighs. "What do you want me to do?"

Callie tossed a look of playful challenge over her shoulder. "Not listen."

"Then I'm going to ask you to pick a safe word, just in case."

Callie quirked a brow.

"Safety first," she said. Not that overstimulation was likely to cause real harm, but if they were going to play with consent, even a little, she didn't take that lightly.

"Unicorn."

"Unicorn?"

Callie lifted her chin, doubling down on the challenge. "Unicorn."

"Unicorn it is." Hudson reached between Callie's legs, mostly to see how wet she was, and let out a low moan. Callie was literally dripping, and her clit was swollen and hard. Callie instinctively shifted her hips, making Hudson ache to be inside her. "I'm tempted to tell you to keep still, but that might be torture for me as much as you."

Callie laughed, but it was raspy and almost desperate. "If it's any consolation, I would try."

Hudson moved her hand back to the cock. She circled Callie's opening a couple of times, lubing up the tip. "It is. But I want you to move. With me, against me—whatever feels good. Can you do that for me?"

"Uh—"

She didn't wait for Callie to get the second syllable out, pressing the tip in. The move elicited a groan from Callie. Hudson pumped her hips slowly, going deeper each time. Each time she pulled out, she marveled at the way the silicone glistened with Callie's wetness.

She planned to take her time, but Callie seemed to have other ideas, thrusting her hips back with impatience—until the entire length was buried inside her and the base pressed insistently to Hudson's clit. "Somebody's greedy."

Callie managed a murmur of agreement before Hudson started fucking her in earnest, timing her thrusts with the movement of Callie's body. She let herself enjoy, grasping Callie's lush hips and letting the push and pull of their joined bodies entrance her.

When Callie's noises became more frantic, Hudson clicked on the vibrator. She reached around and pressed it lightly to Callie's clit.

"Oh." Callie's voice pitched high with surprise.

Hudson held it a little firmer.

"Oh." Callie's voice dipped low, the sound almost guttural.

"That's it. Ride my cock with that pretty little pussy of yours."

"Oh. Oh, fuck. Oh, yes." Callie repeated the phrases, changing up the order and throwing Hudson's name in for good measure, along with more and harder and please.

Despite her release only a few minutes before, Hudson's belly tightened with the promise of another orgasm. When Callie's body tensed, and she called Hudson's name in a way she could only describe as primal, Hudson tumbled over the edge with her.

Callie pushed the vibrator away with force and collapsed on the bed. Hudson dropped it to the floor, barely managing to click it off. She eased out of Callie gently and fell onto the bed beside her, not entirely trusting her legs to keep her upright.

"You didn't say unicorn," she said when the ability to form words returned.

Callie let out a feeble laugh. "I would have if you'd pressed the matter."

"Fair. Do you need help getting the rest of the way into bed?"

"Nah." Callie scrambled onto the mattress—not elegant but completely adorable.

Hudson shed the harness and followed suit, needing a breather if nothing else. "You're ridiculously sexy. Have I told you that?"

"I think so." Callie rolled and curled into the crook of Hudson's shoulder.

"Well, it bears repeating."

"Same," Callie mumbled. "Same."

Hudson's sex-addled brain drifted in the direction of sleep until an unanticipated consequence of their shenanigans had her bolting awake and upright.

"What? What's wrong?" Callie's voice sounded sleepy, sated. A particularly stark contrast to Hudson's panic.

"Lucy."

"Lucy?" Callie came onto her elbows. "What about Lucy?"

"She's home alone."

"Aw. You're so sweet to think of her." Callie's smile was almost enough to distract Hudson from the issue at hand.

"I can take you home. I'm sorry I didn't think about it sooner. We can stay at your place. Or come back here if she's okay with cats." The other, perhaps more logical, option forced itself forward. "Or, I suppose, call it a night."

Callie came to a seated position, her expression coy. "You trying to get rid of me?"

"No." Hudson's already amped up state stole whatever eloquence she might have had left after that last orgasm. "I just…is she fine on her own?"

Callie gripped her forearm. "When it became clear this was where we were going to end up, I texted Sasha and asked if she could keep her for the night."

"Oh." Relief surged but quickly succumbed to realizing the implications of that arrangement. "Oh."

Callie clearly read her thoughts because she laughed. "She's cool, I promise."

She nodded, letting the sex glow return. "I should have known you'd make arrangements."

Callie pinched her side lightly. "Because I'm a responsible dog mom or because I'm the type to assume we'd end up in bed and I'd want to stay over."

Hudson shifted onto her knees, using the newfound leverage to nudge Callie onto her back. She blanketed Callie's body with hers. "Yes."

"What are you going to do about it?"

So, so many possibilities. She started kissing her way down Callie's voluptuous torso. "I've got a few ideas."

❖

Callie woke to a rumbling sensation, paired with the feeling of being trapped. She lifted her head, confusion remaining even as the sleep fog cleared, and looked around. Hudson's room. Right.

The rumbling stopped and the weight lifted. With it, a meow of irritation. Gertrude, the cat. Right.

Callie held out her hand in apology and the cat deigned to rub against it. Gertrude got her fill and sauntered away, and Callie took in the rest of her surroundings. Gray-blue walls and not much in the way of decor. But the dresser matched the headboard and nightstands—richly stained oak in a craftsman style that screamed money. And just like that first morning, Hudson snored away beside her.

Rather than slipping out, Callie took the chance to study Hudson's features. Her eyelashes were long enough to stir a pang of envy, her brows thick and dark. The soft swell of Hudson's breasts set a stark contrast to the muscular lines of her shoulders and arms. The combination had something else stirring, and it took effort to keep her hands to herself.

The bathroom beckoned, however, so Callie extricated herself from the bed. After peeing and pulling on her clothes from the day before, she darted out to get the bag she hadn't bothered grabbing from Hudson's car the night before. She was fully prepared to make a joke about sneaking out, but there was no sign of Hudson when she returned.

She used the downstairs bathroom to change and brush her teeth, then wandered into the kitchen. A fancy-looking coffee pot sat next to an even fancier looking coffee grinder, loaded up with beans. She hesitated only a second before filling the reservoir and poking various buttons until the grinder whirred and the pot gurgled to life.

Despite the running water and noise of the grinder, there was still no sign of Hudson. Even after the whole pot had brewed and the delectable aroma wafted throughout the downstairs, nothing. Callie helped herself to a cup, stealing a spoonful of brown sugar from a mason jar in the pantry and a splash of milk from the fridge.

She contemplated bringing a cup to Hudson but decided to let her sleep. She took hers onto the back deck, glad she'd stuffed a hoodie into her bag along with the leggings and T-shirt. The yard was small but tidy, complete with the sort of generic landscaping one would expect with a rental. It made her appreciate her lush, if slightly haphazard, attempts at making a garden of her own space.

Callie leaned on the railing, watching the chickadees and titmice flit to and from the feeders. Feeders as in multiple. Four hung from branches scattered around the yard, along with two suet cages. There was also a bird bath and a tiny fountain with wide flat rocks where birds could perch and have a drink. Definitely not rental house standard, and the fact that Hudson clearly prioritized making her yard a bird oasis made her smile.

"I thought you'd left."

Callie turned. Hudson stood in the doorway wearing boxers and a tank top, hair in glorious disarray. Callie would swear she sounded relieved to be proven wrong. "You were sleeping so soundly, I didn't want to wake you."

Hudson canted her head. "Not a morning person. I'm glad you made yourself coffee. Have you been up long?"

"Less than an hour." Callie swept her arm over the yard. "I've been enjoying your little nature preserve."

"I confess I'm a bird nerd in addition to being a literature and otherwise general nerd." Hudson hung her head briefly, but her smile made it clear she wasn't truly embarrassed.

"I love that for you. Well, us, really. My setup isn't this intense, but I've got a couple of feeders, too. Lucy and I find it very therapeutic."

Hudson's smile widened, like having that in common pleased her. "It totally is."

Hudson remained in the doorway, but Callie could see goose bumps covering her arms. She flicked a finger up and down. "You're not wearing enough clothes to be out here."

"I could get some," Hudson said. "Or you could come in and let me make you breakfast."

Given how quickly Hudson bolted that first morning, the invite felt extra nice. "Dinner and breakfast, after that picnic lunch? You're pulling out all the stops."

"I could take you back to bed instead if it would make you more comfortable."

She laughed, loving that Hudson's confidence finally seemed to have crept fully out of the bedroom. "Do I have to choose?"

"You do not." Hudson's smile was sly, but she didn't wait for Callie to answer.

Callie followed her inside, amused at the beeline Hudson made for the coffee pot. She poured a cup, took a deep inhale over the steam, and took a sip. No audible "ah" but Hudson closed her eyes and her shoulders sagged slightly, driving home the contented sigh vibes. "Maybe I should be offering to make you breakfast," Callie said.

Hudson opened one eye, then the other. "May I redeem that offer after a future sleepover at your place?"

The prospect of making a habit of the things they got up to last night delighted her. "Deal."

Hudson's slow smile mirrored Callie's sentiments. "Excellent. So, for this morning, I can offer you a smoothie, an omelet, or waffles."

"Waffles?"

"Yes?"

She chuckled. "No. I mean, sure. Or whatever sounds good to you. I was just having a one of these things is not like the others moment."

Hudson's eyes narrowed. "You're not accusing me of being a health nut, are you?"

Callie lifted a shoulder. "You did come here from California. And you drink your coffee black. Oh, and you seem like you like to work out."

"Guilty. But mostly because it makes me feel good. I love excess. In moderation."

They hadn't spent enough time together for her to observe that was literally the most Hudson thing possible to say, but she was tempted to nonetheless. Not that she didn't embrace balance herself. It was just so…Hudson. "A smoothie would be great."

"You don't have to say that," Hudson said.

"I mean it, though. I'm supposed to be at yoga at eleven, and I don't ever eat heavy before that."

"Oh. I'll get on it, then." Hudson set down her cup.

"No rush. It's pretty informal, so I don't have to be exactly on time. But I do hate to miss." And as tempting as it was to try to coax Hudson back to bed, something told her Hudson spent her Sundays on things like laundry and prepping her classes for the week.

Hudson was already pulling fruit and a bag of what looked like spinach from the freezer. "It's all good. This'll just take a minute."

"You're sure you don't mind?" She couldn't quite read Hudson, but notes of disappointment seemed to be part of her vibe.

"Of course not." Hudson flashed her a smile. "I'd love a day of waffles and more sex, but my week will go better if I get some things done today."

Callie laughed before she could stop herself. So Hudson.

"What?" Hudson asked.

She shook her head, but continued to smile. "Nothing."

Chapter Twelve

@shitprofessorssay: I'd be a better adviser, but it requires time and effort.

Between the hiking and the fucking, it was all Hudson could do to rally for a Sunday afternoon of housework and grading. And after staying up until nearly one finishing said grading, it was all she could do to haul herself out of bed in time to make it to campus in time for her nine o'clock class. But the discussion of Eudora Welty's "Why I Live at the P.O." proved livelier than expected, the double espresso she snagged on her way to office hours hit the spot extra, and the maple trees that lined the quad hinted at the blaze of color to come.

She fielded three students wanting to talk through rewrites of their first paper and one senior putting feelers out for an honors thesis advisor. By the time she propped her feet on her desk and tucked into the leftover chicken she'd packed for lunch, the phrase "having it all" sauntered through her brain like Gertrude paraded around the house after an epic nap in a sunbeam.

Well, relatively speaking. Hudson wasn't an idiot. Actually having it all was a myth. She meant having "all" a first-year professor who'd stumbled into a sexually gratifying pseudo-relationship could ask for. A low bar in relative terms. But she liked that about herself—appreciating the simple things even as she worked her ass off.

Today was no exception. She'd signed up to attend a two-hour advisor training session that sucked up most of the time between office hours and her afternoon class. It would mean scrambling around campus, but it also meant getting to spend a good chunk of her Monday staring at Callie. And learning about advising, of course. She wouldn't get advisees until spring at the earliest, and probably not until next fall, but she liked being prepared.

Hudson strolled into the Faculty Development and Innovation Center, wondering if the person who founded it intended to give it the same acronym as the Federal Deposit Insurance Corporation. It seemed impossible that they hadn't, but as one of two doctoral students on her previous institution's ad hoc Academic Success and Student Engagement group, she'd learned not to assume such things.

It wasn't her first time at the FDIC, or at least Coteau's version of it. She'd stopped by once simply to introduce herself to the director, figuring it was good form for new faculty. She'd also attended a workshop on the course management system. It was practically identical to the one she'd used at Berkeley, but she was an unabashed nerd about such things, and figured it would earn her some brownie points to be eager.

Eager beaver.

Callie's teasing tone popped into her mind and made her smile. Teasing or not, being one had served Hudson well most of her life. Including with Callie. She wasn't about to stop now.

She found a few people already in the conference room, and a few others joined as she scouted a spot and set down her bag. She recognized some faces from the orientation a month before, but others were unfamiliar. It made her wonder if they were new or new to advising. Or, perhaps, she wasn't the only eager beaver on campus, and some of her colleagues simply liked staying current.

Hudson observed and filed away details. It was in her nature, but it also kept her from staring too obviously at Callie after saying a professionally casual hello. She wore a maroon dress today. It had a deeply scooped neckline and flared at the waist. The fabric swayed as she stepped away from the teaching station to glance at what was being projected onto the screen. The move gave Hudson a glimpse of tall boots in chestnut brown and a completely appropriate yet somehow salacious few inches of bare leg.

"What are you doing here?" Gwyn slid into the seat next to her.

Hudson shifted her attention from Callie and her delectable legs. "Hey."

"Hey yourself. Aren't you off the advising hook until year two, or did they change that?"

"Just wanting to get a head start."

Gwyn rolled her eyes but laughed. "Of course you are."

She and Gwyn had hung out a few times since that first meeting at the gym. Often at the gym, with coffee or a quick breakfast at the campus café after. It was nice to have a friend who was also a colleague but not one in her department. Gwyn got the particularities of life as a professor—which was great—but Hudson didn't have to worry about maintaining the proper and professional front she felt compelled to show the other members of the English faculty. It was also nice to have a workout buddy who held her accountable without being a dick, and who could share her lighthearted amusement over some of their fellow gym regulars. That said, it also meant Gwyn had plenty of ammunition to tease her about those very same eager beaver tendencies Callie had called out. "I also have the hots for the presenter."

Gwyn turned her full attention, complete with quizzical brow, Hudson's way. "Callie Shaw?"

Hudson tipped her head, more satisfied than embarrassed given her weekend. "Do you blame me?"

"Not even a little." Gwyn, a fellow admirer of femmes, lifted her chin. "You going to do something about it?"

She'd had every intention of keeping things with Callie to herself, but Gwyn was a friend. Besides, Callie had told Sasha, and her criteria had been a simple "she's cool." Gwyn certainly fit that profile. "Maybe I already have."

"Dude." Gwyn elbowed her none too gently in the ribs. "Way to bury the lede."

Hudson shrugged.

"Um, details, please."

The room had filled, and Callie chose that exact moment to welcome everyone. "How about you come fishing with me this weekend and I will?"

Gwyn wrinkled her nose. "I'm not sure that's a fair trade."

"Sure it is. I've got more than enough equipment for both of us. We'll stand in the river and drink beer and talk about women."

"Couldn't we just sit at a bar and drink beer and talk about women?" Gwyn asked.

"But what's the fun in that? You come fishing with me, and I'll let you take me shopping for a weightlifting belt."

Gwyn considered. "And you'll let me teach you how to use it?"

The topic had crept into more than one of their conversations, with Gwyn nudging Hudson to up her game, aka her capacity to bench, squat, and deadlift what Gwyn considered weights worthy of any butch who bothered with such things. She wasn't opposed, obviously, she'd simply yet to take the leap to being serious about it. "Yes."

"Deal."

It struck her that was the second time in as many days that a woman had said that to her. "Excellent. Now, let me pay attention so I can make a good impression and maybe get laid again."

"By all means." Gwyn made a sweeping gesture, enough to draw Callie's attention.

Callie had a friendly smile for Gwyn before her gaze landed on Hudson. The friendliness remained, but it was more than that. Hudson felt it low in her belly. She also felt it in her nipples, which hardened unbidden. She resisted the urge to look around, to worry about whether anyone else noticed. Instead, she returned the smile—equal parts I'm here to learn and I'd like to rip your clothes off. Because as she'd just said to Gwyn, she wanted to do whatever was in her power to make what they'd gotten up to over the weekend happen again.

❖

Hudson lingered after the session, after everyone else had gathered their things and filed from the room. Callie clicked out of her presentation and shut down the teaching station—not taking her time, exactly, but enjoying the sensation of Hudson's eyes on her.

She tucked the flash drive into her bag and looked at Hudson. "You're really earning that eager beaver rep."

Hudson angled her head. "It's a good rep to have, I've decided."

She might want to, but Callie found it hard to argue with that. "Just don't become your department's yes man."

"Are you worried I might?"

She wasn't protective of Hudson—not yet at least—but she'd been around long enough to know how things could play out. "Not worried. Simply aware of how departments work."

"Is that a dig at faculty?" Hudson asked.

A tingle of truculence skittered up her spine, but Callie promptly ignored it. "Not at all. Any office would be the same without good leadership. Including mine."

Hudson lifted her chin in what appeared to be playful challenge. "But yours has good leadership."

"I mean, I don't have a degree in management or anything, but I've done my homework." And tried to learn from her mistakes. Which was more than she could say from some department chairs. Hell, some deans.

"That's hot."

And just like that, any whisper of tension evaporated. The bad kind of tension, at least. "Professor Greene, are you hitting on me at work?"

Hudson didn't blanch, but she did pause, as though considering the question seriously. Eventually, she smiled. "I think I am."

Such a delightful departure from that painfully formal email in August. "Well, since I know you're a stickler for such things, let me be sure to voice my enthusiastic consent."

Hudson didn't come closer, but the smile remained. "That's hot, too."

Callie could have happily passed the next hour doing that, but the Faculty Writing Accountability Group had the room booked. Various harried-looking professors had already begun to arrive, clutching their laptops and cups of coffee like the fate of their careers depended on how many words they managed to pound out in the next hour.

She reluctantly parted ways with Hudson and headed to her office to collect the materials for the first Academic Review Committee of the fall semester. The group was tasked with considering all petitions for exceptions to college policy. Well, all the ones that didn't fall into the dozen or so precedent categories she'd been authorized to approve on their behalf. They also made the deciding call over cases of academic separation, but that only happened at the end of term.

The three or four meetings during the semester tended to be brief, unless they got caught up in debates over equity and accountability or went down a rabbit hole of discussion about changing a policy. That decision, of course, would have to be made by Faculty Senate, but it didn't stop passionate arguments over matters like the pass/fail policy and the GPA required for dean's list. Callie took most of it in stride, reminding herself to be grateful that the people making the decisions cared enough to haggle over them.

As an ex officio member, she didn't technically get a vote on the matters the committee reviewed. But with six years as dean of advising under her belt, the group followed her recommendations more often than not. The exception to that rule was when someone's two-year term ended and a new faculty member cycling on got a bee in their bonnet about her purview.

"The curriculum belongs to the faculty," she'd been told on more than one occasion, complete with a haughty look and condescending tone. As though she'd been trying to wrest it from their cold, tenured hands.

For the most part, it all worked out. On more than one occasion, she'd been spared having to be the one to crush a student's hopes by pointing out that the decision regarding their petition wasn't hers to make. But as with so many things, it came down to whether the faculty members around the table considered her an equal or a minion.

Callie got to the conference room early, pulling up the petitions to be considered and any supporting documents students included in their requests. She artfully arranged the browser tabs so she could easily click through, then settled at the chair closest to the teaching station with the wireless keyboard and mouse. Sasha, the committee's other ex officio member, came in with a pair of travel mugs, one of which belonged to Callie.

"Hello, lovely." Sasha extended Callie's mug. "Look what I'm finally returning to you."

Callie grinned. "You could have kept it. I'm pretty sure some of your Tupperware is on permanent loan in my kitchen."

"Yes, but how else could I have brought you a dirty chai in an environmentally sustainable way?"

She took the mug and sure enough, it had the heft that came with being full. "You brought me a chai?"

"It seemed like a fitting beverage for the occasion. But you can have my London fog if you prefer. That felt fitting, too." Sasha lifted her own mug.

"Questionable euphemisms, but a total treat. Thank you." Callie took a sip and let out a hum of pleasure. "Definitely called for at the first ARC meeting of the semester."

Sasha settled into the seat next to her. "How many newbies?"

Callie grimaced. "Four."

"Yikes," Sasha said.

It was only ever supposed to be two cycling on or off at a time for the sake of continuity, but an early retirement and a sabbatical had mucked things up. "Maybe they'll be cool?"

Sasha's grunt conveyed her doubt. She'd been on the email chain and knew the names as well as Callie.

As if on cue, members of the committee trickled in. Cassandra Njani from Psychology was both an ARC veteran and one of her favorite faculty members on campus, so that helped. Janice Kim was new, but Callie had worked with her on a persistence program in the STEM fields at Coteau. A chemistry professor who wanted students to thrive in organic chem sat pretty high on her list of decent people. A couple of people she knew and a couple she barely considered acquaintances rounded out the group.

Callie was about to pass around the agendas she still found useful enough to bother printing when she realized they were missing someone. George Payne. Or, as he signed his emails, G.W. Sexist son of a bitch if she ever met one. Condescending, too. To her a couple of times, but to pretty much anyone he considered beneath him. If the stories she'd heard were anything to go on, that included most of his colleagues and all but a handful of students. Maybe she'd luck out and he'd be on the committee but never bother to show up.

She'd no sooner glommed onto that possibility than he sauntered in. "Looks like I'm in the right place."

Casandra glanced at her watch. "And almost on time."

G.W.—because it was absurd to refer to him that way so Callie's brain had insisted on it—didn't bother to respond. He took a seat near the door and proceeded to look bored. Cassandra glanced at Callie with a shrug that might as well have been an eye roll. Callie sucked her teeth in agreement.

Everyone but G.W. looked at her expectantly. She cleared her throat. "Welcome to the first meeting of the Academic Review Committee. For anyone who doesn't know me, I'm Callie Shaw, dean of advising. I'm an ex officio member of the group, but I run the logistics, since petitions flow through my office and we oversee academic actions like probation and separation. I put the agenda together and circulate the materials."

Callie turned to Cassandra, hoping she'd take things from there. Cassandra offered a knowing smile. "Callie also knows policy inside and out. She's modest about it, but she gives us well-considered recommendations and makes our work a whole lot easier."

Callie gave her most self-deprecating smile, not because she disagreed with the assessment but because she'd learned the hard way that some faculty didn't appreciate any insinuation that she—sans PhD—was the one calling the shots. "I try to share precedent and any personal knowledge I have of the cases."

"In other words, she keeps us in line," Cassandra said with a laugh. "We should probably do introductions since half the group is new, and we need to elect a chair before we get to the agenda."

They went around the table, then Cassandra took the lead in explaining the role of the chair. She volunteered to do it as the longest-serving member of the committee, and everyone seemed happy to let her. Callie let out a sigh of relief. She didn't spend a ton of extra time with the person in that role, but it was enough to make the prospect of someone like G.W. stepping up borderline dreadful.

With the housekeeping done, she launched into the agenda itself. Mostly the usual fare—students wanting to triple major or withdraw from courses from the prior term. Cassandra ran the meeting like a champ, despite the self-important ramblings of G.W. For a guy who had no clue about the work of the committee, he had plenty of opinions.

Callie bit her lip and avoided eye contact, not wanting to be caught smirking or rolling her eyes. She also scribbled a couple of phrases that would make great fodder for SPS posts. Because if she had to sit through such inanity, the least she could do was wring some material from it.

Chapter Thirteen

@shitprofessorssay: Teaching is like fishing. A lot of showmanship just to get them to bite.

Despite the ramped-up nature of their text flirting—not to mention their post-hike hookup—Callie was surprised when Hudson asked if she wanted to meet for lunch. Pleasantly surprised, but surprised. Like Hudson might finally be settling into the prospect of dating. It helped her with her own settling in, honestly. She might have been the one to put it on the table, but it still felt a bit out of character to be dating a professor in earnest.

She grabbed her grain bowl from the pick-up counter in the food court and scanned for Hudson. No sign of her yet. But since it was after one on a Friday, fewer than half the tables were occupied, and she had no trouble finding one near the windows and with good chairs. Maybe not as nice as the Faculty Club was rumored to be, but in the ways that counted, so much better.

Hudson strode in a moment later, hair disheveled from the brisk breeze and her signature leather briefcase slung over her shoulder. Callie lifted her hand in a wave. She thought Hudson might swing by one of the food places first, but she made a beeline for where Callie sat.

"Hi." Hudson's smile had a knowing warmth to it, like maybe she wanted to kiss Callie but thought better of it.

"Hi."

"I hope you haven't been waiting long. I had a student linger during office hours." Hudson set her bag in one of the empty chairs and slid out of her jacket.

"Just got here." And while she would have enjoyed a kiss in the middle of the campus food court, she didn't genuinely expect one.

"I haven't even ordered yet. What did you get?" Hudson peered at her bowl.

She described the contents, and Hudson whipped out her phone. "Sounds good to me."

The introduction of an ordering app at the various carts and cafés around campus had been touted as a fancy upgrade to dining services. But it had quickly become an all-or-nothing situation, meaning it was impossible to order in person even if you were right there. Hudson punched in her meal and headed to the counter to wait for it.

Rather than starting without her, Callie simply watched. The camel-colored pants and plaid button-down walked the line between preppy and outdoorsy to perfection. She wouldn't have said either were her type—not that she really had a type when it came to things like style—but the combo suited Hudson. For that reason, if perhaps no other, it was enough to make Callie's mouth water.

Hudson returned a moment later, and Callie opted to keep her more salacious thoughts to herself. Hudson might have settled into the idea of being seen on campus together, but it remained unlikely she'd welcome an out-loud account of what Callie would like to do with her.

They ate and chatted, not unlike she would with any number of colleagues on campus she considered friends. But despite the lack of overt flirtation, there was a distinct vibe, and Callie was certain she wasn't the only one feeling it.

"So, what are your plans for the weekend?" she asked during a lull in the back-and-forth about their respective days and goings-on.

"Oh." Hudson seemed surprised by the question. "I have plans to go fly fishing with Gwyn. Bywood. From Gender Studies. Do you know her?"

The words registered. Technically, their meaning did, too. Yet, she couldn't quite make it make sense. "You're going fishing with Gwyn Bywood?"

Hudson frowned. "Is that weird?"

"Not at all." Unexpected, but really, she was still very much in the getting to know Hudson phase. Other than staying on top of her grading in true eager beaver fashion, she had no clue how Hudson spent her free time. And she liked Gwyn, obviously. But even on her best days, Callie found her intimidating.

"It is. Or at least you think it is. I can tell by the look on your face."

"It's not." Callie said, as the mental image of Hudson and Gwyn standing side-by-side in suspendered waders came into focus.

"Wait. Should I have invited you instead? Do you fish?"

The sincerity of the question sobered her. "No. I mean, you could. I do know how to fish. It's not my favorite, though, so I'm not sad to be left out."

"So, what is it?"

Did she confess her real thoughts? That the idea of two professors fishing together felt a little too provincial? That Gwyn struck her as the type of woman who'd eat someone like Hudson for breakfast? "She's such a powerhouse is all. It's weird to think of her as someone you'd take fishing."

"Okay, fair point. She's never been, actually. But she's been helping me up my lifting routine at the gym, so I invited her." Hudson chuckled. "Cajoled might be more accurate, but I'm not splitting hairs."

"Sure, sure." Callie nodded, as though that explanation wasn't a case study in random.

"We're just friends." Hudson lifted a hand. "For the record."

Hudson didn't need to say that, and Callie wouldn't have asked. Certainly not two hookups and only a couple of pseudo-dates in. "It would be okay if you weren't. For the record."

Hudson smiled then, and it warmed Callie from the inside. "I'm not looking to have the are-we-exclusive conversation, but I don't tend to date more than one person at a time."

She didn't either, but it had to do with logistics and the relative size of her dating pool more than anything else. "Same."

"Cool." Hudson gave a casual head bob.

Callie sipped her tea, trying to decide where to take the conversation that wouldn't feel like a clunky ass segue.

"Oh, I almost forgot." Hudson said. "Have you heard of *Shit Professors Say*? It's a social media account that makes fun of faculty."

Clearly, Hudson had no such worries. Callie cleared her throat, more at the question itself than the transition. It wasn't the first time someone had asked her. Only the third, but still. It was enough to spare her being taken completely by surprise. Which meant she'd already sorted how to respond: noncommittal and not dishonest. "I have."

"It's hilarious, isn't it?"

Relief washed over her in a wave. "I think so. I'm surprised you do?"

Hudson matched her quizzical tone with a curious look. "Why do you say it like that?"

"It pokes fun at professors and you're so…"

Hudson folded her arms but looked more amused than put off. "So what?"

"Earnest."

Hudson laughed. "I feel like I should be offended, but it's too accurate for me to argue."

"It's not an insult." Callie let herself smirk. "Not entirely."

"And there it is." Hudson gave a beleaguered sigh, but even that seemed good-natured.

She shrugged. "You're hot, though. And great in the sack."

True to form, Hudson looked around to make sure no one had overheard. Once satisfied, she fixed her gaze on Callie. "You might be the first woman who's wanted me for my body and not my brains."

Callie leaned back, bracing her hands on her thighs. "You say that like those things are mutually exclusive."

"True." Hudson nodded soberly, as though considering the intellectual merits of the assertion. "I definitely want you for both the sex and the stimulating conversation."

"You're such a sweet-talker."

Hudson lifted her chin. "I can be."

Callie shook her head but laughed, and her gaze caught the clock mounted on the far wall. "Crap."

"What?" Hudson asked.

"As much as I hate to leave when things are getting good, I should get back."

Hudson glanced at her watch. "I should, too. I've got a meeting with Henry at one."

They stood, and Hudson gathered up the trash and containers to be recycled. Earnest, but kind of chivalrous. It was the sort of thing Callie didn't usually put a lot of stock in, but she couldn't bring herself to dismiss it. "Since you're spending tomorrow with another woman, does that mean I won't see you this weekend?"

Hudson's expression turned serious. "I won't be home too late Saturday evening, but I probably won't be good for much. What's your Sunday look like?"

"I have dance class in the morning, then plans to help Sasha paint her living room."

"Dance class?" Hudson quirked a brow. "Like ballet? Or tap?"

She chuckled, thinking of how desperately she'd wanted those kinds of classes as a kid. "Not exactly."

Hudson's left brow rose to meet the right. "Please don't tell me pole."

"Please don't tell me you're a prude about things like that."

Hudson cringed. "No. Sorry, you're right."

"So, you're cool with it?" Callie asked.

"Um, yeah. Totally."

She gave Hudson a lot of credit for backtracking so quickly. "I'll keep that in mind. For future reference."

"So, it's not pole dancing?" Hudson asked.

"No. Not yet, at least."

"Modern?" Hudson looked genuinely confused, which was downright adorable.

"Belly, actually."

"Oh." Hudson's lips held the shape.

Callie smirked, enjoying the turn of the conversation immensely. "I could give you a little demo sometime."

"Oh," Hudson said again. "I'd like that very much."

"I'll keep that in mind, too. As for getting together, how about next weekend? Saturday? We can do something fun in the afternoon, then I'll make dinner." By rights, it was her turn. Though, honestly, both felt like little more than foreplay.

"I'd like that very much, too."

Callie lifted her chin. "You know what I'd like?"

"What's that?" Hudson asked.

"I'd like if you packed a bag."

❖

Gwyn peered inside Hudson's tackle box and shook her head. "Okay, you officially have more lures than I do pairs of earrings. I'm never letting a butch tease me about my accessory fetish again."

Hudson made a stopping gesture with both hands. "Okay, first, I would never tell a woman she has too many earrings. Second, you need different flies for different situations."

Gwyn arched a brow.

"Different times of day, different seasons and kinds of light. Sometimes you need them to be light, sometimes you need them to be dark."

"I see, I see." Gwyn picked up a fluorescent green fly with gold glittery wings. "So, they're like eye shadow."

"Um."

"Sometimes, you get an eye shadow but it's too sparkly for daytime. You can save it for nighttime, or you can layer it with something more muted, soften the effect."

She hadn't expected the analogy to work, but she probably knew even less about makeup than Gwyn did about fishing. "Yes. Okay. Exactly. Flies are like eye shadow."

Gwyn clasped Hudson's wrist. "I feel like we both learned something important today."

"And we haven't even cast a line."

"Which you're going to show me how to do right now."

Hudson prepped a rod for Gwyn first, going with something more natural looking than the fluorescent green fly. She demonstrated a series of casts, talking through the ideal release point and the speed for stripping the line back. She reeled in the excess line and passed the rod to Gwyn. "Remember, late is better than early or you're going to spend your day untangling your hook from the bushes."

Gwyn smacked her lips. "That's what she said."

Hudson's jaw dropped but she quickly snapped it shut. Scandalized might be her default for crass jokes, but she and Gwyn had a vibe. Besides, it was funny. Terrible but funny. She cleared her throat. "Exactly. If you're stuck in the bushes, you're definitely doing something wrong."

Gwyn cackled, then made a show of schooling her features into a serious expression. "Let's see if I can land me a big one."

Hudson swallowed the observation that many of her fishing trips ended with a glorious sense of relaxation and exactly zero bites. They'd cross that bridge when they came to it. She watched Gwyn cast a couple of times and offered suggestions for small adjustments. Gwyn was a natural, though, which Hudson imagined was generally the case when it came to anything Gwynevere Bywood set her mind to.

Hudson got her own rod ready, and they cast for a while in easy silence. It was one of her favorite aspects of fishing—that perfect blend of companionship and quiet.

"So, you and Dean Shaw are spending time between the sheets," Gwyn said without any sort of lead in.

Hudson balked, though she'd been the one to disclose it. "Maybe."

"Word on the street is she spent the night at your place last weekend. I sure as hell hope you got up to something."

"Where did you hear that?"

"Not from my new best friend who insisted I go fishing with her this weekend to get the scoop." Gwyn gave an over-the-top disapproving look that ironically softened the blow of her words.

"I've told you more than I've told anyone else." She frowned. Callie mentioned telling Sasha, but had it gone further?

"Don't worry. I don't think your girl is dishing at the Deans and Department Chairs meeting. Your next-door neighbor is the admin in my department. When I told her we were hanging out, she asked if I knew you and Callie were a thing." Gwyn cocked her head and smirked. "She saw Callie leaving your place, and I think she wanted to make sure you weren't stringing me along."

Hudson squeezed her eyes shut and cringed. "Of course she does. And did. And assumed I'm the player in this situation."

"Hey, relax. She's not a gossip. We're tight."

"Right." She opened her eyes but couldn't bring herself to make eye contact. "Right."

"Though, you should probably expect it to make the rounds. I mean, Ryekill is tiny, and Coteau even tinier. And you know academics are worse than hairdressers when it comes to dishing dirt."

"Is it really dish-worthy, though?" She looked at Gwyn, wanting the answer to be no.

"Sure it is. You're a hot new professor. Dean Shaw has a pretty high profile on campus." Gwyn ticked each detail like it was part of an itemized list.

"But, like, is it bad?" God, she'd just stopped freaking out about the prospect of all this and here it was, waiting to bite her in the ass.

"Dude, I'm teasing you. No one cares. Correction." Gwyn lifted a finger. "Wait. That's not accurate. A few people will care because they like to be in the know about everything, but you're only a minor bullet point in the grand scheme of gossip. And a few will care because they care about you or Callie as people and want you to be happy."

Hudson studied Gwyn, looking for what her body language might be saying that her words weren't. "Do you mean that or are you trying to talk me off the ledge?"

"Who says it can't be both?"

She laughed, at Gwyn's cleverness and her own absurdity. "Fair."

"Freakout averted?"

How could someone she'd known barely a month know her so well? "All good."

"Good. Because you owe me some details."

Hudson had friends, but not like this. Friends who teased her and called her out and made her feel good about it at the same time. It made her a little sad to think that her own tendency to take everything so seriously had something to do with it. She made a mental note to lighten the fuck up already, especially with the people she did consider friends.

"Are you going to leave me hanging?"

Hudson started, not sure exactly how much time had ticked by. "Sorry. Yes. I mean no. I mean, yes, we're dating."

That got her the incredulous look she deserved.

"We hooked up at Pride. Well, we met at Pride. Hooked up after. You know what I mean."

Gwyn's lips formed a perfect little O. Combined with her flawless hair and makeup, flannel shirt, and waders, Hudson couldn't help but imagine she was, in that moment, the personification of more than a few sexual fantasies. "Say more," Gwyn said.

"I didn't know who she was."

Gwyn snorted. "Sorry." Then she grinned, making it clear she wasn't all that sorry. "Of course you didn't."

"Yeah, but I didn't have a morning revelation, either. We didn't talk at all about what we did or where we worked." Hudson closed her eyes and shook her head, this time letting herself be amused by the whole thing. "And then she sashayed into new faculty orientation and I just about fell off my chair."

Gwyn laughed. A full belly laugh that had her clutching an arm around her middle and folding over. "Oh, you poor thing," she said, righting herself and wiping her eyes. "Was she as surprised as you?"

"She said she figured I was affiliated with the college somehow because why else did people move to Ryekill?" Which, in hindsight, made total sense. She'd just been utterly—or perhaps willfully—naive.

"So, you had a one-night stand, didn't see each other for two months, and now you're dating."

"Basically." Hudson's casual shrug belied the angsting that had gotten her to this point.

"Classic." Gwyn's terse reply seemed to belie something, too.

"Wait. What do you mean?"

"I mean, academics, dude. We can't get out of our own way most of the time, but we make it work."

She sure as hell couldn't argue with that assessment. It felt like her mantra in a lot of ways. Well, maybe not mantra. Brand. Having Gwyn cite it as a universal proved oddly comforting. "Yeah."

"You give me hope for my own sad sack of a social life."

Hudson shot her an incredulous look. "I thought you'd slept with all the single queer people in town already."

"Not all." Gwyn gave a dismissive shrug. "And not the one I really want."

"Who?" She blurted the question like an eager tween and didn't even care.

Gwyn perseverated, tipping her head and flipping her wrists. "We're all entitled to a few secrets, aren't we?"

Had she not just spilled her own beans about Callie, Hudson might have let her get away with it. "In life? Yes. In this moment? Absolutely not."

"I'll show you mine if you show me yours."

"I already did!" Again with the tween vibes. She was pretty sure she hadn't channeled those even when she was a tween.

"I want to know how it's going, whether you have feelings, and if she's as good in bed as I imagine." Gwyn ticked each item off on her fingers.

"Great, getting there, and better." Hudson did the same ticking of fingers, then lifted her chin. "Now you."

"Damn." Gwyn nodded slowly. "Yeah. Okay."

"Uh-huh."

"I may or may not have a thing for—" The tip of Gwyn's pole flexed, and her eyes went huge. "A fish. I have a fish."

It may have been a perfectly timed stall tactic, but Gwyn wasn't lying. She did have a bite. Hudson pulled in her own line so she could assist. "You do. You got this."

"What do I do?" For all Gwyn's usual swagger, she looked genuinely panicked now. Thrilled, but panicked.

"Relax. Keep tension on the line and keep stripping the line in. Let him tire out a little but keep the line tight. See if you can get him to swim toward my net."

Gwyn followed her instructions, and within a couple of minutes, they'd reeled in a beautiful little brook trout. Well, not so little. It was a solid ten inches. Hudson freed the hook and showed Gwyn how to hold it so she could snap a picture.

"Now what?" Gwyn asked.

"I usually throw them back, but I can show you how to gut it if you want to take it home."

"You bet your balls I want to take it home. I'm going to have this bad boy for dinner."

"Okay, then." She slipped the fish into a bucket of river water so it would keep until they were done for the day.

They got set back up, and Hudson waited a beat, not wanting to seem obnoxious but with no intention of letting Gwyn off the metaphorical hook.

"Sasha," Gwyn said, seemingly out of nowhere.

"Sasha?" Hudson asked, knowing only one Sasha in Ryekill. The one who happened to be Callie's best friend.

"Crane. The registrar. She's the one I have a thing for."

She glanced at Gwyn, who kept her gaze on the river. Not sure whether disclosing Sasha's connection to Callie would help or hurt the situation, she settled for, "Is she queer?"

"Oh, yeah. She and her wife broke up a year ago."

The observation answered a couple of questions and begat several more. "How bad?"

"How bad was the divorce or how bad do I have it for her?" Gwyn asked.

"Both?"

"Pretty bad." Gwyn chuckled. "On both counts."

Chapter Fourteen

@shitprofessorssay: I love my colleagues, until they open their mouths.

Sasha took a step back and frowned. "I don't think I like it."

Callie regarded the sagey green, then Sasha. "It'll get darker as it dries."

Sasha continued to frown. "I still don't think I'll like it."

"This is why I told you to get samples." The response counted as neither empathy nor problem solving, but she had suggested it, and Sasha had dismissed her.

"They're such a waste of money." Sasha full-on pouted now.

"They're cheaper than two gallons of paint you decide you hate."

"I don't hate it." Sasha sighed. "It's fine. I can live with it."

Rather than deflated, Sasha looked almost defiant in her decision to settle. Callie could abide a lot of things. Settling was not one of them. "You can and you should are two different things. Come on, we're going to the store."

"That's silly." Sasha shook her head. "You're here. We've already started."

"And repainting this room is a symbolic fuck-you to Lynn and her love of all things soft gray."

Sasha let out a snort, then her expression sobered. "Yeah. Okay."

"You're going to pick out four samples, and I'm going to buy them for you like I should have from the start. Then you're going to pick the one that makes you happy."

"Yes. Okay." A definitive note registered in Sasha's tone now, which mattered a hell of a lot more to Callie than the color that ended up on the walls, or how long it took them to get it there.

Callie offered to drive since she'd essentially blocked Sasha in, and off they went. "Did I tell you what Hudson is doing this weekend?" Callie asked.

"Other than not banging you, you mean?"

Callie lifted a hand, full stop. "I promised to help you paint. I'm not going to abandon you so I can get laid."

Sasha mirrored the gesture. "It's not abandoning if I give you my blessing. One of us should be getting laid."

She tried for a stern look, the sort that usually sent students scrambling to act like the adults they technically were. Only Sasha had seen that look so many times, it had lost any semblance of effectiveness. "I'm still not doing it."

"Suit yourself." Sasha shrugged. "So, what's Hudson doing besides lamenting not having sex with you?"

"I'll have you know I tried to get together with her yesterday, and she was the one who was busy. Which I was trying to tell you before you so rudely questioned my choices."

"Oh, well. Pardon me." Sasha twitched this way and that, feigning remorse.

"She's fishing."

Sasha wrinkled her nose.

"With Gwyn Bywood."

The grimace gave way to a look of curiosity, the kind that tried not to look as intense as it was. "That's…interesting."

Callie laughed—at Sasha's weak attempt at subtlety and at the descriptor that managed to say everything and nothing. And perhaps, despite the dust settling on her own attempts to wrap her head around the idea, a little at the situation itself. "Right?"

"Whose idea was it?"

She'd resisted trolling for too many details, despite wanting them. "Hudson's. Apparently, they've become gym buddies and Gwyn's been helping Hudson with her form. Hudson wanted to repay the favor."

Sasha sighed. "I'd like her to help me with my form."

The euphemism wasn't much to write home about, but the sentiment behind it landed soundly. Sasha had been crushing on Gwyn for close to a year but had never worked up the gumption to have more than a passing conversation. She blamed her divorce, but with a couple of glasses of wine in her system, she'd admit that Gwyn terrified her. "Maybe you should ask her."

Sasha rolled her eyes because Callie's simplistic advice had about as much effect as her stern looks. "She's so out of my league."

"Lies. You're gorgeous."

Since Sasha knew better than to argue that point—it was literally a rule between them—she let out a pouty sigh. "But I'm not an internationally respected gender studies scholar."

Callie smirked. "You say that like it's a bad thing."

Sasha merely groaned.

"I'm just saying, a woman like Gwyn might find a woman like you very refreshing." She'd applied the same argument to Hudson and stood by the logic. Brainiacs needed a break from admiration and competition with other brainiacs.

"Well, maybe one day I won't feel like a sad sack divorcee, and I'll work up the nerve to talk to her, and we'll see."

It was more than Sasha had been willing to venture only a couple of months ago, so Callie didn't press further.

They got to the hardware store, bought the samples Sasha had been so stubborn about in the first place, and went back to her house. Half an hour later, they went to the hardware store again, this time for two gallons of Raging Sea, a bolder shade of green with more blue undertones than gray.

"You were right," Sasha said after they got the first coat done.

Callie wasn't in the habit of gloating, at least not out loud, but their conversation from before had lingered in her mind. "About the paint or about how Gwyn might think you're a hot little ticket?"

"The paint. I'm only talking about the paint. Just because you're having good sex doesn't mean everyone is hot for everyone else."

Technically, she and Hudson had only had sex twice. She planned to multiply that number by a factor of as many as possible, obviously, but that wasn't the point. From where she sat, people spent a lot of time getting in their own way, overthinking and second-guessing themselves out of most of the fun life had to offer. If she could convince someone like Hudson to let loose a little, she sure as hell should be able to convince her best friend. "No, but it does mean I'm in a perfect position to remind you that flirting and dating and hooking up aren't the same as getting married, and you can do any or all of them solely for their own sake."

Sasha narrowed her eyes. "You realize you're advising me right now. Like I'm a student afraid to take an art class."

Callie shrugged, uncowed. "Apparently, recently divorced kick-ass women and chronically overachieving but stifled eighteen-year-olds have a lot in common."

Sasha's shoulders sagged, but she laughed. "I deserved that."

"You did." She set the paint roller she still clutched in the tray and gave her friend a hug. "And you deserve to get laid. By Gwyn Bywood or anyone else your heart desires."

❖

With the semester in full swing and midterm rapidly approaching, Hudson found herself fully in the groove. She was caught up on teaching, grading, mentoring, and writing. On many levels, it was her ideal existence—doing what she loved with people she mostly liked. And yet, even as she giddily drove to her first departmental cocktail party, she was already thinking about her date with Callie the following day.

She reminded herself one didn't need to cancel the other. She could be the rising star professor and the person sleeping with the dean of advising at the same time. Well, maybe not literally the same time. Talk about awkward.

The idea made her laugh and reminded her to relax. Those were the vibes she wanted for the next few hours. Because social graces might not be an official part of the tenure review process, but collegiality was. And if she'd learned anything from having a world-renowned economics professor for a dad—not to mention her own years as a grad student and post-doc—it was that collegial was an umbrella term that included sparkling cocktail party conversation.

Hudson parked out front of Esther's house, double checking the address despite the seven or eight cars already parked in the driveway and on the street. With its fussy trim work and quirky paint colors, the Victorian suited Esther to a T. She bounded up the porch steps and knocked, clutching a bottle of Malbec and thinking back to the house parties she'd attended in Berkeley.

Most of those had been with her fellow grad students, when cheap wine and chunks of cheese from Trader Joe's were the order of the day. Sometimes, if there was something to celebrate or commiserate over, a bottle of bourbon would appear and the jokes about becoming Ernest Hemingway would start up. A few times, she'd been invited to faculty parties. The food would be upgraded—fancy jams and olives and such to go with the cheese—and none of the wine would be in boxes. Those were the parties she liked most, where a light buzz and intellectual banter made her feel like the professor she aspired to be.

And now here she was. Achievement unlocked.

The door opened, and someone Hudson didn't know stood on the other side. Though he could have passed for an eccentric academic, with his long hair pulled back in a low ponytail and neatly trimmed soul patch. He looked vaguely familiar, but she couldn't quite place him. For the briefest of moments, she thought perhaps she'd gone to the wrong house after all.

"You must be Hudson." He thrust his hand at her. "Doug Drummond. I'm Esther's partner."

Hudson smiled and accepted the handshake. The gym. She knew him from the gym. "Great to meet you."

"Come on in. Most of the gang's already here."

She followed him into the house, filing away details. Like the gorgeously maintained oak banister and staircase that led to the second floor and the fact that Doug appeared to be at least a decade—if not two—younger than Esther. Oh, and the fact that he referred to members of the department as "the gang."

True to Doug's word, most of her colleagues had arrived. George and Henry hovered near the bar, though it looked like George had Henry cornered more than anything else. Amber and Layla chatted with Esther, who stood at the island arranging a charcuterie board.

Esther abandoned the bocconcini she'd been piling next to a mound of shaved prosciutto and came over to wrap Hudson in a hug. "I'm so happy you're here."

"Thank you for the invitation." Hudson handed over the bottle of wine.

"Oh, you didn't have to do that," Esther said. "But thank you."

"My mother would never forgive me if I arrived at a party empty-handed."

"A woman after my own heart." Esther passed the bottle to Doug. "Honey, get Hudson a drink."

Doug gestured to the bar. "We've got lots of options. I can also open this if you'd like."

Hudson did a quick survey. "I'll have a glass of red, but whatever you've already got open is fine."

Doug laughed. "She says, as though they won't all be drunk before the night is through."

Hudson chuckled politely, not sure if he was making a joke or a prediction. Esther smacked him on the arm, and he loped in the direction of the bar. So, joke. Hopefully. "You have a beautiful home," Hudson said.

"Thanks. I've been here for close to twenty years." Esther rolled her eyes. "Along with a few of the cobwebs."

The house was certainly lived in. The furniture had a worn, welcoming vibe. Books, tchotchkes, and framed photos filled the bookshelves that covered most of the walls in the living area. But Hudson detected no dust, which made her wonder who kept it that way. Her own parents had hired a cleaner for as long as she could remember, but that was because her father was hopeless, and her mother had insisted that her own career and raising two kids counted as more than enough jobs for one person.

Doug returned with two glasses of wine and extended one to her. "It's a cab franc from a winery a buddy of mine owns up on Seneca Lake."

"Thanks." Hudson accepted the glass with a smile and took a sip.

"I know what you're thinking. Since when does the Finger Lakes make a decent red? But I've really been leaning into the locavore scene and took a drive up that way last summer and found this really cool guy who grew up in California. He followed his wife here when she got recruited by Bausch and Lomb, and he decided to buy a vineyard. He hired a buddy of his and they've been playing mad scientist together for the last twenty years."

"That's so cool." Hudson nodded and continued to smile. She didn't know enough about Finger Lakes wine to have an opinion one way or another, but this one was solid, and she was always happy to hear New York was doing something well.

"I feel like I know you from somewhere." Doug stroked the tiny patch of hair under his lip.

She chuckled. "I had that same thought when you opened the door. I think we've crossed paths at the gym."

"The gym." Doug pointed at her, air gun style. "You lift with the Amazon."

Hudson laughed in earnest then, mostly because Gwyn would get a kick out of some random dude referring to her that way. "I do."

"Tuesdays and Thursdays, right? And the occasional Friday afternoon?"

"Uh, yeah." How did he know that? "You're very observant."

Doug waved her off. "I spend a lot of time there. You start to notice the comings and goings."

Her instinct was to ask him what he did for a living, but she had a feeling the answer would be house husband—house partner—and she didn't want to inadvertently disparage that arrangement.

"I'm in a band," he said, as if reading her thoughts. "Local gigs mostly. And I dabble in filmmaking."

Hudson didn't disparage that, either, though she did struggle to relate to something so precarious in terms of income. What really got her was trying to imagine Esther with someone like that. Of course, she'd have been the first to call Esther eccentric—in her mannerisms, her style. Why wouldn't that extend to her choice of partner?

The doorbell rang, and Doug excused himself to go answer it. Hudson smiled as he strutted away, deciding to find the whole thing charming, then went in search of another conversation to join.

While her preference would have been to join Layla and Amber, George caught her eye and motioned her over. Henry looked relieved, so that counted for something. And Lawrence had appeared from somewhere and joined them. All in all, not a bad group to sidle up to.

"How's the semester treating you?" Lawrence asked.

It was a strange question coming from someone she expected to bump into more days than not. But other than one of the two department meetings that had taken place over the last month, she'd seen neither hide nor hare of him—on campus or otherwise. "It's good," she said with the joviality she had for the semester, if not for Lawrence specifically.

Henry clapped a hand on her shoulder in a way that made Hudson feel like his teenage son. "Your first observation was stellar. And word on the street is you put in an appearance at the advising intensive at the FDIC last week."

Hudson, once again, resisted laughing at the acronym. Instead, she focused on how Henry knew she'd attended the session. Which was silly, really, since she should be paying attention to the compliment about her teaching. "Thank you. We had a great class discussion that day."

"I have to say, I was a little dubious about an all-female syllabus for a survey class, but even the young men seemed on board."

George curled his lip. "You're teaching an American lit survey without Hemingway or Faulkner or Poe?"

Hudson lifted a shoulder and tried for an easy smile. "How many survey classes have been taught through the years without Welty or Wharton or Morrison?"

Lawrence tipped his head, as though conceding the point. Henry smiled, though she couldn't tell if it had more to do with her class or the mild dressing-down she'd given George. George, of course, remained unimpressed and impassive. "Nothing surprises me these days."

Hudson didn't have world-weary on her obnoxious professor bingo card, but perhaps it counted as merely a subset of bored. Not that she should be thinking about any of her colleagues that way. But people like George made it impossible not to. Even at her most goody-goody, she couldn't fake more than basic pleasantries. At least he was a lone wolf in that regard. The rest of her department was great, and as she glanced around the room and took them all in, it struck her that she couldn't have landed in a better place.

Chapter Fifteen

@shitprofessorssay: I've never had a student bring me an apple. I have to say, it kind of hurts my feelings.

Callie knocked on Hudson's door promptly at eleven. It was the time they'd agreed on, but the precision of it made Hudson smile. Callie was such a mix of carefree and conscientious. Hudson had never met anyone like her.

She opened the door with a smile. "Come on in. I just need to put on my boots."

Callie—looking adorably outdoorsy and femme in her own pair of hiking boots, snug jeans, and a lumberjack flannel—stepped inside.

"So, are you going to tell me where you're taking me?" Hudson asked.

Callie grinned. "Apple picking."

"Yeah?" Hudson mulled the idea. "I've never been."

"Seriously? You've never gone apple picking? You're from New York."

"Long Island," Hudson said, pretty sure that explained it. "It wasn't really a thing."

Callie humphed, seeming to dismiss the idea of it not being a thing, but perhaps also Long Island in general.

"Am I overdressed?" Hudson asked.

"That's fine." Callie gestured to the jeans and sweater Hudson already wore. "You probably don't even need a jacket."

Hudson looked down at her outfit, then at Callie. "Okay, then. I'm game."

"Yay." Callie clapped her hands together the way a child might, and Hudson was quite certain there was nothing ironic about it.

"Do you want to drive, or would you like me to?" She didn't want to assume that the butch always drove.

"I will. That way you can bask in the foliage." Again, Callie seemed dead serious.

"Bask in the foliage?" Hudson asked.

"You're obviously autumnally deprived. I want to give you the full New York in the fall experience."

Hudson lifted a finger. "Full upstate experience you mean. I'm still technically from New York."

Callie made a face. "You can't call Ryekill upstate. We're not even in the Catskills."

"Who made you the geography police?"

"No one." Callie stuck out her tongue. "I'm just from legit upstate and we take it personally when people think fifty miles out of the city constitutes the upper half of the state."

Hudson resisted the urge to point out that technically both counted as upstate. She was more interested in finding out what part of upstate Callie called home. They'd danced around the edges but hadn't gotten into the specifics of origin stories. Well, not past Callie poking fun at her Long Island roots. "Wait. Where are you from?"

"Adirondacks, remember? The real upstate."

Was this where she confessed having never been farther north than Albany? Probably not. "Oh, right. Where, exactly?"

"Saranac Lake." Callie quirked a brow, and Hudson couldn't tell if she was being playful or not. "Let me guess, you've never heard of it."

"Of course I have. Great beer." Hudson gave an enthusiastic thumbs up.

"I want to be mad about that but I'm not," Callie said with a shake of her head and a smile.

"It's one of my many talents. Now take me apple picking and tell me I get to stuff my face with cider donuts before the day is through." Because she liked apples, but she loved cider donuts.

"That can most definitely be arranged."

They got on the road, and Callie put her in charge of music. Hudson felt the weight of making the right selection. It needed to suit the mood, but whatever she picked would say a lot about her taste. She scrolled playlists, hovering her thumb for a moment over show tunes before settling on the mellow but mighty mix of female artists ranging from Stevie Nicks to Brandi Carlisle.

"Nice," Callie said with a nod when "Right on Time" gave way to "Rhiannon."

"I know this is technically Fleetwood Mac, but I consider it a Stevie Nicks song."

"Fair."

Callie sang along, not super loud but with feeling. Hudson simply stared. Callie had a nice voice for sure, but it was the confidence that Hudson found riveting. The complete and utter ease with herself. Such a turn-on. And she was pretty sure Callie didn't even realize it.

"What?" Callie's gaze flicked from the road to her. "Do you not sing in the car?"

"I do." Hudson cleared her throat. "But only when I'm alone."

Callie smirked. "Is that your roundabout way of asking me to stop?"

"No, no," she said in a rush. "Not at all. I was enjoying it actually. A lot."

"Then you should sing, too."

"I would if I sounded like you." Maybe.

"You don't have to sound good. That's the beauty of singing in the car. You can turn up the volume and drown yourself out." As if proving her point, Callie tapped the volume button on her steering wheel. "Come on, Greene. Show me what you got."

Hudson joined in as the second verse started. She kept her eyes on Callie, who kept hers on the road. Callie swayed her shoulders and started singing again, like she genuinely didn't care whether Hudson sounded good or not.

Four songs later, they pulled into a gravel lot with a weathered barn that had been converted to a farmstand. Callie put the car in park and regarded her with a knowing grin. "Wasn't that better?"

Hudson chuckled. "Yeah."

Callie reached behind the seat and pulled out a couple of canvas totes. "Come on. Let's go pick some apples."

She'd planned to let Callie take the lead, but when Callie sniffed the donut-scented air and let out a happy smile, Hudson suggested they start with that. "Fuel for the harvest, right?"

"Right."

They housed a dozen between them, though as Callie pointed out, they were small. Small and hot from the fryer. Sprinkled with cinnamon sugar and absolutely glorious. As was the spiced cider Callie insisted they needed to wash them down.

By the time they wandered into the orchard, Hudson was rocking a pretty amazing sugar buzz. But even in her rather hyper state, she couldn't help but stop to take in the view. Row after row of trees, their branches heavy with apples in red, gold, and green. The rolling hills in the distance ablaze with fall color.

"Chop, chop," Callie said. "They aren't going to pick themselves."

"Yes, ma'am." Hudson gave a playful salute and hurried over to the tree Callie indicated. She managed to get five or six apples in her bag before an almost giddy feeling took over. "I know I'm supposed to be focused on the task at hand, but I have to tell you that I'd really like to kiss you right now."

Callie tugged a branch down far enough to peer at Hudson through the leaves. "Who's says you can't?"

Hudson looked around. She could make out voices in the distance, but no one was close enough to see. "Can I? May I?"

"You just have to catch me first." Callie grinned and disappeared into the next row.

Hudson darted after her, prepared for a chase. But Callie stood only a few feet away. Hudson reached for her, but she evaded. They did that a few times before Callie slipped between two old trees with leaves and branches thick enough to conceal her from view. Her top half, at least. Hudson slid in beside her. "Gotcha."

"And? What are you going to do about it?"

Callie's bedroom eyes had Hudson wanting to do a hell of a lot more than their current surroundings would allow. How did they keep getting themselves into that situation? Fortunately, the limits of public decency didn't mean she couldn't enjoy what was available. Hudson slid a hand into Callie's hair and leaned in for a kiss.

She brushed her lips over Callie's, debating between what she wanted and what she considered appropriate. It struck her that she spent a lot of time thinking about what was appropriate, what was expected. That she held back more often than she didn't, not wanting to come on too strong or be too much.

Callie was different. Freer. Almost like by simply being, she dared Hudson to break out of her mold.

With that thought blazing in her mind, she took the kiss deeper. Callie's lips parted and Hudson slipped inside, teasing and exploring with her tongue. Callie's arms slipped under the hem of her sweater and around her waist, and Hudson used her free arm to pull Callie against her.

Callie tasted like apples and cinnamon, comforting and yet somehow provocative. Hudson sucked Callie's bottom lip into her mouth and Callie moaned. Hudson's clit thrummed with longing.

The warmth of their bodies and the chill in the air made for a deliciously stark contrast. Callie's scratched lightly across her lower back. She snuck her own hand under the tail of Callie's shirt, tracing the dip at the base of her spine.

She wanted more than a hand on Callie's skin. She wanted Callie's body on hers without a scrap of fabric between them. She wanted to explore every inch with her tongue, as though steeping herself in Callie might finally sate her. She wanted more and more and more and wasn't sure she'd ever be able to get enough.

The squeal of a child pierced her lustful thoughts. Callie broke the kiss but didn't let her go. Hudson's vision came back into focus, and she found Callie smiling at her with mischief in her eyes. "Almost got carried away there," Hudson said, not quite wanting to admit how close she'd been to taking Callie against a tree.

"Almost." Callie canted her head. "I'm trying not to be disappointed."

She was, too. Fears of getting caught notwithstanding. "I can see the headline now."

"'College Professor and Administrator Arrested for Public Indecency at Local U-Pick Orchard.'"

"You'd enjoy that, wouldn't you?" Hudson asked, not entirely joking.

Callie's expression turned haughty, though she'd yet to let go of Hudson's waist. "I have a reputation to maintain, too, you know."

She immediately felt like a jackass. "I didn't mean—"

"I'm kidding." Callie released her but gave her butt a pinch in the process. "I might be more inclined to entertain such thoughts, but we're both adults who, by and large, act accordingly."

Hudson relaxed into the playfulness of the exchange, happy they were—by and large—on the same page. "Who said I didn't entertain them?"

Callie nodded slowly, as though conceding the point. "What kind of thoughts are you entertaining now?"

She made a show of looking Callie up and down. "The kind that involve taking you home and getting you out of all those clothes."

"Well, look at you with all these brilliant ideas all of a sudden."

"We should finish picking apples, though. Seems a shame to come all this way and go home with barely a dozen between us." Hudson definitely wanted sex more than apples at this point, but she had a shred of impulse control.

"Better make quick work of it, then."

❖

In the end, they managed to finish picking apples and stop at a brewery for an early dinner. They ordered beers and big salads and settled at a cozy little table near the fireplace. They chatted about work and life and everything in between—Hudson's favorite student and her most challenging one, Callie's choice of belly dancing as her primary form of exercise. Realizing that salad greens could be a bone of contention.

"You can't actually like it," Callie insisted, indicating the kale that made up the majority of Hudson's salad.

"I do. I love the way it squeaks against my teeth."

Callie shuddered.

"At least it's really a salad. You might as well get a cheeseburger," Hudson said.

"I don't eat Cobb salads because they're healthy." Callie jabbed her fork in Hudson's direction. "I eat them because they're delicious."

"Oh. Well, then."

"Though I'd argue it brings more fiber and nutrients to the table than a cheeseburger would, along with protein and at least some good fat. Though cheeseburgers have their place. Food shame is bullshit."

Hudson nodded soberly. "Bullshit."

"You're one of those good all the time types, aren't you?" Callie narrowed her eyes and used air quotes around the word good.

Hudson's grimace said more than any words could have. "Not all the time."

"It's that eager beaver streak. Chronic overachiever." It normally didn't appeal to her, but something about Hudson compelled her to make an exception, again and again.

"Guilty as charged." Hudson took a bite of kale, making it squeak loud enough for Callie to hear.

In spite of—or perhaps because of—those tendencies, it was Hudson who asked if Callie wanted to spend the night together. Callie was quick to agree, but since she hadn't made arrangements for Sasha to take Lucy for the night, she suggested they stay at hers.

She dropped Hudson at home to feed Gertrude and get some fresh clothes along with her car. Despite the frantic vibes of their make-out session among the apple trees, there was something almost domestic about their arrival at Callie's, one right after the other.

Callie let Lucy out, scooped her kibble, and made sure she got her thyroid pill before she ate. Hudson meandered the living room, asking casual questions about the family photos scattered among the books and tchotchkes on the shelves. Like the night at Hudson's but flipped.

"Do you want to sit?" Callie asked after letting Lucy out a second time. "Go through the motions of putting on a movie?"

"Or?"

She tipped her head in the direction of the stairs. "Or we could skip all that and go upstairs."

"Seems more efficient," Hudson said with a casual shrug.

"Is that what we are? Efficient?" She didn't have anything against that, but it was starting to feel like what they did—what they had—was more.

Hudson shook her head slowly. "I prefer to think of it as having my priorities in order."

Callie folded her arms but kept her expression playful. "And what are those?"

"Spending less time getting you into bed so I have more time having you in bed."

Hard to argue with that.

"Besides," Hudson said, "we spent the day together not having sex. Dawdling now would be overkill."

Callie let out a guffaw. Definitely not the Hudson of that first night. "Well, then what are we waiting for?"

"Not a damn thing." Hudson grabbed the overnighter she'd brought in and followed Callie up the stairs to her bedroom.

"Did you pack me any surprises in that bag of yours?" she asked.

"I've got some really cute boxers."

"Not exactly what I had in mind."

"How about a nice thick cock I've been wanting to fuck you with since the last time you let me?"

Just Hudson saying the word cock had her clit twitching. Perhaps because she'd been wanting it again since the last time, too. "That's more like it."

"I thought so."

"Do I get to go down on you again before you do?" The prospect had heat rushing to her core.

"Would you like that?" Hudson's voice was like bourbon—rich, smooth, and intoxicating.

Callie licked her lips and nodded.

Hudson opened her arms. "Then you better get me out of these clothes."

Since they'd ditched their boots downstairs, Callie reached for Hudson's belt. What was it about the tug of leather through a buckle that turned her on so much? She took her time, knowing Hudson's gaze was fixed on her. But rather than sliding it through the loops, Callie left it, turning her attention to the button and zipper of Hudson's jeans.

As much as she wanted her mouth on Hudson, and as much as she wanted Hudson's cock inside her, the access proved impossible to resist. She slid her hand in and found Hudson hot and wet. "Wanna bet I can get you off without removing a single thing?"

Hudson's hips bucked. "Sounds like a losing proposition to bet against it."

Callie worked Hudson's clit as much as the limited access would allow. She gripped Hudson's shoulder, and Hudson rode her hand. Going down might be her go-to, but this was proving to be pretty damn effective at turning her on to the point of struggling to see straight.

It didn't take long before Hudson went rigid and let out a feral groan in Callie's ear. Callie eased her hand away. "Yeah, looks like we both won."

Hudson tore at her clothes then. Okay, she didn't literally tear, but she had Callie buck naked in under a minute and took about the same amount of time to shed her own clothes. She went to her bag and pulled out the harness and cock.

Callie expected her to slink off to the bathroom, but Hudson tugged it on right there in front of her, tightening the straps in a way that made Callie's mouth water. Hudson went to the bed and made a show of making herself comfortable. After a fair amount of butt wiggling and pillow fluffing, she curled a finger in Callie's direction. "You let me ride you, and now I'm going to repay the favor."

Callie's pussy clenched. She didn't usually start off being on top, but she had no doubt she was wet enough to. She took her time sashaying across the room, keeping her eyes locked on Hudson's.

Once in the bed, Callie swung a leg across Hudson's hips and straddled her. She reached between her legs and positioned the tip of the cock, rubbing it along her clit a few times before guiding it into her waiting pussy. She shifted her pelvis, taking the length of it deep.

She loved being taken from behind, but this was a close second. It made her feel powerful, and each undulation of her body filled her and created the perfect pressure against her clit. And she could tell from the way Hudson's eyes rolled back each time Callie ground against her that the feeling was mutual. It drove her to the edge almost as much as the fucking itself.

And then there was the way Hudson's fingers dug into the flesh at her hips. Possessive, raw. She quickened the pace, knowing it wouldn't take much to make her come. They had all night, after all, and she had it on good authority that Hudson could coax several out of her without breaking a sweat.

Well, maybe a little sweat. Like the bead that trickled between her breasts. Like the light sheen on Hudson's chest below her collar bones.

Callie rode Hudson until the heat gathered low in her belly, until it spread like fire through her limbs, igniting everything in its path. She closed her eyes and let it take her until her whole body felt like it might melt into a puddle of satisfied delight.

Not trusting herself to hold her position, Callie collapsed onto the bed next to Hudson and worked on sucking in as much oxygen as her lungs could hold. "I'd like to state for the record that I like your priorities."

Chapter Sixteen

@shitprofessorssay: I don't keep tissues in my office because it gives students the notion it's okay to cry to me about their problems.

"Do you have a minute?"

Hudson looked up to find Pav, a student in her Am Lit survey course, hovering in the doorway. She wasn't technically holding office hours, but she went out of her way to tell students that an open door equaled an invitation. Besides, she'd been daydreaming about Callie more than getting any work done. "Of course."

Pav stepped in, then hesitated. "Do you mind if I close the door?"

She generally preferred open-door meetings—for reasons—but a closer look at Pav made Hudson think she was on the verge of tears. "Totally fine. What's up?"

Pav pushed it shut and sat. "I had a huge fight with my parents, and I don't know what to do."

Hudson nodded slowly, certain this was completely out of her lane, not to mention her area of expertise. "That sucks. I'm sorry."

"I told them I wanted to major in English and not be premed anymore and they flipped out. Like, seriously flipped. Said I was ruining my life, disappointing them, throwing away everything they worked hard for. The whole nine yards." A tear escaped, and Pav didn't bother wiping it away.

Okay, so a tiny bit more in her lane. She'd never experienced it herself, but she could at least appreciate the parental pressure to choose a major based on prestige or practicality. "Hey, it's not the end of the world."

"Could have fooled me." Pav slumped in the chair, but then just as quickly bolted upright. "They said they weren't going to pay for me to get a degree that wouldn't even get me a job."

Hudson bristled at the insinuation. She debated between sharing a moment of righteous indignation and making a logical argument about the marketability of written communication and critical thinking skills. "Well…"

"The thought of studying science for the next however many years it takes to get through medical school makes me want to kill myself."

Both options evaporated. Pav might be joking, but she might not. Either way, Hudson knew without a doubt she was in over her head. "Hey, that sounds pretty dire. Have you considered meeting with someone at the counseling center?"

Pav shook her head and started to cry in earnest.

Since that was the extent of Hudson's crisis management skills, her own panic meter ticked up a few notches. "How about the advising center? Have you been there?"

Pav nodded and sniffed. "Once. About my schedule."

"Would you be okay if I called one of my colleagues there? She might have some good ideas."

Another nod. Hudson held out her box of tissues and Pav took one. Then she grabbed Callie's card from the top drawer of her desk, dialed the extension, and said a little prayer to the goddess that Callie picked up.

Callie didn't, but a student working the front desk of the advising center did. After an excruciatingly long minute on hold, Hudson got assurance Dean Shaw would be available if Dr. Greene and her student wanted to come over. When they got there, Callie was waiting for them in the reception area. Hudson had no doubt the reassuring smile was for Pav, but she saw no reason she couldn't take some comfort from it, too.

"Is it okay if Dr. Greene stays?" Pav asked.

Callie flicked her gaze to Hudson before returning it to Pav. "That's entirely up to you. And Dr. Greene."

Despite the little voice in her head telling her to finish the warm handoff and hightail it out of there, Hudson nodded. "Dean Shaw is amazing, but I'm happy to stick around if you want."

Callie smiled. "It's easier sometimes to have someone you already know there, isn't it?"

Pav nodded.

They all filed into Callie's office and, even though Pav remained front and center in her mind, Hudson took in the details of Callie's space. A cozy little seating area in addition to the more formal setup at her desk, a rug that definitely wasn't standard office issue, and probably a dozen plants. Not more personal than hers, but different. Callie motioned them to the little table.

"I understand you're having a rough time. Do you mind giving me the highlights?"

Pav had stopped crying on the walk over but looked like she might start again at any moment. She told Callie much of what she'd told Hudson, with the addition of the fact that she'd bombed her first organic chemistry exam. "And by bomb, I mean I got a C. Of course, it might as well be an F as far as medical schools are concerned."

Callie listened and asked a few clarifying questions. She seemed more interested in giving Pav space than pitching possible solutions, and Hudson made a mental note to remember empathy could be just as important as problem-solving.

When Pav seemed to run out of words, Callie waited a beat, then another. "So, there's definitely some brainstorming we can do around your academic goals and trying to align them with your passions, plus the matter of your parents' expectations. But that feels like getting ahead of ourselves a little. Do you mind if we take a step back for a minute?"

Pav shrugged, obviously uncertain about what Callie had in mind.

"Have you been sleeping?" Callie asked.

Pav shook her head.

"How about eating and showering?"

Pav winced.

Callie's features softened. "Hey, it's okay. We've all been there. Self-care takes more than you've got some days."

Hudson hadn't been there. Not once. Even at her most stressed, she'd never lost her basic routines. It struck her how privileged that was.

"I just feel so hopeless," Pav said.

"That makes everything hard. Especially studying for classes you hate." Callie paused. She took a slow breath that Pav seemed to mirror without even thinking about it. "I know this might feel like an awkward question, but I have to ask it. Have you thought about hurting yourself?"

Pav didn't say anything.

"You're not in trouble even if the answer is yes." Callie pressed a hand to her chest. "But I need to make sure we get you connected to help right away if that's the case."

"I haven't, like, planned it or anything." Pav sucked in a breath and blew it out, shaky once more. "Just, you know."

Callie didn't ask for clarification or fill in the gaps herself. She simply waited.

"I have thought it would be easier if it all went away." She winced. "Me included."

Hudson's heart lodged in her throat, and it took every ounce of energy she had not to whip out her phone and dial 911. Callie didn't even flinch. She canted her head and offered a gentle smile. "Easier, maybe, but definitely not better."

"Yeah. I know. I wouldn't ever do anything. My poor parents. Talk about disappointed." Pav rolled her eyes and let out a defeated laugh.

"I'd still feel better if you talked with someone sooner rather than later. What if we walked over to the counseling center together?"

Pav shook her head. "My parents made me sign a FERPA waiver. I really don't want them finding out. They would truly lose their shit." She cringed. "Sorry."

Callie smiled fully, then. "No apologies needed. And I'm happy to say the counseling center is a HIPPA operation and not a FERPA one, so your secrets are safe with them."

"Wait. For real?"

Callie's smile was both encouraging and genuine. "A lot of students miss that during the onslaught of information at orientation."

Pav raised a hand. "I swear I paid attention."

Hudson chuckled at that. A nerd after her own heart.

"I believe you," Callie said. "So, what do you say? Drop-in hours are until three."

Hudson racked her own memory for the plethora of information she'd been fed at her own orientation. What Callie was casually referring to as "drop-ins" was officially called crisis walk-in hours. Hudson's respect for Callie ticked up another notch.

"Yeah," Pav said eventually. "Okay."

"Great." Callie gave a decisive nod. "I'd love to meet again, too, if you're open to it. Academic soul searching is kind of my jam."

Pav laughed, and the sound sent a ripple of relief through Hudson. "I'd like that," Pav said.

Callie stood, so Hudson followed suit. Pav did, too, but then she lifted both hands. "You don't have to go with me. That's extra."

Callie shrugged, casual enough that Hudson almost bought it. "You can decline, but I'm perfectly happy to get a walk and some fresh air. They don't let me out much during the day."

Callie winked, and Pav nodded her agreement. Hudson cleared her throat. "I'll walk with you, too, if it's not weird. I haven't been to the counseling center in person, and it would be good for me to know where it is."

Pav looked from Hudson to Callie and back. "Not weird. Or not any weirder than me sort of wishing you were my parents instead of my actual parents."

Callie pressed a hand to her heart. "I'm going to take that as a compliment to my coolness and not a dig about my age."

Pav's eyes went huge. "I didn't mean—"

"Kidding," Callie said. "Just lightening the mood a little."

"Thank you." Pav took a deep breath and looked like she might be, once again, on the verge of tears. "For everything."

Hudson took a deep breath of her own, the emotional swings of the last hour pushing the limits of what she could reasonably handle. Callie sent a quick message to her admin, and the three of them headed out of the advising center and across campus. The walk was pleasant, a crisp breeze stirring the fallen leaves scattered across the quad. If the circumstances were different, Hudson would be grinning like a goof and resisting the urge to take Callie's hand.

She lost herself a bit in the swirl of those thoughts until they arrived at the building that housed the college's health and wellness services. Callie told Pav what to expect, going so far as to walk her inside and introduce her to the person behind the desk. In a matter of minutes, Pav was taken back, and Callie and Hudson were retracing their steps.

"You're really good at that." Hudson willed her adrenaline to wane. "Are you as calm as you look?"

Callie smiled. "Not quite, but not too far off. You okay?"

"Yeah. I've never asked a student if they were thinking about suicide, though. I've always been terrified to bring it up."

Callie tipped her head back and forth. "I feel you. You just have to remember it's never a power of suggestion thing. If they're in that place, pulling it out of the shadows is always better. And it opens the door to connect them to help. I don't pretend to be that help, but I can connect like a boss."

Hudson chuckled, a surge of a different sort of emotion swelling in her chest. "I'm glad I've got you on speed dial."

❖

Callie didn't see Hudson the rest of the week, which was a bummer since she could have used the release a couple of good orgasms could bring. They'd done weeknight sleepovers a few times, but between Hudson's schedule and hers, they'd managed little more than texts since the afternoon Hudson brought Pav to her office.

To make up for it, she invited Hudson to come over after work on Friday. But by the time it rolled around, she was beyond beat. Still, the company was welcome, with or without the energy to do much with it. Callie got home a little later than usual thanks to one of her advisers needing to process a difficult student, which meant she managed to let Lucy out and change into comfies before Hudson arrived, but not much else. Since it was barely five thirty, she decided they both deserved a glass of wine before she got started on dinner.

She handed Hudson one of the glasses and settled next to her on the couch. She took a long sip, letting the smoky notes of the Rioja play across her tongue. She let her head fall onto the back of the sofa and released a sigh. Much better.

"You okay?" Hudson asked.

She righted herself and blinked a few times. "Yes. Midterm grade panic meets the course withdrawal deadline meets advising for registration, but yes."

Hudson cringed. "Why does that happen all at once?"

She chuckled. "Because that's the way the academic calendar works."

"I guess it makes sense in some ways, right?"

"It does. It just makes for a brutal couple of weeks for people in my line of work. Which is why I'm extra grateful for weekends." She took another swig from her glass. "And wine."

Hudson set down her glass. "What about girlfriends who rub your feet?"

"Depends. How would said girlfriend feel about rubbing my neck instead of my feet?"

"This girlfriend would be more than happy to do that." Hudson poked her thumb into her chest. "You calling me your girlfriend?"

Callie laughed at the delivery more than the question. She didn't put a ton of stock in labels—or at least not rushing them—but she warmed to the idea. She lifted her chin in playful challenge. "Maybe."

Hudson grinned. "Well, then, let me get on that."

She motioned Callie into place and Callie happily settled on the floor between her thighs. "Is this okay?"

"Perfect. Let me know if it's too much pressure or not enough."

Hudson had barely pressed her thumbs to Callie's traps when Callie let out a moan. Or perhaps it would be more accurate to say her first moan. "Oh. Oh, that's good. Just right."

Hudson continued the massage—thorough and with more skill than Callie had experienced outside of an hour with a paid professional. Callie continued to moan, and occasionally groan, her appreciation. Every semblance of tension drained away.

"Do you want to talk about it?" Hudson asked.

Callie forced her eyes open. "Talk about what?"

"What has your shoulders in knots? You seem more stressed than you were letting on."

She chuckled. "I promise I'm not. Only one vexing meeting, really. Mostly it's having enough back-to-back student appointments to test even my most extroverted self interspersed with email goblin shoulder hunch."

Hudson's hands stilled. "Email goblin?"

"I don't like to admit this because it's embarrassing, but impeccably professional, friendly but firm email is my superpower."

Hudson laughed then. Really laughed. And then she said, "I'm not sure whether I should feel pity or envy."

Callie gave a little bow. "Both are acceptable responses."

"So, what does a person have to do to get one of these emails? I confess the idea kind of turns me on."

She shook her head. "Nope. You do not want to be on the receiving end. I have patience for students because their brains aren't baked, but when I have to send one to a fellow adult, it's not pretty. Well, not pretty if you have the rhetorical savvy to see through my impeccable professionalism. The snark is strong with me."

"Okay, now I'm genuinely frightened. Please warn me if I'm ever in danger of getting one so I can brace myself."

It was her turn to laugh. "You're doing all right so far."

"Whew." Hudson resumed the massage.

"Of course, if you want to rub my shoulders on the regular, your chances of staying in my good graces go up exponentially."

"Noted."

Hudson continued to work her magic, and Callie found herself on the verge of nodding off. She said as much and wiggled away, since Hudson showed no signs of stopping on her own. "Do you want me to do you?" she asked.

"I'm good, I think."

"Rain check, then. I don't think I can give as good as you did, but I'm all about reciprocating."

"I'll note that too," Hudson said with a smile.

"There's one problem with a glorious massage before dinner." Callie stood and rolled her now deliciously loose shoulders.

"What's that?" Hudson asked.

"I have zero desire to cook now."

"That's not really a problem, though, right? Your house is in the delivery radius of at least half a dozen decent options." Hudson quirked a brow. "Though I wouldn't be sad to eat a bowl of cereal and call it good. Or skip dinner altogether."

Callie considered both options. "Are you not hungry, or are you trying to be sweet?"

Hudson smacked her lips and looked Callie up and down. "Maybe I'm hungry for something besides food."

The salacious tone made her giggle even as it turned her on. "Is that so?"

"Yes, though I completely understand if you're beat."

Callie indulged in her own slow once-over of Hudson. "You really are sweet, you know that?"

"Yes." Hudson smirked. "But if the rest of your week entailed even a fraction of the emotional labor that went into that meeting with Pav, I'd be a first-rate dick not to pamper you however I could and put you to bed."

"How would you feel about a shower, a quickie, and being asleep by ten? After your choice of cereal or takeout." She had no idea what time it was, but it had to be before seven still.

Hudson glanced at her watch. "I want you to have enough dinner to sleep well, but my vote is definitely cereal."

Never had the prospect of a bowl of Special K held such appeal. "Then it's unanimous."

After poking some good-natured fun at her selections, Hudson conceded that Golden Grahams made for a completely legit late-night snack. Callie poured them each an oversize bowl of Special K Strawberry, and they settled back on the sofa to eat. Lucy waited patiently for her bowl licks, then Callie fed her and let her out. It was all said and done by quarter to eight.

"I'm looking forward to seeing how much I can squeeze into the next two hours," Hudson said as they climbed the stairs.

"I thought we'd agreed to a quickie."

"Yeah, but you said asleep by ten, which gives me a solid two hours even after a shower. Considering how long I'm otherwise inclined to keep you up, it totally counts as a quickie."

Callie couldn't fault the logic. Not that she even wanted to. Hudson managed to be sweet and smart and sexy as fuck—all at the same time. And, apparently, sweet and smart and sexy Hudson wanted to be her girlfriend. It was way more than she'd bargained for when they started hooking up. Not to mention more than she ever expected from dating a professor.

Perhaps it was time to come clean about her alter ego. After all, Hudson was proof in spades that not all faculty were fickle or farcical. Soon. Tonight, she had minimal bandwidth and other priorities. And who wanted to talk about social media when soapy skin-on-skin, sex, and sleep were on the docket?

Chapter Seventeen

@shitprofessorssay: We are convening a committee to discuss the prevalence of excess committees. Meetings will be weekly.

Saturday brought a lazy breakfast and a few hours back in bed that had nothing to do with sleep. Or with being quick. As tempted as Hudson was to make a whole weekend of having her way with Callie, she had a bucketload of grading to do before heading to Long Island for Thanksgiving. So she suggested lunch out, figuring it would be easier to part ways from a public place than any space in close proximity to Callie's bed.

Callie suggested Ivy, since it was walking distance from her house and she liked them for brunch even more than happy hour. "It's usually overrun with students on the weekend, but most of them have already cleared out for break."

"I remember that phenomenon from my Cornell days." Hudson shook her head as they walked the few blocks to the restaurant. Most of the leaves had faded and fallen, but they remained scattered along the sidewalks and made for a satisfying crunch underfoot. "Though at the time, I was one of those pesky undergrads all the townies couldn't wait to get rid of."

"I love students, but I confess I resemble that remark. Mostly at the end of May, though. By the time the spring semester ends, I'm definitely ready for some peace and quiet."

"My research agenda and I feel the same." Though she was making decent headway, her fall teaching load was a course lighter than it would be in spring. "Do you get summers off?"

Callie tipped her head. "Uh, no. Most of us lowly staff have to work all twelve months of the year."

"Uh, you're a dean. There's nothing lowly about that."

Callie let out a dismissive sniff. "I might have the title, but I'm required to keep regular business hours twelve months of the year. And I don't get sabbaticals."

Hudson's instinct was to point out that sabbaticals were for research, not vacation. Or that she worked plenty in the summer, even if that didn't include teaching any courses, but she knew it wasn't the same. She got to set her own hours and work from home in her pajamas if the mood suited. She might be the type to show up to her office most days, but she got that it was a choice. Still, Callie had made her choice when she went into administration, right? "Yeah, okay."

"It's different, though," Callie said, clearly not picking up on any of Hudson's underlying defensiveness. "Campus is a ghost town. We get to work on big projects and, with faculty gone, the number of committee meetings I have to go to is like half."

Hudson was all about the work of shared governance but had a feeling Callie sat on a lot of committees. She didn't begrudge Callie wanting a break. "Fewer meetings is definitely cause for celebration. My chair is nudging me to avoid any until next year, but there's a DEI advisory group that I heard about through the Rainbow Alliance that I might join."

Callie smiled at that. "You should. I'm on it and it's definitely the least soul-sucking meeting I go to."

She chuckled. "High praise."

"Low bar, but that, too."

"I've heard horror stories about Faculty Senate." Though she'd also heard that was the doing of a couple of particularly intractable members more than the group as a whole.

They arrived at the restaurant and, as expected, found fewer than half the tables occupied. Hudson asked for a table near the fireplace, more for ambiance than warmth. Once they'd placed their orders, she found herself wanting to talk about something other than work.

"So, are you going to your folks' for Thanksgiving?"

Callie nodded. "You?"

Hudson mirrored the nod. "It's the one meal a year where my mother goes all out. She's a great cook but generally considers it more trouble than it's worth."

Callie laughed. "I don't share that sentiment, but I can appreciate it."

"She made sure my brother and I were fed, despite having a career just as demanding as my father's. I'm pretty sure my father would have let us starve. Not out of malice, but he's one of those absent-minded academics who'd forget to feed himself if left to his own devices." One trait, thankfully, she hadn't picked up from him.

Callie shot her a side eye. "Am I allowed to roll my eyes at that?"

"Absolutely. We put up with his eccentricities but not without making it a running family joke."

"I suppose that counts for something," Callie said.

Since Hudson wasn't entirely sure Callie meant that, she opted to shift the focus. "What about your parents? Who runs the ship in your family?"

"Oh, definitely my mom. Though she lets my dad think he does. No one is fooled, especially him."

She smiled at the description. "And you have sisters, right? Only sisters?"

"Yeah. Tammy is the oldest. She's a nurse and rocks all the older and wiser vibes without being obnoxious about it. Becca is the baby. A middle school teacher and a total ball-buster."

"In a good way, I hope," Hudson said.

"She can be extra, but we love her."

Hudson chuckled. "I think my brother might say the same about me."

"You? Extra?" Callie raised a brow, clearly dubious.

"More the ball-buster part."

Callie's expression morphed into one of pure disbelief. "I'm going to need you to elaborate."

She angled her head one way, then the other. "Let's just say that, in addition to my early love of female writers, I also developed a fondness for feminist scholars."

Callie squeezed her eyes shut and pressed her lips together. Hudson assumed it was to suppress a laugh, but when Callie's gaze fixed on her a moment later, delight shone in her chocolate-brown eyes. "Why is it so easy to picture a fourteen-year-old you chasing some hapless boy around with a copy of bell hooks?"

She smirked. "Maybe because it's not far off from how things actually went down."

"I approve this message."

Hudson spared a moment to remember that time in her life with fondness. "He was a good sport about it, all things considered. And I like to think he's one of the more woke stock analysts roaming around Wall Street."

"Okay, I definitely approve of that." Callie smiled, as though having a fond memory of her own. "So, will you see him, too?"

"Yes, he and his wife will come out from the city, but only for the day most likely. I'll spend the whole week with my parents."

"Nice."

The server arrived with their food, punctuating the conversation once again. Callie tucked in to her chicken sandwich and fries, citing the need to make up for the cereal they'd had for dinner despite the bagels she'd toasted them for breakfast. "Plus I have rehearsal with my dance group this afternoon. Shimmying for an hour requires carb loading."

"I'm with you," Hudson said. "Gwyn has me lifting almost double what I was at the start of the semester. I'm ravenous literally all the time."

"Except last night." Callie licked her thumb, drawing Hudson's attention to her lips.

"I was plenty ravenous. I was simply prioritizing my hierarchy of needs."

Callie's thumb hovered at the corner of her mouth, like she knew the effect it had on Hudson and didn't care. Or maybe she cared plenty and simply liked it. "I think Maslow might have something to say about that."

"I think if Maslow took one look at you, he'd understand."

Callie licked her lip and bit it lightly. Hudson resisted the impulse to squirm. "That's quite a come-on. How would little feminist Hudson feel about grownup Hudson dropping such lines?"

Callie was clearly teasing her, but Hudson took the question to heart. "I think she'd take one look at you and be thoroughly impressed with the girlfriend grownup Hudson has managed to snag."

❖

Callie didn't make it to her parents' until Wednesday night, but she arrived just in time for the traditional pizza and wings from Sal's, plus a little too much wine and a rather raucous game of Scrabble. Since Tammy lived nearby, she and her kids, plus husband Greg, went home for the night. Since the bedroom that had been Tammy's—and then briefly Callie's when Tammy moved out—had since been claimed as a sewing room slash office, that left Becca and her to share their childhood room. It was kind of fun, aside from the fact that Becca snored like an elephant.

Snores or not, Becca's internal alarm had its own agenda, and Callie woke up alone. Despite being up and downstairs before seven, she was the last one to the table. Even Tammy beat her there, leaving the kids and Greg home to watch the parade while she came to help with dinner prep. Which meant Thanksgiving morning, much like the night before, felt like it had for the better part of her life.

She settled in her usual spot, one that looked out the picture window to the collection of bird feeders hung around the yard. No fewer than thirty flitted about, starting their days with seed and suet. She indulged in a long, lovely inhale before sipping her coffee and releasing a contented, "Ah."

Callie loved Thanksgiving, but mostly, she loved being home.

"Nice of you to join us," Becca said.

Sisterly niggling notwithstanding. "You're just jealous that I can sleep past five."

Becca stuck out her tongue. "Someone has to educate the youths."

"And we're all eternally grateful you do."

Tammy lifted her mug. "We all do our part."

Becca lifted hers as well. "And we all deserve a day off."

"I'm so glad you girls still come home for holidays," their mom said with affection.

"Yeah." Dad lifted his chin. "You turkeys are much more exciting than our resident ones."

"Still no suitors?" Tammy asked.

A flock strolled through the yard most afternoons courtesy of the corn and other treats put out for them. Seven hens but no tom. After a couple of months, their parents started calling them the golden girls, and more than a few lesbian jokes had been made. Dad shook his head. "They seem perfectly content without."

"Speaking of suitors." Becca looked pointedly at Callie. "You're still dating the professor?"

Callie gave her sister a bland look. It was a terrible segue. Besides, Becca knew full well she was still seeing Hudson. The question was simply her way of making sure everyone else at the table knew. They did, but of course Becca had to make a show of it. "I am."

"I never thought I'd see the day." Becca set her coffee to the side and leaned in, propping both elbows on the table. "Does she know your secret identity?"

Dad looked up from the crossword, and Mom stopped stirring her coffee. Callie huffed out a breath. "I don't have a secret identity."

No one said anything, but looks were exchanged. Becca, troublemaker that she was, took it as her cue to press on. "You manage an internationally popular social media account whose sole purpose is to make fun of professors. No one but your closest friends and family know this fact. If that's not a secret identity, I don't know what is."

A combination of head tilts and tongue clicks made it clear everyone agreed with Becca, even if Becca was the only one saying it out loud. Callie offered a simpering smile. "I think calling SPS 'internationally popular' is a bit hyperbolic, no?"

"I think criticizing my word choice is a bit of displacement, no?" Becca mimicked Callie's delivery perfectly.

"Hey." Tammy lifted a hand. "Let's not let Psych 101 sparring distract us from what's important."

"Yeah," Callie said. "It's the holiday of gratitude and togetherness."

Tammy wagged a finger. "While true, I was talking about your new girlfriend. Other than the fact that she's an English professor, you've been very tight-lipped."

"I have not." Callie frowned, mostly on principle. "There's not a whole lot to tell."

"So, it's not serious?" Mom asked, all innocence.

"It's not…anything," Callie said.

"So, you're fuck buddies," Becca said.

"Becca!" Callie and Tammy hollered in unison.

Becca shrugged. "What? It's a legitimate question."

Callie glared at Becca, shot a pointed gaze at their father, then resumed glaring.

Becca rolled her eyes. "He's not a prude, you know."

It wasn't the first time they'd argued over what level of sharing was appropriate in front of their parents. Becca might be the baby, but instead of the precious little princess, she was a little bit like the son their parents never had. A little loud, a little crass. Daddy's little ballbuster. It was mostly hilarious, if weird. And occasionally inconvenient.

Callie looked once again at their father. He'd resumed the crossword, adamantly keeping his gaze down. "She's not that."

"Friend with benefits?" Becca asked without missing a beat.

Callie pinched the bridge of her nose. "We're dating. It's something adults do. You should try it."

Tammy, who'd married her high school sweetheart and was pregnant with her third child, cackled. "I'm not sure our allergic-to-third-dates girl is down for that."

Becca gave a simpering ha-ha, and Callie laughed in earnest.

"Is that all we're going to get?" Mom, not usually one to pry, raised a brow.

Callie had a pretty open relationship with her family—both siblings and parents. They might not get into some of the more explicit details like what she'd share with Sasha, but they were her people. They helped each other navigate all the ups and downs of life. This sort-of relationship she had going with Hudson was no exception. "I like her. More than I thought I would."

"So, she's not an esoteric narcissist?" Becca asked.

"She's not." Callie pursed her lips. "Most of them aren't. Not really."

Becca arched back in her chair like she'd been walloped with some shocking revelation. "Oh, my goddess, she's going soft."

"Stop." Callie punched Becca's arm. "You make fun of the ridiculous people in your profession, too."

"Well, sure. But it's not the same. Teachers are entitled to be neurotic."

Callie didn't disagree. Teachers put up with all manner of abuse. Plus they worked insane hours and were chronically underpaid. But if Becca was going to poke holes in her logic, she sure as hell was going to return the favor. "How many times have you threatened to start a Shit Parents Say?"

Becca gave a cringey smile. "Yeah, but there are already so many, how would I stand out?"

Becca had a point. Plenty of accounts parodied life in the public school system. Hell, there were sitcoms about it. And while hers wasn't the only one that highlighted the foibles of academia, it had a niche. Its content resonated with way more people than she could have imagined when she'd started posting after a particularly absurd email from a faculty member trying to foist his entire advising load on her. "Yeah. I guess you'll never manage to be as cool as me."

"Wait." Tammy raised a hand. "Did we establish whether or not Hudson knows you're Shit Professors Say?"

All eyes fixed on Callie. Even Dad. He did that lowered chin thing so he could study her over the top of his reading glasses. She sighed. "No."

"No, we didn't establish it or no, she doesn't know?" Tammy asked.

She wanted to be annoyed by how literal Tammy could be sometimes, but it was a fair question. One she'd undoubtedly pose if the tables were turned. "No on both counts. Though I guess now only the second."

Dad's eyes narrowed, like it took him a second to parse her meaning. But then he gave the slightest head shake and went back to the crossword. Callie frowned. It was subtle, but she had no doubt he was disappointed. Why was she so freaking susceptible to that?

"Have you considered why that is?" Mom asked gently.

Both Becca and Tammy closed up like clams, knowing better than to get in the way of their mother's unique capacity to unravel flimsy arguments without batting an eye. Callie swallowed any and all witty retorts that presented themselves. She knew better, too. "I will." She picked at the edge of the cotton tablecloth. "If we get serious."

No one said anything. Becca didn't observe that she'd believe it when she saw it. Tammy didn't offer an encouraging smile and say she hoped that turned out to be the case. It was unsettling, the quiet conveying so much more than a continuation of the ribbing. Like they all sensed she was on the precipice of something and didn't want to jinx it.

Eventually, Mom braced both hands on the table and stood. "Who wants breakfast before we start working on dinner?"

The weird spell of silence shattered, like hitting play on a paused TV show. Becca asked whether pancakes were a possibility, and Dad got up to put on a second pot of coffee. Callie picked up the crossword, scanning for the blanks whose clues had stumped her father on the first pass.

By all obvious accounts, she was off the hook, at least for now. But as her family bustled around her, the comfort and familiarity of a holiday at home took a back seat to the question of whether she and Hudson were serious. Whether she wanted them to be.

Callie didn't make a show of shunning relationships, but she didn't make a show of seeking them out either. She went with the flow, enjoying the ride and not taking anything too seriously. Except the things that mattered, of course. Only then did it strike her she'd started to take that category—things that mattered—for granted. She relied on a gloriously black and white differentiation that gave her life and her work meaning while tuning out or poking fun and the absurdities that were part and parcel of that life and work. Things rarely shifted from one category to the other, and that was exactly how she liked it.

For all that, she couldn't deny her relationship with Hudson felt decidedly gray.

She expected that revelation to fill her with unease, to leave her grasping for purchase and longing for certainty. Only it didn't. It felt…refreshing. Like going into a situation with decidedly low expectations and being pleasantly surprised. She'd thought that more than once with Hudson. Hudson revealing her inner confidence, Hudson showing the sort of self-awareness often lacking in career academics. Having as much fun with Hudson out of bed as in it.

Callie got up to start frying bacon or whatever other task her mother gave her and let that idea settle over her like a comforting blanket. Maybe that's what her whole relationship with Hudson was turning out to be—a pleasant surprise.

Chapter Eighteen

@shitprofessorssay: Thanksgiving break is like the eye of a hurricane. Just when you think you've survived, you realize the worst is still to come.

With her sous chef duties done, Hudson excused herself to shower and dress for dinner. Since her brother and his wife wouldn't be arriving for another hour, she took her time in the bathroom, then shed her towel and flopped on her childhood bed naked. She grabbed her phone and rolled onto her stomach, suddenly feeling sixteen again.

Going with the vibe, she tapped over to her text thread with Callie. *I hope it's okay to tell you I'm thinking about you.* Send. *Because I am.* Send. *Thinking about you.* Send. *And telling you about it.* Send.

They'd texted throughout the week and even talked on the phone once. Still, today was the holiday proper, so Hudson didn't expect a reply. At least not right away. But the little dots appeared before she could even swipe to another app.

If it's not okay, then we're both in trouble. She added the winking emoji with the heart, making Hudson smile.

Hope you're having a good time with the fam. Be sure to stuff yourself just shy of a food coma.

Callie's reply, once again, came instantly. *Go big or go home. Food coma all the way.*

Hudson laughed, and it struck her how much she did that around Callie. Laughed, relaxed, took herself a little less seriously. Things she could do, but that didn't always come naturally.

They hadn't really talked about their relationship beyond the initial agreement to date. Even that was more the result of deciding to spend time together in addition to having sex than any sort of agreement. But when push came to shove, Hudson was pretty far gone. She woke up thinking about Callie and fell asleep doing the same—whether or not they were together.

It was weird for her on some levels. She liked things being concrete, at least as far as her own life was concerned. Nuance was for textual analysis. Callie was different, though. The carefree spirit that had been so sexy that first night they met seemed like a mantra for life and not merely sex. Hudson would be lying if she said it didn't leave her uncomfortable still. But like so many things she'd learned to appreciate, discomfort was an essential part of the process. What that meant for her and Callie remained to be seen, but it helped to wrap her head around her own feelings.

The sound of car doors closing outside broke Hudson from her reverie. She chuckled and hauled herself out of bed. There'd be plenty of time for pensive musings after gorging herself on turkey. She got downstairs just as her brother and sister-in-law finished exchanging hugs with her parents. She took one look at Milton, then dropped her gaze to her own outfit. Of course.

He looked at her, and his head dropped to the side. "Dude."

"Don't look at me." Hudson pointed to their mother. "I'm not the one who bought us the same shirt."

They both looked at Evelyn, who shrugged. "It's a nice shirt. I thought it would look good on both of you."

Everyone laughed because it was funny, but also because it wasn't the first time she'd done that. Combined with two children always looking to earn good child points by wearing gifts they'd been given, it was a wonder they hadn't stumbled into twinning before. "I can go change," Hudson said.

"Oh, please don't." Mom clutched her hands to her chest like she was a trad housewife more than a woman who managed multi-million-dollar portfolios. "You look so adorable."

Adina nodded eagerly. "Agreed."

Both Hudson and Milton rolled their eyes but didn't argue. They knew what hills to die on, and this wasn't one of them.

Everyone tried to help with the final touches on dinner, but Mom shooed them out until it was time to carry dishes to the table and pour wine. They all became her little minions then, equal parts eager to please and eager to eat. By the time grace was said and the food passed, that feeling of being a teenager had returned. Only now she got to talk about the grades she gave rather than the ones she was getting, and she didn't have to ask permission for wine.

"Everything looks amazing, Mom. Truly." It struck her how lucky she was—for the over-the-top meal but also for a family who loved and supported her.

"Cheers to that." Dad lifted his glass and they all joined in.

Conversation meandered along with the meal. Hudson loved how unhurried it all was. She liked to think of herself as someone who stopped to savor the little things, but she fell victim to food as fuel more often than she cared to admit.

Dad asked her about working with Lawrence, and Hudson kept her answers vague instead of outing her father's best friend as a completely absent mentor and rather disappointing colleague. Fortunately, she was spared follow-up questions by Milton and Adina's big announcement that they were expecting a baby in the spring. Baby talk dominated the remainder of their time together, and Hudson didn't mind in the least.

"You ready to be an auntie?" Milton asked when he pulled her into a hug as he and Adina said their goodbyes.

"Are you kidding me? I've been sitting on a book of feminist bedtime stories for close to a decade."

He shot her a dubious look. "You have not."

"Okay, not a decade, but I do have one." She grinned. "I picked it up when I was in San Francisco one time with your future baby in mind."

Milton shook his head. "Adina and I weren't even married yet."

"Which is why I kept it to myself until now. No way was I going to insinuate if or when you two decided to breed."

That got her an eye roll. "There's the sister I know and love."

"I try."

Milton and Adina headed back to the city, and Hudson helped her father with cleanup. Much like she and her brother had worn the shirts gifted to them by their mother, her dad now sported the Real Men Do Dishes apron she'd gotten him for Father's Day. She'd expected him to get a laugh out of it more than wear it, but since dishes were one of his primary household duties, it seemed to be serving a purpose after all.

With the dishwasher loaded and running, and everything else washed, dried, and put away, Frank Greene declared their work done for the day. Mom was already in the living room with her feet up, so they filed in and joined her.

Hudson settled into her corner of the sofa, wondering if nine was too early to call it a night. She tuned out the latest medical drama her parents were streaming these days and pulled out her phone. After a token check of her email, she clicked over to her social media feed and scrolled her carefully curated collection of accounts—laughing at cute animals, saving a couple of recipes she could maybe make for Callie, and bookmarking an online fly-tying workshop that would be fun to do over winter break.

Her feed also included a couple of nuggets from Shit Professors Say. As usual, they were a mix of funny and cringe-worthy. One caught her attention; it was weirdly similar to something Callie had said in passing the week before. Of course, it had to do with professors wanting "someone" to intervene in the prevalence of students missing class in the days leading up to break. Not a unique gripe by any stretch of the imagination.

She scrolled on, but it didn't take long for boredom to set in. Her attention span for scrolling had never hit doom levels—for which she was equal parts grateful and proud. That pretty much left her with the cadre of word games she fell back on when procrastinating and picking up her text convo with Callie. It didn't take long to settle on the latter.

How's the food coma?

When the reply dots appeared not five seconds later, Hudson smiled. *Semi-conscious and happy with my choices. You?*

She laughed. *Same.* Then, *When are you back?*

Saturday afternoon. You?

Hudson typed another *same* and asked if Callie had any interest in getting together. That felt safer than delving into how much Callie had been in her thoughts or how a week of not seeing her at all felt like far too long. Callie's reply—instant and enthusiastic—made her feel like maybe she wasn't alone in those sentiments. It warmed her from the inside, more than any amount of turkey and stuffing could.

❖

Callie spent Friday helping her parents get and decorate their tree for Christmas and Saturday morning sorting through a box of things her mother insisted she take with her or toss. Both were great, but by the time she made her way to 87-South, she was ready to be home.

Because she was stubborn like that, she attempted to bring everything into the house in a single trip. Not her finest moment. Especially her attempt to unlock the door without losing everything on the front step. Fortunately, the only one around to witness the ruckus was Lucy.

Once they made it inside, she unhooked Lucy's leash and dropped the pile of bags on the bench by the front door. She jutted out her elbow, allowing the dog bed tucked under her arm to fall. "Girl, we need to talk. You travel with more crap than I do."

Lucy ignored the comment and hopped on the couch.

"Yeah, go ahead. I can see you're exhausted from the three-hour nap you took in the car."

Lucy settled with a happy sigh and Callie couldn't help but laugh. She might spend a lot of time making fun of how cushy college professors had it, but they didn't hold a candle to spoiled old dogs.

After putting things away and starting a load of laundry, she considered her options. One was to take a nap of her own, but she always woke up feeling like she'd been hit by a bus and then not being able to fall asleep when she wanted to. Not worth it.

She spent a few minutes poking around the kitchen, investigating whether she could rustle up something good for dinner that didn't require going to the store. A decent selection of veg, a log of goat cheese. Could she be bothered to whip up a pie crust? Why not?

She got the squash and onions roasting and used the down time to take a shower. Hudson might be beat by the time she arrived, but Callie wanted to feel ready for any friskiness that might ensue. A week with no sex shouldn't have her wound up and wanting, but there it was.

With sex on the brain as much as dinner, she threw the tart together and got it in the oven. Too bad she hadn't stopped for some fresh greens. On the heels of that thought came the memory of her shopping trip the week before, when she'd decided to take one for the team. She went to the fridge and tugged open the crisper drawer, smiling at the bag of baby kale staring back at her. It hadn't even gone slimy. She chuckled and reluctantly added a tick mark to the kale column.

Hudson texted an ETA of a little after five and, because Hudson was Hudson, pulled into the driveway at 5:03. Callie opened the door, knowing full well Hudson would be standing on the other side but feeling a jolt of excitement nonetheless. "Hi."

Hudson's smile seemed to echo the sentiment. "Hi."

Callie grabbed her hand and pulled her inside. "I know it's totally silly to say this, but I feel like I haven't seen you in ages."

"A week, ages. Same difference." Hudson didn't even bother shrugging out of her coat before pulling Callie into a kiss. "Too long."

In addition to the surge of arousal she always got when Hudson kissed her, a different sort of surge radiated from a bit higher. It might have been more accurate to call it a flutter. Not wholly unexpected, but the intensity of it caught her off guard. She'd missed Hudson—had said as much in their text chats and the one phone call they'd managed when they both happened to have a moment to themselves. But it was more than that. Hudson coming over now felt like Hudson coming home.

Hudson broke the kiss long enough to take off her coat and boots, and Callie used the opportunity to study the woman she'd been spending more and more time with. That dark hair, so prone to looking unkempt despite Hudson's best efforts. Deliciously defined shoulders. And those hands. God, what Hudson could do with those hands.

Hudson stood, locked eyes with Callie, and smiled. "There. That's better."

Instead of making a joke about better being when they tumbled into bed naked, Callie concluded her study with those hazel eyes. They communicated so much—apprehension, delight, desire. More green than brown tonight, they shone with what Callie perceived to be simple happiness. It made the flutter in her chest swell. "Much. I'm glad you're back."

Hudson grinned. "Me, too. I love my family, but all I could think about was getting back to my little house and my little office. And you."

The sweetness of the sentiment reinforced Callie's read. "I know exactly what you mean."

Hudson took both of Callie's hands in hers. "So, what do you want tonight to look like? Do you want to order dinner and watch a movie? Fuck until we're famished and eat cereal in our underwear?"

"Hmm…" Both options appealed, as did the fact that Hudson suggested them.

"Wait." Hudson sniffed a few times, pointing her nose in the direction of the kitchen. "Something smells good. Did you cook?"

In addition to settling on the galette because she had the ingredients on hand, it happened to be something they could eat hot or at room temperature. "It's this tart thing with roasted squash and goat cheese. I thought we could have it with a little salad. I needed a break from turkey and stuffing."

"That sounds amazing."

Callie tipped her head. "I even bought baby kale."

Hudson's eyes narrowed briefly, as though waiting for the punchline. When Callie merely smiled, she pressed a hand to her chest. "Be still my heart."

It was a joke, obviously, but like the happiness that seemed to reflect back at her in Hudson's stare a moment earlier, the phrasing and the gesture hinted at the same sort of feelings swelling in Callie. Not capital-L love, perhaps, but something on the path to it. She didn't mind it. She didn't mind it one bit.

CHAPTER NINETEEN

@shitprofessorssay: I don't know why students are always going on about the cost of tuition. They're thrilled when you cancel class. Oh, and no class tomorrow. You're welcome.

Zeke, Callie's first appointment of the day, lurched forward in his chair. Frustration radiated from him. "He hasn't answered any of my emails. He canceled office hours the week before break, no-showed to class Monday, and he canceled class this afternoon. I'm freaking out. I can't fail this class."

Callie kept her expression calm and collected, since that was the professional thing to do. Inside, however, she seethed. While she chalked up the majority of student complaints to mutual missteps, this was the third student she'd met with about Lawrence Michaelson in as many weeks.

The first didn't like the feedback he'd gotten on an essay. After ensuring it hadn't crossed any lines, she'd encouraged him to meet with the professor to try to get some clarity and demonstrate his commitment to improving his approach on the final. The second had been the gripe about office hours. Callie had been on her side, especially with only two weeks of classes to go before finals.

Even then, though, she'd made excuses as much as she'd channeled empathy. Maybe Professor Michaelson had a perfectly valid reason for his actions. In the more likely case that he didn't, she'd still do well to hold her tongue. Because no matter her title, she never lost sight of one of the universal truths of her position. Making enemies of faculty didn't do her—or her students—any favors. Besides, helping students navigate their way into adulthood came with the territory, including the fact that the world wasn't always fair. She took that responsibility seriously.

Much like baseball, however, she had a three-strike rule. She might not be able to call anyone out, but she could alert the people who could. At least theoretically. No one with tenure got ousted for anything short of a felony indictment. Hell, she'd seen one survive even that. But she believed in due diligence, and in her line of work, that meant bringing in the department chair. Clearly, the time had come.

"I'm sorry to hear you're experiencing this. From where I sit, we've got two related but distinct issues." Callie went on with her usual spiel, separating out having trouble with a class and wanting to lodge a complaint about a professor. She hated thinking of it as a spiel, but she delivered it often enough that the descriptor fit. Students needed to understand their options, as well as how each of those options might play out.

Zeke, for his part, listened intently. She could tell that being heard—and having options—went a long way in helping him feel less trapped. She led with the complaint part, explaining that he could let her convey the sentiments or put something in writing, that he could entrust it to her or meet with the department chair directly.

"I don't want him to know it was me." Zeke shook his head with fervor. "He'd totally fail me then."

She made a point of not promising things she couldn't guarantee. That included retaliation. "He won't. That's the perk of my position and the advising center. We're here to help, but we also pass along concerns that come up. Coming from me, the department chair will know to take it seriously, but I have the luxury of delivering it anonymously."

The assurance seemed to calm Zeke down. "Yeah. Okay."

"That doesn't do anything immediate for the problem at hand, I'm afraid."

Zeke's shoulders slumped. "Right."

Callie dug deep into the well of her professionalism. "My advice is to keep trying office hours. Make a note of times you're there and he isn't. And keep a file of whatever emails you've sent and any replies. The grade appeal process doesn't open until after final grades are submitted, but if the end result of all this is that you feel you were not assessed per the terms of the syllabus or that you were assessed differently than other students, you have a path to request review."

Very few formal grade appeals made their way through the system after any given semester, but for a lot of students, knowing it existed provided enough reassurance to turn down the dial on their anxiety. At the end of the day, the true worriers often ended up with decent grades and were happy to move on. And the rote complainers hit the wall of not meeting the appeal criteria laid out in the policy.

By the time Zeke left, Callie's next student appointment was waiting. That was followed by two more students and a meeting to plan the abbreviated orientation program for students transferring to Coteau midyear. When the academic piece was squared and the student affairs folks started discussing the challenges of designing icebreakers for introverts, Callie clicked over to her email and dashed off a missive to Henry Hazelton.

Since she knew better than to hit send on something written with half her attention and all her ire, she relegated it to drafts until it could get a proper proofread in her office. She tuned back into the meeting in time to vote in favor of a proposal to allow students to self-select into a low-stimulation version of the Get to Know Coteau event that had students learning about both college traditions and each other. If it went well at Winter Welcome, they'd roll it to the larger format program in the fall. She might not identify as an introvert herself, but she'd taken on the care and feeding of enough of them through the years to know it would be a hit.

When the meeting ended, she recognized the need for a break and dashed off a quick text to Hudson to see if she was free for coffee. By some magical alignment of the universe, Hudson had wrapped up her office hours on time and offered to meet Callie at the library café. Even better, Hudson beat her there and had chai waiting. "Bless you," Callie said with a small bow.

"I'm never going to pass on the chance to see you and caffeinate in the middle of the afternoon." Hudson lifted a finger. "Please note you got billing over caffeine."

She took a sip of her gloriously sweet and spicy drink, letting it warm her from the inside. "That's very noble of you. I suppose I'll say same."

Hudson chuckled. "How's your day, aside from having to trek across campus in the snow?"

For the briefest of moments, she considered confiding her current conundrum. It didn't feel right, though. One, because Hudson had a personal relationship with Lawrence, and muddying those waters felt like a bad idea for everyone involved. Two, Hudson didn't suck, but she was still faculty. It felt weird to vent when she'd yet to disclose being behind SPS. It was one thing to omit, another entirely to talk about something that would likely turn into a post or two. And then not acknowledge said post.

Hudson shifted in the seat across from her, moving more directly into her line of sight. "Should I have started with an easier question?"

Maybe. "No. Sorry. I think my brain is frozen along with the rest of me. It's good. I'm good."

Hudson settled back and sipped her coffee, seemingly satisfied with that answer. "It's going to be even colder tonight. I'm tempted to invite myself over so I can sit next to your fireplace."

They didn't often do weeknights together, but Hudson only had early class on Mondays and Wednesdays. And since Callie was already used to starting her day while Hudson slept in, it wouldn't be weird to leave her in bed to get to work on time. "I could save you the trouble and invite you myself."

"How about I bring takeout?"

Even better. "You don't have to bribe me. I already signed on to the plan."

"Yeah, but I'm willing to bet money you eat girl dinner on the regular, and I don't want you to feel compelled to do more than that if I'm there."

It was a valid point, so she didn't argue. "Sold. I'll even let you surprise me."

"With dinner or is that a more general consent?"

She could have asked for clarification or gone with a coy "it depends." But much to her surprise, Hudson hadn't disappointed her yet—in the bedroom or otherwise. If anything, Hudson's surprises to date had either been totally sweet or next-level sexy. Why would she turn down the chance for more of that? "Let's consider it a blanket declaration unless specified otherwise."

Hudson's smile was slow, packing a whole lot more sexy than sweet. "I can work with that."

❖

Hudson spent longer at the gym than expected. She'd run into Doug, who seemed a lot more interested in chatting her up than his circuit of the weight machines. Gwyn showed up right as she was leaving, which required more chatting since they hadn't seen each other since before the holiday.

Since it was going on six by the time she left campus, Hudson called in her "little bit of everything" order to Za'atar and headed directly there. It was only after picking up the food that she realized she could smell herself almost as much as the fresh-from-the-oil falafel. Hopefully, Callie would still let her through the front door.

She'd no sooner crossed the threshold and kissed Callie hello than Callie leaned back in and gave her a sniff. "Someone's come right from the gym."

Hudson winced. "I should have stopped at home. But I called in dinner, and it was going to be ready way quicker than I thought and I didn't want it to get cold."

"Oh, I'm not complaining. I like a little well-earned sweat."

"Is that so?" Was it wrong for her mind to race to the ways they might work up a sweat together?

"Absolutely. Besides, I do have a shower." Callie tipped her head. "And I have on good authority we shower well together."

"Does that mean you'll be joining me?" The prospect had her juices flowing, sweaty stench notwithstanding.

"How about I let you take this one solo? Something tells me we'll be wanting another before the night is through."

Hudson tsked. "Promises, promises."

"Go. I'm sure it will take you all of two minutes." Callie took the bag and gave it a little shake. "I'll get this situated and pour wine."

"Can I trouble you for a big glass of water, too? If I don't hydrate, I'm going to be hurting tomorrow." Hudson leaned in for a kiss, taking care not to get any of her sweat on Callie.

"Of course. It's a good reminder for me, too, even if I didn't spend my afternoon pumping iron."

By the time Hudson showered and tugged on the sweats and tee she'd left the last time she stayed over, Callie had turned her kitchen table into a Middle Eastern feast. "I may have gone a little overboard," she said.

Callie shook her head. "No such thing."

Hudson slid into one of the chairs, and what she could only describe as an old man grunt escaped. She winced. "Sorry."

"Don't apologize. Do you want some ibuprofen with your falafel?"

She chuckled feebly. "How sad is that?"

"Eh? We're in our thirties. It's all downhill from here." Callie got up and disappeared into the kitchen, returning with a pair of orange caplets.

"Please don't remind me." Hudson laughed at the absurdity of it. And by absurdity, she sort of meant reality.

They tucked into the food, little hums of pleasure taking the place of conversation for a while. With the first few falafel devoured—still crispy and hot despite transport—Hudson felt reasonable venturing back to words. "So, Henry is hosting a holiday party for the department. It's an annual thing, complete with significant others."

"Okay." Callie nodded, but Hudson wouldn't say she looked enthused. In fact, she looked anything but.

"I was hoping you'd be my date." She hoped the phrasing, and the addition of her version of pretty-please eyes, would win Callie over.

"You're difficult to say no to. You know that, right?"

Hudson frowned. "I want to take that as a compliment, but I'm not sure I should."

Callie smiled. "It is."

"But you're saying yes because of that and not because you have any desire to go." Which sucked, since she had every indication that Callie liked socializing more than the average person. Or at least the average academic. Was better at it, too.

"Maybe, but that doesn't have to be a bad thing. I'm happy to be your plus-one."

An unpleasant thought occurred to her. "Do you have bad history with Henry? Or someone else in the English department?"

"No. Nothing like that," Callie said. There was a "but" clearly hovering below the surface, but she didn't continue.

"Come on. You can tell me. Wait. Is it George?" It had to be.

"What makes you say that?" Callie asked with a look that said she already knew the answer.

"He's a dick. The question is, did he do something specific to you?"

Callie shook her head. "Nothing to me. He's on Academic Review Committee this year, so I have more direct contact than I would otherwise, but that's more insult by association than anything personal."

She didn't like the idea of any sort of insult being lobbed in Callie's direction. "You'll tell me if he does? Insult you personally, I mean."

"You gonna defend me from the playground bully?" Callie batted her eyes.

Hudson didn't relish making an enemy out of anyone who might have a voice in her tenure review, but she sure as hell wasn't going to stand by. "If it comes to that."

"I promise I can take care of myself, but you totally get brownie points for offering."

Hudson wanted to press the matter—to say she wasn't looking for brownie points or that Callie shouldn't have to deal with George's assholery even if she could. But she didn't want to lose the thread of the initial conversation. "How about, you be my plus-one, and I promise to not so subtly interrupt if he attempts to corner you in conversation?"

"I accept these terms." Callie smiled, but it didn't quite reach her eyes.

Hudson studied her for a moment, debated and promptly rejected leaving it at that. "Is it something else? You seem squirrelly."

Callie hesitated, convincing Hudson she was on to something. But Callie composed herself quickly, her usual easy smile in place as if it had never faltered. "Not at all. Just ready for bed I think."

Hudson slowly shook her head, deciding to go with Callie's words if not her vibe. "No complaints here."

They put away the leftovers—easily twice as much as they'd managed to eat—and Callie fed Lucy and let her out. Callie hesitated at the top of the stairs. "Should I shower? I feel like I should shower."

"You should let me have my way with you, then you can shower. Imagine how good you'll sleep."

"Mmm. You make a compelling case."

In the bedroom, Callie flicked on the lamp she always did when they were getting ready for bed. She turned down the bed, then looked to Hudson with a mixture of deference and wanting.

Hudson would have happily taken either. The combo did wicked things to her, especially since deference was pretty much the last thing Callie showed the rest of the world.

"So, I took your comment about surprises to heart." She took the velvet pouch from her bag. "But I don't want you to feel pressured to say yes. Or you can say yes in theory but no thanks for tonight."

Callie quirked a brow. "Color me intrigued."

Hudson handed her the pouch.

"It's heavy." Callie squinted, as though she might be able to peer inside.

"They," she said, less to correct and more to continue the game.

Callie gave the pouch a squeeze. "Are these what I think they are?"

"Depends. What do you think they are?"

Rather than reply, Callie loosened the drawstring and tipped the glass spheres into her hand. "Ben Wa balls."

Hudson hoped the slightly breathy tone had to do with excitement and not distaste. "Have you played with them before?"

Callie shook her head. "I may have read a certain terrible straight erotic romance back in the day that had them in one of the scenes. I never bought any, though. I'm not sure why."

"Well, now you have a pair of your very own. We can try them now if you want, or another night. Or maybe you'd like to experiment on your own."

Callie looked from Hudson to the glass marbles. When her gaze returned to Hudson, her brown eyes were hot with arousal. "I want to try them now."

The certainty in Callie's voice wiped away any concern lingering in Hudson's mind over the party invite and Callie's reticence to accept. She'd said yes, after all. And every other aspect of their relationship seemed to click perfectly. That's what mattered—in this moment and in the grand scheme of things. She had no reason to do anything but enjoy it.

Chapter Twenty

@shitprofessorssay: Academia is like kink but without a safe word. Only with more performance and less getting off.

It may have been a matter of minutes, but thoughts about Henry and Lawrence and everything else were long gone. All that remained was Hudson and her—the heat between them and the promise of more to come. Callie had exactly zero complaints.

Hudson hadn't so much as touched her, but Callie's clit thrummed. Arousal and anticipation pulsing out a persistent beat. In her mind, it sounded a lot like Hudson. Over and over and over. She leaned into it, and away from the niggling voices. She and Hudson clicked in the ways that counted. There was no need to worry about the rest.

"What do I do?" she asked, her voice breathy and pleading in her own ears.

"Do you trust me?" Hudson asked in return.

Such a loaded question, and yet the answer was almost disarmingly simple. "Yes."

"Lie down. Relax."

Hudson's own achingly simple direction washed through her, wiping away any need she might have felt to call the shots or, hell, know what she was doing. Tonight was about giving herself over, about letting go. Callie did as she was told, easing onto the bed and trying to keep her breath steady. At least for now.

Hudson touched one finger to the inside of her thigh, just above the knee. "Be a good girl and open your legs for me."

One sentence and any semblance of steady breathing went out the window. Any chance of being anything but putty in Hudson's hands promptly followed. Callie did as she was told.

Hudson ran that finger all the way up, to where Callie already dripped with wanting. "I'm going to get some lube. Just a little. I know you're already wet for me."

Holy fucking fuck. What the hell switch had Hudson managed to flip? Callie was a puddle. Literally. Okay, not literally, but it felt like it. Her bones had melted, leaving her powerless to do anything but follow Hudson's lead. Hudson's command. "Okay."

She felt Hudson's absence keenly, though it lasted only seconds. When Hudson returned, Callie tensed instinctively, unsure of what to expect.

"Shh. Relax. I've got you." Hudson's words were honey. The return of Hudson's fingertips to her skin a reassuring balm.

Callie nodded, not wanting Hudson to think she was having second thoughts. "I know."

"I've tried to warm these in my hand. I hope they're not too cold." Hudson ran the first sphere of glass along Callie's opening, coating it with her wetness.

Callie tuned in to the sensation—hard, smooth, and surprisingly warm. The hum of anticipation came unbidden, but it seemed to signal all the right things to Hudson. The ball slipped inside her, and her muscles pulled it in and held it tight. The hum became a moan.

"Are you ready for the second?"

She had no idea what to expect, what it would feel like, but a single word reverberated through her. More. "Yes."

Just like with the first ball, Hudson teased her with it first. Up and down her slit, over and around her clit. Callie clenched instinctively. Having something inside to grasp sent her into overdrive.

Hudson pressed the second sphere into her. Callie gasped. Hudson gripped her thigh. "Are you okay? Talk to me."

"It's…it's good." Forming even those meager words took all the concentration she had. Or perhaps more accurately, all the concentration she could spare.

Her body clenched and relaxed, tightened and released. Each time, the balls shifted. Each sensation new and a little different from the one before. It was as mesmerizing as it was erotic. And somehow deeply intimate, despite it not being Hudson inside her.

"I'm going to touch you now." Hudson's voice lilted through the trance. "You'll tell me if something doesn't feel good."

It was a statement more than a question, but Callie nodded anyway. She wanted Hudson to know she'd heard, and the task of forming words proved more than she could manage.

At the first brush of Hudson's finger over her clit, Callie tensed. As it always did. Only this time, it had something to hold onto. Like a cock but not. More nuanced, and completely internal.

Every nerve in her body seemed to come alive at once, every sense heightened. The mattress beneath her, the cotton sheets against her skin. The cool air of the room, the warm glow cast by the lamp next to the bed. And Hudson—kneeling beside her and staring at her with an intensity that should have left her feeling exposed. Only it didn't. It made her feel seen. Safe.

Before Callie could delight in the novelty of it, she came. Hard and fast, it had her hips bucking off the bed and her back arching in a way that would make yoga her proud.

"Fuck," she said around the ragged attempts to suck in enough oxygen.

"Does that mean you're done?" Hudson's voice practically dripped with self-satisfaction.

Callie considered, then shook her head.

Hudson smiled. "Would you let me put my mouth on you?"

She nodded.

"You seem to be at a loss for words," Hudson said.

Callie tipped her head. "I know that might be hard for someone like you to understand, but I promise it's a good thing."

Hudson chuckled. "Rendering the dean speechless is quite an accomplishment."

"Well, you don't seem to be in need of advising."

"I've been told I pay excellent attention."

Callie smiled at that. "You most certainly do."

Hudson gently nudged Callie's legs apart and settled between them. Callie took a steadying breath and tuned back in to her body. Hudson kissed her thighs before pressing her tongue to Callie's clit. Callie let out a moan.

Hudson hummed her approval. She licked and sucked—gently at first but with increasing fervor as Callie ramped toward another release. Like before, the balls shifted and moved inside her, and her muscles worked them in time with the thrust of her hips.

"Yes," she said, voice all panting and pleading.

Hudson's tongue continued to work, but her fingers joined the party. She circled Callie's opening, dipped inside. The tip of her pinky pressed Callie's other opening without penetrating.

"Oh. Ohh." The pressure in Callie's belly began to build.

Hudson lapped at her clit, fast and firm.

The orgasm ripped through her like a tornado. But instead of destruction in its wake, it left only pleasure. The sort of bone-melting pleasure that left Callie dazed and dizzy.

Hudson rested her forehead on Callie's thigh. "That was hot."

"Uh-huh."

"You're incredible," Hudson said.

"Uh-huh." Callie swallowed. "I mean, you too."

Hudson crawled up the bed until she was face to face with Callie. "Thank you."

"Oh, no. Thank you." Heavy emphasis on the you. "I think I'm done now. With these at least."

Hudson nodded. "You'll need to push them out. It might be easier standing. If and when you think you can."

Callie winked one eye closed, then switched. As the throbbing subsided, she was able to focus on the muscles she had the capacity to control. One sphere popped out, then the other.

"Or maybe your vaginal walls follow your every command."

She laughed at that and, after Hudson collected the balls from the mattress, squeezed her thighs together. "Fuck," she said again, mostly for good measure.

Hudson slipped into the space beside her, resting her palm between Callie's breasts. "Thank you for doing that with me."

"Thank you for introducing me to something I should have tried a long ass time ago."

Hudson chuckled. "I'm not sad to be your first."

The sentiment of that landed, not heavy exactly, but full. Solid. She rolled to her side. "I'm not, either. More a where has that been all my life sort of feeling."

"I understand."

"What about you?" she asked.

"What about me?" Hudson stared at her now, in all her earnest glory.

Callie willed her vision to focus along with her thoughts. "Is there anything you want that you haven't done before? Or haven't done in a while?"

Hudson traced a finger along Callie's jaw, earnest expression holding firm. "That."

It was hot to think Hudson took as much pleasure in giving as Callie took in receiving. But even as it thrilled her, it left her antsy. "Do you want to do it, you know, the other way?"

"No," Hudson said without the slightest hesitation.

"I kind of figured." She tried for a sheepish smile. "But I thought I should ask."

"I like that you did. And I like that you—confident, sexy, independent you—let yourself come undone a little around me. I can't tell you how much of a turn-on that is."

Callie ran her leg up and down Hudson's, leaving it to drape over Hudson's thigh. "That's just it. I don't only want to turn you on. I want to leave you as sated and satisfied as you leave me."

"I see." Hudson's serious look remained, but suddenly there didn't seem to be anything earnest about it. "You could go down on me, if it would make you feel better."

Callie chewed her lip. "Would it make you feel better?"

"You going down on me always makes me feel better."

And delightfully, it was as simple as that. "Before I do, I should probably warn you."

"Yes?" Hudson asked.

"Having my mouth on you invariably turns me on. I might need you to fuck me when I'm done." Even after what they'd just done, she had no doubt she'd want Hudson again.

"I'm pretty sure that's an incentive more than a warning."

"In that case..." Callie hooked her foot on the far side of Hudson and used the leverage to come to a straddle over Hudson's hips. "I should get on that."

Hudson's hands came to rest on the swell of her ass. "You absolutely should."

❖

Hudson woke to sunlight streaming in and no one next to her in bed. She stretched a hand into the spot where Callie had last been and found it cold. Right. It was Thursday.

She dragged herself to a seated position and looked around the room. Everything was as it always was—a goodly portion of Callie's clothes piled on the chair in the corner, Callie's jewelry and makeup scattered over the dresser. Oh, and Lucy—in her bed, one eyebrow perked. "Good morning, girl."

The perked brow lowered, and the opposite one went up.

"Don't look at me. If it was my house, I'd let you sleep in the big bed."

Lucy lifted her whole head at that, and when Hudson got up, Lucy happily followed. After a stop in the bathroom, she beelined for the kitchen to see if Callie had left any coffee behind. She had, of course, along with a mug and a note.

Lucy might like to go out, but don't let her convince you she didn't get breakfast. She's a dirty liar. Also, feel free to make fresh coffee if you'd prefer. Wasn't sure how you ranked fresh vs. easy.

Callie hadn't signed the note, but she'd put a little heart at the end. Hudson's own heart did a little flip at the sight of it. Silly, really, but she didn't try to talk herself out of it.

She let Lucy out and opted to reheat a cup of the coffee Callie had left. It seemed wrong to waste it. And she could make a small pot for herself at home when she got there, before heading to campus.

As predicted, Lucy went to her bowl and gave Hudson the most forlorn look imaginable. Hudson didn't feed her because she could be the adult in situations like this, but she did sneak a couple of treats from the jar Callie kept on the counter.

She loaded the dishes Callie hadn't bothered with the night before but otherwise resisted the urge to fritter her day away. It wasn't like she was lacking for work to do.

Hudson told Lucy to be good the way she'd seen Callie do once or twice, the way she did with Gertrude. Though she got the feeling Lucy actually listened. Not that Gertrude misbehaved. More that her choices had little to do with Hudson's preferences or directives.

At her place, she showered and dressed for the day. Her fall uniform had transitioned to winter, which meant layering sweaters over her standard button-downs. Callie had definitely teased her about it once or twice, but since hardly a day went by that Callie didn't sport some variation of tights and ankle boots, Hudson gave as good as she got, and it all seemed like butch-femme appreciation more than anything else. And since she couldn't seem to get enough of Callie—in bed or otherwise—she decided to text Callie to see if she might eke out a little more. *Hey, I managed to put myself together at a reasonable hour. Any chance you're free for lunch?*

Hudson headed to campus without waiting for a reply. Even if Callie wasn't free, she could pop into the Faculty Club for a big salad and a cup of soup. Now that the weather had turned, she'd made a habit of doing that at least a couple of times a week. It helped her from getting bored of the soup she made at home—giving her a reason to freeze a bunch rather than eat it every day for a week.

By the time she made it to her usual parking spot, Callie had replied. *Sorry. I've got a meeting with your chair momentarily, and back-to-back students with all manner of issues the rest of the day.*

Hudson texted back a *no worries* because that was the reasonable thing to do, but her mind started turning. Why would Callie be meeting with Henry?

There was an independent director of academic integrity, whose office was adjacent to Callie's but not part of it. She'd asked about that specifically when she'd gone to his spirited, if not entirely satisfying, workshop on navigating student use of AI. She'd gotten the sense everything in his shop stayed separate and confidential unless an official sanction was entered into the student record. But maybe Callie had more involvement than Hudson knew.

Or maybe it was about something else entirely. Maybe it was about her.

Hudson shook her head. She'd know if she'd truly fucked up, the kind of fuckup that required secret meetings. She had to trust that. And trust that Callie would share something that affected her if she could. Hell, maybe even if she technically couldn't.

Somewhat mollified, Hudson resisted texting again. She did go to her office via a slightly circuitous route that took her past Henry's, but finding his office door closed—with the lights on and murmurs of conversations discernible from the hall—made her regret her choices. She didn't even know if it was Callie's meeting with him or something else, but it left her uneasy regardless.

It was fine. It would be fine. And if, by some weird stretch of the imagination things weren't fine, Callie would tell her.

She settled in to do some work before lunch, only to have her phone flash with a text from Gwyn. *Please tell me you're free for lunch.*

Hudson frowned at the urgency of the request, especially since she and Gwyn were due to work out together later that afternoon. *Just made it to campus. Faculty Club at noon?*

When Gwyn replied with nothing more than a thumbs up emoji, Hudson gave in to her unease and asked if everything was okay. Another thumbs up came in reply, followed by: *Big news. BIG. NEWS.*

Since Gwyn didn't seem inclined to share anything more, Hudson tried to focus on work. She found it easier to manage curiosity than concern in general. Besides, she only had to sit in suspense for the next hour. Hopefully, whatever it was would be a nice distraction until she could see Callie again and get assurances that everything with them was thumbs up as well.

Chapter Twenty-One

@shitprofessorssay: Feel free to take your complaints to the chair. It's not like he has the power to do anything about it.

Callie took a fortifying breath and strode into Storey. The dark wood walls and frosted glass doors felt like a movie set—a far cry from the mid-aughts reno her own building had undergone. She climbed the stairs to the offices of the English Department. At Henry's office, she hovered for a moment, then rapped lightly on the doorframe when Henry didn't look up. He instantly bounded from his seat. "Dean Shaw. Always a pleasure to see you."

He might not feel that way by the time she'd said what she came to say, but she appreciated the genuine warmth he was channeling now. "Thank you so much for agreeing to meet with me."

"Absolutely." Henry extended a hand, which Callie shook. "Thank you for coming to me."

She smiled. "Well, you did promise me a coffee."

Henry chuckled. "It usually does the trick. What can I get you? Espresso? Latte?"

"Latte?"

Henry stepped to the side and gestured to the contraption behind him. "I confess getting the deluxe model was gilding the lily, but I decided to treat myself with my overload payment from last semester."

Of course he did. "I'm not going to turn it down if you're offering."

"Then I can admit with impunity that I bring fresh milk from home twice a week."

Callie laughed politely. "Your secret is safe with me."

He pressed a button and the grinder whirred to life. Seconds later, the aroma of fresh espresso teased her senses. A froth of milk, a spoonful of turbinado sugar, and the next thing she knew, he was handing her an elegant cup complete with a leaf design in the foam. "I'm still working on my latte art."

Callie admired the effect and took a sip. It beat the library café by a mile. "It's good to have hobbies."

"That's what I tell my wife." Henry shrugged. "She says I should take up something that would be more helpful around the house."

She empathized with his wife's plight a bit more than his but didn't tell him that. "I appreciate being the beneficiary of this one."

He finished preparing his own cup and lifted it her way. "Cheers."

"Cheers." She mirrored the gesture and took another sip.

"So, now that we're settled in like civilized people, how can I help?"

Callie cleared her throat. "Like I mentioned in my email. I've met with a couple of students regarding concerns about a faculty member in your department."

Henry cringed. "Is it George Payne? I've washed my hands of that. Any new complaints can go directly to the dean of faculty or to Title IX."

She pressed her lips together, trying not to look horrified since, honestly, she'd want to wash her hands of him, too. "It is not."

"Oh." He frowned, clearly not expecting that. "Who is it about?"

"Lawrence Michaelson."

Henry closed his eyes for a moment, and his head dipped slightly. Callie wondered if it was a show of surprise or merely disappointment. When he opened them, he regarded her with the look of a man defeated. "Go on."

"He's been canceling both class and office hours. When I hear complaints from one student, I take it seriously, but with a grain of salt." She took a fortifying breath. "And typically pass the details along to the chair as an FYI and leave it at that."

Henry had gotten a few of those emails from her through the years, but this was the first time she'd requested a meeting. He frowned. "That's not the case now."

"I'm up to three, just in the last couple of weeks. They're similar, but not identical in the way that makes me think students coordinated their effort."

He chuckled. "I've had a couple of those. Like they compared notes and made a script to drive home the key points."

"Exactly." Callie cleared her throat. "I don't assume malicious intent."

Henry set his coffee down, as though the conversation had taken the pleasure out of it. "On the students' part, or Lawrence's?"

It was her turn to chuckle. "Lawrence. What I mean is that I've seen situations where professors are going through something health related or at home that impacts their work, but they've hesitated to tell anyone or ask for help."

Henry smiled, but it had a rueful quality to it. "That's generous."

It was, though she'd seen cases of the absentee professor caused by pregnancy, divorce, and one battle with cancer. So as much as she didn't love cutting slack to people who already had such massive flexibility, she tried her best to get all the information before passing any real judgment. "Maybe."

"I'm not sure that's the case here," Henry said.

She never in a million years expected him to admit as much. Chairs tended to be protective of their faculty. Faculty like G.W. Payne notwithstanding. "It's not my place to judge one way or another. I'm simply advocating for the students affected."

"Are you sure you wouldn't like to give Professor Michaelson a stern talking-to? I could arrange it for you."

It might be fun to fantasize about such a thing—or to joke about it via the safe distance of social media—but the prospect of telling a grown man to do his job sat pretty low on Callie's list of things she wanted to do. "I'm going to pass on that."

"Yes, I imagined you would." Henry let out a rather beleaguered sigh. "Do you want me to meet with the students? Do you think it would help?"

She shook her head. "They'd rather remain anonymous, and I'd prefer to respect that if it's all the same to you."

"Yes. Yes, of course."

"Thank you."

Henry frowned again, as though the reality of having to be a boss who wasn't really a boss hit him all over again. "I'll circle back with you, though. Does that make sense?"

Callie barely resisted the laughing at the choice of phrase. It was the sort of corporate lingo that seemed prevalent in business schools. Coteau didn't even have a business major. Perhaps he'd been spending time with the enrollment marketing team. They were all about things like circling back and being nimble. Not to be confused with closing the loop, obviously. That was assessment lingo. "Of course," she said quickly, realizing she'd slipped down a rabbit hole of amusing herself.

"Excellent." Henry stood, then seemed to catch himself. "Was there anything else?"

Callie stood as well. Henry might rank above average on the pleasant to talk to scale of department chairs, but she had no desire to linger. Even if his coffee was top-notch. "Not at all. Thank you for taking the time, and for taking these concerns seriously."

"I can't promise how much difference it will make. Between you and me, I get the feeling Lawrence is thinking about retirement. But I promise I'll try."

She knew better than to think otherwise. "Thank you."

Callie left Henry's office and contemplated stopping by Hudson's. If she was remembering Hudson's schedule correctly, her afternoon class didn't start for another hour. But instead of strolling by, she headed to the stairwell at the opposite end of the hall. She told herself she didn't want to chance interrupting Hudson's office hours. The truth had more to do with not wanting Hudson to ask about her meeting.

Because if Hudson asked, Callie wasn't sure how to answer in a way that wouldn't put at least one of them in an awkward position. She didn't want that for Hudson. And knowing there was at least a small chance Hudson would come to Lawrence's defense, she really didn't want that for herself.

❖

Gwyn slid into the seat opposite Hudson. "It happened."

Hudson waited, assuming something in the way of context would be forthcoming. But Gwyn didn't say anything more. She simply sat there, grinning like a fool. "Should I know what you're talking about?" Hudson asked.

Gwyn's smile was so sly, Hudson couldn't help but wonder if she'd gotten up to something illegal. "What have I been dreaming would happen for, like, the last year and a half?"

Hudson's first thought was that it had to be something professional—a prestigious journal acceptance or conference keynote invitation. That's what would get her all aflutter. Then it hit her. "Book deal?"

Gwyn rolled her eyes. "Seriously, dude? You think I'm going to act like a giddy schoolgirl over some work thing?"

Most academics she knew would. She sure as hell would. Then another possibility smacked her upside the head. The only thing besides professional accomplishments that would make her heart race these days. "You and Sasha."

Gwyn nodded buoyantly, her exaggerated smile showing more of her teeth than Hudson had ever seen.

"You hooked up?"

Gwyn stilled, and her brow furrowed. "Slow down there, cowboy. Some of us don't go zero to sex in sixty seconds."

The fact that Gwyn teased her about being the sort of person who did felt equal parts hilarious and ludicrous. As did the implication that, of the two of them, she was the one who had more game. That didn't mean she'd hold back on giving Gwyn shit. "Oh, so you talked to her, you mean. Did you tell her you think she's pretty?"

Gwyn glared for a moment, but her protest on principle didn't stand a chance. The grin returned. "I asked her out on a date, and she said yes."

Not that it wasn't great news, and not that Gwyn didn't deserve fantastic first dates and more, but she couldn't help but feel like they were teenagers talking about crushes. Though, honestly, not in a bad way. "I'm so happy for you. Also, it's about damn time."

That got her a more typical Gwyn response—a withering look paired with an exasperated sigh. "It's a big deal."

Hudson softened then. "It is. I don't mean to make fun."

"I don't know what it is about her that terrifies me so much." Gwyn shook her head. "But asking her out was harder than a six-hundred-pound deadlift."

She chuckled at the analogy, since both fell fairly far outside her comfort zone. Current relationship with Callie notwithstanding. "Some women have that effect. I'm thrilled you went for it, and that she said yes."

A server came to the table then, and they paused long enough to order drinks and let her know they' be partaking of the soup station and salad bar. Gwyn suggested they grab food, so they paused long enough to fill plates.

Back at the table, Gwyn gave an uncharacteristically sheepish smile. "Thank you for indulging me. I had to tell someone, and I really didn't want to do it at the gym."

They'd both overheard more than a few nuggets of juicy gossip while doing the weight circuit or hoofing it on the treadmill. It had become a running joke that no secrets were safe at the fitness center. Especially with people like Doug, who seemed to spend more time hanging out than working out most days. "I respect that choice."

Gwyn dove into her salad. Hudson did, too. She debated airing her low-grade qualms about Callie's meeting with Henry, feeling silly and self-conscious. But if Gwyn could bare her underbelly, Hudson figured returning the favor was the least she could do. "Do you think it's weird that Callie is meeting with Henry?"

Gwyn stabbed a bite of chicken with her fork and pointed it Hudson's way. "Like, outside of work?"

"No, no. Nothing like that," Hudson said.

"You're going to have to give me more to go on then."

She filled Gwyn in on the specifics, not that there were many.

"Not weird," Gwyn said without taking even two seconds to think about it.

"You're just saying that to make me feel better."

Gwyn shook her head. "I'm saying it because you have zero reason to assume it has anything to do with you and because you're a worrier by nature."

Hudson could feel herself pout and didn't even try to stop it. "I'm pretty sure that's a subset of trying to make me feel better."

"Barring something truly egregious—which I'm pretty sure you'd know if you'd done—I can't imagine her not coming to you first."

It was pretty much the same rationale she'd made to herself. "You're right." She shook her head, willing the apprehension to fall away. "Thanks."

"I got you, cowboy."

Hudson chuckled, at her tendency to borrow trouble and at the pet name Gwyn had taken to using with her. "Same."

"Speaking of…" Gwyn said.

"Yes?" Hudson raised a brow. She had literally zero idea where Gwyn would go with that.

"Not to be weird…" Gwyn wrinkled her nose.

"You should totally be weird. It's one of my favorite things about you."

"Ha-ha."

"No, really. But sorry. Go on."

Gwyn took what appeared to be a fortifying breath. "Would you ask Callie if there's anything I should know about Sasha?"

"Anything you should know?"

"Not betraying confidences or anything. Just, you know, is there anything she loves that I should make a point of asking her about? Should I acknowledge her divorce or not mention it? Does she kiss on the first date?"

Hudson was torn between laughing and wishing she'd had that sort of insight into Callie before they'd gotten involved. "Okay, okay. Do I have to be subtle about it, or can I own that I'm fishing?"

Gwyn frowned.

"I mean, it's not like we haven't talked about you two already. I'll couch it as a vibe check and go from there."

"You think I'm ridiculous, don't you?"

Hudson smiled. "I think you're adorable."

Gwyn shook her head. "You don't have to say that. I know I'm pathetic."

"Well, sure. But in the current situation, it's endearing."

"Thank you. And thank you for meeting me"—she made circles with her hands—"here."

Hudson snickered. "For what it's worth, I'm sure Doug would find you adorable, too. Though, I'm not sure I'd entrust him with any vibe checks."

Gwyn rolled her eyes. "Dude is nothing but vibes."

She polished off the last of her butternut squash soup and swooped the spoon at Gwyn. "Truth."

Chapter Twenty-two

@shitprofessorssay: After an in-depth analysis of your rhetorical choices and the application of an epistemological framework honed by years of study, my only possible conclusion is that you're an idiot.

Hudson let out a low whistle. "Damn, woman."

Callie looked down at her dress and winced. "Too much?"

Hudson shook her head. "Only if by 'too much' you mean leaving me worried about other people trying to pick you up all night."

It really wasn't that suggestive, falling almost to her knees and showing no more cleavage than she would at the office. "I feel compelled to point out that there isn't a single member of the English Department I find remotely enticing. Aside from you, of course."

"Not even Amber Jones?" Hudson asked.

"Ooh, I forgot she was in your department." Callie tapped a finger to her lips. "Will she be there tonight?"

"Rude."

Callie shrugged. "She's hot. Are you telling me you don't think so?"

"Oh, no." Hudson nodded with fervor. "She's gorgeous. I just happen to know I'm not her type."

"Sigh. I've seen her at a couple of Pride things and figured she was at least bi."

"She is," Hudson said. "What I happen to know is that she prefers her partners—male and female-identified—on the more feminine side. And only bottoms."

"Why didn't you say so? I'm going to go put on something more revealing." Callie tipped her head toward the stairs.

Hudson grabbed her before she could make a move and pulled her close. "That's cold. I'm not saying I blame you, but still. Cold."

She ran a finger down Hudson's chest. "I promise you're the only one I want to go home with at the end of the night."

"Now, see. That's sweet."

"And true," Callie said to drive home the point. "Amber Jones is more the admire from afar type for me. I'm definitely not edgy enough for her."

Hudson's eyes narrowed. "Sure you are. You're way edgier than me."

Callie pressed her lips into a line. "A sandwich is edgier than you."

"Hey," Hudson said with enough feeling that Callie worried the joke had cut the wrong way.

"Like a funky sandwich, though. Peanut butter and pickles."

Hudson shook her head. "You're making it worse."

"Wanna squeeze my boobs before we go?" Callie asked.

"Are you serious?"

Callie lifted a shoulder. "If it would make you feel better."

Hudson shook her head again, this time closing her eyes. "What am I going to do with you?"

"Take me up on my offer?" She gave a little chest shimmy.

It was fun to watch Hudson's brief internal debate before palming Callie's breasts. "You're right," Hudson said. "I do feel better."

"Good. Now, play your cards right and you can do it again when we get home."

Hudson quirked a brow. "And more?"

"And more."

The drive to Henry Hazelton's house was short. The gorgeous old craftsman sat a few blocks from campus on what Callie thought of as the swanky street. Because of course. She and Hudson were some of the first to arrive, and Callie found herself in the kitchen with Isa, slicing lemons and limes for the bar.

"I think I'm supposed to feel bad putting you to work," Isa said.

"Trust me, I like being helpful." She waited a beat, then took a chance. "I'm happy to be Hudson's plus-one, but faculty parties aren't usually my scene."

Isa, an interior designer, laughed. "You and me both. Let's be friends. I'll save you from any conversation that gets too esoteric if you promise to do the same for me."

Since Callie had a lemon in one hand and a knife in the other, she gave a decisive nod. "Deal."

After helping in the kitchen until there was nothing left to do, Callie reluctantly joined the party. Other members of the department had arrived, and Hudson was now tête-à-tête with Lawrence. Since she didn't want to touch that with a ten-foot pole, she put on her edgy girl panties and insinuated herself into a conversation with Amber and Layla.

Whatever edgy reputation Amber had, her actual demeanor was welcoming and warm. Well, welcoming, warm, and laced with snark. She and Layla made Callie feel right at home, even going so far as to share select snippets of gossip about some of their crustier male colleagues. It was all Callie could do not to whip out her phone and type up some SPS posts on the spot.

Esther Fielding and her partner, Doug, joined their little group, and the conversation grew decidedly duller. She took that as her cue to excuse herself and visit the bathroom. By the time she returned to the party, that group had fractured, leaving Callie to strategize her next move.

When Wesley Roberts sidled up to her, Callie breathed a sigh of relief. As long as he didn't start quoting Blake, she could do worse. "Good fall semester?" she asked.

"Other than particularly pervasive Dread Pirate Roberts jokes, it has been." Wesley frowned, clearly serious about the existence of said jokes and his opinion of them.

Callie suppressed a chuckle, mostly because she'd been guilty of referring to him that way herself. Only to Sasha, of course, but still. "Just when you think cultural references might not pass to the next generation."

G.W., who'd looked to be passing by them with disinterest, paused. She should have known the phrase 'cultural reference' would be like catnip to him. She shifted her stance to allow him into the conversation, figuring he and Wesley would talk amongst themselves and she could slide into observer mode before making a graceful exit.

Ha.

Ten minutes later and they were still going. Callie wanted to walk away, but she was transfixed. Her gaze bounced between Wesley and G.W. as they volleyed for superiority points. It was like the best and worst of reality TV, but with big words. They fed off of each other, that unique flavor of toxic masculinity specific to highly educated white guys who considered themselves above all that but in truth had elevated mansplaining to an art form. And since neither of them bothered to say a word to her, it gave her the chance to file away enough lines for a dozen or more SPS posts. She might have to sneak off to the bathroom again to make notes.

"I'm just saying, your interpretation of Kubrick's motives come from a singularly visual place. You're completely ignoring the linguistic implications of Hal's poetic cadence." Wesley stuck out both hands for emphasis, seemingly forgetting that one of them held a Manhattan.

Callie instinctively curled back, saving her dress, but leaving her feet open to the splatter of whiskey and vermouth. She sighed, regretting the choice of suede ankle boots for the evening.

"Oh, God. I'm so sorry." Wesley had the grace to look mortified.

"It's fine," she said. It would be a pain to clean them, but they'd seen worse.

"Maybe you should work on your own poetic cadence," George said with a sweep of his hand that managed to be condescending to both of them.

"It really is okay." She put a hand on Wesley's arm.

Wesley stopped glaring at George and gave her an apologetic smile. "I can pay to have them cleaned."

"I'll give them a little scrub when I get home. Trust me, they're not that nice."

Wesley frowned. George looked bored.

She flashed a smile. "How about a few napkins to clean this up so no one slips?"

Wesley started, like the thought had never occurred to him. "Right."

He scurried away, and Callie figured G.W. would pounce on the excuse to go talk to someone other than her. Only he didn't. He lifted his chin. "What's your PhD in again?"

The "again" was funny, since they'd never had a conversation in which she would have discussed her degrees or credentials. And she had no illusions he considered her bio interesting or important enough to look up on the college website. She mirrored the gesture. "I don't have a doctorate, actually. My master's is in higher ed administration."

"They let someone without a doctorate be a dean?"

G.W. gave her a look of disdain that, in her younger years, would have sent her slinking to a dark corner. Even now, a tiny voice in the back of her mind whispered that he had a point. That she—with her blue-collar background and state university diploma—didn't measure up in circles like these.

In her brain, she knew that was utter bullshit. Her heart, where the squishiest and most vulnerable parts of her lived, was another matter.

"You are only in charge of advising undergraduates, I suppose," he said.

Callie opened her mouth, but the clever retorts—the ones that came so easy when she was talking about, rather than to, dismissive faculty—wouldn't form. In fact, no words came at all. She simply stood there, probably looking like one of the students he liked to humiliate in class.

George quirked a brow. "I'm going to go refresh my drink."

Since his glass remained more than half full, Callie didn't doubt he simply wanted to leave the conversation. Fine by her.

As if summoned by the fact that it was all over, Hudson appeared by her side. "Sorry, I saw you stuck with the two of them, but I couldn't seem to extricate myself."

The perfectly reasonable yet utterly unsatisfying explanation landed heavy in her chest. Callie took a deep breath and reminded herself it would be a cold day in hell before she cried at a cocktail party full of faculty. "You missed all the excitement."

Hudson turned to Callie with a confused look. "What happened?"

"Male academic posturing led to actual posturing, which led to a spilled drink." She gestured to the puddle still at her feet.

"Oh, no." Hudson frowned.

"You laugh, but look at the state of my poor boots." She gestured to her feet.

Hudson cringed. "Sorry. Though, to be fair, I feel almost as bad for Wesley. Expecting him to carry on a normal conversation in the presence of a gorgeous woman is a recipe for disaster."

"I'll have you know he and George were carrying on like I wasn't even there."

"Well." Hudson canted her head. "Not talking to you doesn't mean they weren't talking for you. I'm sure they were both in top form."

Callie rolled her eyes. "They were in some kind of form."

"I shouldn't have left you unattended, especially after promising to keep George from cornering you."

"He was particularly condescending this evening." She shrugged. "Or maybe I noticed it more because it was directed at me."

Hudson blanched. "What did—"

Callie lifted a hand. "I've worked in academia for more than a decade. I can handle a couple of pompous manboys." That was what mattered, even if the thought of Hudson coming to her rescue had been nice.

Hudson's eyes narrowed, but then a smile slowly crept in, and she lifted her chin. "Remind me to stay on your good side."

"I'll tell you one way you could do that," Callie said.

"Yeah?" Hudson asked.

"Spare me anymore highbrow chitchat and take me home."

"Just take you home?" Hudson's innocent tone implied the exact opposite.

Normally, Callie would leap at the chance to pick up what Hudson was putting down. At this moment, she couldn't even muster the will to fake it. "I—"

"Sorry, I got waylaid." Wesley reappeared, fistful of napkins raised like a trophy.

Callie took a step back, if for no other reason than Wesley's attempt to wipe up the mess brought his face uncomfortably close to her crotch. Hudson stepped to the side and let out an exaggerated sigh.

Wesley stood, clutching the used napkins but staring at Callie's boots. "Are you sure there's nothing I can do about those?"

"They're fine, I promise." Callie tried for a friendly smile. "And for the record, I thought Hal's cadence was unsettlingly poetic."

Wesley flushed, clearly pleased but also embarrassed. "Yes. Yes, it's exactly that."

Hudson shot her a quizzical look, then Wesley. "Do I even want to know?"

Wesley opened his mouth, and Callie had no doubt he was prepared to rehash the entire thing, so she took matters into her own hands. "You had to be there." She turned to Wesley. "You go get rid of those and get yourself a fresh drink."

He frowned briefly but headed back to the kitchen without further comment. Hudson's questioning look returned, but Callie merely shook her head. "Where were we?" she asked.

"I think you were asking me to take you home and do sordid things to you."

"We should do the home part at least." Callie blew out a breath. "Like, now."

Hudson winced. "I should do a round of goodbyes."

Callie resisted the urge to scrub a hand over her face. "Yeah, okay. I'm going to let you do that solo. Please give Isa my regards."

"You okay?" Hudson asked.

Not really, but she didn't want to prolong things or, worse, force Hudson's hand. "Just tired."

Hudson lifted her hand and kissed her knuckles. "I'll hurry."

Despite those promises, Hudson seemed to make of point of stopping and speaking to everyone in the room. It went on so long, Callie had time to seek out Isa herself. It managed to kill some time, but not enough to stop her from noticing a particularly jovial exchange between Hudson, Henry, and G.W.

She shook her head and went to the door to slip on her coat. So much for chivalry.

❖

Hudson expected the party at Henry's to feel like a festive end to her first semester, but life felt anything but festive. The last week of classes brought with it a pair of rejections from top-tier journals and a whole lot of students looking for a whole lot of guidance on their final papers. The rejections weren't really a surprise—the submissions had been long shots to say the least—but they still stung.

On top of that, Callie seemed unusually withdrawn. She'd confided the asinine comments George had made but insisted they were no big deal. Hudson wasn't so sure. But for the moment, she was too busy to do anything about it. Teaching evaluations would be rolling out in a matter of days, and she had every intention of hitting the "highly effective" ball out of the proverbial park.

Derek, a kid who'd been hit or miss most of the term, nodded for the twentieth or so time and picked up his bag. "I will, Professor Greene. Thank you."

Hudson wasn't entirely sure he would, if his papers up to this point were anything to go on. But the ball was in his court now. He'd pull off a solid paper or he wouldn't, and she'd grade him accordingly. That, at least, wouldn't happen until after evaluations were in. She pinched the bridge of her nose and blinked a few times, willing her mind to clear along with her vision. She'd no sooner blown out an exhausted breath when another knock came at the door.

"Kianna. Come on in." Unlike Derek, Kianna was one of her rock stars. Hudson had already looked over a draft of Kianna's final paper—an analysis of racial identity in Wharton's "The Old Maid" and offered feedback. "What can I do for you?"

"I don't want to be neurotic, but I wanted to ask about length. You said eight to ten pages, but I'm hovering just over eleven, and I don't want to get dinged for not following the directions."

Hudson chuckled. "You will not be penalized for going over."

Kianna smiled, her sigh of relief audible. "Thanks."

"However." Hudson lifted a finger.

Kianna's worried expression returned. "However?"

She wondered vaguely about whether the college should offer a class on composure. Poker Face 101. Maybe the Psychology Department could teach it. "However, I think it might be good practice for you to try to whittle it down, even if only a little."

Kianna frowned then.

"You're looking to go into copywriting, right? Marketing or advertising?" Since Coteau didn't have any formal business programs, English often picked up students looking to go into those fields. Critical thinking and communication skills for the win.

Kianna nodded with enthusiasm. "I've got an internship already lined up for next summer."

"Well, it's probably not as rigid as journalism, but I'm guessing when it comes to ad copy, the same rules apply. Every word counts."

Kianna blushed, but the smile crept back in. "Yeah."

"Your concentration is creative writing?"

Another nod. "I want to be a writer, but, well, it's not the most practical."

Hudson made a mental note to have a follow-up conversation about that in the spring. Hopefully, Kianna was aiming for a balance of her practical and creative selves, not abandoning the creative altogether. But at least one other student hovered in the hall, so that would have to wait. "That tells me you're used to cutting the fluff."

She sighed the sigh of a nerdy kid who'd been caught fibbing the teacher. "I am."

"Same goes for academic writing. Don't stress about it but promise me you'll try."

Kianna agreed and went on her way. Asher popped in next. They'd neglected their final paper to cram for organic chemistry and had worked themself into a borderline panic. Hudson offered them a one-day extension, assuring them she'd rather get a good paper a day late than a crappy one on time. She reminded them that was the exception rather than the rule, one they'd earned with being diligent and attentive all semester.

And so it went for the next two hours—an hour longer than even the extended office hours she'd scheduled for the week. She didn't regret her offer to meet with anyone wanting to talk through their rough draft, but damn. She was beat. And she still had an afternoon class to teach.

She was about to pack up for her lunch date with Callie when her phone flashed with a FaceTime request from her mother. Hudson considered her options and decided to plop back at her desk. She had a few minutes still and sitting at her desk outweighed trying to hold her phone aloft while trudging across campus in the snow.

She flipped her laptop open and clicked Accept. "Hey, Mom."

"Hi, honey. How's your week?"

Hudson indulged in an eye roll. "Remind me to stop assigning final papers."

Evelyn tutted. "I'm not sure you can get away with that in literature classes."

She tipped her head back and forth. "Remind me to get a PhD in something that can be graded with Scantron forms."

"Oh, honey. Not even your father uses those anymore." Her mom offered a sympathetic smile. "And I'm pretty sure that ship has sailed."

"I'm pretty sure getting another doctorate would be easier than grading the number of papers I've got coming in. And don't even get me started on the papers students haven't even started writing yet."

That got her a laugh. "A professor's work is never done."

"Says the financial planner."

Another laugh. "Touché."

"Is everything okay? You don't usually call on weekdays. And during the day no less." Texts, sure, but calls were for the weekend. It had been that way since her own undergraduate days.

"Yes, yes. I wanted to talk with you about our trip."

After considerable back-and-forth, her parents had settled on renting a villa in Greece for the family holiday. Milton and Adina would only be able to join them for a week, but since both Hudson and her dad had close to a month between semesters, her mom had decided to take two full weeks off. "What about it?"

"Well, your father's been invited to give a talk at an economic summit in Turkey right after New Year."

It wouldn't be the first time his speaking gigs had cut into family vacation. But he'd never bailed entirely, and other than not having him around for half their trip to Disney World when she was ten, she'd never felt compelled to hold it against him. "Please tell me we're cutting it short and not canceling altogether."

"Definitely not canceling." Mom rolled her eyes. "No offense, but I need sun almost as much as I need to see my children."

"None taken because same," Hudson said.

"Anyway. We've got the house booked for two weeks, and it's already paid for. I wanted to let you know as soon as possible so you can decide whether to change your flight or be the eccentric academic recluse holed up writing all by herself for a week."

"That does sound appealing." She might be happy to be back on the East Coast—including the snow that came with it—but she'd lost her fortitude for the gray skies and short days that came with winter.

"I thought it might."

"Hey, would it be okay if I invited Callie to come?"

Mom's eyes lit up. "For the whole trip? We'd love to meet her."

Hudson cringed. "I was thinking just the second week."

"Oh, right. Sure."

"I'm not opposed to you meeting her, but spending Christmas together is pretty big in her family." Which was true. Callie had said as much.

Evelyn tutted. "And a week together in a foreign country probably isn't what you had in mind for that first meeting."

"Exactly." She should have known her mother would know what she was thinking even if she kept it to herself.

"Well, I think it's a lovely idea. And if we all happen to overlap by a day, I wouldn't be sad."

"I'll keep that in mind." Hudson smiled. "Let me see if she wants to come first."

"Fair point. I've got to run, but keep me posted. I'll call you this weekend."

"Sounds good. Love you, Mom."

"Love you, too. Happy grading."

Festive feelings restored, she slipped into her coat, tucking her scarf in and buttoning it all the way up. It would be short notice, but hopefully Callie wouldn't hesitate to say yes. Even if it was a little early in their relationship to be traveling together.

She strode out of Storey into the blowing snow, not even minding as the wind whipped at her face. She'd been looking forward to spending the holidays in Greece since her parents first suggested it. It wasn't the first time they'd traveled over winter break. If anything, that felt like more of a tradition than anything tied to her childhood home. The prospect of some down time with Callie—in a sun-drenched villa no less—was icing on the cake.

Chapter Twenty-three

@shitprofessorssay: My contract is for ten months, but I only work about eight of them. If students aren't working, neither am I.

Callie looked around, taking stock of the space and the people in it. Cozier than she expected, to be honest, but still casual. A wee bit pretentious, of course, with its piped-in elevator music and waitstaff dressed in black. Though, truthfully, she could just as easily call it dated. The place definitely hadn't seen an update since the nineties.

"You've seriously never been to the Faculty Club?" Hudson asked.

"I'm not faculty."

"But it's open to staff. And you're an administrator. That's practically the same thing."

Callie laced her fingers together and leaned back in her chair. "I think there are quite a few faculty members who'd beg to differ."

Hudson rolled her eyes. "You know what I mean."

She did, which made it all the more important to drive home the point. "That might be true for deans who started as faculty. Maybe even the provost, though I'm sure plenty of faculty have their stones to cast at her."

"But not you?" Hudson looked genuinely curious.

"Have stones to cast? No. I don't agree with all of Provost Marsh's decisions, but I respect her and think she's got more integrity than a lot of people in her position."

Hudson smiled. "Yes. Same. But I was talking about feeling welcome at the Faculty Club."

"Oh. Well. I didn't start as faculty. And I don't have a doctorate. There are plenty of faculty on campus who don't regard me as an equal."

Hudson's smile fell, and she shook her head. "I'm sorry George is an asshole."

It wasn't anywhere near as simple as that, but teasing out the social hierarchy of academia wasn't on her bingo card for the day, so she gave a wry smile of her own. "Thanks."

"And I, for one, think you absolutely should come here anytime you damn well please."

Callie was tempted to differentiate between her vague—or perhaps not so vague—sense of not belonging versus worrying someone would try to check her credentials at the door. But again, not a winning lunch conversation. "Well, if the soup is half as good as you've been telling me it is, I'll have to take that under consideration."

Hudson's easy smile returned, effectively closing the matter. "You won't regret it."

They ordered—Callie going with a grilled cheese and Hudson a tuna melt. When the server left, Hudson hurried over to the soup station to get them each a bowl. She looked on with anticipation as Callie tasted the tomato bisque, then grinned when Callie nodded her approval. "Amazing, right?"

"You did not steer me wrong," Callie said.

"I do my best."

"Why do I get the feeling you're talking about more than soup?"

Hudson's expression turned sly. "So, I know it's ridiculously short notice, but what are you doing the first week of January?"

Callie narrowed her eyes. "Besides work, you mean?"

"You have to work?" Hudson frowned and looked genuinely confused.

"I mean, I'll be off the week between Christmas and New Year's. The college closes that week. But I'll be back in the office on the third."

"Huh."

"They're called regular business hours. Most of us work them." She went for a chuckle, but it had an edge she felt a little bad about.

"Could you take that week off? Students aren't around, so you won't have that much going on, right?"

The eager optimism in Hudson's voice should have made whatever she had in mind feel exciting—whether or not Callie could say yes. But of course it didn't. It felt like Hudson had no clue how her job worked. How most people's jobs worked. Like Hudson was playing into the very stereotype of faculty Callie had convinced herself Hudson wasn't. And perhaps worst of all, like Hudson assumed nothing Callie did while classes weren't in session could be all that important. Which was probably an overreaction, but knowing that didn't stop the knot from forming in the pit of her stomach. "I've got academic status review. Not to mention prepping for spring orientation."

"Oh." Hudson's shoulders slumped. "I'm sorry. I didn't even think about all of that."

The quick apology made her feel better, even as it made her feel like a jerk for having such an intense reaction. "Yeah. It's a quick turnaround this year, too, with MLK falling early and classes starting mid-January."

Hudson rolled her eyes. "Tell me about it. I've been working on my spring syllabi so I don't have them hanging over my head all break."

It was a small consolation, to know that Hudson considered the time and the work to be done. Callie didn't begrudge Hudson the flexibility of her schedule. Well, mostly didn't. "What were you hoping to do?"

"I'm spending Christmas with my family in Greece. My parents booked the villa for two weeks, but they need to be in Turkey right after New Year for a talk my father's been invited to give."

It was Callie's turn to say. "Oh."

The server brought their sandwiches, briefly interrupting the awkward.

Hudson picked hers up but set it down without taking a bite. "I know it's a little soon to be vacationing together, but I thought I might be able to talk you into flying over for the week."

Callie paused, dunked corner of her grilled cheese halfway to her mouth. That hadn't even occurred to her. She was still hung up on the Christmas in Greece part. And the villa part. And the fly halfway around the world on a few weeks notice part. Hudson might as well have been speaking Greek for all that it made sense to Callie. "Yeah, I can't pull that off."

"Is it too soon to say I'd love to be lounging on a beach with you? Preferably with a cocktail and very little clothing between us?"

The flirty vibe was almost enough to pull Callie back to level ground. Almost. "You certainly paint a pretty picture."

"Not half as pretty as you'd be in a bikini, I'm sure."

Callie couldn't help but chuckle. "That's a terrible line."

Hudson lifted her chin. "But you're going to let me get away with it because I'm cute, though, right?"

"Yeah, I am." And also because it was more fun than picking apart the flash of ickiness from before.

"Let me buy you dinner, too?"

A flicker of the ickiness returned, but Callie shoved it aside. It was a turn of phrase. She and Hudson had taken turns the few times they'd eaten out. Just because Hudson came from a family that vacationed in Greece together, it didn't mean Hudson was out of touch with her world, her reality. And it didn't mean that a trip to Greece couldn't be her reality if she wanted it to be. With reasonable planning and pre-arranged PTO.

"Other plans?" Hudson asked.

"Huh? Oh, no. No plans. Dinner would be great."

"Sushi?"

Callie angled her head and pretended to consider. "Only if gyoza are part of the offer."

"I happily accept these conditions."

They finished lunch and walked together to the quad. Hudson peeled off to head to her afternoon class and Callie continued on to her office. Snow swirled, muffling the sounds of students hurrying to a final or the library for an afternoon of studying. Despite the amped up stress levels the last week of the semester brought, campus had a peaceful quality to it. Like even the buildings knew things were wrapping up for a month of quiet.

Callie got to her office, but rather than settling in to tackle the afternoon's to-do list, she paced the space behind her desk a few times. She could only manage two strides before hitting one wall or the other, though, so the move proved less than satisfying. She flopped into her desk and unlocked her computer, only to pick up her phone and spin to face the window.

Would you jet off to Greece on a moment's notice? She stared at the text for a moment, then copied it before hitting send. After Sasha, she pasted the identical text in a message to Becca and Tammy. She spun back to her computer and dropped her phone on the desk.

Work. She had work to do. Mulling over her disappointment at not being able to run off to Greece at the drop of a hat wouldn't get that work done. Much less angsting over whether or not to be thrilled that Hudson wanted her to go or annoyed that Hudson had been so myopic in her invitation.

❖

For the third day in a row, Hudson emerged from her office to find the hallway dim. She shook her head and waved an arm to activate the motion sensor. It was barely three in the afternoon, but Storey was already a ghost town. It was the middle of finals, to be fair, and classes had been done for almost a week. Still. Didn't people have grading to do? Or meetings with students about final papers and projects?

She chuckled at her instinct to be a fuddy-duddy about such things. Eager beaver with a judgmental streak. That's what Callie would say. Or perhaps she was simply being a junior faculty member, trying to do and be everything her professors and advisers said would solidify her career and land her tenure. Callie teased her, but as much as having tenure provided a security blanket, getting it was far from guaranteed.

The chuckle faded, leaving her standing alone, shoulders slumped, in the quiet building.

All joking aside, the last week had felt a little like walking a tightrope—at least a few of her colleagues insinuating she worked too hard and Callie seeming to think she didn't work hard enough. Or at least that faculty in general didn't work hard enough. No matter which way she leaned, she seemed to disappoint someone.

Or maybe that was her insecurity talking.

All she wanted was to do everything expected of her as well as she possibly could. The problem was that she couldn't make everyone happy. She knew that was a bad way to think about things, but she wanted it anyway.

At least Callie was coming over for dinner. It was the last night they'd have together before not seeing each other for more than two weeks. She hoped they could spend some quality time together and put the stresses of the semester behind them. Her fifty-six papers to grade and Callie's academic status review notwithstanding. Feeling good about that mission, she headed home to start dinner.

With the roast chicken in the oven, Hudson turned her attention to Gertrude. The cat had warmed to Callie in the last few months, but when Callie brought Lucy with her, like she'd be doing tonight, Gertrude took the invasion as a personal affront and would stubbornly hide until they'd gone. She would have been more sympathetic if Lucy had shown even a hint of interest in chasing or even trying to be friends. But Gertrude was set in her ways and Hudson didn't blame her, so she plied Gertrude with treats and pointed her to the office.

At Callie's knock, Hudson went to the door, thinking it was probably time they dispensed with such formalities. She opened it to find Callie smiling at her, scarf wound snugly around her neck and cheeks pink from the cold. "Hi," Callie said. "I'm starving, and I brought wine."

Hudson pulled her in and took the bottle from Callie's gloved hand. "You didn't have to do that."

Callie shrugged, and her eyes sparkled in a way that made Hudson think maybe she'd been overreacting about Callie being distant. "I didn't, but it's been a week and I have every intention of downing the better part of a bottle myself, so it only seemed fair."

The words didn't match Callie's expression, leaving Hudson floundering. "That bad?"

Callie hung up her coat, then bent to unclip Lucy's leash and take off her boots. "I'm exaggerating. But the semester is officially over now, and that's cause for celebration."

Hudson smiled at Callie's thoughts tracking so closely to her own. "Now that, I can get behind."

"Whatever you're making smells amazing."

Hudson headed to the kitchen and poured them each a glass from the bottle she had open. "Just roast chicken."

Callie, who'd followed her, accepted the wine. Her smile hadn't waned. "That's the thing, though, isn't it? The simple things are often the best things."

She soaked that in, and the unspoken assurances it seemed to offer. "Can't argue there."

They ate at the table, chatting about work and whether Sasha and Gwyn were ever going to make it past first base. Everything about the evening felt cozy and normal. Domestic. Much like that first night back after Thanksgiving, it left Hudson with the sense that, while she hadn't been looking, this was exactly what she wanted. For a semester, for a year. Forever.

It was all she could do not to laugh at herself—waffling between certainty and doubt, wondering if Callie felt the same. She craved the black and white of knowing where they stood, of articulating what they had and where they were going. But she knew relationships didn't always work that way. Hell, very little in life did.

Was she, once again, playing the eager beaver to Callie's go with the flow?

"You look awfully serious right now," Callie said.

Hudson looked up from her plate and found Callie regarding her with that playful expression. Worries aside, there was something to be said for Callie knowing her so well. "I think that might just be how I look."

Callie clicked her tongue. "You have a point."

"Is that your way of telling me you're tired of me?" It was about as far from a direct question as she could get, but oh well.

Instead of answering right away, Callie took a minute and studied Hudson. The playful look faded and a serious one took hold. Hudson braced herself for an answer she wouldn't like. But then Callie's features softened, and Hudson would swear there were love vibes in the air. "I'm not," Callie said eventually.

There was definitely more to it than that, and Hudson wanted to know what. "You don't sound sure."

"I'm actually pretty damn fond of you." Callie sighed like it was some sort of concession. "Maybe more than fond."

She didn't love the trace of reluctance, but perhaps it had more to do with their relationship turning out to be more than Callie bargained for at the beginning. Hudson could appreciate that. "If it helps, that feeling is mutual."

Callie's smile seemed to mirror Hudson's thoughts. "Yeah. It does."

They sat in silence for a little while, and then Callie launched into a story about a student who'd stopped going to class in October and showed up at her office that afternoon hoping to salvage the semester. Rather than downplaying, the shift seemed to reinforce the significance of what had been said. Maybe Callie was hesitant to fall in love; maybe she was simply reticent to use the word. Oddly, Hudson felt like she could work with that. Because for all that she might be an eager beaver, when it came to winning life's races, she was far more tortoise than hare.

Chapter Twenty-Four

@shitprofessorssay: Grades are posted. I will not be taking further questions.

Much like Thanksgiving, Callie's Christmas passed in a blur of warm and fuzzy family time. Requisite ribbing notwithstanding. Yes, it felt a little weird to video chat with Hudson on a sun-soaked veranda around a seven-hour time difference, but it was nice to know Hudson made it a priority to connect with her. By the time she and Lucy made it home, she found herself ready for Hudson to be home so they could pick up where they'd left off.

Since she couldn't be on that sun-soaked veranda, it helped that most of her work at this time of year was with people she liked. Like today's planning session to finalize transfer student advising and registration during winter orientation. A lovely mix of student affairs and academic affairs folks—and not a faculty member in sight.

They'd no sooner ended the meeting than Sasha grabbed her arm. "We need to catch up," Sasha said.

"Lunch?" Callie asked.

Sasha shook her head. "I'm covering the phones for Stan. He got Covid for Christmas."

Callie wrinkled her nose. "Ew."

"I'm just glad he kept it, and himself, home. But Jenny is out, too, so we're stretched pretty thin."

"Drinks?"

"Yes." Sasha squeezed her eyes shut. "I've got so much scoop for you."

When Sasha deigned to call something scoop, it usually was. "Do tell."

"Not here."

Callie balked. "Not even a hint?"

Sasha shook her head.

"It better be good."

Sasha held up a finger. "One is about work." She added as second finger. "One is about me. Neither are safe for work."

Callie's mind spun with possibilities. "How early can you leave?"

Sasha winced. "Four?"

It was better than either of them could usually manage during the semester. "Perfect. Ivy?"

Callie hesitated.

"You know it'll be dead," Sasha said.

Like most of Ryekill when school wasn't in session. "Right."

"So, yes?"

There was something to be said for small graces. "Yes. Go answer phones and I'll see you soon."

A few hours later, Callie snagged a pair of old-fashioneds from the bar and headed to the little high-top table Sasha had snagged. Though snagged might be a bit of an overstatement. She counted fewer than a dozen people at Ivy, including both the restaurant area and the bar. Students weren't the only ones who cleared out for the break.

She set the drinks down, and Sasha immediately picked hers up. "Here's to the lull between terms."

Callie mirrored the gesture. "Cheers."

They each sipped and let out a sigh. The time between the fall and spring semesters wasn't exactly a lull. Academic status review, processing dean's list and grade changes, and preparations for the upcoming term kept them both busy. Still, the absence of both students and faculty lent a peaceful quality to campus. It made getting work done and getting a drink after much easier.

"How was your time with the fam?" Sasha asked.

"Seriously? That's what you're leading with?"

Sasha shrugged. "Humor me."

"Good." Callie smiled thinking about it. "You?"

"The fam was the fam." Sasha closed her eyes briefly and shook her head. "They mean well but can't get out of their own way most of the time."

She'd learned through the years of being friends with Sasha that was code for conservative but trying. Sasha tried to give them points for the trying but rarely felt truly understood or supported. "Sounds exhausting," Callie said.

"Yeah." Sasha shook her head, like she regretted taking the conversation in that direction.

"You ready to share your scoop now?"

Sasha laughed. "I really did want to know about your holidays."

Callie waved her off. "Come on. Dish."

"Okay, fine. The first isn't scoop so much as material for SPS."

She grinned. "I'll take that."

Sasha whipped out her phone and started tapping at the screen. "It's too good to explain. You have to see it for yourself."

Callie took it from her and skimmed the email Sasha had pulled up. Essentially, Lawrence Michaelson had not only enlisted his TA do his final grading—which was explicitly against college policy—he'd given her his login to enter those grades into the system. Also against college policy. When that failed to work because of the dual authentication system, she'd reached out to him. Only he was on holiday in the Caribbean—sans computer—and couldn't manage to enter them himself, so he missed the submission deadline altogether. Instead of individual grade change forms, which was the standard consequence of not submitting grades on time, he'd simply forwarded the list to the registrar. And to top everything off, he hadn't even attempted to cover his tracks. He'd simply hit forward on the email from his TA, including the spreadsheet of grades she'd originally attached.

The whole email was only three sentences, but it encapsulated everything Shit Professors Say was about: the cluelessness, the condescension, and the sheer cojones. Callie let out a low whistle. "Damn."

"Right?"

She winced. "Are you going to report it?"

"I kind of feel like I have to," Sasha said.

Given her own experiences with—or more accurately about—Professor Michaelson this semester, Callie was even less inclined to be generous than she might be otherwise. "Well, at least to Miles."

Miles, the associate provost for academic affairs, was both Sasha's and her direct supervisor. Passing it along to him would count as due diligence and hopefully shield Sasha from having to deal with any fallout. Sasha nodded. "Yeah."

"Ugh. I'm sorry you had to deal with that," Callie said.

Sasha waved her off. "Just the usual bullshit."

Sadly, it was. Callie cleared her throat. "Okay, what's the personal scoop?"

"Are you still moping about Hudson jetting off to Greece without you?"

She bristled at Sasha's use of the word mope, mostly because it was accurate. And she did not mope. Like, by definition. "She's not jetting. She's spending the holidays with her parents. It just happens to be in Greece."

"Funny, that's not what you said when she invited you like it was NBD."

Callie went for another sigh, but it came out more like a whine. "Okay, fine. She's jetting, I'm moping. Are you happy now?"

Sasha sucked her teeth, then took another sip of her drink. "Did you have spectacular send-off sex before she left?"

"What does that have to do with anything?"

"I'm trying to gauge my own situation." Sasha pressed her fingers to her chest. "I, for example, had fantastic send-off sex. And now I'm super mopey that I won't see Gwyn for the next month. She's jetted to California, though, not Greece. I'm not sure whether that makes a difference."

Callie's mouth fell open and she let it. "You hooked up with Gwyn?"

Sasha's answer came in the form of a coy smile.

Irritation at Lawrence and Hudson's trip and the weather all faded, and sheer delight took hold. "Oh, I'm so happy for you. You deserve all the great sex and all the good things."

"Thank you." Sasha's smile turned a little dreamy, but then she straightened her spine and squared her shoulders. "Not that it's a relationship or anything like what you and Hudson have."

Callie sat up a little straighter, too. "What does that mean? What Hudson and I have."

Sasha folded her arms, and her expression had major don't-even vibes.

But rather than laughing it off, Callie sat with the insinuation. Things with Hudson had certainly gotten more serious. Hell, Hudson had invited her to Greece. If that wasn't a relationship move, she didn't know what was. Still. The nescience of the invite itself had stirred up some feelings. And Hudson liked and respected people like Lawrence. The cognitive dissonance of it left her antsy. Maybe that was her problem. She'd gone and fallen for Hudson but wasn't entirely sure she and Hudson made sense long-term.

"Ahem," Sasha said.

"What?" Callie asked.

"What is it you and Hudson have?"

More questions than answers, perhaps, but no point pretending things remained casual. "Great but complicated?"

Sasha smiled, all sympathy now. "That sounds about right."

❖

Hudson stretched out on one of the loungers by the pool and pulled out her phone. As usual, she started with a text to Callie—even though she knew Callie wouldn't be able to answer—then toggled to her email. Satisfied nothing there needed her attention, she switched to social media and started to scroll.

She skimmed, letting the pictures and posts lull her into relaxation. Until one from SPS stopped her in her tracks. She squinted at the words on the screen and tried to ignore the flash of recognition.

@shitprofessorssay: I missed my TA's text that she'd finished grading but couldn't log in with my credentials and missed the grade deadline. I'm in St. Lucia without my laptop, so please see attached. Sent from my iPhone

Lawrence was in St. Lucia. He'd been talking about it since before Thanksgiving. And he had zero qualms using his TA for grading. But even he wouldn't be stupid enough to leave official grade submissions to an undergraduate student. Would he?

Sharing a login to the student information system was a flagrant violation of IT policy as well as academic. Admitting it, in writing no less, would be a truly idiotic move. And yet. Lawrence hadn't shown much in the way of discernment or discretion in the few months she'd known him professionally.

She stewed over the possibility—and her rising irritation at him—for a good minute before the other shoe dropped. If the post was talking about Lawrence, then someone at Coteau put it there. Was submitting things if not posting directly.

Hudson shook her head. She was overreacting, maybe even imagining things. She'd find a way to ask Lawrence discreetly about his grades for the term, then not so subtly remind him that people paid attention to things like that, and he should be more mindful, especially about what he put in writing. As for Shit Professors Say, it was probably a coincidence.

But what if it wasn't?

It meant that, at the very least, someone at Coteau was sharing not just faculty foibles, but things that could land someone in legitimate hot water. Even as she told herself to let it go, Hudson clicked over to the account page. She scrolled the posts with a different eye.

Most were generic enough they could come from any asinine professor anywhere. A few very clearly couldn't come from Coteau—references to teaching in business schools or taking advantage of graduate students. But a lot felt weirdly familiar. Maybe it was confirmation bias. Or maybe it wasn't.

A brief drill-down told her SPS took submissions from anyone, and noted that only things that maintained anonymity would be accepted. She was deep in the rabbit hole, now, though, and there was no room to be reassured.

"Hudson, are you coming?"

The sound of her mother's voice yanked Hudson back to reality. She'd lost nearly an hour doomscrolling, and it was officially five minutes past the time she and her parents were supposed to leave for dinner. "Sorry. Be right there."

At the restaurant, Hudson sipped her wine and stared at the ocean. But not even the combo of alcohol and a sunset over the water could still her racing thoughts. Did any of this matter? Was it her place to intervene? And perhaps most pressing, if SPS was run by someone at Coteau, who?

That last question nagged her all through dinner and had her going back to the SPS archives until well after midnight. It was during that second read-through that the truly damning evidence came.

@shitprofessorssay: Yes, my dad's best friend was on my hiring committee. What does that have to do with my opposition to legacy admissions?

She'd said that. Well, not exactly that. It had actually been a self-deprecating comment about not going to her dad's alma mater so she never had to wonder about being a legacy admit. But the sentiments were similar enough. And her father's best friend technically hadn't been on her search committee. But how many people wound up working in the same department at the same institution as a family friend?

The prospect of one of the posts being about her needled Hudson enough to keep her awake most of the night. It needled her when she got up to use the bathroom and pop some ibuprofen, and it was waiting for her when she woke up with more of a hangover than she'd nursed in quite a while, though the raging headache likely had more to do with lack of sleep than alcohol.

She managed to set it aside long enough to enjoy a final breakfast with her parents and see them off to the airport. It wasn't like she could talk to them about Lawrence's unprofessionalism or her own fears of being a nepotism hire. By early afternoon, she was at the villa alone and left completely to her own devices. When a dip in the pool—code for swimming twenty laps—didn't clear her mind, she decided to text Callie. When she didn't get an immediate reply, she shot a similar query to Gwyn. Gwyn, goddess love her, texted back right away.

I don't remember how I discovered SPS. But I swear I know half the people they quote personally.

Gwyn likely didn't mean that literally, but it didn't help Hudson's squirrelly thoughts. *What if you do?*

That got her a series of question marks in return.

For all that Hudson wanted to hash out the possibility, putting her paranoia into words left her queasy. But she couldn't exactly drop it now. *I have this weird feeling someone at Coteau is behind it.*

She expected to be shot down, fast and furious. But instead of asking what she'd been smoking, Gwyn simply said *Say more.*

Hudson sent screenshots of a few that felt obvious in hindsight, ones that used the same lingo for things like faculty senate and gen ed requirements. Gwyn remained intrigued but didn't make the leap to convinced. Hudson hesitated only a moment before sending the one that started it all. In for a penny, in for a pound.

I may know of a professor, currently in St. Lucia, who's alluded to not doing his own grading.

Gwyn's response—a simple *damn*—didn't come with a request for specifics. Hudson appreciated that. It did come with a different follow-up question, though. *Who do you think it is?*

Hudson hadn't gotten that far and said as much. Gwyn threw out a couple of ideas, but none of them seemed right. They agreed it likely wasn't a faculty member, though the notion felt ironic more than impossible. It had to be someone privy to the kinds of details that showed up in the posts. The possibility struck her like a Norton anthology to the temple. Not only a viable candidate, but the person she'd actually joked with about Lawrence being a family friend. The person Gwyn had recently started dating.

What about Sasha?

She wanted Gwyn to dismiss the notion, but of course her reply was a deflating *Ooh.*

Hudson scratched her temple, wanting rather badly to be wrong. But Sasha sat in on all the high-level meetings related to things like curriculum and academic policy. She also likely sat on the receiving end of a boatload of faculty bullshittery in the form of email. And she knew about Lawrence.

Should I go to HR? Her finger hovered over the send arrow for only a second. She trusted Gwyn, and Gwyn's opinion. She might not trust Gwyn's ability to be unbiased, but beggars couldn't be choosers.

Why?

Because some of this could get someone in genuine trouble. Like, someone she knew personally.

It's anonymous, though. There's no way to connect it to a real person unless you already know the specifics.

Hudson scowled. *Are you saying that as my friend and colleague or the person who recently started sleeping with the registrar?*

Gwyn's reply: *BOTH*

Gwyn's logic mollified Hudson's inner stickler, in part if not entirely. *I guess you're right. It just bugs me.*

Once again, Gwyn came back with a simple *Why?*

She took a minute then, peering past her initial instinct to protect Lawrence. She didn't entirely like what she saw. *It's too close to home. It feels personal.*

Gwyn's response took no time at all. *It's only personal if you're saying something idiotic enough to be quoted.*

When it came down to it, Gwyn had a point. Biased or otherwise. It wasn't her behavior being shared for eye rolls and amusement. Not really. If Lawrence wanted to make that bed, it would be his to lie in.

But even as she texted as much to Gwyn, the whole thing remained firmly stuck in her craw. Posts on Shit Professors Say might be personally about her. At the very least, she was increasingly convinced they were personally connected to her. Not because of her affiliation with Coteau or even her relationship with Lawrence. Sasha Crane wasn't merely the registrar, she was Callie's best friend. If Sasha was the true face behind the SPS profile picture, the degrees of separation between it and Hudson had officially landed in uncomfortable territory.

You're stewing, aren't you?

Gwyn's follow-up question made her laugh even as it made her cringe. *I have no idea what you're talking about.*

That got her a string of laughing emojis but not a press to elaborate. Hudson considered confiding further but, in the end, decided not to. She'd already created more layers of complication than she cared to. And since she planned to indulge in some of that stewing Gwyn alluded to, she didn't need someone hanging around and poking holes in her logic.

She asked about Gwyn's break, whether she'd made any headway on the revise and resubmit she'd gotten right before finals. How much goofy texting she and Sasha had been up to. Gwyn didn't give her a hard time about changing the subject, and they signed off with plans to grab a drink when Hudson got home.

Without the distraction, the ruminating returned. Along with a complete reread of the last six months of SPS posts, trolling for more phrases that might even loosely allude to her. Coming up empty should have been a relief, but it was almost as though she wanted to find something. Evidence that would justify the indignation still swirling around in her gut.

Hudson did the time zone calculation, already knowing the answer but wanting it to be different. She grabbed her sunglasses and headed to the beach, figuring she could fill the time if not enjoy it. Callie would be at work for another two hours at least, which meant a conversation with her would have to wait. Whether that conversation turned into a consolation or a confrontation remained to be seen.

Chapter Twenty-five

@shitprofessorssay: What are you going to do, tell the provost? I have tenure. You can't touch me.

"The young man writes a very compelling letter." G.W.'s voice dripped with condescension.

Callie resisted pointing out he likely didn't write it. She couldn't prove it, obviously, and it probably didn't matter to someone like G.W. Payne. "I'm not disagreeing with you. I'm—"

"Overstepping." George sat back in his chair, arms folded. "I don't think he should be punished for extenuating circumstances that were clearly beyond his control. And I don't think you should be trying to usurp the committee's opinion."

Heat flamed in Callie's cheeks, and she hated herself for it. "Academic separation is not a punishment. It's a pause button meant to give students the time and space to work through the challenges impacting their ability to be successful."

"If you're in a hole, stop digging." Cassandra gave her an encouraging smile. "It's not a new concept, George."

George gave a dismissive shrug. "If his parents have enough confidence in him to write the check, who are we to say otherwise?"

He wasn't the first person to use that logic. She'd even been swayed by the argument once or twice herself, though those instances had more to do with toxic family dynamics and believing a student would be better supported on campus than at home. But this student's circumstances were a far cry from that. This case involved a sophomore from Westchester who spent most of his time getting high and playing video games. Callie didn't doubt he suffered from anxiety, but she wasn't convinced by his plan to magically start spending four hours a day in the library.

Callie pressed her index fingers to her temples. But instead of alleviating some of the tension that had built over the last two hours, the added pressure only seemed to exacerbate it. "Of course I defer to the committee's authority to make that decision."

"Then I call a vote to approve Cedric Holloway's appeal for reinstatement. All in favor?"

Four hands went up.

"Opposed?"

Three, including Janice Kim from Cedric's own department.

Cassandra shot Callie a sympathetic look before saying, "I believe that wraps academic status. Are there any petitions for consideration?"

Callie walked through the five requests for exception to academic policy. The committee had received them all in advance, so there was little discussion. All the decisions skewed lenient, which she didn't love but would take over harsh adherence to the letter of the law. Thoughts on academic separation notwithstanding.

The meeting ended, and the room cleared. Callie started clicking out of systems and closing tabs. Sasha lingered. When only the two of them remained in the room, Sasha gave her a knowing look. "You okay?"

"It's pointless to be anything else, right?"

"Maybe, but it's possible. Probable. Understandable." Sasha shrugged. "You got steamrolled. And insulted."

It wasn't the first time in her career that had happened. She didn't imagine it would be the last. "Such is the plight of staff who carry the mantle of middle management."

Sasha let out a snort. "Sure, but some of those assholes couldn't manage their way out of a paper bag."

Callie cracked a smile then. She had to. She wouldn't survive in her line of work if she lost her ability to find humor in the absurd.

"Seriously, though. That got a little heated. Do you want to talk about it?"

"Nah. I think G.W. is wrong. G.W. thinks my opinion isn't worthy of consideration. He gets a vote at ARC. I do not."

Sasha sniffed her disdain. "You should have all the votes. You're never wrong."

Callie smirked. "Of course I am. Remember Blake Mooney?"

Sasha rolled her eyes. "Okay, once. You were wrong once."

She'd been wrong plenty. It was impossible to know for certain which students would get their acts together and which ones wouldn't. She'd improved her instincts over the years, though, and was right more often than not. "I am but a lowly member of the staff. What are fifteen years advising experience to the infinite wisdom of a tenured professor?"

"I'm not answering that. Do you want to go out for drinks?"

A glass of wine held more than a little appeal. But decision letters wouldn't send themselves, and after her staff had spent the morning preparing for the ARC meeting, she'd sent them all home early. "I'm going to plow through letters so I can put this particular instance of being put in my place behind me."

"Okay, let me know if you want me to come over later to burn some effigies."

Callie headed back to her office. With everyone gone, she didn't hesitate to crank the music. Between the mundane task of formatting form letters and the solid tunes, her mood lifted enough to do a little desk dancing.

When her phone rang—with the picture she took of Hudson on their last hike filling the screen—she quickly paused the song and clicked to accept the call on her computer. Apparently, she'd lost track of time, too. "Hey."

"Shouldn't you be home by now?"

"Academic Review Committee met this afternoon. I wanted to stay and get the letters out." Because she might not agree with all the decisions made, but she did believe students deserved to know what they were sooner rather than later.

Hudson frowned. “Shouldn’t your admin be taking care of that?”

“Yes, but she’s hourly and I don’t have the budget to offer her overtime.”

The frown intensified. “I was hoping to talk to you about something.”

Callie leaned back in her chair. “Go ahead.”

“I was hoping you’d be at home.”

“Well, by the time I get home, I’m going to want a glass of wine and a hot bath, so this is what I’ve got to offer.”

“Okay.” Hudson nodded, expression serious. “You know Shit Professors Say, right?”

Callie kept her face impassive despite the tickle of apprehension along her spine. “Yeah.”

“Well, there was a post that I’m pretty sure is about Lawrence Michaelson. It’s too specific to be a coincidence. So I went back through the last few months, and I know some of the quotes come from other places, but I think it might be based mostly on Coteau.”

“Okay.” Without knowing where Hudson was going, she didn’t have much else to say.

“I think it might be Sasha. She’s got a position that would give her access to the kinds of things that get shared.”

Callie’s stomach tightened, but still she resisted anything more than an “And?”

“And it’s a total violation of confidentiality. Not to mention professionalism,” Hudson said.

“Is it?” When Hudson simply balked, she added, “I mean, it’s all in good fun. And it’s not like any names are attached.”

Hudson straightened then. “It’s not fun for the people being made fun of.”

She tried for a wry smile. “Pretty sure it’s not for them.”

“Yeah, but it’s about them, and some of the stuff isn’t just cringey. It’s fireable.”

A dozen or more justifications popped into Callie’s mind, but she swallowed them and settled for the vaguer, “That feels like a stretch.”

"I don't think it is. And if it is Sasha, I don't think I can let it go. People's reputations are at stake. Their jobs even. I considered going to HR, but I'm not sure what they'd do. And it's not like I want her to get fired or anything. I thought since you were her best friend, you might be able to—"

"Hudson," Callie said.

"Maybe talk to her about—"

"Hudson," she said again, this time louder. "Stop talking."

Hudson started, clearly taken aback by the sharpness in Callie's voice. To be fair, Callie was a little taken aback herself. Hudson folded her arms. "Why? So you can try to talk me down?"

Callie closed her eyes and pinched the bridge of her nose. "It's me."

"What are you talking about?"

She looked up. Hudson's startled expression had given way to confused. "I'm Shit Professors Say. It's my account."

"I don't understand."

It bugged the crap out of her when people said that, because they did understand and simply didn't like what had been said. It bugged her even more that she'd backed herself into a corner of her own making and Hudson had every right not to like it. Though, in that instance, bugged might not be a sufficient word. "I am the person behind Shit Professors Say. The quotes come from a bunch of different people, from colleges and universities all over. But I'm the one who compiles and posts them."

Hudson's expression turned dark. "Except the ones you write yourself."

"Those are anonymous, too." Callie stuck out both hands, as though that might make her defense more compelling.

"Not so anonymous that I couldn't put the pieces together."

Hudson had every right to be mad that Callie had kept it from her, but the implication that the site itself was the problem made her hackles rise. "And?"

"And you posted something that could damage the career of someone who is both a friend and a colleague."

Irritation gave way to genuine anger. "If your friend and colleague actually did what was referred to in the post, he's got much bigger problems than being outed on social media."

"Are you serious right now?"

Something about the scandalized tone flipped a switch in her. The desire to smooth things over evaporated. In its place, a simmering frustration that erupted into a boil. A little bit of it was Hudson, a little bit was every dismissive or condescending thing said to her by every jerky professor she'd ever encountered. But none of those professors were there. Only Hudson. And maybe she should know better, but her feet were still wet from her slog across the unplowed campus, G.W.'s digs still echoed in her mind, and she had two snarky parent emails in her inbox. She simply didn't have it in her to be the bigger person. "I don't know. It's hard to take you seriously from your spot on the beach, so my sensors might be off."

"You could be on this beach, you know," Hudson said, expression turning stoic.

"No, Hudson. I couldn't. I had to be here, having a shitty day deciding the fates of students with a committee of faculty who think of me as the help."

Hudson's features softened, if only a little. "What happened?"

"I really don't want to talk about it, especially with someone who thinks of me the same way."

"That's not fair," Hudson said.

"No? Let me ask you something. Why is it you were prepared to go on a witch hunt over a stupid social media post but not the behavior that inspired it?"

Hudson's mouth fell open, but she snapped it shut instead of saying anything.

The gesture only served to fuel Callie's ire. "Seems to me like you have a double standard when it comes to how you think of your faculty colleagues and how you think of the staff."

Hudson shook her head. "No more than you do."

"What is that supposed to mean?"

"It means you're quick to critique the faculty you work with as being conceited and out of touch, but you're the one looking down on them."

She bristled, though it was hard to tell whether she was annoyed by the generalization or the fact that it held a kernel of truth. "Only the ones who bring it on themselves."

"Like me?" Hudson asked.

Callie's indignation wavered for the briefest of moments. "Not that I've seen, save maybe this conversation."

"But it didn't stop you from posting about my connection to Lawrence. Implying that I got my job because he's friends with my father."

She'd forgotten all about that post. Even though Sasha had technically hit the button, she'd been complicit. And even though she and Hudson hadn't been serious yet, there was enough between them that she'd hesitated. Hesitated but gone along with it. "I didn't mean—"

"Am I just a joke to you? Source material and a good fuck?"

The stark departure from Hudson's generally magnanimous demeanor made the insult land extra hard. "Hudson."

Hudson shook her head. "I need to process all this. I'll let you get back to your letters."

The call ended, leaving Callie staring at the spreadsheet and document she'd been working on when Hudson called. She scrubbed a hand over her face and let out a groan of frustration. She snatched up her phone and started a text to Sasha, only to delete it before typing a single sentence.

What a complete and utter clusterfuck. And the worst part? She'd done it to herself.

❖

Whoever said it was impossible to be miserable on vacation had clearly never had a massive fight with their girlfriend in the middle of one. Hudson spent her final days in Greece skulking about, vacillating between drafting apologies in her mind and crafting increasingly scathing dress downs.

It was the question she hurled out at the end that clung to her like a bad case of static electricity. The one about Callie using her for material. Oh, and a good fuck.

She knew it wasn't true, knew it was an unfair question even to ask. But Hudson hadn't been able to take it back, and she'd been too full of indignation to try. Or to apologize.

But even as she sloshed around in her own regrets, Callie's obstinance needled her. She hadn't been willing to give an inch. Which left Hudson to close the entire gap. Assuming, of course, that was the end goal. At this point, she wasn't sure. And now, on top of the mess that was her personal life, she'd come home to crappy weather, a cat hell-bent on holding a grudge, and a summons to a meeting with the provost for God only knew what reason.

Instinct told her in must have something to do with Callie's post. She'd insisted to Callie there was every possibility that could happen. That someone could trace it all back and there'd be real and serious consequences. The indignant part of her wanted that to be true even as the rational part of her knew better. Both parts were terrified by the possibility.

Too bad she didn't know which part to listen to.

On the day of the meeting, Hudson hovered at home rather than going to her office and chancing a run-in with anyone. Not that anyone but Betty was likely to be in a full four days before classes started. Either way, she went right to the administration building and sat in the waiting area, doing her best not to fidget like a twelve-year-old summoned to the principal's office. Not that she'd ever been summoned to the principal's office. She was an OG good kid. Perhaps that was why her current predicament had her all but crawling out of her skin.

She waited, then waited some more. She pulled out her phone and checked her email, hoping to mask how slowly the minutes ticked by. Eventually, a door opened, and Henry emerged.

He offered her a nervous smile. "You, too?"

Shouldn't he know that? Or, maybe, whatever this delicate matter was had nothing to do with the department. But then, why would he be here? Hudson shrugged and tried to return the smile, pretty sure she managed little more than a grimace.

"It'll be okay." Henry nodded the way a dad might to a kid who'd just blown the championship game—encouraging but not convincing.

What was with all the disappointing child analogies? If she hadn't been so despondent, she might have laughed. Before she could think of something banal to say in return, the young guy behind the reception desk cleared his throat. "Dr. Greene?"

Hudson leaned past Henry to make eye contact. "Yes?"

"Provost Marsh will see you now."

She stood. "Thank you."

Henry clapped a hand on her shoulder as she passed him but didn't say anything further. Hudson took a steadying breath and headed down the hall.

Eliza Marsh was a take-no-prisoners sort of woman who probably could have made a killing in the corporate world had she deigned to set foot in it. The only senior administrator at the college with a business degree—aside from the CFO—she ran the Division of Academic Affairs with a practical, no-nonsense approach Hudson respected. Even if the prospect of falling on her bad side proved utterly terrifying.

"Dr. Greene, thank you for coming in today. Please, have a seat."

Hudson did as she was told.

"Do you know Elaine Bitterman, Coteau's general counsel?"

Hudson was certain that she blanched, but there wasn't a damn thing she could do about it. Fortunately, Elaine, for all her starchy lawyerly appearance, offered her a warm smile and extended a hand. "I don't believe we've met," Elaine said.

Hudson shook Elaine's hand and tried for a genuine smile. "Not formally. I saw your presentation at new faculty orientation."

Elaine chuckled. "I promise I'm more fun than that half hour would imply."

"Do you know why I asked to meet with you?" Provost Marsh asked, clearly impatient with the small talk.

Was that a trick question? "Only that there was a matter of some delicacy and urgency."

The provost nodded. "I understand you have a personal relationship with Lawrence Michaelson."

Fuck. Fuck fuck fuck. A wave of rage swelled alongside the anxiety already roiling inside her. Fuck Callie and her stupid Shit Professors Say. "He's, um, a family friend, if that's what you mean. He and my father went to school together."

"Right. Yes." Elaine cleared her throat. "We understand that this might make some of our questions difficult, but I hope you understand how important it is that you answer honestly."

It was Hudson's turn to nod. "Of course."

"Are you aware that Professor Michaelson used his teaching assistant to grade papers for his courses?"

How bad would it come back to bite her if she lied? Even as that question swirled in her mind, another swooped in. How much did she want to put her own reputation on the line for someone who'd clearly checked out professionally? The answer to that one came in loud and clear. "He mentioned it to me in passing, though I wasn't certain whether he meant it or was making a joke."

Elaine scribbled notes on her legal pad. The provost's lips pursed. "Did Professor Michaelson share with you how long this had been his practice?"

Hudson shook her head.

"Do you—"

"Wait," Hudson said.

"Yes?" Provost Marsh laced her fingers together, and Hudson couldn't help but notice the way her knuckles turned white.

"He joked that he hadn't graded a one-hundred-level essay in a decade." Hudson shook her head. "Again, I wasn't sure if he meant it, but that's what he said. It was right before the fall semester began."

Elaine and the Provost exchanged glances, and Hudson didn't need to read minds to know that Lawrence was up shit creek. They asked her more questions, ones about the culture of the department, her experiences with Henry as chair. Nothing like the bombshell of where the conversation started, but it left her frazzled and more than a little queasy.

When Elaine asked if she had anything else to share, or any questions, Hudson cleared her throat. She didn't want to ask, but she had to. She needed that nail in the coffin that would give her clarity if not consolation. "May I ask how this…issue…came to light?"

Provost Marsh looked to Elaine, who gave an almost imperceptible nod. "We received a complaint from a student."

Relief washed through her. Followed swiftly by the pang of feeling like a complete asshole. "I see."

Provost Marsh offered something resembling a smile. "For the record, student complaints don't generally get to our level. This one is particularly serious, obviously, but it also came through the family's attorney."

"Oh."

"Exactly," Elaine said. Her smile seemed to come easier, making Hudson wonder if it was her personality or feeling overall less frazzled by threats of legal action. "I think it goes without saying, but this entire matter is strictly confidential."

"Of course." Hudson coughed. "So, what happens next?"

"That's confidential, too, I'm afraid." Elaine closed her pad folio.

"Right. Sorry." She shook her head. "I shouldn't have asked."

"It's understandable." Provost Marsh's expression softened, as though appreciating Hudson's predicament. "He's a friend as much as a colleague."

Hudson frowned, suddenly willing to draw a line in the sand she hadn't before. "Like I said, he's a friend of my father's. I'm not sure how much he and I have in common at this point."

Both women nodded, and Hudson was glad she'd put that distance between herself and Lawrence. Whatever loyalties she might have didn't extend to things that undermined her reputation. Or her values. "If there's anything else you need from me, I assume you'll be in touch."

"Absolutely." Elaine stood and extended her hand again. "It was great to meet you, even if the circumstances weren't ideal."

Hudson followed suit. "Same."

Provost Marsh joined in with a "I hope your first semester was a good one. We're really happy to have you on the faculty."

Hudson didn't presume Provost Marsh knew much beyond the fact that she was a new hire in the English Department, but she appreciated the sentiment all the same. "Thank you. I'm really happy to be here."

Current train wrecks in multiple areas of her life notwithstanding.

Chapter Twenty-six

@shitprofessorssay: If it's not in the minutes of a faculty senate meeting, it didn't happen. I can't be responsible for things buried in the policy manual.

"You'll never guess what a little birdie told me." Sasha blew on then took a bite of the soup Callie had brought for them both to have for lunch. "This is fantastic by the way."

"Thank you." It was a new recipe for her, one she'd planned to try out on Hudson. Stupid Hudson.

"Don't you want my hot gossip?"

"Huh? Oh, yeah. Tell me." Callie took a bite of the soup, pleased with how the flavors had developed overnight in the fridge. She made a mental note to always make it a day ahead.

"There's an investigation brewing in the provost's office. It seems like our Professor Michaelson got himself on the wrong side of a student with snowplow parents and legal representation." Sasha punctuated the declaration with an exaggerated crunch of tortilla chip.

Callie stilled, spoon hovering between the bowl and her mouth. "Seriously?"

Sasha wagged her spoon, on a roll now. "Apparently, his poor TA let it slip to her boyfriend that she'd messed up grade submissions and felt bad about having to disturb the creep on his vacation. The boyfriend's little sister happens to be a first-year at Coteau who's in his intro Shakespeare course. He told her, she told the parents, and the parents looped in the Offices of We're Gonna Sue Your Asses and Associates."

A snort of laughter escaped at that last bit, but the twist of emotions coiling in her chest proved more complex. Relief that behavior like Lawrence's wasn't going unchecked, relief that the person who brought it to light had nothing to do with her or SPS, relief that Hudson wouldn't have even more fuel on the fire of her indignation. But with the relief came a wave of sadness. For all her poking fun at the absurdities of academia, things that damaged students sat heavy. And, grudgingly, things that damaged faculty, too. She loved a little Schadenfreude as much as the next person, but she'd prefer if people didn't behave badly in the first place.

And Hudson. For all her mixed emotions over how things between them went down, she didn't see how this would help. If anything, Hudson would magically find a way to make it all her fault. Or, at the very least, hold firm in her assertions that Callie was the bane of the academic profession and want nothing to do with her ever again.

"Really? That's all you're going to give me?"

Sasha's question brought Callie back to her office, back to the soup, and back to the fact that, while she loved gossip, the reality of it often left her uneasy. "Sorry. My brain went a thousand places, you know?"

Sasha nodded, eyes full of empathy. "Yeah."

"Do you think he'll get fired?"

"Hard to say. It'll depend on the exact circumstances, obviously." Sasha shrugged. "Maybe they'll nudge him to retire."

It wouldn't be the first time Coteau—or anywhere else—had used that method to get rid of someone. She bristled at the idea of people being forced out of jobs simply because they were old but, in a world where tenure afforded immutable job security, old so often equaled antiquated ideas and ways of doing things. And in those cases, good riddance. Whether or not they deserved the graceful exit. "Maybe."

"Word is people are being brought into the provost's office. Fact-finding."

"That's gross." Not that the facts didn't need to be found. More that the token slaps on the wrist she'd seen doled out didn't give her a lot of faith in the system. Going through the motions and then doing nothing? That was the worst of all.

"Did you get summoned?" Sasha asked.

"No." Based on the conversation with Henry about canceled classes and no-show office hours, she very well could have. Dodged a bullet there. "Did you?"

Sasha shook her head. "Miles did, though."

"Better him than you." At least he had the title and paycheck to go along with the administrative drama.

"Truth." Sasha paused. "Are you going to reach out to Hudson?"

Callie started at the mention of Hudson's name, despite Hudson being front and center of her thoughts. "Why would I do that?"

"To say told you so?" Sasha smirked.

Callie scowled.

"Kidding. I meant to, like, see how she's doing."

It didn't take long to come up with a list of reasons why that was a terrible idea. "Considering I shouldn't know anything about this, I'm going to go with no."

"And she probably wouldn't take it as sincere anyway," Sasha said in her matter-of-fact way.

"Gee, thanks." Callie rolled her eyes even though that was on the list, too.

"Seriously, though. Are you just never going to talk to her again?"

The possibility landed like a lead weight. "God, I hope that's not the case. We didn't even break up. Not technically at least. Hudson said she needed to process."

"Huh."

"I'm trying to let the dust settle." Hudson obviously felt betrayed, and Callie had to accept responsibility for that. She would, because it was hers to own. But Hudson had managed to make her feel like shit, too. Even if she was inclined to forget the harsh words, the underlying reasons for it remained.

Hudson might think the biggest problem between them was a social media account, but the underlying impetus of SPS was a dissonance with the way many college faculty saw the world, moved through it. How they treated people without their rank and pedigree. That came down to values.

Though, really, Hudson could make the same argument. She had, in a way, when she questioned whether Callie took her seriously. Respected her. At the end of the day, if they didn't respect each other, it didn't leave room for much else.

Which were all nice and tidy and rational arguments to make to herself but did nothing to ease the ache in her heart. To lessen just how fucking much she missed Hudson. It had been barely a week since they'd argued and only three days since Hudson had landed back in New York. But having Hudson absent—from her texts, from her bed, from her life—hurt like hell.

"Gwyn says Hudson is taking it pretty hard." Sasha lifted a shoulder. "Actually, she said really hard. Full on moody and reflective."

Callie took a small bit of satisfaction in that. Mostly because that's exactly what she'd been. For all her indignation, withholding SPS in a way that could quite reasonably be construed as lying left her feeling like a jerk. She didn't want to be that person with people she didn't like, much less people she did.

"The fact that you're not gloating says a lot," Sasha said.

"Do you think I should apologize first?" Callie asked rather than agreeing with or arguing the point.

"Do you think you should apologize at all?"

Of course Sasha had to go and be mature and ask the much harder question. Callie sighed. "Yeah. For sure."

"Then order feels pretty irrelevant."

She hated when Sasha was right. Or perhaps more accurately, she hated when Sasha being right meant she was in the wrong. "Yeah."

❖

Not twenty-four hours after her meeting with the provost—and a scant forty-eight before the first day of classes—Hudson opened her email to find a message from Henry at the top of her inbox: Announcing the Retirement of Professor Lawrence Michaelson. She took a fortifying breath and clicked on it.

Dear colleagues,

It is with mixed emotions that I share the news that an esteemed member of our department will be retiring at the end of the spring semester. Professor Lawrence Michaelson has been a member of the Coteau faculty for over thirty years, teaching courses in British literature and Shakespeare to literally thousands of Coteau students. He has been a friend and colleague to many.

Since Lawrence is one year past due for a sabbatical and was slated to take a two-semester leave next academic year, the provost has graciously approved an exception to policy and will allow him to take this well-earned rest in his terminal semester. Wesley has graciously agreed to cover a second section of Intro to British Literature on overload, and I will teach Shakespeare.

Please join me in extending congratulations and well-wishes to Lawrence. And stay tuned for information regarding retirement festivities later this spring!

Warmest regards,

Henry Hazelton

Hudson read the email again. Its contents weren't complicated. Nor were they surprising, given everything that had unfolded. It felt fast, obviously. Especially for higher ed, where a minor tweak to the curriculum could easily turn into a yearlong affair. She'd be lying if she denied the sense of relief over not having to walk an impossible tightrope any longer. But more than anything, the whole business made her sad.

She slumped back in her chair, the universally preferred position for mulling and sulking.

Obviously, she was disappointed. In Lawrence, not the decision to have him retire. But there was more at play.

If Henry had the time to compose the email—and no doubt have it vetted by the esteemed Elaine Bitterman—that meant

Lawrence had known it was coming and didn't even bother to tell her. Though, would she reach out personally to share a hastily thrown together retirement plan that clearly had its roots in some unrelated circumstances? Hard to say since she couldn't fathom doing the things Lawrence had done to get himself into the situation in the first place.

And not that she had the time or the inclination to cover either of Lawrence's spring classes, but the fact that Wesley was meant he'd been brought into the loop before her. Yes, it was beside the point, but it added insult to injury. Because that's what it felt like. Injury. She'd looked up to Lawrence for years and, not six months after becoming his colleague, he had to go and blow what remained of his career.

Maybe she'd been a fool to look up to him in the first place.

Hudson pressed the heels of her palms to her eyes. She needed to tell her father. Or did she? She dropped her hands and considered which he'd take worse—hearing the news from her or hearing it otherwise and realizing he hadn't heard it from her first.

He should hear it from her. Because then he could reach out to Lawrence and make sure he was okay. Better her father than her at this point. Hudson didn't even know what she'd say to Lawrence if given the chance.

She picked up her phone to start crafting a text but was distracted by another email popping into the top of her inbox. Same subject as Henry's, but this one came from the provost. Hudson clicked on it. The text was essentially the same, minus the specifics about course coverage and with a few flourishes about Lawrence's research accomplishments thrown in. It had gone out to the entire campus community.

It was real then. Official. Hudson's stomach sank further, and she decided to forward the email to her dad rather than text him. A bit of a copout, but it was all she had in her at the moment.

When her phone flashed with a notification, her heart leapt and not in a good way. She snatched it up, already scrambling for what to say to her dad's confusion and disappointment. Only the text wasn't from her dad. It was from Gwyn.

Isn't Larry Mike your dad's BFF?

Even in her sorry state, Hudson smiled. The only thing that irritated Lawrence more than being called Larry was when people shortened both his names. *Yup.*

Rather than a follow-up text, Gwyn called. "Hey," Hudson said, weirdly relieved to have someone who wasn't her father to talk to.

"Do you know what happened? Is he sick or is there a scandal?"

Her first instinct was to protect Lawrence. Her second was to follow the strict instructions she'd been given about confidentiality. Too bad neither of those instincts had served her particularly well of late. "I think it's a number of things."

Gwyn hmphed her opinion of Hudson's non-answer.

"I'm not supposed to talk about it."

"Okay, so, scandal," Gwyn said.

Hudson couldn't help but laugh at Gwyn's simplistic but obviously accurate deduction. "Low-level."

"Nothing Title IX, then."

Though Title IX referred to all manner of gender bias and related misdoings, Gwyn was clearly using it as code for sexual impropriety. "No, thank the goddess."

Gwyn chuckled at that. "Wait, does it have something to do with what you and Callie had that big fight about?"

"Yes and no."

"Dude. Give me something to work with." Gwyn paused. "Actually, don't. We should be talking in person. I'll be in your office in five."

The prospect of processing her many and mixed feelings collided with the possibility someone in Storey might overhear them. "I'll come to you. Neutral territory. I'll bring coffee."

With a detour to the library café, it took Hudson fifteen minutes instead of five. And her feet and fingers were good and frozen by the time she arrived at Gwyn's office. But Gwyn's cozy space and empathetic smile made the trek more than worthwhile.

Rather than the abbreviated version she intended to tell, Hudson started at the beginning. Idolizing Lawrence as a kid. That first lunch with him in August, his never being around. Since she'd already looped Gwyn in on the SPS debacle, she skimmed over that and the specifics of her fight with Callie and focused instead on her meeting with the provost and general counsel.

"Dude, that sucks. Nothing worse than when our heroes crash and burn."

"Yeah." It was true, but the more she thought about it, the more she realized Lawrence wasn't that. Yes, she'd looked up him as a child and yes, he represented everything she wanted to become as a teacher and scholar. But he wasn't what he represented, and maybe he never had been. She didn't actually know him well enough to know one way or another.

"What?" Gwyn asked. "You're stewing. I can tell."

She chuckled at being so transparent. "I think I'm more upset about things with Callie. Lawrence made his bed and now he has to lie in it. It's not really my problem."

"But the Callie thing is the bed you made. And you're not liking having to lie in it."

The metaphor might be crap, but it landed with all the heaviness of being one hundred percent true. "She made it, too, for the record."

Gwyn raised a brow.

"But I'm the one who flipped out, hung up on her, and haven't talked to her since."

Gwyn's brow lowered and she gave a knowing nod.

"Do you think she'll take me back?"

"Did you break up?" Gwyn asked.

Hudson made a series of faces as she replayed the awful conversation in her mind for the hundredth or so time. "Not officially."

"Then it sounds like you should start with an apology and go from there."

"You make it sound so simple," she said, feeling like it was anything but.

Gwyn grinned. "Groveling usually is."

Chapter Twenty-seven

@shitprofessorssay: Don't tell my colleagues, but I actually sort of like students.

The final days of break passed with the sort of low-intensity fanfare that came with fresh starts in the dead of winter. New students arrived, Callie's probation students trickled in, and she very quickly got a sense of who took their situation seriously, and who did not. She knew she needed to reach out to Hudson but put it off. Telling herself she was busy and would get to it over the weekend.

Sasha, in all her new relationship glory, continued to poke at her. "I don't understand why you won't just apologize already," she'd say. "You've already admitted you were wrong."

That was the thing with being wrong, though. It was one thing to know it, to acknowledge in the safe space slash cone of silence that was one's best friend. Owning it to the person who'd basically called her a self-serving jerk? That was another matter entirely.

Not helping matters was the two-thirty appointment on her calendar.

"How are you?" Callie tried to keep her tone from straying too deep into concerned territory, but the last time they'd met, things had been pretty dire.

"I'm good." Pav nodded slowly, then with more vigor. "Really good, actually?"

"Yeah?" She was happy to hear it, if a little dubious.

“I’ve been meeting with a counselor, which has been really good. So, thanks for that.”

Callie smiled. “I only made the suggestion. You’re doing the hard work.”

Pav laughed, then. “You know, I never got it when people said that, but now I do.”

“I promise the payoff is worth it.” A sentiment she felt comfortable slotting into the universal truths category.

“Totally. And I’ve been meeting with Hudson—I mean Dr. Greene—every week, too. Sometimes twice. We even Zoomed over break.”

“If she’s encouraged you to call her Hudson, it’s okay to refer to her that way.”

“Yeah, okay. Hudson.” Pav ducked her head, sheepish now. “She’s helping me explore ways I might be able to have my cake and eat it, too.”

Callie was fond of the idiom, but hearing it from a nineteen-year-old felt out of place, dated. More like something Hudson would say. “And was Hudson the one who used that phrase? The one about having your cake and eating it, too?”

Pav cringed. “It’s one my mom always uses. Mostly to tell me I can’t. Hudson said she respectfully disagreed.”

Callie couldn’t help but chuckle. “I see. So, what does that look like for you?”

“Oh, my God.” Pav’s eyes lit up. “So many possibilities. Like, I could stick with bio as a major and do a minor or even a double major in English. That would keep the med school door open, but I could maybe go into science writing. Or I could write medical thrillers with a level of expertise a lot of writers don’t have.”

Pav rubbed her hands together with almost maniacal delight at that last one, making Callie laugh in earnest. “That’s a lot of options. Really good ones, too.”

“Right? My parents aren’t sold.” Pav lifted a finger. “Yet.”

“Well…” She searched for the right reassuring-but-realistic truism.

"But they aren't threatening to pull me from school until I get my priorities straight."

Callie went for a cringey smile. "Win?"

"Total win. Besides, if I keep taking at least some of the premed requirements and get my GPA over three-point-eight, I haven't closed that door—which I'm saying now instead of killed that dream—completely."

"I support every aspect of this plan." Because as easy as it was to tell a nineteen-year-old to follow her dreams, the reality was that she—and most of the students she worked with—relied on their families for financial support. Finding a way to strike a balance when personal and parental priorities didn't line up sometimes felt like the biggest win of all.

"Thanks." Pav gave a definitive nod, reminding Callie that her own endorsement carried weight too, sometimes.

"So, do you need help changing your schedule?"

"Hudson helped me with that, actually. I just wanted to check in." Pav reached into her bag and pulled out a small box of chocolates. "And to thank you for your help last semester. I was a mess."

Callie accepted the gift even as she shook her head. "I hope you know you didn't need to do that. Supporting you is literally my job, and helping students in general is my favorite part of what I do."

"I know. It's okay, though, right? I'm not breaking any rules or anything?"

"It's totally fine. And thank you." She glanced at the box. "Ooh. Caramels are my favorite."

"Hudson said the same thing." Pav's smile was sly, like she was sharing some sort of secret.

Callie swallowed with more intention than the moment called for, so many thoughts about Hudson and secrets suddenly swirling in her mind. "Well, Professor Greene clearly has excellent taste."

Another smile, as sly as the first, and Pav stood.

"Don't be a stranger, okay? I'm here to help, but I also like to hear how you're doing, good or bad."

Pav's nod was eager this time. "I can do that."

"Good. I also want to know if you land yourself a publishing deal before graduation."

"I promise you'll be the first to know."

"Well, second or third would be okay, too."

Pav looked confused for about five seconds, then understanding spread as wide as her grin. "You got it."

Pav left, and Callie found herself with fifteen minutes before her next appointment. Since the advising center was a hub of activity at this time of year, she'd normally head out to the front to see if she could help with walk-ins. This time, however, she simply sat. Well, simply might be a bit of an overstatement. The thoughts about Hudson swirled with renewed vigor, and for the hundredth or so time in the last couple of weeks, she felt like a complete and utter heel.

Callie picked up her phone to text Sasha but found herself toggling to SPS instead. She made several attempts, deleting each while mumbling swear words under her breath. It was hard to be clever while also being humble.

In the end, she settled on simple. Because she'd made this mess and there was no getting around needing to clean it up. And because some situations left no room for error.

@shitprofessorssay: I care about your academic success but also your happiness. I want to help you find both if I can.

Callie followed the post with comments, providing some context and the sort of observation that would be true to the good-natured spirit she tried to bring SPS. But also something that Hudson couldn't possibly read as anything other than an apology. Assuming, of course, Hudson saw it at all.

❖

Looks like someone is trying to make nice.

Hudson stared at the text, trying and failing to understand what the hell Gwyn was talking about. The screenshot came a few seconds later. A post from SPS. She groaned on principle, then read what it had to say. Her throat tightened.

Gwyn followed up with two more screenshots—a pair of comments on the original post:

@shitprofessorssay: *This account started as a way to let off some steam. It grew into something that resonated with a lot of people. I told myself it was all in good fun, but I've recently had to confront the fact that poking fun doesn't always land as innocently as one might like. I apologize for any harm or hurt feelings the posts here have caused. 1/2*

@shitprofessorssay: *2/2 Don't worry, the account isn't going anywhere. We all need to delight, and occasionally despair, at the lack of tact and good judgment that surrounds us. But as I've recently been reminded, the good truly outweighs the bad and, with only a few exceptions, we're all on the same team. -your faithful and ever so slightly less fickle moderator*

Hudson flicked through the images, reading the entirety of the post a second, then a third, time. It wasn't the apology she'd been hoping for. And yet, it was somehow also better. Public. Like Callie wasn't trying to make nice in private but then carry on like nothing had happened.

What are you going to do?

She chuckled at Gwyn's impatience. *Think about it for a hot minute.*

As it did so often, Gwyn's reply came in an instant. *What's there to think about? Kiss and make up. Have all the sex. Live happily ever after.*

Hudson couldn't help but laugh at the distilled take on the situation. But even as she dismissed it as not that simple, she started to wonder. What if it was?

She'd be the first to admit her reaction in the moment had been intense. Worry that Lawrence might have taken a step too far paired with Callie's revelation about pulling the strings behind the scenes of Shit Professors Say had tipped the scales of her ability to think—much less behave—rationally. But even in the heat of the moment, she'd said she needed time to process, not that that she didn't want to be with Callie at all. It wasn't like they'd broken up.

Right?

Despite the encouraging vibes of Callie's latest post, reality remained. They hadn't talked since that disastrous video chat in Greece. That had been over a week ago. And while she might like a personal apology, she couldn't argue that the need to clear the air was a two-way street. She'd done nothing on her side to make things right.

Dude. Seriously. I need you two to work things out so we can go on double dates.

Hudson rolled her eyes, but the prospect of the four of them spending time together appealed. Not at the top of her list, obviously, but on it. She chuckled. When it came to appealing things about being with Callie, if she took the time to write everything out, it would be a really long list.

The simple truth of that hit her a lot harder than Gwyn's relationship equation. She liked more about Callie—about being with Callie—than she had about anyone else in a long time. Maybe ever. And perhaps just as importantly, she liked who she was with Callie. A little less uptight, and a little more playful.

She dashed off a promise to Gwyn that she was on it, then scrolled to her thread with Callie. *I saw your post. Posts.*

After hitting send, she regretted not giving herself that hot minute to think. Because it was one thing to know her feelings, but another entirely to be eloquent about it. She started and stopped, then wanted to kick herself when the reply bubbles appeared. What if Callie thought that was all she had to say? What if it wasn't good enough?

Hudson gave up trying to string words together and held her breath.

It needed to be said. But please don't think I expect that to count as the personal apology I owe you.

The carbon dioxide that had started to strain Hudson's lungs came out in an audible whoosh.

Callie continued: *I'd like to do that in person if you're amenable.*

Hudson's pulse—that had been thudding with trepidation a moment before—thudded for an entirely different reason. Though flutter might be more accurate. Hope really was the thing with feathers. *I would like that, and I'd like to offer an apology of my own.*

Callie responded with the two pink hearts emoji, which prompted Hudson to ask Gwyn what that meant. Gwyn sent the shrug emoji with a *Hold please.*

Hudson waited, wondering whether Gwyn's research consisted of asking Sasha. Which in turn let to her wondering if Sasha would turn around and ask Callie. She made a mental note to cease and desist teasing students about their convoluted communication styles.

A moment passed, then another. Unwilling to leave Callie on read, she asked if they might get together over the weekend. Callie's reply: *Can you do dinner tonight? My place?*

The immediacy of the invite, paired with the intimacy it implied, made it difficult for Hudson to sit still. Not that she expected Gwyn's formula to magically come to fruition. But she really would like to kiss and make up and have all the sex and live happily ever after. Talking at Callie's place was a far cry from meeting up on campus, giving her hope that Callie might want those things, too. If that was the case, Hudson had every intention of making the most of it.

Chapter Twenty-eight

@shitprofessorssay: There's nothing a little Hegelian dialectic can't cure.

Callie blew out a breath, trying and failing to remember a time she'd been more nervous to have a conversation. Or when it felt like a single conversation had so much at stake. It was the at stake part that got her.

Somewhere along the way of the last semester, she'd gone and fallen in love with Hudson Greene. It had crept up on her, the sort of subtle knowing that felt as natural as breathing. She liked to think she was more self-aware than the average bear, but it took the prospect of losing Hudson to bring the truth of it into focus. Hopefully, Hudson reaching out—not to mention alluding to an apology of her own—meant her feelings were somewhere in the same ballpark.

The knock on her front door was so soft she almost missed it, and Lucy, as usual, was no help. When she opened it to find Hudson standing on the other side, looking as hesitant as she had that night back in June, it took everything Callie had not to yank her inside and into her arms.

"Hey." Hudson's smile looked as reticent as the rest of her.

"Hey." Callie stepped back to let Hudson in, sans yanking.

"Thanks for inviting me over," Hudson said as she slipped out of her coat.

"Thanks for coming over." Callie stood awkwardly while Hudson bent to take off her boots.

Hudson stood, but before Callie could so much offer her a seat, she launched in. "I'm sorry for reacting the way I did. Even if I felt blindsided, it doesn't excuse my implying that you were only using our relationship for material." She winced. "Or sex."

Callie shook her head. "I should never have put you in a position to be blindsided. I lied by omission, and there's no excuse for that."

Hudson gave her a wry smile. "You assumed I wouldn't take it well, and I proved you right."

"But if I'd told you when you first asked me about SPS, it never would have gotten to that." It almost felt like they were arguing over who was more sorry—absurd but oddly reassuring.

Hudson lifted a finger. "But we'd only just started dating. It's completely reasonable that you wouldn't have confided in me then."

Callie shook her head again. "But I could have told you a thousand other times since then. I also could have shared my concerns about Lawrence with you sooner. I knew you had a personal connection. Maybe you could have talked some sense into him."

"You had other concerns?" Hudson asked.

She winced. No holding back now. "Some students complained about him canceling class and blowing off his office hours. I took it to Henry because that's how I handle things like that, but I also could have confided in you. Trusted you."

This time it was Hudson shaking her head. "No, you were completely right to leave me out if it."

"Even if that's true," Callie said, "I didn't have to post about it. Anonymous or not, it spilled onto you and put you in a bad position. I never meant for that to happen."

"Lawrence spilled it on himself when he decided to be an idiot on top of being an ass."

It was the harshest Callie had ever heard Hudson speak about Lawrence, and it went a long way in sharpening the lines that separated the kind of person Hudson was from the likes of people like Lawrence. "Still. I was wrong, and I'm sorry."

Hudson took a deep breath and blew it out slow before fixing her eyes on Callie's. "I'm sorry, too."

Callie blinked a few times, letting the words sink in and the relief take hold. And then it struck her that they'd laid all that out standing in the little space she called a foyer but didn't really qualify, with Lucy standing between them like she was waiting to see why no one had bothered to come sit on the couch and rub her belly.

Hudson's gaze followed hers down to Lucy, and Lucy looked back and forth between them. With both of them now watching her, Lucy's tail started to wag. She rocked side to side, paws lifting in her geriatric version of a happy dance. "I think she's glad we made up," Hudson said with a smile.

"Have we? Made up, I mean." Callie wanted that to be the case, but it felt almost too easy.

"I think so?" Hudson's smile faded. "Do you?"

She took a deep breath of her own. "I also need to apologize for the post about you."

"Oh. Right."

It seemed like maybe Hudson had forgotten, and Callie almost regretted bringing it up. She'd learned that lesson, though. The hard way. "It was obviously inspired by something you said rather than a direct quote."

Hudson nodded.

"It was still a shitty thing to do. I just…it wasn't really about you, you know. It was the idea of having that sort of double standard. None of which is you."

Another nod. "I accept your apology."

So simple, yet so huge. "Thank you. For what it's worth, I felt weird about it even then. Ironically, Sasha posted that one so I didn't have to."

"So you are in cahoots."

Callie laughed, mostly at the use of cahoots. "We consult."

Hudson's eyes narrowed. "If I ever start a Shit Administrators Say, that's going to be my first post."

Callie opened her mouth and promptly closed it again. Because yeah. She sucked her teeth. "Yeah. I definitely deserve that."

Hudson grinned. "So, made up?"

"I'd like that. I think we probably need to do some talking about communication and expectations and the future and stuff, but we probably needed to do that anyway. Oh, and insecurities. I have a few of those."

Hudson chuckled. "You sound like me."

All things considered, she could do worse. "Is that a bad thing?"

"No, but I don't want you to be more like me. I like you the way you are," Hudson said.

Callie's shoulders fell, and her whole body relaxed. "I like you the way you are."

"I like that you get me to take things a little less seriously."

Tears welled then, but Callie did her best to blink them away. "I like that you remind me that some things are worth being taken seriously."

"Like what?" Hudson's question seemed genuinely curious rather than leading.

"Like how I feel about you." She shrugged. "Like us."

"And how is it you feel about me, exactly?" Perhaps a little leading this time, but Callie didn't mind.

"Do you really want to have this conversation right here by the front door?"

It was Hudson's turn to shrug. "Seems like as good a place as any."

Callie thought back to that first night she brought Hudson home. Hudson had hovered in that very spot, waiting for Callie to make the first move. Hudson had taken the lead on plenty since then, but it felt fitting to come full circle. "I'm pretty in love with you," she said.

Hudson lifted a brow. "Only pretty?"

"No, not only pretty. Completely. Totally. Terrifyingly in love with you."

Hudson took a step toward her. "And here I thought nothing terrified you."

Callie's pulse tripped. "Oh, no. Plenty does. I'm just good at hiding it."

"Maybe stop hiding around me." Hudson threaded a hand into Callie's hair.

What a novel concept. "Okay."

"I love you, too, for the record." Hudson smiled. "Completely. Totally. And most definitely terrifyingly."

No amount of blinking could keep the tears at bay then. Callie sniffed and let them fall. "I'm glad."

Hudson nodded, and it seemed like her eyes might have gone a little glassy as well.

"So, do you want to come in and stay a while?" Callie tipped her head toward the living room.

The glassiness cleared. In its place, something resembling mischief. "Depends. Are you going to offer me a drink or skip the pretense and take me upstairs?"

Callie's heart swelled even as her desire surged. "That's a pretty good line. I'm surprised you didn't use it that first night."

Hudson wagged a finger. "You know I need clear and enthusiastic consent before I take charge."

"I see." Callie twitched her lips one way, then the other. "In that case, I'm not all that thirsty."

"Ah." Hudson clicked her tongue. "Is that your way of asking me to take you to bed?"

"So enthusiastic. Much consent."

Hudson extended a hand. "We might need to work on your structure, but your thesis is excellent."

Callie took it, and let Hudson lead the way up the stairs. "You know, I've never been a fan of hot for teacher, but in this exact moment, I think I get it."

"That's convenient," Hudson said when they'd reached Callie's bedroom. "Because I'm very hot for a very particular dean."

"What are you going to do about it?"

Hudson pulled Callie close, bringing her mouth mere inches from Callie's. "Let me show you."

❖

With the lights off and the blankets tucked snugly around them, Hudson pulled Callie tighter against her and kissed the top of Callie's head. She breathed in the scent of Callie's shampoo—a botanical blend she never bothered trying to tease out. It, paired with Callie's citrusy perfume and the lingering scent of sex, relaxed her even as it had her revving for more.

Pure bliss.

"Gwyn is going to be insufferable," she said, as much to herself as Callie.

"How so?" Callie didn't bother lifting her head.

"Oh, just smug. Lots of 'I told you so' and 'you make things harder than they need to be' vibes." Hudson chuckled. "To be fair, I've been pretty damn insufferable to be around the last couple of weeks."

Callie lifted her head and looked Hudson right in the eye. "Yeah?"

No point denying it now. "I knew I owed you an apology. But I wanted one in return, and I wasn't sure you were going to offer one. I couldn't decide how that would play out, so I went with emotional paralysis."

Hard to say whether that was better or worse than emotional flailing. "You're very self-aware. Stubborn as fuck, but self-aware."

Hudson cringed. "Thank you?"

"Definitely a compliment. Or more compliment than not, at least."

"Laced with a little 'takes one to know one' perhaps?" Hudson asked.

Callie laughed. Hard. As in, rolled onto her back, laced her fingers together over her belly, and cackled. By the time she stopped, she had to wipe tears from her eyes. "Absolutely. And for what it's worth, Sasha is going to be pretty smug, too."

Hudson chuckled. "I'm glad they finally got up the nerve to stop dancing around each other and get together already."

Callie raised a brow. "Unlike us, you mean."

"Exactly. We got a little sidetracked, but we both knew a good thing when we saw it and acted accordingly."

"Oh, is that what we did?"

It was Hudson's turn to laugh. Not a full cackle, but not far off. "That's the story I'm going to tell our grandchildren."

Callie rolled back to her side and then draped herself across Hudson. She cupped Hudson's breast in her palm and rested her chin on it. "So, you're planning our children and grandchildren now?"

"Figure of speech," she said.

"Ah."

"Which isn't to say I'm not open to the idea."

Callie tutted. "That's a double negative, Professor."

"Ahem. Let me rephrase. While I don't want to rush things, I should confess I've allowed myself to entertain all sorts of future possibilities that include you. Feature you. Prominently."

She thought Callie might balk, but Callie merely smiled. "I like that."

"To be fair, I haven't put a lot of thought into grandchildren yet."

Callie chuckled. "That's probably for the best."

"I have, however, given spring break quite a bit of consideration."

"Have you?" Callie asked.

Not exactly how she planned to have this conversation, but sooner was probably better than later. Especially since she'd wanted to broach the subject as soon as she got home from Greece. "I know you don't get those days off, and I'm not presuming you'd want to use vacation time, but I would love to spend spring break with you. Or as much of it as I can."

"Really?"

She hesitated but only for a second. "If going away is an option, I'd love to plan something for us. No pressure, obviously. I'd rather be here with you than on a beach by myself."

Callie gazed out the window at the swirling snow. "I'm not sure I would."

Disappointment flashed, but Hudson did her best to hold it in check. "For what it's worth I'd be perfectly happy to cook dinner and give back rubs if you have to work. I mean, technically, I have a paper I should be working on myself. It would probably be good for me to spend some time in my office anyway."

Callie laughed. "I meant that last part. I'm not sure I'd pick here with you over on a beach by myself."

"Oh," Hudson said.

"Though, on a beach with you would definitely be my top choice."

Hudson relaxed. "Yeah?"

"Yeah." Callie leaned in for a lingering kiss. "I'm sorry you might doubt that."

"Well…"

"I know." Callie brought Hudson's hand to her lips and pressed a kiss to her palm. "But I promise you don't need to tiptoe around me, even when it comes to time off and lavish vacations."

"Whoa. Who said anything about lavish?"

Callie canted her head. "Where were you thinking we might go?"

Hudson winced.

"Go on. I can take it." Even in the dim light, Callie's eyes gleamed.

"The Bahamas?"

"Mm-hmm. Not lavish at all."

"Okay, fine. It is indulgent. But I suggested it because anywhere we could go in the US that would be warm enough to enjoy a beach will be teeming with college students, and I don't think that would be relaxing for either of us."

"You have a point." Callie tipped her head, as though weighing a formal proposal on the matter.

"And the Bahamas is the most accessible destination in terms of time and money, so I thought it would be reasonable." Hudson lifted a hand. "Again, not assuming you'd be able and want to go, just wanting to have something in mind in case you said yes."

"One condition," Callie said.

She told herself not to get excited until Callie actually agreed. "What's that?"

"We stay on Eleuthera."

"Wait. What?"

"I want to stay on Eleuthera. It's one of the islands."

Hudson frowned. “I know.”

“Have you been there?” Callie asked.

“I haven’t. I’ve been to Grand Bahama and Exuma. I was going to suggest the latter because it’s less touristy.” Hudson spiraled her finger in front of Callie. “But you seem to know what you want, and I’m totally on board.”

“To be fair, I’ve never been.”

Hudson’s eyes narrowed. “But you have thoughts on which island is best.”

“My sisters and I used to watch this house show where people were house hunting in the Bahamas. In between heckling the obscenely rich people buying vacation homes, we developed strong opinions about which of the islands we’d deign to consider.”

Hudson shook her head but laughed. “Of course you did.”

“For the record, Exuma is my second choice.”

“I’d love to experience Eleuthera with you. Wait. Was that hypothetical, or did you just say yes?” It wasn’t a big relationship decision, like moving in together or—ack—getting married. Yet, somehow, it felt weighty. Perhaps because shadows of the Greece debacle still loomed. They’d both learned something from that, though, about themselves and each other. And she really liked where they’d ended up.

“I’m absolutely saying yes.”

Chapter Twenty-nine

@shitprofessorssay: The key to a successful spring break is going somewhere students don't. Preferably to a conference somewhere tropical on the university's dime.

"I knew you weren't a morning person, but this is pathetic." Callie lifted her coffee in Hudson's direction. "You're practically comatose."

Hudson's eyes drifted closed once again. "You made me get up at four."

"Damn right I did. We're going to be on the beach by noon. It's practically a bonus day."

Hudson opened her eyes long enough to take a long swig from her cold brew. "I'll thank you when we get there. And I'll buy the first round of whatever cocktail your heart desires."

She didn't need thanks, and she wasn't really giving Hudson a hard time. And to be fair, she'd been the one who'd kept Hudson up til almost midnight. What should have been an evening of packing and an early bedtime had turned into a fuck fest courtesy of a new vibrating cock Hudson had procured but hesitated to pack without a consult. Callie had insisted the only way to know was to test it out and that had been that. Suitcases tossed to the floor and laundry abandoned. But it had been so worth it. "I'll absolutely let you get the first round and I'll also give you the window seat on the plane so you can nap."

Hudson pressed a hand to her chest. "You really do love me."

The gate area had started to fill, but Callie didn't care. She leaned in and planted a noisy kiss on Hudson's lips. "I really, really do."

Two flights, a nearly missed connection, and a questionable shuttle ride later, they arrived at the hotel and got checked in. Hudson swiped the key card to unlock the door and held it for Callie to go first.

Callie swept in and dropped her suitcase with a thud. She resisted flopping onto the bed, but barely. "I kind of want to go to the beach, but I kind of want a nap."

Hudson closed the distance between them and wrapped her arms around Callie's waist. "You said that like you have to choose."

"I don't, do I?"

Hudson shook her head. "You do not."

She'd hesitated when Hudson suggested a resort. She was more of a cozy little rental traveler and put a lot of stock in exploring local neighborhoods. But Hudson had found a place that seemed to offer the best of both worlds—ample amenities and access to local shops and restaurants. Oh, and a beach with loungers, umbrellas, and full food and beverage service. "Let me change."

Hudson tipped her chin. "Let me watch?"

Callie swatted her arm. "It's nothing you haven't seen before. And I'm not waiting a minute longer than I have to for that cocktail you promised me."

Hudson hung her head but only for a second. She looked at Callie and grinned. Then, without breaking eye contact, she unzipped her bag and pulled out a pair of board shorts. "You might not know this about me, but I'm great at multitasking."

"Is that so?" Callie sauntered to her own bag and pulled out the two-piece she'd bought special for the trip. Not a true bikini, but it showed off plenty of skin. And since she planned to wear it all day most of the days they were there, she could go to the bathroom without an interpretive dance of wiggling in and out of the cute but convoluted wrap number she'd worn the last two summers.

"Uh-huh." Hudson kicked off her shoes and dispensed with her pants. "See?"

Since she'd already shed the cardigan she wore on the plane, Callie grabbed the hem of her tank top and worked it up. But instead of efficiency, she went for effect. Slow and sinuous, she undulated her torso and hips. By the time she had the shirt off, Hudson's attention had settled solely on her. She stood there, rocking a full Winnie the Pooh aesthetic. Callie smacked her lips. "Yep. A real pro."

Hudson was on her in an instant, pushing her to the bed and settling a knee between Callie's thighs. "I can't help it if you choose not to play fair."

Callie lifted her chin. "Are you asking me not to take my clothes off in front of you?"

Hudson made a show of considering. "When you put it that way."

"I thought so," Callie said with a laugh.

Hudson kissed her, long and slow. She palmed Callie's breast and pressed her thigh to Callie's center. Callie's nipples went hard, and a moan escaped before she could stop it. Beach? What beach? Who needed a beach when she could have this?

But instead of finishing what she started, Hudson broke the kiss and all but bounded out of bed. "Just remember two can play that game."

Callie let out an entirely different sort of moan. "Not fair."

Hudson extended her hands and, when Callie grabbed them, hauled her to her feet. "You'll thank me when your toes are in the sand."

She pouted.

Hudson tipped her head toward the bed. "And I promise lots more of that later."

"Fine." Callie didn't keep the whine from her voice, but it was all for show. There was little she could imagine enjoying more than an afternoon of lounging in the sun and playing in the ocean, followed by something bright and fresh for dinner and a night of naked shenanigans with Hudson.

Hudson pulled on her board shorts and swapped her shirt for a racerback swim bra. She slipped her feet into a pair of flip-flops and stuck out her arms. "What's taking you so long?"

"Sorry. I was too busy staring at you." She hurriedly put on her own bathing suit and flops and grabbed her sunglasses. "Ready."

"Aren't you forgetting something?"

She made a show of patting her boobs and then her butt. "Pretty sure you're going to have to be in charge of the room key."

Hudson patted the little zippered pocket on her shorts. "Already have it."

"Oh. Sunscreen."

"Got that, too." Hudson lifted one of the cotton string bags she used for groceries.

It was cute how prepared Hudson always was. Not to mention convenient. "So, what am I missing?"

Hudson pointed to the floppy sunhat Callie had fallen in love with at the airport. Such a silly and impulsive purchase, but the second she'd picked it up and tried it on, Hudson had insisted on buying it for her. Callie scooped it up and perched it on her head. She struck a pose, complete with kissy lips.

"Much better." Hudson slipped an arm around her waist and pulled her close. "Perfect, I'd say. Downright irresistible."

Hudson's grip was deliciously tight. Callie gave a little shimmy, savoring it and imagining all the ways Hudson would hold onto her later. Since she didn't have a lot of wiggle room, she dropped her head to the side and looked Hudson up and down. "Same goes, Professor. Same goes."

❖

After four days in Eleuthera with Callie, Hudson seriously considered what would happen if they quit their jobs and decided never to leave. Okay, maybe not seriously considered, but the fact that she considered it at all counted as a massive departure.

Callie seemed to agree, soaking up the sun as much as her winter skin and SPF 70 would allow, wanting to try every local delicacy, and reading no fewer than three romance novels. And that said nothing of what they got up to in their room. Hudson had never had so much sex in a single week in her entire life.

On their last afternoon on the island, Hudson couldn't help but find herself a little sad. She glanced over to Callie, who'd settled herself on a lounge chair under a massive umbrella. "You know, for someone who doesn't do spring break, you seem to be really good at it."

Callie turned her head and slid her sunglasses down far enough to peer over them. "Just because I don't spring break doesn't mean I don't know how to vacation."

A valid point, but she wanted Callie to admit there was something uniquely delicious about this vacation. "I never doubted that for a second. But come on. Middle of the semester? Ryekill in the throes of a Nor'easter? It's extra, right?"

Callie slid her glasses the rest of the way off and sat up. She took her time folding them closed. "Okay, yes. Perhaps spring break has a few things to recommend it."

Hudson chuckled. "Thank you."

Callie smiled then. "And you have orchestrated a truly memorable, luxurious without being stuffy, utterly perfect specimen of a spring break."

She was clearly teasing, but Hudson felt a swell of pride at the kernel of truth she knew sat at the center. "Careful, now, or all that praise is going to go right to my head."

Callie turned to face Hudson and folded her arms. "You have a praise kink, don't you?"

Hudson straightened and mirrored the gesture. "I have no idea what you're talking about."

"Mm-hmm."

Hudson grinned. God, she loved this woman. "So what if I do? You have a problem with that?"

"Not in the slightest."

Hudson swung her legs around so she could lean across the space between the lounge chairs. She captured Callie's lips in a lingering kiss. When she pulled back, Callie's eyes were smug, like she'd orchestrated the kiss. Callie smiled. "Good," Hudson said.

"Know what kind of kink I have?" Callie asked.

"No, but I really hope you're going to tell me."

Callie leaned in like she was sharing a major secret. "I have a thing for earnest academics who come out of their shell around me. Who act all prim and proper until the bedroom door closes then toss me around and have their way with me like I'm a plaything."

Even as her arousal surged, Hudson paused. Not out of any real concern but not wanting to let Callie off the hook. "Academics, huh? Plural?"

Callie tipped her head in a playful concession. "Got me. One. One very singular, very specific academic."

"Whoever it is should consider themselves damn lucky," she said, feeling like the luckiest human on the planet about now.

"I don't know. I think the luck goes both ways."

Hudson pressed her fingers to her chest. "Well, I can only speak for this particular academic, but she's ridiculously in love with the most gorgeous, most amazing dean of advising ever to walk this earth."

"Even if that dean of advising has a pesky habit of calling out shit professors say?"

Hudson considered. The thing was, professors had a habit of saying shit they shouldn't. Who was she to pretend otherwise? And when push came to shove, the dean of advising in question—the one she was so madly in love with—happened to have one of the highest bars for personal and professional integrity Hudson had ever seen. She found herself in awe of Callie day after day and spent a fair amount of her time trying to be more like her. "Even then."

"Sounds like we might be the perfect match," Callie said.

Hudson certainly wouldn't have said so after that first hookup, or any number of other times in those early days. Mostly because she could be her own worst enemy sometimes. And, to be fair, because Callie got her own way on a couple of occasions, too. Yet, here they were. And there was nowhere in the world she'd rather be. She debated popping the question that had been on her mind for the last month and decided now was a good a time as any. "Perfect enough that you might consider moving in together at some point?"

Callie quirked a brow. "Define some point?"

"Um, after May but before August the following year." Which basically meant this summer or next. She wasn't in a rush, but she also like the idea of going to bed with Callie every night and waking up with her every morning.

"I like the sound of that. Let's discuss in earnest once we're back in the real world."

Hudson could think of nothing that sounded better, return to the real world notwithstanding. "Whatever you say, Dean Shaw."

About the Author

Aurora Rey is a college dean by day and award-winning lesbian romance author the rest of the time, except when she's cooking, baking, riding the tractor, or pining for goats. She grew up in a small town in south Louisiana, daydreaming about New England. She keeps a special place in her heart for the South, especially the food and the ways women are raised to be strong, even if they're taught not to show it. After a brief dalliance with biochemistry, she completed both a BA and an MA in English.

She is the author of the Cape End Romance series and several standalone contemporary lesbian romance novels and novellas. She has been a finalist for the Lambda Literary, RITA®, and Golden Crown Literary Society awards but loves reader feedback the most. She lives in Ithaca, New York, with her dog and whatever wildlife has taken up residence in the pond.

About the Author

Books Available from Bold Strokes Books

Feeling Lucky by Krystina Rivers. What happens when, despite suddenly having enough money to buy almost anything, Lucy and Tanner start to discover that maybe all they need is each other? (978-1-63679-876-9)

Iceberg by Gun Brooke. When Lady Arabella hires Zandra, she never expects to find love, especially not as a disaster looms on the horizon. (978-1-63679-908-7)

It Happened One Semester by Aurora Rey. After a Pride night hookup, can eager new Assistant Professor Hudson Greene and Dean of Advising Callie Shaw overcome the odds and ace falling in love? (978-1-63679-814-1)

It's Kind of a Bad Idea by Sarah G. Levine. What happens when an emotionally unavailable serial dater meets the one woman she can't help but fall for—who happens to be the one woman who told her not to? (978-1-63679-920-9)

Thankful for You by Tagan Shepard. Everyone deserves to find their person, maybe Karen has finally found hers? (978-1-63679-884-4)

What Happens on Location… by Nan Campbell. How can Helen produce a successful movie when its director is the woman responsible for the demise of her marriage? (978-1-63679-904-9)

When Love Comes Around by Radclyffe and Ronica Black. Can Maya Sanchez and Nolan Wright trust each other enough to build something real, or will the past tear them apart? (978-1-63679-930-8)

Anywhere with You by Margo Glynn. On a road trip through the Great American Southwest, two friends discover nature, hope, and each other. (978-1-63679-907-0)

Burning Bridges by Lesley Davis. Can Clancy and Jude crack the case of eight missing women—and the secrets of their own hearts? (978-1-63679-872-1)

Dreams Entangled by Sophia Kell Hagin. Amid self-doubt, secrets, a pandemic, fear of attack and attempted murder, Pirin and Gracie's attraction turns to love and their lives will never be the same. (978-1-63679-892-9)

Echoes of Love by Catherine Lane. As Hazel's and Jo's paths intertwine, they're swept up in a whirlwind of long-buried secrets, sizzling chemistry, and memories that won't be denied. (978-1-63679-835-6)

Moonlight Obsession by Sheri Lewis Wohl. All it takes to stop a clever killer is moonlight, love, and a silver bullet. (978-1-63679-831-8)

My Boyfriend's Wife by Joy Argento. Amid betrayal and heartbreak, can two women discover a love that could heal their pasts and rewrite their futures? (978-1-63679-866-0)

Tapout by Nicole Disney. A struggling MMA fighter finds her edge in an underground ring, but as she falls for the magnetic and ambitious promoter behind the matches, their dangerous world threatens to destroy everything they've fought to rebuild. (978-1-63679-924-7)

The Fame Game by Ronica Black. Wild child Hollywood actress Luna Kirkman begins dating Hollywood's leading man, only to fall for his straitlaced sister instead. (978-1-63679-858-5)

An Extraordinary Passion by Kit Meredith. An autistic podcaster must decide whether to take a chance on her polyamorous guest and indulge their shared passion, despite her history. (978-1-63679-679-6)

That's Amore! by Georgia Beers. The romantic city of Rome should inspire Lily's passion for writing, if she can look away from Marina Troiani, her witty, smart, and unassumingly beautiful Italian tour guide. (978-1-63679-841-7)

The Unexpected Heiress by Cassidy Crane. When a cynical opportunist meets a shy but spirited heiress, the last thing she plans is for her heart to get involved. (978-1-63679-833-2)

Through Sky and Stars by Tessa Croft. Can Val and Nicole's love cross space and time to change the fate of humanity? (978-1-63679-862-2)

Uncomplicate It by Kel McCord. When an office attraction threatens her career, Hollis Reed's carefully laid plans demand revision. (978-1-63679-864-6)

Vanguard by Gun Brooke. Beth Wild, Subterranean freedom fighter, is in the crosshairs when she fights for her people and risks her heart for loving the exacting Celestial dissident leader, LaSierra Delmonte. (978-1-63679-818-9)

Wild Night Rising by Barbara Ann Wright. Riding Harleys instead of horses, the Wild Hunt of myth is once again unleashed upon the world. Their ousted leader and a fey cop must join forces to rein in the ride of terror. (978-1-63679-749-6)

Heart's Appraisal by Jo Hemmingwood. Andy and Hazel can't deny their attraction, but they'll never agree on the place they call home. (978-1-63679-856-1)

Behold My Heart by Ronica Black. Alora Anders is a highly successful artist who's losing her vision. Devastated, she hires Bodie Banks, a young struggling sculptor as a live-in assistant. Can Alora open her mind and her heart to accept Bodie into her life? (978-1-63679-810-3)

Fearless Hearts by Radclyffe. One wounded woman, one determined to protect her—and a summertime of risk, danger, and desire. (978-1-63679-837-0)

Forever Family by L.M. Rose. Two friends come together after tragedy to raise a baby, finding love along the way. (978-1-63679-868-4)

Stranger in the Sand by Renee Roman. Grace Langley is haunted by guilt. Fagan Shaw wishes she could remember her past. Will finding each other bring the closure they're looking for in order to have a brighter future? (978-1-63679-802-8)

The Nursing Home Hoax by Shelley Thrasher and Ann Faulkner. In this fresh take for grown-ups on the classic Nancy Drew series, crime-solving duo Taylor and Marilee investigate suspicious activity at a small East Texas nursing home. (978-1-63679-806-6)

The Rise and Fall of Conner Cody by Chelsey Lynford. A successful yet lonely Hollywood starlet must decide if she can let go of old wounds and accept a chance at family, friendship, and the love of a lifetime. (978-1-63679-739-7)